$\mathcal{Y}$OU still want ̶ ̶ ̶ don't love you?"

"Stop talking like a schoolgirl. I haven't said anything about love. You can give me what I need, that's all."

"And what's that?"

He smiled. "Women are still scarce in the Nevada territory. You can learn to cook my meals . . . wash my clothes . . . share my bed, and you'll be willing and agreeable."

He released her, and she took a step backward.

"And in return," Adam went on calmly, "I'll see that you get to San Francisco and won't go hungry. That's my proposition. Take it or leave it."

Shannon's shock and hurt gave way to cold, numb despair. What choice did she have? She looked away. "I'll go with you, Adam. . . ."

Love's Promised Land

Diana Haviland

A FAWCETT GOLD MEDAL BOOK • NEW YORK

LOVE'S PROMISED LAND

Published by Fawcett Gold Medal Books, a unit of CBS Publications, the Consumer Publishing Division of CBS Inc.

ISBN 0-449-14000-8

Printed in the United States of America

10 9 8 7 6 5 4 3 2 1

Love's Promised Land

ABOUT THE AUTHOR

Diana Haviland was born in New York City, and is a graduate of Queens College. She has also lived in Pennsylvania, New Jersey, and North Carolina. When she is not doing research for her historical novels, she enjoys reading about American social history, in particular about the early years of New York City, where she now lives with her husband, who is also a writer, and two cats.

1

SHANNON CAVANAUGH STOOD at the rail on the upper deck of the riverboat *Amaranth,* the night breeze billowing her full pale-gray cotton skirt around her slender body. A strand of honey-colored hair whipped across her face, and she tucked it back under her straw bonnet, not taking her eyes away from the shoreline. In the moonlight, she could make out the towering shapes of the cypresses, the water-oaks and sweet gum trees that lined the banks of the twisting, flood-swollen Alabama River.

She leaned forward, hoping to catch a glimpse of one of the white, many-columned houses that stood on the bluffs above the river.

Back in Boston, where Shannon had been a pupil at Miss Colter's Academy for Young Ladies, she had read everything she could find about the mansions of the delta country, for she had always been sure that one day she would return there and live in such a house.

Aunt Kate, who had cared for Shannon until her eighth birthday, had cautioned the child against such daydreams.

"But my father is a planter. You told me so," Shannon had protested.

"Maybe I shouldn't have told you. You mustn't get a lot of fancy notions, dearie. That's what ruined your poor mother, rest her soul."

"But if my father's rich, if he has a fine, big house, why can't I live with him?"

Aunt Kate had hesitated, then she had said: "Because your name's Cavanaugh, same as your mother's. You got no right to your father's name, nor to his property, neither, and don't you go forgetting that."

Then, seeing the hurt in the child's face, she had added: "Not that he's shrugged off his duty to you, like some would've done. He pays the rent on the house here."

"This house?" Shannon's voice was scornful as she looked around the shabby kitchen of the cottage set in the pine woods west of Mobile Bay. "He lives in a mansion, and keeps me here?"

"You're too young to understand about such matters. When you're older—"

"You said I had no right to his name." Shannon looked steadily at her aunt. "Tell me what his name is and I'll find him and—"

"Be still. He don't want you to know his name. You have a roof over your head and food in your belly, and that's more than you've a right to expect."

But then, a few days after Shannon's eighth birthday, a stout, red-faced gentleman in a fine, plum-colored coat and shiny black boots had come to the cottage and talked to Aunt Kate, and a short time after that, Shannon had gone to Miss Emily Colter's Academy in Boston. Aunt Kate had not accompanied her, but had given her into the care of the red-faced man. When Shannon had asked him if he was her father, he had gone even redder and had explained that he was not. "I'm the family lawyer."

"What family? What's my father's name?"

But the lawyer, like Aunt Kate, had refused to tell her that. "It's my client's—your father's—wish that you should receive a good education to fit you for a respectable position."

Although Shannon was not sure what that meant, she was convinced that her father must love her. Otherwise, why would he be concerned about her future?

Now, leaning against the rail of the riverboat that was carrying her back to Mobile in this spring of 1859, Shannon's full lips tightened and her eyes grew thoughtful. She was remembering the letter she had received from Aunt Kate only a few weeks ago; she had read the words so often that she knew them by heart.

> Your father died a few months back, and there's no more money for your schooling. But your Uncle Jethro says he'll give you room and board here at the tavern. You can mind the bar and keep the rooms clean to pay your way.

Shannon had never met Jethro Rawlinson, for Aunt Kate had married the tavern-owner less than a year ago. Shannon had been surprised at the news, and had guessed that Aunt Kate must have grown tired of spinsterhood and poverty. Shannon realized that was her aunt's affair, but on one thing Shannon was decided: nothing would make her go to work in a tavern, to serve drinks in a taproom, and clean up after her uncle's overnight guests. By the age of sixteen, Shannon had made excellent progress in her studies; she knew, too, that she had the look of good breeding, and that she was pretty.

Aunt Kate had once told her that she had inherited her looks from her mother. "A real beauty, our Peggy was, with a fine, trim shape and hair the color of honey, like your own." Aunt Kate had smiled sadly. "Her eyes were blue, though. Like the river back home that she named you for."

"But my eyes aren't blue."

"They were when you were born, like most babies' eyes. You have your father's eyes now."

Her father's eyes: hazel in certain lights, and a deep, mysterious gold in others, slightly tilted at the corners and set under dark, curving brows.

Now, on the deserted deck of the *Amaranth*, Shannon stood in the moonlight and thought about the father she would never know. She felt a stir of pain and a sense of loss, for although she should hate her father, she could not.

She had to know his name, and somehow she would force Aunt Kate to tell her. Surely he had made provisions for her future. He would not have wanted her to work in a waterfront tavern in Mobile.

She half-turned, hearing footsteps behind her, and saw a ship's officer in a dark-blue coat and visored cap. "It's getting late, miss," the officer said politely. "Damp, too, with all this fog."

"I'll be going below soon," Shannon assured him.

He touched his cap, said good night, and moved on. But Shannon stayed where she was, reluctant to go forward to the crowded, stuffy ladies' cabin.

There, she would be jammed in with a crowd of female passengers who could not afford the luxury of one of the private cabins. Shannon's cot stood between two others, with scarcely more than a foot of space on either side. To the right was a girl, younger than herself, who had worked in one of the cotton mills near Montgomery, and who was returning home, desperately ill, with a wracking cough. On Shannon's left, the cot was occupied by a plump, overdressed girl with red hair, piled up into elaborate curls, puffs, and waves, augmented by a false fringe in front. Her lips and cheeks were bright pink, and even Shannon, unsophisticated in such matters, knew that the coloring was not natural; the scent of her strong heliotrope perfume lingered on the warm, damp air of the cabin, mingling with other, even less pleasant smells of unwashed bodies, unaired linen and babies' diapers.

The red-haired girl had introduced herself to the others as soon as she had come aboard at Montgomery. "My name's Clarisse Jenkins. I'm an entertainer. Going to work in Mobile."

Shannon noticed that the other women, many of them the wives of farmers from the hill country of Kentucky and North Carolina, who were following their men to the new settlements to the West, drew away from Clarisse Jenkins. One thin-faced, bony woman, trailed by her brood of whining, fretful children, had said to nobody in particular: "Entertainer, my foot. That one's going to entertain sailors in one of them fancy houses."

Then, seeing Shannon's bewilderment, the farm woman had added: "You're the innocent, aren't you? Why, everybody knows the Mobile waterfront's full of them sinful places. Near as bad as New Orleans or Natchez-under-the-Hill."

Shannon, after her years of virginal seclusion at Miss Colter's Academy, had only a vague notion about such matters but the farm woman's words had made her more determined than ever not to remain at Uncle Jethro's tavern.

Shannon's thoughts were interrupted with swift violence as the *Amaranth*, which had been moving smoothly down the river, now gave a sharp, sickening lurch, and swerved around in a wide arc, so that she was thrown to her knees on the deck. The rail on which she had been leaning was ripped away with a splintering sound, and there were other noises all around her. She heard the boat's side grate against something hard and solid, heard the canvas awning, rigged over the rear portion of the upper deck, tear loose and flap noisily in the night wind.

On her hands and knees, she backed away from the broken railing and the dark, swirling river beyond, until she felt herself held fast by her full skirt, which had caught on the end of the splintered rail. The next violent movement of the boat would throw her into the water that was washing up over the deck.

She cried out in terror, and a moment later, she felt

an arm around her, and heard a man's voice. "Don't be frightened. You're all right now."

The uproar was increasing, as the officers shouted orders to the crewmen, as frightened women screamed and children wailed, and men, roused from sleep, staggered out on deck, cursing.

Shannon tugged at her skirt until the man who was holding her tore the fabric away with his free hand. Then he helped her to her feet and half-dragged, half-carried her into one of the private cabins.

She leaned against him, trembling and bruised. A throbbing pain shot along her leg and side.

"Sit down," the man said. "Do you feel faint?"

"A little." She let him lead her to a rosewood and velvet settee, where she relaxed gratefully against the soft cushions. She took off her bonnet and smoothed her hair. The man poured a glass of amber wine from a bottle he took from the marble-topped cabinet beside the bed.

Shannon studied him with interest. Although he was only a little above medium height, he was impressive, because of his proud carriage and easy grace, his slender, well-muscled body. He wore a dark blue brocade dressing gown over his shirt and trousers, and his coat was flung across a chair.

His hair was light, the color of ripe wheat. She thought of the heroes in those paper-covered novels that had been smuggled into the school to be read secretly by candlelight, after bedtime. Like the men in the books, this man, too, was slender, graceful, with a look of elegant wealth.

Shannon was aware, however, that she should not

be here at all, after midnight in a private cabin with a strange man.

Then, hearing the uproar from the deck, the crashing of timbers, the splintering of glass, the pounding of the sailors' boots across the sun-dried planks, she decided that this was no ordinary situation, and perhaps Miss Colter's rules did not apply here.

"Are we going to sink?"

The young man's gray eyes met hers and he smiled. "Of course not, Miss—"

"Shannon Cavanaugh."

"I'm Bruce Lathrop."

He sat down beside her. "We've only run into the trees. Happens all the time when the Alabama overflows its banks."

"I might have been swept overboard."

"Drink your wine, and try not to think about it."

She sipped the golden sherry, and wondered whether the warm sensation that was coursing through her was caused only by the wine.

"You see," Bruce Lathrop explained, "the higher the waters rise, the narrower the river channel becomes. It's true that the swamps and lowlands are flooded, but the boat still has to pass between the two rows of trees on the banks, and right around here, their branches almost touch overhead. In the dark, the slightest miscalculation can send the boat in among the branches. Sometimes a branch catches on the woodwork or comes crashing through a cabin window."

He smiled. "You must be new to this part of the country, or you would have known."

"I've been away at school in Boston, but I was born near Mobile."

"Then let me be the first to welcome you home, Miss Cavanaugh." He hesitated, then said softly: "Shannon. A lovely and unusual name."

"My mother named me for the river, back in Ireland. She thought my eyes would remain blue, like hers, but—" Shannon stopped, thinking that she must be tipsy to be speaking so freely to this young man.

"I like your eyes exactly as they are. The color of that sherry. Tawny gold and warm."

"I—think I'd better leave now," she said.

"Not yet. You need time to recover. But if you wish, I'll get one of the crewmen to find your maid."

She was about to tell him that she had no maid, that she had traveled alone by train and coach and now by riverboat, all the way from Boston; that she was a second-class passenger with a cot in the ladies' cabin below. But the words would not come. If Bruce Lathrop knew her circumstances, he might consider them a barrier.

Swiftly, she changed the subject. "Are you traveling all the way to Mobile, Mr. Lathrop?"

"Only as far as Cypress Bend."

"Is that a plantation?"

He shook his head. "Cypress Bend is the name of the landing on the river. We share the dock there with the Duvals of Beau Rivage. My own home is called Jessamine."

"Is it far from here?"

"Right above Mobile. We should be there by tomorrow at noon. And you, Miss Cavanaugh? How far are you going?"

"Right through to Mobile. My aunt and uncle live there."

"Are you visiting them, or—"

"It's only a visit." The words came swiftly, instinctively. Uncle Jethro might think she was going to stay at the tavern and work as a barmaid, serving drinks to crewmen from riverboats and flatboats, to trappers from the back country and passing slave traders, but he was mistaken.

"I don't believe I know any Cavanaughs in Mobile. Are they newcomers to the city?"

"My uncle's name is Rawlinson, not Cavanaugh. My mother's name was—" She stopped in time, her face burning with vicarious shame.

The girls at the school had known nothing about her birth, for Miss Colter, if she had known the truth, had guarded it well. The school in Boston had been far enough from Mobile so that there had been little likelihood of an embarrassing revelation. But although Shannon had been treated exactly like all the other young ladies, she had known that she was different. Sometimes she had lain awake at night, tormented by that sense of being different. When she let herself think about the circumstances surrounding her birth, she remembered the harsh, ugly word the other children had called her when she had lived with Aunt Kate in the pine woods.

If Bruce Lathrop knew the truth, would he think of her in that same way? Would he use that word in his own mind?

She stood up. "Now, I really must get back to my cabin."

He rose and said: "I'll escort you."

"Please don't. It's only a short way."

Let him think she was occupying one of the private cabins, like his own. If he took her back to the ladies' cabin, he might catch sight of Clarisse Jenkins, with her red hair and too-pink lips and cheeks, wearing one of her revealing lace-trimmed wrappers.

Clarisse had been pleasant enough to her, but the farm woman might have been right; perhaps Clarisse *was* going to work in a fancy house on the Mobile waterfront.

Shannon started for the door, but Bruce held her arm.

"Please don't rush off like this."

"I'm tired. I must get some rest."

He was all concern. "Of course you must. But you will allow me to call on you in Mobile, won't you?"

"You can't do that."

"Why not? Surely if you tell your uncle about me, he won't object." He spoke with quiet assurance. "I think he's heard of the Lathrop family. And of Jessamine."

As if Uncle Jethro would object to any man calling at the tavern, so long as he had the price of a drink, Shannon thought bitterly.

She seized on the first excuse that came to her. "My aunt is very strict. She might not allow me to—"

"But your parents—"

"They're dead. My aunt and uncle are my only relatives now."

He did not release his hold on her arm. His touch was gentle, respectful, but firm.

"Please speak to your aunt. Promise me you will."

Shannon had had no experience with men, but

there was no mistaking the warmth in his eyes, the ardent tone of his voice, and she responded, not with her mind, but with the swift, hot currents of her blood. Until she remembered her mother, who had yielded to another ardent young man, years before. Who had not waited for marriage.

Shannon made herself say: "I'll think about it, Mr. Lathrop. Now, I must go." He released her.

"Thank you for helping me," she said. "Good night."

Her voice was as formal, her manner as restrained, as even Miss Colter could have desired.

She lifted her torn skirt and hurried out onto the deck, hardly aware of the other passengers milling around her, of the sailors who were slashing with heavy axes at the branches that held the *Amaranth* imprisoned in the trees, of the officers shouting commands.

If only she could have let Bruce escort her back to her cabin; if only she really had a private cabin, with a maid. How she had longed to tell him he might call on her in Mobile. Tomorrow he would be leaving the boat, going home to a plantation called Jessamine, and she might not see him again.

Bruce had been right when he had predicted that the *Amaranth* would not be delayed long by the accident. Before the dawn turned the river to crimson and gold, the boat was moving again, the shattered woodwork repaired temporarily, the smashed panes of glass in the dining salon replaced with boards.

Shannon had remained in the ladies' cabin during the morning, and Clarisse Jenkins had brought her coffee and hot rolls. Although the first-class passengers did not dine with those in the ladies' cabin, Shannon did not want to run into Bruce accidentally.

Her only suitable dress, the gray cotton, had been ruined, and although she had two others in her carpetbag, neither was suitable for the warm, sultry Alabama spring.

"I'll lend you one of mine," Clarisse offered, but Shannon declined. Although she knew she should have nothing to do with a girl like Clarisse, she could not make herself feel unfriendly, for, in spite of Clarisse's flamboyant appearance, she had a warm, natural generosity; she was not dour and careworn, like most of the other ladies that shared the cabin.

She kept up a stream of chatter as Shannon drank the hot, strong coffee. "Listen to that. We're going to make a stop at one of those fancy plantations."

Shannon heard the *Amaranth*'s bell clanging to announce the landing.

"That's the worst of these boats," Clarisse went on. "They stop at every big plantation to drop off cargo and take on passengers." She fastened a puff of artificial red curls over her forehead. "Same on the Mississippi. Takes us second-class passengers twice as long to get where we're going."

"You've traveled a lot, haven't you?" Shannon asked.

"Lord, yes. All up and down the Mississippi from St. Louis to Natchez. That's one hell of a lively town, Natchez. And I've worked in New Orleans."

"And now it's Mobile. Will you be staying long?"

"Probably not. I've been thinking about going on to San Francisco. That's the place to be right now."

"I heard about the silver boom out there," Shannon said, "but you don't plan to become a miner, do you?"

Clarisse laughed good-naturedly. "Lord, no. There's plenty of money for girls like me out there. Why, when those miners come in from the back country, they haven't seen a girl for weeks. They're ready to pay for what they want, so I hear. They throw nuggets right up onto the stage, even if a girl has a voice like a crow—as long as she's pretty."

Shannon, aware that the other women were looking at her disapprovingly because she was talking to Clarisse, said: "I think I'll go up on deck for a while."

She took off her wrapper, and stood in her petticoats, then sighing, she put on her brown flannel dress, with its high neck and long sleeves.

"I'll go with you," Clarisse said.

Shannon felt a swift, sinking sensation, for she had hoped to see Bruce again before he left the boat, but she didn't want Clarisse with her. She sighed, and climbed the short flight of stairs to the upper deck, Clarisse right behind her.

The sailors were putting down the gangplank. The air was warm and rich with the mingled scents of spring: the rich black earth that made this part of Alabama one of the most fertile cotton-growing areas in the South, the budding shrubbery, and the trees that covered the rise of land beyond the dock—water oak, pecan, cypress and sweet gum.

Shannon tilted her head back and tried to catch a glimpse of the house on the top of the rise. She saw the gleam of white pillars, hidden by golden jessamine, purple wisteria and pink crabapple trees bursting into bloom. Was that Bruce's home, Jessamine?

Or perhaps it was the other house, with the French name. Beau Rivage. Bruce had said that the Lathrops shared this river landing with another family, the Duvals.

She turned to see Bruce coming across the deck, and she shrank out of sight in the shadow of the newly replaced awning. He was dressed in cream-colored trousers, fashionably narrow and strapped under his shoes. An elegant waistcoat of striped blue and cream, with a fine linen stock knotted under his chin, completed the picture, and Shannon was dazzled by him. His silver-blond hair glinted in the sunlight.

He was looking about, and she wondered if he was seeking her. She wanted to go to him, but she fought the impulse.

"Look there," Clarisse said. "We're takin' on cargo."

Shannon did not grasp her meaning at first, for there were no bales of cotton, no crates piled on the dock. But a moment later, she understood.

Four black men and one woman, a light-skinned quadroon in a flowered muslin shift, were standing down on the dock, looking up at the boat. She saw, too, a white man who was obviously in charge of the slaves. He was a big, dark-haired man whose shirt was open at the throat, his jacket slung over his shoulder, his wide-brimmed Panama hat pushed back on his head. He stood with his booted feet set well apart, and Shannon thought there was a look of arrogance about him. He gestured, and the black men moved forward, but the quadroon girl hung back, as if reluctant to go on board the *Amaranth*.

Shannon forgot Bruce Lathrop for the moment.

She felt her throat tighten with pity for the slaves, but she was angry, too. Her years in Boston had made her forget that down here in Alabama slaves were cargo, to be stored on the lower deck along with the bales of cotton, the crates of plantation supplies, the firewood for the boat's engines.

Now, as the quadroon girl in the flowered muslin continued to stand still, her head down, one of the black men leaned toward her and said something. Slowly she shuffled forward.

"Look over there," Clarisse was saying. "Now that's a fine rig, isn't it?"

"What?"

"That open carriage comin' down to the dock. Liveried driver and all."

It was, as Clarisse had said, a fine rig, and the occupant was no less elegant: a girl, who sat back against the leather cushioned seat, her pink skirts spread around her, a dainty parasol held in one hand. The liveried driver brought the carriage to a halt at the foot of the dock, sprang down from the box and helped the girl to alight.

"Looks like a princess, don't she?" Clarisse said.

With small, graceful steps, her pink skirts swaying, the girl approached the gangplank.

At the same moment, Shannon became aware of a flurry of movement on the steps leading up from the lower deck. She saw a flash of brightly flowered muslin. The quadroon girl had escaped from the cargo area, and was now leaning over the railing.

"Miss Odalie—Miss Odalie—help me—please—"

The quadroon was calling to the girl in the pink dress, who now made her way up the gangplank with a leisurely step, calm, unhurried. She held her pink parasol over her head to shield her delicate, ivory-white complexion from the blazing sunlight and, with her other hand, she lifted her pink skirts so that they would not brush the wood.

From the lower deck, booted feet now came pounding up the stairs, and Shannon saw the white man in the Panama hat, who had been in charge of the slaves. "All right, girl. That's enough. Quiet down, now."

There was a crisp ring of authority in the man's voice, and passengers who had been lounging on the upper deck now began to form a small crowd around him, and the quadroon.

"Please, sir, please let me talk to Miss Odalie there. She'll tell you. It's a mistake. Missus wouldn't sell me, not without tellin' me."

The tall man shook his head, his sunburned face impassive.

"There's no mistake, girl. I have the papers from Mrs. Philippe Duval, all in order. Too bad she didn't prepare you, but you've been sold. That's the truth, and you might as well get used to it."

"Kincaid, what's the trouble here?" Bruce Lathrop forced his way through the crowd.

The tall man shrugged. "Mrs. Duval sold this girl, but the wench won't believe it. I'd show her the bill of sale, but she can't read, of course. Maybe if you were to read it to her, she'd take your word, Lathrop."

But the quadroon turned and ran to the head of the gangplank, where the young lady in the pink dress was coming on board, helped by the captain.

"Miss Odalie, let me talk to you, please—"

"Now, don't you go botherin' Miss Duval," the

captain said sternly. "You heard Mr. Kincaid. The papers are all in order."

As Odalie Duval looked at the quadroon, her pretty, doll-like face, shaded by the pink parasol, was faintly troubled.

"I'm sorry, Tina," she said, "truly I am. But there's nothing I can do. Mother has made the arrangements."

"Sold me away from Beau Rivage?"

"I'm afraid so." Odalie turned to Mr. Kincaid. "Tina is a house servant," she said. "Born here on the place. I hope you won't—treat her harshly."

Kincaid took off his hat and bowed. "Don't you worry, Miss Duval. So long as Tina does as she's told, she has nothing to fear. I give you my word on that."

"That's all right, then." She turned to the quadroon. "Now, Tina, go below with the others and don't make trouble." It was plain that Odalie Duval had already dismissed the incident of the slave girl. She turned to Bruce.

"Welcome home," she said, and hearing the easy intimacy of her tone, Shannon's insides twisted with envy and resentment. This girl knew Bruce well, that was plain enough. Why not? Jessamine and Beau Rivage stood side by side on the bluff above the river; the Lathrops and the Duvals shared the landing, Bruce had said so last night. These two must have grown up together.

"Dare I hope you've come down to greet me?" Bruce asked, smiling warmly at Odalie.

"Why, Bruce Lathrop. As if I'd do any such thing. The fact is, I was expecting a package, a cashmere shawl I ordered on my last trip to Montgomery."

The captain shook his head. "It wasn't on board this trip, Miss Duval. But I'll keep an eye out for it on my next run."

Odalie sighed. "How provoking. I most particularly wanted it to wear to your sister's party next week, Bruce." She looked up at Bruce, her long lashes shading her brown eyes. "But as long as I'm here with the carriage, perhaps you'd like to drive back with me."

"Nothing would please me more."

Bruce gave his arm to Odalie, and they moved away, followed by a black crewman who carried Bruce's luggage.

"What made your mother sell Tina?" Shannon heard Bruce ask.

"I'm sure I have no idea. You know what Mother's like when she gets a notion into her head. Now, I want to hear all about your trip."

Shannon turned her face away, grateful for the purple shadows that had concealed her under the awning. She was unable to watch the pair as they descended the gangplank.

"Handsome couple, ain't they?" Clarisse remarked.

Shannon could not answer.

"What's wrong? That business about the quadroon got you upset, honey?"

"Yes, I suppose so."

"If you're goin' to live down here, you'll get used to seein' a lot worse than that, believe me. Besides, somethin' tells me that little wench won't have too bad a time of it."

"What do you mean?"

"She'll be spreadin' her legs for that good-lookin'

fella—what's his name, Kincaid. She could've done a lot worse, I'd say. Now, that's a man. Big, and husky, and I'll bet he's randy as a stud bull in spring." Clarisse giggled. "Now, don't look so shocked, honey. I've known enough men in my time to be able to tell by lookin'."

Shannon had never heard any girl talk the way Clarisse Jenkins did.

"No matter," Clarisse rattled on. "You couldn't take your eyes off that blond fella in the striped waistcoat, could you? No use lookin' at that kind. They're not for the likes of us."

"I don't know what you mean," Shannon said stiffly. She might be traveling second-class, but that certainly did not make her similar to Clarisse Jenkins.

"Down here," Clarisse said, "marriages are all arranged according to who your grandpa was and how much cotton land your folks own. Don't matter how pretty a girl is, unless she's got money and family."

Was Clarisse right? Here, in the stratified society of Mobile, would Shannon be forever barred from associating with Bruce Lathrop?

Through a swift blur of hot tears, she looked down at the dock. Odalie Duval was seated in the open carriage and Bruce was climbing in beside her. The liveried coachman cracked his whip, and they started off, the bay stepping out smartly.

A few minutes later, the engines of the *Amaranth* coughed, sputtered and made explosive sounds, as the high-pressure steam escaped into the air. The side wheels began to turn, agitating the yellow water of the river.

"You're lookin' kinda pale," Clarisse observed.

"Not used to the heat down here, I suppose. And that dress. Honey, you'll swoon wearing that thing. Better borrow one of mine."

"No, thanks," Shannon said quickly. Better to swoon than to arrive in Mobile in one of the gaudy satin dresses belonging to Clarisse. The girl might be well-meaning, but Shannon hesitated about becoming too friendly with her.

"You could return the dress when we're both settled in Mobile," Clarisse persisted.

It was hard to resist Clarisse's warm smile, the honest friendliness in her eyes. Shannon had never had a real friend among the girls at school.

She found herself smiling back. "Maybe you're right. This dress was comfortable enough back in Boston, but here—"

"That's what I've been saying. Come on, I have a yellow organdy that'll be perfect for you."

"You're very kind," Shannon said. She followed Clarisse back down the steps to the ladies' cabin, and tried to push aside the memory of Bruce, driving off with Odalie Duval.

Maybe she's in love with him, Shannon thought. *How could she help it? He's so handsome, so—so romantic-looking. But all the same, he's still free. I have a chance with him, too.*

2

THE WHARF at Mobile was crowded and noisy, and although it was already sunset, Shannon still felt the heavy, humid air pressing down; even in the low-cut organdy dress that Clarisse Jenkins had finally persuaded her to borrow, she was uncomfortably warm. Still, it was certainly more suitable than her high-necked brown flannel.

Shannon had seen this part of Mobile only once before, when she had passed through it eight years ago, on her way up north. She was bewildered yet fascinated, by the city, so different from Boston.

She breathed the mingled odors of hemp and tar, of muddy water and decaying garbage. Some of the long, low two-story buildings had a foreign look, with their intricate ironwork balconies. The air itself was different, she thought: soft and seductive, filled with the moist heat of the tropics. She wondered if the gulls that wheeled and swooped overhead had come up from the Gulf of Mexico, only a little way to the south.

Shannon shaded her eyes against the glare of the setting sun, and searched for a glimpse of Aunt Kate down on the wharf. She had written informing her aunt of the probable time of her arrival in Mobile, but the *Amaranth* had been delayed. Still, Aunt Kate should have waited, shouldn't she?

As the last of the passengers made their way down the gangplank, Shannon sighed and picked up her carpetbag. Maybe she would find Aunt Kate down on the wharf after all.

But down below, she found herself jostled by the crowd. She watched as the other passengers were met by friends, and whisked off in fine, open carriages, and she began to feel uneasy.

On those occasions when she had gone out for daily walks in Boston, she had been accompanied by the other girls, and chaperoned by one of the teachers, or by Miss Colter, the headmistress; in a neat, double file, the girls had stepped briskly along the pavement, eyes cast down. Now, Shannon was uncomfortably aware that she was on her own.

In this maze of warehouses, livery stables, taverns and other buildings she could not identify, there was no Miss Colter to ward off a predatory male with one icy look.

The wharf and the surrounding streets and alleys of Mobile's waterfront were filled with sailors, big, hulking men from the flatboats and keelboats, officers from the riverboats. The sailors were no sooner ashore than they were approached by men in brocaded satin waistcoats and tall hats, who engaged them in low, hurried conversations. From one of the buildings, close by, Shannon could hear the sound of a tinkling piano, and high-pitched feminine laughter.

The Mobile landing was thick with vessels: flat-boats laden with wheat and corn, turkeys and pigs; keelboats, barges and skiffs, all of them discharging their crews.

She looked over at the livery stable, wondering if she might hire a public cab to take her to the tavern, for Aunt Kate was still nowhere in sight. As she debated the matter, she saw a man drive a wagon and team out of the stable. He made straight for the wharf and she had to step aside quickly to keep from being splashed by the scummy, greenish water in the puddles.

"This ain't no place for a lady to be standin'," said a sailor, a bearded man in cotton duck trousers and a greasy hat with a red turkey feather stuck in the band. From the smell of him, Shannon guessed that he had come off a flatboat carrying pigs.

"Come on with me, honey," he said. "I'll buy you a drink, and then we can—"

His hand closed on Shannon's arm, and his body pressed close to hers. "Leave me alone," she said, trying to pull away.

"Got my pay right here," he said. "I'll show you a good time."

"I'm waiting for someone." Fear made her voice high and shrill.

"A girl as pretty as you don't need to be kept waitin'. Come on, now."

His heavy arm encircled her waist, and his hand cupped her breast. She cried out, sickened and terrified. "I told you, I'm waiting for—"

"The lady's waiting for me." It was the driver of the wagon that had nearly splashed her. A moment later, he was off the high seat.

The sailor frowned but looked uncertain. By the flickering light of the torches now lit along the wharf, Shannon recognized the wagon driver. He was Mr. Kincaid, who had brought the slaves aboard the boat at Cypress Bend. Kincaid was a head taller than the sailor, his shoulders wide and heavy with muscle, and there was a steely glint in his hard blue eyes.

The sailor shrugged, then, as a dark-haired girl, her face bright with paint, moved past, he turned and followed her, leaving Shannon alone with Kincaid.

"Is someone really meeting you?" he asked.

"I thought my aunt would be here. I wrote her, but—"

"Where does your aunt live?"

"At Rawlinson's Tavern. Perhaps you know where it is."

"Everybody down here knows Rawlinson's place." She did not like the way he said that, or the look he gave her, familiar, impudent.

He pushed his hat back on his head. "I'm going past Rawlinson's place. If you wait in the wagon while I take care of some business, I'll drive you there."

"I couldn't possibly. I—"

"Why not?"

"I don't know you."

He swept off his hat in a half-mocking gesture. "Adam Kincaid, at your service."

"I'm Shannon Cavanaugh. My aunt is Mrs. Rawlinson."

"All right, now we're properly introduced."

He took the carpetbag out of her hand, tossed it onto the seat of the wagon, then, grasping her around the waist, he lifted her with one easy movement, holding her against him for a moment before depositing her on the seat. She felt the hard, masculine body pressed against hers; the warmth of his hands through the thin organdy of her dress. She was aware of a swift, hot tide of sensation never felt before. "Make yourself comfortable," he said, when she was seated. "I'll be back as quickly as I can."

Shannon stared after him, taken aback by his cool certainty that she would ride with him, and disturbed by the strange, frightening feelings she had had during that brief moment when her body had been pressed against his.

Her impulse was to get away, but she realized that she could not climb down from the wagon unaided without showing an indecent glimpse of petticoats and pantelettes. She moved back into the shadow of the canvas shed, open at either end, at the back of the wagon.

Perhaps she should be grateful to Adam Kincaid for rescuing her from the sailor's advances, but she did not like his arrogance. He was not a gentleman, like Bruce Lathrop, of that she was certain.

Still, she had to get to the tavern, and she did not know if the money that remained in her purse after her long journey was enough to pay for a hired cab. Why hadn't Aunt Kate been here to meet her?

Shannon started as she heard a shrill scream; it came from the upper balcony of one of the rickety waterfront buildings close by. Leaning forward, she saw that a girl, wearing a silk wrapper, open to the waist, crouched on the balcony.

A moment later, a man, wearing only a pair of cotton pants, lurched out on the balcony, and seized the girl's arm.

"You bitch, you robbed me," he cried.

The girl responded with a torrent of French and English, protesting her innocence until the man dragged her back inside.

Shannon was shivering, in spite of the humid heat. She had never heard a man speak to a woman that way; but the scene had attracted little attention from the crowd and she decided, with a sinking sensation, that perhaps such scenes were common here. She felt a swift pang of homesickness for Miss Colter's Academy, for the neat parlor where one of the girls would be playing the piano, now, in the early evening, while the others embroidered or crocheted.

She had only been in Mobile once before, briefly, passing through on her way to Boston; she had scarcely been aware of her surroundings then, for she had been carried away with excitement at the prospect of her new life at school. If only she could have been allowed to stay there, safe and sheltered.

Turning away, she looked back toward the *Amaranth*, and saw that Adam Kincaid was returning now, leading his cargo: the black men and the quadroon girl. She had forgotten all about the slaves.

"Move along," Adam was saying.

"Get up there in the back of the wagon," he ordered.

The men obeyed, then the girl. In the glare of the torchlight, Shannon saw that the girl's thin, flowered shift clung to her, revealing the outline of her small, pointed breasts and rounded hips. Shannon averted her eyes, feeling embarrassed at her thoughts: the quadroon was Adam's property. His, to use as he pleased.

"There," he said to Shannon. "I told you I wouldn't be long." He swung up on the seat beside her, closed the canvas flaps of the shed, so that the slaves were hidden from view, picked up the reins and cracked his whip. The mule team started forward.

"Mr. Kincaid, wait. I don't think I can ride with you after all."

"Why not?" There was a flicker of amusement in his blue eyes.

"I can't ride with your—cargo."

"They're not dangerous. They're tame as these mules here."

"They are human beings, Mr. Kincaid. Not mules." Her voice trembled with indignation.

"Are you a Yankee, Miss Cavanaugh?"

"I was born down here, but I've been away for eight years, at a female academy in Boston."

There was mockery in his half-smile. His eyes flicked over the bodice of her borrowed dress and she was aware of how she must look to him in the yellow organdy, trimmed with cheap lace and sleazy green satin bows.

"If it'll make you feel better, those men back there aren't my property. My partner and I leased them from Mrs. Duval to work in our lumber mill."

"And the girl? I was on deck on the *Amaranth* when she tried to get away from you. She was terrified."

"She was a little scared, I guess. Never been away from her mother. It was foolish of Mrs. Duval not to tell her she was being sent to Mobile. But the girl's getting used to the idea. She'll be all right."

"I don't believe you. How can any woman get used to the idea of being sold, like an animal?"

"Look here," Adam said impatiently, "I'm not forcing you to ride with me. If you want to get down and walk, go right ahead."

Shannon's panic at the thought of making her way along the waterfront in darkness must have shown in her face, for Adam said: "I thought not. Don't look at me that way. Those blacks will be allowed to keep part of their earnings. And, if Mrs. Duval is willing to give her consent, they can buy their freedom one day."

"I didn't know that."

"You've been away a long time. Why not wait before you pass judgment?"

His condescending tone irritated her.

"I suppose you're going to tell me that the girl, Tina, will be working in your lumbermill, too."

He laughed. "Hardly, Miss Cavanaugh."

"Then what are you going to use her for?" She spoke without thinking and was dismayed by the effect of her words.

Kincaid gave her an impudent smile. "What a bold question. Are all young ladies educated up North so outspoken?"

She looked away, remembering what Clarisse Jenkins had said about the probable fate of the quadroon girl. *She'll be spreadin' her legs for that good-lookin' fella.*

Was Adam Kincaid good-looking? His black hair

waved crisply over his broad forehead, and his nose was short and straight, his mouth wide, full-lipped. It was a sensual face, and a hard one. Shannon thought that she would not have wanted to become his property. She felt her face getting hot.

"I didn't mean to pry. But—she looks so young."

"About your age, I'd say." His eyes rested on Shannon's high, rounded breasts with a look of frank appraisal, making her feel that she was on the auction block.

"Aren't we near my uncle's tavern yet?" she asked, hoping to divert him.

"We'll be there soon enough. Tell me, will you be staying long at Rawlinson's place?"

"No. I simply can't."

"Why not?"

"I wouldn't expect you to understand," she said stiffly.

"Do you have other relatives you can stay with?"

"No. But surely, in a city this large, I can find more suitable employment."

"What are you trained to do?"

"Why—I—"

"Surely, you must have learned to do something useful during all those years at school."

"I can read and speak French quite well. And a little Latin, too. I've studied elocution and dancing. I embroider nicely and I play the piano."

She broke off when she saw that he was laughing at her. What a horrid, rude man. "A formidable collection of skills. But hardly marketable. You're much too young and pretty to work as a governess." He shook his head. "I'm afraid you'll have to tend bar for your uncle." He flapped the reins to speed up the mules. "What made that tight-fisted Jethro Rawlinson pay for such a fancy and useless education?"

"My uncle didn't pay for my education."

"Who did, then?"

Her eyes went narrow and blazing golden, like the eyes of an angry cat. "It's none of your business."

She hated her uncle, although she had not yet met him, hated Mobile, but most of all, she hated this big, arrogant man who sat beside her, making no effort to hide his amusement at her plight.

She thought of her education at Miss Colter's Academy, and of the dismal future that Jethro Rawlinson had planned for her. It wasn't fair. Her father would not have wanted it this way.

"You're quite right, it isn't any of my business," Kincaid agreed. "But you didn't hesitate to question me a little while ago. Now, shall we declare a truce?"

"As you wish."

"Fine." He smiled down at her. "Because I want to take you out driving."

She looked at him in surprise.

"Not in this wagon," he explained. "I have a new buggy and a high-stepping little mare. I'll drive you over to the other end of Mobile, the part with the gardens and the fine houses."

"Thank you, but I—don't care to see you again."

"Maybe after a week tending bar you'll have changed your mind."

"I won't be tending bar. I can't. No one can force me to—" She was close to tears. She tried to turn her face away, but Adam put a hand under her chin, and forced her to look at him. She was surprised by the unexpected gentleness in his voice. "All right, calm down. Maybe there's something else you can do. You said you knew how to embroider?"

"Oh, yes. And I can use a sewing machine, too. Miss Colter let me use hers to make my own clothes."

Adam nodded thoughtfully. "There's a new dressmaker in town. Miss Harwood. My partner's wife gets her dresses made there. She says the old lady's swamped with work and hasn't been able to get an assistant to suit her. Maybe you could get the job."

"Do you think so?"

"No harm in trying. And if you fail, there's always the tavern." He put an arm across the back of the seat. "You know, a girl as pretty as you are would do a lot for Jethro's business. Lizzie, the girl he just let go, was willing enough, Lord knows. Made the sailors feel right at home. But she didn't have your looks."

"I don't know what you mean."

But even as she spoke, she was remembering the scene on the balcony down by the wharf: the half-naked girl, the angry man. Vague, frightening pictures forced their way into her mind. If only she had listened to certain furtive, whispered conversations among the older girls at school.

Adam moved his arm, so that it was around her shoulders. "If you don't get the job at Miss Harwood's shop, you'll do well enough at the tavern. Once you drop those fine lady's airs. You weren't really a pupil at that school, were you? More likely a maid or a seamstress's helper who was able to pick up some scraps of learning and manners. I think—"

She glared at him. "I don't care what you think."

"You should. Because I like you, Shannon, and I'm

going to see you again. You might even learn to like me, too."

"Don't flatter yourself."

"All right, then. But you might need a friend. Jethro's a hard man, and if you end up working for him, and run into trouble, the lumberyard's only a few blocks from the tavern."

"Whatever happens, I can't imagine turning to you for help."

She tried to draw away, but his arm tightened around her and his hand was on her shoulder. His fingers were warm, strong.

"All the same, if you need me, I'll be there." He took his arm away, and, pointing with his whip, he said: "Look, over that way. That's the tavern, right up ahead."

Shannon saw a long, rambling, two-story building with a faded blue and gold sign that said *Rawlinson's.* Oil lanterns blazed at either side of the swinging doors.

Before Adam could stop the mules, Shannon had stood up and her movement threw her forward; then, losing her balance, she fell across his knees. He jerked the mules to a stop, and held her. She saw his face above hers, saw the swift hunger in his eyes. He bent his head, and she said, "Please don't—please—"

To her surprise he smiled and let her go. "I'll be damned," he said slowly. "I think you really are what you say—a finishing-school miss." He shook his head. "You'll have a rough time ahead."

"I can take care of myself."

"For your sake, I hope so." He got down from the wagon and lifted her out, and once more, she was aware of his hard strength. "I'd still like to take you driving."

"You've been most helpful, but I do not think there is any reason for us to meet again, Mr. Kincaid."

"You must have learned that speech in school," he said. "But I don't think they taught you to dress that way."

"The dress is borrowed, and I'm not going to wear it one moment longer than I have to."

"It's a little gaudy, but it's not too bad. Shows off your charms. Still, you might wear something a little more concealing when I take you for a drive. We don't want to shock those high-toned ladies at the other end of town."

"You are the most arrogant—the most—"

"And you are obviously at a loss for words. No matter. By our next meeting, you'll have found something suitably scathing to say to me, I'm sure."

She turned away.

"Wait," he called. "You're forgetting your carpet-bag."

He took the bag down from the wagon, and she snatched it away from him. "I don't want to delay you any longer. You must be in a hurry to get home with your—merchandise."

"My what?"

"The girl. Tina."

"Why, Shannon, I do believe you're jealous of the wench."

Her face went scarlet and she turned away quickly; but although she kept her head high, and her back poker-straight, as she had been taught to do in Miss Colter's classes on posture and deportment, she had the uncomfortable feeling that she had lost her dignity. Adam's laughter, following her, confirmed her suspicion.

She could still hear him laughing as she pushed open the tavern doors. Then she was inside the noisy, crowded taproom, that reeked of tobacco smoke, spilled whiskey, and unwashed men. She forgot all about Adam Kincaid.

"Shannon, is it?"

She drew back from the barrel-chested man who confronted her. He wore no jacket and his shirtsleeves were rolled up to his elbows. He was under middle height, and his potbelly bulged over his heavy, tooled leather belt, but she could see that there was muscle under the layers of fat.

"Yes, I'm Shannon." She tried to back away.

"I'm yer uncle, Jethro. No need to be bashful." He seized her arm and hurried her through the crowd over to the bar that ran the length of the rear wall.

"Kate," he shouted over the uproar. "Get yer arse over here. It's Shannon."

Aunt Kate came from behind the bar, wiping her hands on her soiled apron, and pushing back a lock of faded blonde hair that had straggled down over her brow. Her plump face was flushed with the heat.

"Shannon, dearie." She threw her arms around Shannon, then held her away a little to get a better look at her.

"Why, it's a real young lady you are," Kate said. "And a beauty like your mother."

Jethro nodded, his small eyes flicking over Shannon. "She's got a good shape on her. Damn good.

And you don't mind showing it, do you? Kate'll learn you all you need to know about tendin' bar."

"I'm not going to tend bar, Uncle Jethro."

"What kind of nonsense is this? Course you're goin' to wait on the trade, and help your aunt around the place. I got no room for a fine miss who don't want to earn her keep."

"Now, Jethro, Shannon's tired, that's all. And hungry, I'll bet. Once she's had a bit of supper and a night's sleep, she'll see things different." Aunt Kate gave Shannon's arm a warning squeeze. "She'll want to help out, and she'll be a good worker, you'll see."

"She damn well better be," Jethro went behind the bar and took over, while Kate hustled Shannon from the taproom into the cluttered kitchen, a low-ceilinged room, heavy with the mingled smells of boiled pork, simmering greens, spilled ale and rancid fat.

"Sit down at the table, dearie," Aunt Kate said. She busied herself at the ancient black stove, heaping a cracked earthenware plate with a thick slice of fatty pork, a pile of collard greens, and a couple of biscuits, topping it all with gravy.

Shannon, watching her aunt, saw how much she had changed during the past eight years. Those years had robbed Kate of the last traces of a slender, graceful prettiness, had put streaks of gray into her ginger-blond hair and had caused her chin and jowls to sag, her waistline to thicken.

Shannon remembered what Adam Kincaid had said about Jethro. Bad-tempered. Tight-fisted. She felt a stab of pity for Aunt Kate.

Her aunt set down the plate, and poured two mugs of ale, then seated herself next to Shannon.

"You must be careful what you say to your uncle," Kate warned. "He's a good enough man, as men go, but sometimes he—he ain't too easy to get along with." She forced a smile. "He took a real fancy to you, though, I could see that. And why not? You'll be a regular ornament to the tavern."

"I meant what I said about not working here."

"Now, Shannon, don't talk foolish. Eat your supper and drink some of this ale."

The coal stove made the kitchen almost unbearably hot, and, although Shannon was hungry, the fatty meat and thick, lumpy gravy were not appetizing, but the ale did help to quench her thirst.

"I'm not ungrateful, Aunt Kate, and I'm willing to work hard. But surely you must know that I wasn't trained for this kind of work."

"Why, the tavern's a fine place. We do a good business here."

Shannon set her chin at a stubborn angle, and there was determination in her golden eyes. "My father wouldn't have wanted me to work in a tavern."

"Shannon, you never knew your father, so how can you be so sure what he would have wanted?"

"He paid for my education at Miss Colter's Academy, I know that much. He wanted me to be a lady. I am a lady."

She was not yet ready to tell Aunt Kate about Bruce Lathrop, her need to see him again, and to impress him with her respectable surroundings. She could not do that if she stayed here.

"You've learned nice manners, to be sure," her aunt

was saying, "and an elegant way of speakin'. But you got no money. You'll have to work here, dearie. Besides, Jethro went and fired Lizzie, the regular barmaid, soon as he knew you were on your way."

Shannon set down her mug of ale. "Then he'll have to hire her back or find someone else."

She did not want to quarrel with Aunt Kate, not now, after their long separation. She knew that she owed her aunt a debt of gratitude for having cared for her as a child; true, her father had paid the rent on the cottage where she and her aunt had lived, but he had not been able to pay for the love and kindness that her aunt had lavished upon her during those early years.

But she could not stay at the tavern, for she was thinking of Bruce Lathrop and she knew she could not have him calling on her here. She felt sick even thinking of having Bruce see her behind the bar, serving drinks to her uncle's customers.

"Shannon, dearie, I did the best I could. You'll get used to livin' here. You'll have to jolly the men along, flirt with them a bit, but nothin' more. I'll see to that."

Shannon thought of Bruce, driving off with Odalie Duval in a fine carriage with a liveried driver perched on the box. She remembered the pretty, rose-colored dress Odalie had worn, the elegant little parasol held over her head.

I'm as much a lady as she is, Shannon thought. *And I'm prettier—I'm sure I am.*

The ale was making her lightheaded, for she was not used to drinking. "I won't work here," she told her aunt. "I'll have a house with servants and fine clothes and a carriage. I want—"

"You want what your poor mother wanted, I know," Aunt Kate interrupted. "Peggy had fine notions, too, and look how she ended up. Dying a year after you were born. If yer father hadn't provided for you, Lord knows how I would have managed to raise you."

"Who was my father?" Shannon leaned toward her aunt, golden eyes blazing. "You never would tell me and neither would that lawyer who took me to Boston. But I have a right to know now. I've got to know."

"Hush, dearie." Aunt Kate's plump, sagging face was filled with panic. "You mustn't ask. You must forget about your father. You mustn't know his name, not ever."

"Why not?" Shannon demanded.

"It could mean danger for you, for all of us."

"But my father might have made some provision for me in his will."

"How could he, without his wife findin' out? A regular she-devil she is, I've heard tell."

Shannon pushed her chair back from the table and sprang to her feet. "I don't care," she cried. "I'm not afraid of her. Tell me who she is and I'll go see her."

"Oh, no. You must be mad, talkin' like that—"

The kitchen door swung open and Jethro strode in.

"What's all this carryin' on here? I could hear the two of ye out in the taproom."

"It's nothin', Jethro. Shannon's foolish and head-strong, but she'll listen to reason."

"Damn right she will," Jethro said. He turned on Shannon. "You still makin' a fuss about workin' here?" he demanded.

He grabbed her by the shoulder, his stubby fingers

holding her in a cruel grip. "I don't know what fancy notions ye picked up in that school in Boston," he said, "but you'd better get over them. You're Peggy Cavanaugh's bastard, and it was a lot of damn foolishness havin' you brought up like a lady." Without releasing Shannon, he turned on Kate. "And you'll not be coddlin' the girl. She either gets to work here, or she can go peddle her tail to the flatboat men down on the wharf."

Shannon wrenched free. "I won't stay here and I won't—" She could not bring herself even to repeat what her uncle had said. "I'll get work. As a dressmaker's assistant. I won't ask you for a penny, so you needn't worry about that."

"And who's going to give you a job, with your airs and graces?" Jethro demanded.

"Miss Harwood. She's a dressmaker. Adam Kincaid told me she needs an assistant."

Jethro looked surprised. "Adam Kincaid, is it? And where did you meet him?"

"Down at the wharf. He gave me a ride here in his wagon."

"Did he, indeed? Well now, you haven't lost any time gettin' acquainted. Smart young fella, Kincaid is. Comes in here sometimes. Him and his partner, Matt Cory, have got a thriving business. So you took his eye, did you?"

"I'm not planning to see Mr. Kincaid again."

"Whyever not?" Aunt Kate demanded. "He's got an eye for a pretty girl. I'd have thought—"

"He asked me to go riding with him, in his carriage, but I refused. He—he's arrogant. And common."

"Common, is he?" Jethro shouted. "He's one of

the most respected businessmen in Mobile. Got more
ready cash than a lot of them planters upriver."

"I'm not interested in Mr. Kincaid or his money.
I'll get work and take care of myself."

"As you please," Jethro said. "But if that dressmaker turns you down, don't come back here and
expect to live off me." He glared at Shannon, but she
did not flinch, and he turned on Kate. "And you get
back out to the bar. Get movin'.'"

"I fixed up Lizzie's old room for you," she said to
Shannon over her shoulder, as she hurried out. "First
one to the right, at the top of the stairs."

"I'll find it, Aunt Kate," Shannon said.

The room set aside for her was small and drab,
and none too clean, the faded paper peeling from the
walls in strips, and the narrow window, overlooking
the stableyard, was uncurtained.

Shannon put her thin cotton blanket over the
window, then removed the yellow organdy dress and
her underclothes. Aunt Kate had left a pitcher of
water and a basin on the nightstand, and Shannon
began to wash herself. She had been able to keep up
a bold front for her uncle, but now that she was alone,
she felt uncertain about the future.

Suppose Miss Harwood refused to hire her?
Shannon had had no experience in a dress shop and
perhaps skill, alone, would not be enough.

She sighed, and lathered her breasts with a bit of
soap. As she did so, she remembered how Adam's
eyes had lingered on her breasts, and she felt hot all
over. She dried hastily. She would get the job with
Miss Harwood and she would never have to see

Adam again. Instead, Bruce Lathrop would come calling on her, at the dressmaker's shop; he would take her riding.

She sighed, in eager anticipation, as she put on her long-sleeved nightgown. Oh, she had to get the job at the shop. She simply had to.

She stretched out on the narrow, lumpy bed and shifted restlessly. It was hard to get comfortable, and although she was sleepy from the long journey and the ale, she found the noises from the stableyard disturbing. A drunk sang lustily, a woman gave a shrill laugh, then cried out: "Easy there, sailor. Can't ye wait 'til we get to my place?"

Shannon shuddered and pushed her head into the pillow, in spite of the heat. She tried to visualize Bruce's face, the chiseled features, the deep gray eyes. She tried to imagine herself seated beside Bruce in a fine carriage, with a dainty parasol held over her head to shield her from the sun.

But instead, as she drifted off to sleep, another image arose: Adam Kincaid, holding her across his knees on the seat of the wagon. The memory of his laughter echoed in her mind, mocking her. But she would show him. She would show everyone. She was a lady, the daughter of a fine upriver planter, and one day soon, all Mobile would know that.

3

SHANNON, HOLDING HER skirt high to avoid contact with the puddles, and stepping carefully around a drunk who lay sprawled in her path, started for the dressmaker's shop. She wished that she had a parasol to shield her from the glaring sunlight, and she sighed when, a short time later, she left the waterfront behind her, and turned into Government Street, whose majestic oaks provided some shade.

She quickened her steps, hurrying past business establishments with neat brick and wooden fronts, and small houses whose ironwork balconies, decorated with fleurs-de-lis or bees, emblems of Napoleon Bonaparte, supported climbing roses and trailing wisteria.

She breathed the fragrance, and her pace slowed as she let herself slip into her daydreams of Bruce once more. Was he engaged to Odalie? she wondered.

She tried not to envy Odalie Duval, as she had

tried not to envy her schoolmates, the girls who went home for the holidays, while she was left behind.

During her first winter in Boston, Shannon had learned that she was different, set apart from the others. The bitterness of that lesson was still with her.

Hetty Davenport, the daughter of a wealthy Boston merchant, had asked Shannon, with whom she shared a room, to come home with her for the Christmas holiday.

But shortly before she was to leave, Shannon had answered a summons from Miss Colter, and had been told that she must refuse the invitation.

"But Hetty wants me—"

"I'm sorry, Shannon. I cannot allow you to go."

"Why not? You've said my work was improving, that my deportment—"

"I'm pleased with your progress," Miss Colter said quietly. "But Mr. Bassett, the gentleman who brought you here, told me you were not to visit the homes of your classmates. Your—father—made that a condition of your attending school here." Miss Colter blushed slightly. "You are too young to understand the circumstances of your birth."

"But I do. Aunt Kate told me."

Miss Colter grew redder. "We'll say no more about it, then. And after the holidays, you won't room with Hetty. You'll be given a room of your own."

"But Hetty's my friend."

"It will be better this way, believe me," Miss Colter said. "It's not fair, perhaps, that you must bear the burden of your parents' indiscretions, but we cannot change the views of our society. One day, perhaps—"

"But if I can't have friends, or visit anyone, what will I do on the holidays?"

"You will devote yourself to your studies, and someday, you will use your education to find a respectable position as a governess. Or perhaps, if your father is inclined to be generous—he's a wealthy man—he might set you up in a school like this one."

"That's not enough. I want—" She wanted the same future as the other girls here: balls, dinner parties, summers at Saratoga or Newport, and later, marriage to a handsome young man.

"We cannot always have what we want, Shannon," the head mistress said, and there was a look on her long, pale face that Shannon did not understand. "Now, shall I tell Hetty that you can't go home with her?"

Shannon shook her head. "I'll tell her."

Even now, eight years later, Shannon remembered the hurt of having to refuse Hetty's invitation. Of moving into a room of her own.

She learned, gradually, to hide the hurt, but she was inwardly angry, rebellious, and lonely.

What good did it do to learn the waltz, the polka, the schottische? Why practice the correct way to enter a drawing room, to make polite conversation suitable for a young lady at her first ball?

Miss Colter, sensing her unhappiness, tried to compensate. One summer, when Shannon was fourteen and left alone at school, the headmistress had taught her to use the new sewing machine.

"It's not difficult," she said. "We'll shop for material and you will make a new wardrobe. You need one, my dear."

At fourteen, Shannon was conscious of her budding breasts, pushing against her now-tight bodices. She was conscious of other mysterious changes in her body. Miss Colter had explained, in a matter-of-fact way, the most frightening of these changes, for Shannon had no friend among the girls to reassure her. Miss Colter had tried to be kind then, as now.

"I'd like to make my own dresses," Shannon had said. And she quickly discovered that she had a talent for sewing, an eye for patterns and colors.

A good thing, too, Shannon thought, as she stopped in front of Miss Harwood's shop. She would be lucky to work here, on this pleasant, tree-lined street, far from the waterfront. Although, she thought with a sigh, even if Miss Harwood hired her, she would still be a long way from the world of Bruce Lathrop. And Odalie Duval.

Odalie and her mother had spent the night in the Creole cottage on the outskirts of Mobile, a pleasant, two-story townhouse with a rosy facade of brick, faded by the blazing sun and the sea air, half-hidden by hedges of Cherokee roses and the arbors of scuppernong grapes. Now they sat side by side in their carriage, parasols held high to keep off the noonday sun. The liveried driver cracked his whip, and the horses trotted more quickly along the winding shell road, past groves of orange trees and magnolias.

Odalie, seated beside her mother, felt uneasy.

Since Papa's death, Mama had changed. There was a bloom about her. She looked younger. And she no longer wore black, but a pale gray half-mourning, over the objections of old Aunt Lucienne, Papa's aunt, who lived with them at Beau Rivage. "That dress is too low in the bosom," Aunt Lucienne had protested the first time she had seen the gray silk dress.

"I won't have my portrait painted wearing black," Mama had said firmly. "Black doesn't become me."

"Is it the portrait you're concerned about?" Aunt Lucienne had snapped. "Or is it young Mr. Sutherland?"

Edward Sutherland, an itinerant artist, had been spending a good deal of time at Beau Rivage, working on the portrait Mama had commissioned.

"I don't like that young man. He's got a bold look. Those eyes of his—"

"Really, Lucienne," Mama had said, "if you were younger, I'd suspect you of being interested in Mr. Sutherland yourself." Then, her voice hard, she had added, "What I do is no concern of yours. I am mistress of Beau Rivage, and you would do well to remember that."

And Aunt Lucienne, a spinster and a dependent, had said no more. But Odalie could not help noticing that Mama emerged from her sessions with the portrait painter flushed, even a little disheveled, not at all like herself.

"You'll have to have a whole new wardrobe," Mama was saying now. "I want you to look your best for Mr. Cunningham's visit."

"Arthur Cunningham's coming to Beau Rivage? But why?"

"I invited him. He'll be here in September."

"But there's plenty of time for a wardrobe then."

"You'll need some traveling dresses at once. I'm sending you to visit Aunt Belle and Aunt Carrie for the summer."

At any other time, Odalie would have protested being shipped off to visit her aunts, in North Carolina, for the two ladies, both widowed, devoted themselves to needlework and church activities. Now, however, faced with the prospect of a visit from Arthur Cunningham, she felt that nothing else was important.

"I hate the man," she said. She shuddered, remembering the portly New Englander with his reddish whiskers and harsh Yankee accent. His voice, loud and alien, stirred memories she had tried to keep locked away.

"Mr. Cunningham was taken with you when he met you on our visit to Lake Pontchartrain. He asked if he might see you again and I said yes."

"But, Mama, I don't want to see him."

"That will do," Mama said, her arching black brows drawing together in a warning frown.

"He's old. And he's a Yankee."

"He's only a little over forty, and a most successful businessman. His cotton mills are profitable, he has great political influence in Massachusetts—"

"How do you know so much about him?" Odalie asked.

"I made inquiries, naturally. He'll be staying at Beau Rivage for at least a month."

"Then I'll remain with Aunt Belle and Aunt Carrie until he's gone," Odalie snapped.

"You'll do no such thing. I'm giving a ball in Mr. Cunningham's honor and you will be there. You will be pleasant to him. You will show him the courtesy due any guest in our home."

"He's crude and vulgar and I—I'm afraid of him."

"What nonsense. You'd better get over those feelings, and quickly."

Surely, Mama was not going to try to marry her off to Arthur Cunningham. She was going to marry Bruce.

"The Lathrops will be at the ball," Odalie began, feeling her way cautiously.

"I suppose so," Mama said carelessly.

"If Mr. Cunningham is overattentive to me, Bruce will be jealous, and you know how hot-tempered he is."

"Bruce has no claim on you."

"But he does. Bruce and I—we're—"

"You are childhood friends, nothing more." Mama looked at Odalie sharply. "You have not allowed him to take any liberties with you?"

"Oh, Mama, Bruce isn't like that. He's a gentleman."

"He's a man," Mama said. "And if you were not so innocent you would know—"

Innocent. Odalie turned away. Mama did not know. No one knew. No one ever would, not even Bruce.

It had happened only a little over a year ago. Papa, stricken with his first heart attack down in

New Orleans had been forced to remain there, and Mama had gone to join him, and make arrangements for his care. He was not to be moved for several weeks.

Odalie, bored and restless at Beau Rivage, with only Aunt Lucienne for company, had slipped out of the house and ridden down to the bluffs to watch the last of the year's cotton harvest being loaded aboard a riverboat under the watchful eye of Craig Judson, the new overseer.

Judson was a loud-voiced, sandy-haired man from New England. No one knew much about him, not even Mama, who had hired him in desperation, after their former overseer had died of fever. Mama, who had been preparing to leave for New Orleans, with the picking season at its height, had considered herself fortunate to find a replacement.

Odalie, watching Judson moving about on the landing, shouting orders, began to grow aware of him as a man. He was not a gentleman, no Yankee overseer could be, but there was something about him that aroused disturbing, unfamiliar feelings in her.

He was tall, heavy-set, with hard muscles under his coarse cotton shirt; his rolled-up sleeves bared his hairy, sun-bronzed forearms.

When the boat was loaded and the slaves dispatched to other tasks, Judson rode up to Odalie, who was seated on her sleek, brown mare.

"Shouldn't think a young miss would be interested in such dull business as loading cotton," he said.

"Beau Rivage will be mine some day. I'm concerned with everything about it." She held her head at an arrogant tilt, as she had seen Mama do when speaking to inferiors. Judson's eyes lingered on her. She knew she looked smart in her jade green riding habit; the costume set off her tiny waist and emphasized the full curves of her breasts. Well-rounded breasts, a little startling for a girl of fourteen. Aunt Lucienne had said that all the Duval girls matured early.

"With Mama away, I should know everything that is going on at Beau Rivage," Odalie said, "so that I may write and tell her."

"Then maybe you'll let me ride back with you, and we can stop at my house. Queenie whelped this morning, as fine a litter of pups as I've ever seen."

The dog and her puppies were in a shed attached to the overseer's neat, whitewashed cottage. Odalie and Judson knelt together to examine the tan, silky little animals. "Oh, how sweet," Odalie said. "So tiny."

"Maybe you'd like one for yourself, Miss Odalie. When they get a little bigger, come down and pick whichever one you like."

Odalie gave Judson a warm smile. "Oh, thank you," she said. A puppy would ease her loneliness, give her something to care for.

Judson gave her a hand to help her to her feet, and as he did so, her breast brushed against his bare arm. She was only half-aware of his swift intake of breath, of the way his greenish eyes narrowed under his sandy brows.

"Come around as often as you want," he said. "It won't be easy to choose among these pups."

After that, Judson stopped by the big house from time to time, to tell Odalie what progress the puppies were making and to speak to her of other events around the plantation, and she was flattered. Mama might treat her as a child, but here was a man who recognized her as a responsible young lady. The thought was a heady one.

The weeks dragged on, Mama was still unable to leave New Orleans, and Bruce and Melora were visiting in New York City. Odalie came to welcome the visits from the overseer.

Then, early one evening, when Aunt Lucienne had retired with a migraine, Odalie had one of the servants saddle her mare and she rode down to Judson's cottage. Although it was already early autumn, the air was still heavy with the mingled odors of jasmine and roses.

She knew Aunt Lucienne disapproved of her friendliness with the overseer, but Odalie was indifferent to her aunt's opinions. She already suspected that Aunt Lucienne's migraines might have some connection with the apricot brandy with which the old lady consoled herself, whenever her homesickness for Paris overcame her.

Odalie dismounted outside the cottage and went into the shed; the light from the one window was dim. Odalie knelt down, tucking the full skirt of her thin white organdy dress under her knees. The day had been close and humid, and she had worn as little as possible under the dress; only her pantelettes and a gossamer-sheer camisole. Even her starched petticoat had been too confining.

Craig Judson, his day's work finished, was preparing to go down to the quarters. For some weeks now, he had had his eye on Sheba, a lithe, coffee-colored young wench with a fine pair of tits and a well-rounded rump. Now, with the harvest over, he would relax and pleasure himself. There was a heavy, warm urgency in his loins as he thought about it; he'd be the first with her, he'd bet on that. Some men preferred a wench with experience, but he didn't. The younger, the better. There'd been that twelve-year-old virgin in that fancy house up in New York. She'd cost him nearly a week's pay, but damned if he'd regretted it. The fear in her eyes, her tears, her shrill cry of pain, these things stimulated him, adding an edge to his pleasure.

Odalie heard footsteps, looked up to see Judson in the doorway. "It's kind of late for you to be riding out alone, isn't it?" he asked.

His voice was different, husky. His eyes were fixed on her in a peculiar way.

"I was trying to pick out the puppy I want."

"Here," he said, lighting an oil lamp on a shelf as she got to her feet. "Now you can get a better look."

The lamp was behind her and its light outlined her body, under the thin white organdy. Her eyes were huge and dark in her small face. "I'd better be getting back to the house," she said uneasily. "If Aunt Lucienne should wake up and find me gone—"

"No hurry. The old girl should be out like a drunken sailor, with all that brandy she drinks."

"How dare you? You're forgetting your place."

"Take it easy. Regular little spitfire you are, when you get riled up."

He moved quickly, so that he was between Odalie and the door leading to the yard. "I want to go home," she said. "If you don't move aside this minute I'll—"

"You'll what?" He was at her side in two long strides. He swung her up off her feet and carried her from the shed into the bedroom at the rear of the cottage. She cried out, and his mouth, hot and wet, covered hers, stifling the sound.

He threw her down on the bed. "No need to go down to the quarters," she heard him say. "We can have us a good time right here."

He was on the bed beside her, pinning her down with the weight of his body. She had to fight for breath.

"Let me go—please—"

Instead, his hands went to her breasts. He cupped them, kneaded them. "You like this, don't you? And this—"

One of his hands moved down, pushed up her skirt, and parted her thighs. "Take your hands off me. I'll tell—"

"Who'll you tell? Your Pa's a sick man. The blacks are afraid of me. Who'll you tell, girl?"

"We have neighbors. You'll be punished for this."

"I'll be long gone by then. Listen, girl, you've been hanging around me, looking at me, coming up here alone. You've been asking for it."

"I never thought—I didn't mean—"

"The hell you didn't. Wiggling your backside at me, like any high-yella girl."

Terrified now, she screamed again, and he struck her across the face with such force that lights danced before her eyes. He was tearing at her clothes, stripping her naked. His hot tongue pushed between her parted lips. He fumbled with his breeches and a moment later, she felt his hardness against her.

Instinctively, she closed her legs but he forced one knee between them, and then he was on top of her.

A moment later he was thrusting himself up inside her, so that she was sure the sharp, searing agony would tear her apart, would kill her.

His voice was hoarse; he was saying words she had never heard, did not understand, moving harder, faster. . . .

Some time during that night, Craig Judson had left Beau Rivage. And before dawn, Odalie had managed to get back to her own room in the big house, where she lay for a day and a night, pretending illness. No one must ever know. Aunt Lucienne was too befuddled with the aftermath of her session with the brandy bottle to suspect, and Tina, Odalie's personal maid, would keep silent.

Odalie was sure she would never be able to let any other man come near her after that. But when Bruce came home that winter, she had changed her mind.

A girl had to marry, or be a spinster, like poor Aunt Lucienne. And nothing was more shameful than spinsterhood. Besides, Bruce was a gentleman. She had known him since childhood. He would never hurt her. He would be patient, understanding.

Even with Bruce, her imagination would not go beyond their wedding. She could see herself in a dress of ivory satin, a veil of creamy lace draped over her dark hair. Beyond that, the future was vague, hazy.

"For heavens' sake, Odalie, can't you answer when you're spoken to?"

"I'm sorry, Mama. What did you say?"

"I said, you must look your prettiest at the ball for Mr. Cunningham. You must dance with him as often as he asks you to."

"Gracious, one would think President Buchanan was coming to Beau Rivage." She forced herself to speak lightly. And, with her talent for dismissing the unpleasant, she made herself forget Arthur Cunningham for the moment, and think, instead, of how Bruce would admire her new ball gown.

4

"I'M AFRAID you won't do, Miss Cavanaugh."

Shannon stood in the showroom of the dressmaker's shop, while Miss Harwood, a tall, bony woman looked at her through gold-rimmed spectacles. "I'm sorry, but—"

"Mr. Kincaid said you might need an assistant—"

"Kincaid. I don't know the man."

"He and his partner, Mr. Cory, own a lumberyard. He said that Mrs. Cory—"

"Oh, yes. Cory and Kincaid." The dressmaker spoke with disdain, and Shannon swiftly decided that the wife of a tradesman, no matter how prosperous, was not a favored customer.

"Most of my ladies come down here from the plantations, or I go upriver to fit them at their homes. Why, only last week, Madame LeVert, Octavia LeVert, assured me that my work was superior to that of the finest dressmakers in New Orleans."

"I've been away from Mobile since I was a child,"

Shannon said, to excuse her lack of recognition of Madame LeVert.

"Indeed? And you've never worked for a dressmaker?"

"No, but I sew well. I made this dress I'm wearing." Shannon refused to give up without trying. "The skirt was badly ripped. I mended it, you see."

"And neatly, too. Yes, indeed." She lifted Shannon's skirt a few inches and examined the seams. "Made by machine."

"I can sew by machine and by hand. And I embroider beautifully. That is, Miss Colter, the headmistress at my school in Boston said so."

"You worked in a girls' school in Boston?"

"No, I was a student there."

Miss Harwood straightened, and threw a sharp, searching look at Shannon. "Is it customary for young ladies in Boston to learn to use a sewing machine? Fine embroidery, yes. But a machine—"

"Miss Colter had progressive ideas. She called the sewing machine one of the mechanical marvels of our century, and said that—"

"It's fast," Miss Harwood said disdainfully. "Speed is everything today, particularly among the Yankees. A bustling, pushy lot."

"I'm not a Yankee," Shannon assured her. "I was born in Mobile."

"And you're living in a tavern, on the waterfront."

"I don't live there. I only stayed overnight."

"No matter. I haven't time to train an inexperienced girl. I do have several orders piled up, but I hardly think—"

"I'll help you catch up. Can't you hire me for a trial? I'm strong and I work hard. You—don't have to pay me a salary right away, only room and board. I can't stay at my uncle's tavern. Oh, please—"

"You want to get away from the waterfront, that's understandable. But I still don't see why you left school and went to such a place."

"There were financial reverses," Shannon improvised.

"You do have a ladylike manner, and a pleasant appearance. That's important, in my establishment." She paused. Then she said, "Come with me. I'll give you a chance to show me what you can do."

She led the way through the showroom, up three steps.

"That is the dressing room," she said, indicating a small cubicle to one side. Shannon noticed that the walls of the dressingroom reached only halfway to the high ceiling, to permit the circulation of air. The cubicle was curtained in front with a length of flowered cotton.

"The workroom's back there," Miss Harwood said. She moved stiffly, as if her legs ached with every step.

The workroom was large and airy, with long windows overlooking the back garden. Shannon felt that she was a world away from the waterfront.

One of the new Singer machines stood in a corner. An open cabinet revealed bolts of glacé silk, organdy, grenadine, tulle and tarlatan. On a long worktable were boxes of buttons, trimmings, laces and sprays of artificial flowers made of silk and velvet. On another table lay a half-basted organdy dress, the sleeves not yet set in.

"I'll give you an easy task," Miss Harwood began. "Take this dress and—"

The shop bell tinkled. "Never mind," she said hastily. "Wait here until I've finished with these customers. Then I'll explain what I want you to do."

Shannon took a seat, relieved that at least she would have a chance to prove her skill.

Miss Harwood departed, as quickly as her stiffened joints would allow. Shannon heard voices from the front of the shop. Then, as Miss Harwood and the new arrivals approached the dressing room, she heard the dressmaker say, "A pleasure to see you again, Mrs. Duval. And you, Miss Odalie."

Shannon's fingers tightened on the arms of her chair.

"Step into the dressing room." Shannon heard the clink of metal rings as the curtain was drawn across the front of the dressing room. Then she heard Miss Harwood, chattering breathlessly from within the cubicle. "So kind of you to come to my shop. My rheumatism has been most troublesome."

"I want a new wardrobe for Miss Odalie. Traveling dresses, to be completed by next week. Then, a ball gown, several afternoon dresses, a theater costume. We won't be needing those until September. For the ball gown, one of those new brocades from Lyons, France, I think."

"That may take time," Miss Harwood said.

"If you can't manage it, I can find another dressmaker."

"That won't be necessary. I'll start on the traveling dresses at once. If the brocade should be late in arriving, I'll put every other order aside to work on it."

"You have an assistant, surely," Mrs. Duval said.

"The fact is, I have not yet been able—"

"Then we must go elsewhere, I suppose," Mrs. Duval interrupted.

Shannon pitied Miss Harwood, and felt an instant dislike for Mrs. Duval: A hard woman who would bully anyone who could not stand up to her. The woman who had sold Tina, the quadroon girl, to Adam Kincaid, without a word of warning.

"Mrs. Duval, I assure you, I was interviewing an assistant when you came in. A skilled seamstress. A young lady in reduced circumstances."

"Oh, very well," Mrs. Duval said impatiently. "But I must have those dresses on time."

"Certainly, Mrs. Duval. Now, let me help Miss Odalie off with her dress."

There was a moment's silence then: "We'll want one of the afternoon dresses in white silk. Another in pale blue organdy. As for the ball dress—green brocade, I think. With a thread of silver in the design. Don't you agree, Odalie?"

"I don't care."

"Odalie, really!"

"If I'm to go to visit with Aunt Belle and Aunt Carrie, I'll stay there until—"

"We've settled all that."

"No, we have not, Mama. I won't appear at a ball in honor of Mr. Cunningham."

Mrs. Duval said smoothly, "Miss Harwood, please go and get some fashionplates to show us."

"Yes. Yes, indeed. There are charming colored plates in the latest number of *Godey's Lady's Book*." Miss Harwood was obviously relieved to make her escape.

Shannon knew that she should not eavesdrop, but she did not close the workroom door, for she had to find out all she could about Odalie Duval.

"Mama, really," Odalie said, "first you tell me that I'm to leave for North Carolina. Then I'm to return to entertain Mr. Cunningham. I don't understand."

"You will, soon enough. And now, since you're not interested in your new wardrobe, I'll choose the patterns and the materials."

There was a long, uneasy silence and even from her seat in the workroom, Shannon could feel the tension between Odalie and Mrs. Duval. Then Odalie spoke. "I think a pale green brocade would make a charming ball gown." Her voice was light, and she gave a little, tinkling laugh. "Too bad unmarried young ladies can't wear red. But after Bruce and I are married I'll have a dozen red dresses. The color is becoming to me and—"

"You will not marry Bruce Lathrop."

Shannon's lips parted. No longer able to remain seated, she rose and went to the workroom door.

"Mama, you can't mean that."

"I do."

"But I love Bruce."

"You're a child. You don't know what love means."

"I do know. I love him. I'll always love him."

Odalie's voice rose, and Shannon sensed the hysteria under the surface.

"You'll marry Arthur Cunningham. I'll see to that."

"But why? A Yankee! I'd have to leave Alabama, all my friends." Odalie stopped short. Then she continued, in a different tone, accusing, angry. "Or is it that you want to get rid of me? That Mr. Sutherland, who comes to Beau Rivage so often. Maybe you don't want him to start thinking about you as the mother of a grown young lady. I've noticed how you make excuses to send me away when he's expected. Maybe you're afraid that alongside me, you look old."

"How dare you?"

"Papa's hardly been dead six months, and you're chasing after a man whose young enough to—"

Shannon heard the sound of a slap, sharp as a pistol shot, then Odalie's soft weeping.

"I'm leaving now," Mrs. Duval said. "When Miss Harwood returns you will allow her to proceed with the fittings." Her voice was trembling with suppressed fury.

Shannon had barely enough time to step back from the open doorway before Mrs. Duval came sweeping out of the dressing room and down the three steps to the showroom. Odalie was making soft, choking sounds, and in spite of herself, Shannon felt sorry for her.

The sobbing continued until Shannon, unable to bear it any longer, left the workroom and pulled aside the dressing-room curtain. "Is there anything I can do?"

Odalie's face was flushed, her eyes swollen. "Who are you?" she asked.

"My name's Shannon Cavanaugh. Miss Harwood's new assistant. At least, I hope to be."

Odalie caught at the back of a small, gilt chair. "I feel dizzy. The heat—"

"I have smelling salts in my reticule." Shannon put an arm around Odalie. "Sit down. Now breath deeply."

"I can't. My stays are too tight."

Shannon handed the smelling salts to Odalie, then loosened her stays. "Better?"

"A little."

"Now, bend your head forward, all the way. That's it. You don't want to faint."

"I don't care if I do. I wouldn't care if I died this minute."

She's childish and spoiled, Shannon thought.

"You're a long way from dying," she said tartly.

"I'd rather die than marry Arthur Cunningham. He's horrible."

"What's wrong with him?"

"He's loud and vulgar. He's a Yankee."

"Not like—"

"Bruce? You heard, then. But, of course, you must have."

"I was waiting for Miss Harwood in the workroom."

"Oh, no!" Now that she was regaining self-control, Odalie was growing aware of the proprieties, too. Her hand went to her cheek, to cover the imprint of her mother's hand.

"Mama's not herself, since Papa died. You understand."

"Of course," Shannon said soothingly. "Perhaps she'll change her mind about—"

"About Bruce? She's got to. He—he's the only man I can ever marry."

How could any girl help falling in love with Bruce? Shannon thought. All the same, she had to suppress the urge to shake Odalie until her teeth rattled. Briskly she said, "Right now, I hope you'll let Miss Harwood proceed with the fittings. If she has a large enough order, she'll have to hire me."

"That's true, isn't it?" Odalie smiled faintly. "You need the work?"

"Yes, I do."

"How dreadful, having to work for a living."

"I enjoy sewing," Shannon said. She would not have Odalie feeling sorry for her.

"Do you? I hate it. You don't look like a seamstress and you don't talk like one. Miss Harwood said you were in reduced circumstances. Does that mean—"

"Miss Cavanaugh, I told you to remain in the workroom." It was Miss Harwood, her arms laden with copies of *Godey's Lady's Book.*

"I had a dizzy spell," Odalie said. "Miss Cavanaugh was so kind. You must hire her." She gave Shannon a conspiratorial smile, and Shannon could not help smiling back.

Miss Harwood sent Shannon back to the workroom, but in a few minutes, she came to join her. "You may help me carry in that bolt of blue organdy, and the white glacé silk. And that roll of Brussels lace. Can you manage all that?"

"Oh, yes. Does that mean you'll hire me?"

"I'll give you a trial," the dressmaker said. "I'll need help, what with this new order. And you haven't lost any time in winning over Miss Odalie."

Although Shannon resented having to feel grateful to Odalie for her new job, she was deeply relieved that she would not have to return to the tavern, thankful that she had left the ugliness of the waterfront behind her.

5

DURING HER FIRST two weeks at the dressmaker's shop, Shannon discovered that she had little time to think about anything except her duties. Miss Harwood, with a backlog of orders, kept her busy from early morning until far into the night, basting, sewing on the clattering machine, embroidering, edging endless ruffles with delicate lace. Although Miss Harwood was still stiff with rheumatism, Shannon was not permitted to wait on customers.

She had been allowed one brief visit to the tavern to pick up her carpetbag, and to inform Aunt Kate of her new position. Otherwise, she had remained in the shop. She was pleased, therefore, when she received a visit from Clarisse Jenkins one afternoon.

Clarisse breezed in with a flurry of magenta ostrich plumes on her silk bonnet, trailing the heavy scent of heliotrope perfume.

"I was going to return your dress—" Shannon began.

"I didn't come for that. I dropped in at the tavern and your aunt told me you were working here. Thought I'd see how you were getting on."

Clarisse eyed the billowing white tulle, the sprays of green satin vine leaves, the yards of lace on the work table. "I guess old Miss Harwood keeps you busy."

"She isn't well," Shannon explained. "Her rheumatism."

"Where is she now?"

"Upstairs, resting."

"And leaving you with all this to do."

"I don't mind," Shannon said. "It's better than working in my uncle's tavern."

"Hope you're gettin' well paid, at least."

"I'm not getting paid at all. But I do get room and board."

"That's all? Listen, honey, with your looks and figure, I could get you hired at the Cherokee Rose. That's the concert saloon where I work. And you'd have more fun than you do here."

"I don't think I'd—"

Before Shannon could finish, Miss Harwood came into the workroom, leaning on her cane. "And who might this be?" she demanded, looking first at Clarisse, then at Shannon.

"This is my friend, Clarisse Jenkins. She lent me a dress when I tore mine, on the *Amaranth*."

"And now she wants you to return it. Very well. Go and get it at once, Shannon. Then get back to your work. This order must be delivered tomorrow. It's for Miss Melora Lathrop of Jessamine. I still can't travel upriver, not with my rheumatism."

Jessamine. Shannon lowered her eyes to conceal her elation. She had known that this dress, and two others, now finished, were for Melora, Bruce's sister, but she had not dared to hope she would be allowed to deliver them. This was her chance to see Bruce again.

She hurried to get Clarisse's yellow organdy, and when she returned, she heard Miss Harwood saying, "I do not permit my assistants to entertain friends here."

Clarisse shrugged. "Shannon, honey, if you ever get a day off, you come by the Cherokee Rose. Not before noon, though."

"I'll show you out, Miss Jenkins," Miss Harwood said.

"I can find my way," Clarisse said, her red curls bobbing as she tossed her head. "Remember, Shannon, come see me."

After Clarisse had departed, Miss Harwood said, "I'm surprised that you have such friends. And what is the Cherokee Rose?"

"It's a—concert saloon."

"Well, really! Little better than a—You're not to visit her there, not if you want to go on working in my shop."

Shannon did not argue the point, for she was too elated at the thought of her visit to Jessamine. She might see Bruce again. And this time, if he wanted to call on her, she could say yes, for the shop was respectable, even elegant. And, although Miss Harwood objected to visitors, she would not offend Bruce Lathrop, the brother of one of her best customers.

Balancing the large, shiny dress box across her knees, Shannon looked out over the fields of Jessamine. The driver of the carriage she had hired at the landing turned onto a road that ran between two fields, where slaves bent to plant the cotton seed in the rich, black soil.

Beyond the fields were smooth lawns, dotted with flowering shrubs, the jessamine that gave the plantation its name. A peacock cried shrilly, unfurled his magnificent tail, and strutted past, followed by his harem.

Shannon sighed. She might have grown up on such a plantation, might have taken such splendor as her natural heritage, if only she had had the right to her father's name.

Even so, she might have been reasonably contented, working at the dressmaker's shop, had she not met Bruce.

"No use lookin' at that kind. They're not for the likes of us."

She brushed aside the memory of Clarisse's warning. She wasn't like Clarisse, not after those years at Miss Colter's Academy. Her speech, her deportment, were those of a lady.

"There it is, right up ahead, miss," the driver said. Shannon saw the house then, with its gleaming white columns, its lacy iron balconies and tall, green-shuttered windows.

A black boy came running up. Shannon explained her errand, and the boy said, "Dis way, please, miss. I'll carry dem boxes."

Melora Lathrop was waiting in the upstairs sitting room, between two tall windows curtained in pale blue silk. Although she looked older than Bruce, Shannon saw the resemblance in the silver-blond hair, the gray eyes, the fine bones of the face. But Melora was too thin, too pale to be pretty, and, at the moment, she had none of Bruce's gracious manners.

"I expected these dresses two weeks ago," she snapped. "Well, don't stand there. Open the box. Why didn't Miss Harwood come herself?"

"I'm her assistant," Shannon explained. "Would you like to try on the white tulle first?"

"Very well. I shouldn't take the dresses at all, considering how late they are."

Shannon bit her lip to keep from snapping back.

"This doesn't fit well," Melora said, looking at her reflection in the mirror. "The bodice is too loose."

Shannon wanted to say that a few rows of ruffles sewn into her corset cover would improve the fit. Or she might try the spiral-spring bosom pads that Shannon had seen advertised in *Harper's Magazine*: "For those who require some artificial expansion to give rotundity to the form."

"Help me off with this," Melora ordered, tugging at the white tulle. "I'll try the blue satin next."

"If you'll let me make those alterations in the bodice—"

"The blue satin. At once."

"But I can—"

"That will do. You may take all the dresses back. And you may tell Miss Harwood to come herself next time."

"She isn't well. Her rheumatism is giving her great discomfort," Shannon said.

"Then she can't do her work. I'll have to go to another dressmaker in future, I suppose."

Shannon's cheeks burned. Damn Melora. She looked away to hide the anger in her eyes. "It's only a temporary indisposition," she said. "I'm to blame for the dresses being late. I've had no experience in a dressmaker's shop, you see."

Miss Harwood had given her a job and made it possible for her to escape from the tavern. She had to do all she could to keep the old lady from losing a customer. But it wasn't easy to humble herself before Melora.

"I see." Melora tapped her foot, her eyes narrow. "Oh, very well. I'll try on the other two dresses."

"Thank you, Miss Lathrop." Shannon almost choked getting the words out; humility did not come naturally to her.

Melora had to concede that the blue satin and the plaid tarlatan were acceptable. She accompanied Shannon to the head of the stairs. "Next time, I expect to see Miss Harwood here, not an assistant."

Shannon hesitated. "There's one more thing," she said. "The account. Miss Harwood hoped you might—"

"I'll settle my account in due time."

"Yes, Miss Lathrop. But Miss Harwood particularly requested—it's been nearly a year since—"

"I know how long it's been. I'll pay when it's convenient. And remember to tell your employer that if she cannot take care of my orders herself, I'll have my dresses made elsewhere."

"Even if you change dressmakers," Shannon said,

her temper exploding at last, "you'll still have to pay Miss Harwood for her work."

Melora began to speak, but something she saw in Shannon's face stopped her. For a moment, the two girls stood on the long curved stairway, the silence stretching between them.

Then Melora said, "You may leave now," and turning, she went quickly upstairs.

Shannon, the dress box under her arm, hurried down to the front hall, blinded by tears of rage. At the front door she stopped and fumbled for her reticule, for it would not do to show the carriage driver a tear-streaked face. The dress box hampered her movements, and she dropped it; white tulle ruffles billowed out. She knelt to pick up the box, then froze as she heard a man's voice, saying, "Allow me."

She raised her head. Bruce stood looking down at her. He bent, tucked the folds of the dress back into the box, and replaced the cover. Then he helped her to her feet.

"Shannon Cavanaugh. I hadn't expected to find you here this afternoon."

"I was just leaving."

"Not yet. You won't get away from me so easily this time."

Although she had thought of him so often since their last meeting, now, when she was face to face with him, she longed only to escape. Surely he must see that she was close to tears. But he gave no sign that he was aware of her distress.

Instead, he looked at the black, flowing script on the cover of the dress box. *"Miss Harwood. Dressmaker.* I don't understand."

"I work for her," Shannon said. "Or I did. But now—"

"Now?" How handsome he was, looking down at her, his gray eyes attentive, a little teasing.

"I've offended your sister. I was quite tactless. If she complains to Miss Harwood—"

"Melora can be a bit high-handed at times, but she cools down quickly." He gave Shannon a reassuring smile. "She won't make trouble for you, my dear. I'll see to that."

Gratitude welled up inside her. "This position means so much to me."

"But I understood you'd be living with relatives."

"I changed my plans." She wanted to linger, but he might ask more questions. She did not want him to know about Aunt Kate and Uncle Jethro, about the tavern.

"I'll have to leave now," she said. "I have a hired carriage waiting, to take me to the landing."

"I'll drive you to the landing."

Before she had time to refuse, Bruce had ordered the black butler to dismiss the hired carriage, had taken Shannon's arm, and a few minutes later, she found herself seated beside him in his shiny, high-wheeled gig. He touched the back of the sleek black mare, and the animal trotted forward.

Shannon relaxed, forgetting about Miss Harwood and Melora, reveling in the delight of being at the plantation with Bruce. She was glad that she had found time to refurbish her gray cotton dress, cutting the neckline lower, so that it revealed the curve of her throat, the whiteness of her bosom. Miss Harwood had given her a small tan straw bonnet with wide taffeta ribbons that tied in a bow under her chin.

"You need a little time to recover from your run-in with Melora," he said gently. "A drive through the gardens, perhaps. I'll get you down to the landing in time, don't worry."

Emerging from a path that ran beneath twin rows of live oaks, they entered the gardens of Jessamine, set on the sweep of descending terraces that led to the river.

"Now this is the azalea garden," Bruce said. Shannon was entranced with the riot of color spread out around her; the blooms shaded from pale pink to cerise, to deep purple.

"Those small shrubs are the dwarf Japanese azaleas," Bruce explained. "My father traveled in the Far East, and brought back many rare flowers and shrubs. He made notes and sketches, too. I have tried to carry out his plans."

The path sloped downward, and Shannon grew dizzy with the heady scents of camellias and crepe myrtle.

"That statue there—it looks like the god Pan," Shannon said, her eyes resting on the marble creature, half-man, half-beast, with pipes raised to his lips, as if playing a soundless tune.

"You've studied mythology then?"

"It wasn't part of the regular course of study, but Miss Colter, the headmistress at school, allowed me to borrow books from her own library."

"Surely, even in Boston, there were more exciting diversions for a beautiful young lady. You are beautiful, Shannon. I'm not the first man to have told you that, I'm sure."

Let him think that her life in Boston had included parties, dances, visits to the theater and the opera. And flirtations with suitable young gentlemen. Better than admitting the truth, that she had been kept separated from her classmates, forbidden to share their holiday pleasures.

"Up ahead," Bruce was saying, "is my favorite spot."

They rounded a bend in the road, and the next moment Shannon was sure that she had been transported to some distant corner of the world. The azalea garden had been bright with color. Here, only white flowers grew. On a small pool, lilies floated, stirred by a light breeze. Around the pond were plantings of white jessamine, white petunias and snowball bushes.

"That curious little building over there is a real Chinese pagoda. We use it for a summerhouse. Here, let me help you down."

He alighted and lifted her to the ground, then, taking her arm, he led her over an arching stone bridge. From the pagoda, windbells made their delicate music.

"It's lovely," Shannon whispered.

He drew her down on a wooden bench beside the pagoda. "I'm trying to find a stone Buddha to put over there," he said. "I'll probably have to travel up to New York for an auction."

"How will you find the time? It's planting season now, isn't it?"

He laughed. "You mustn't judge all planters by

that remark a visitor made, on his first trip to Mobile: 'the planters live in cotton houses and ride in cotton carriages. They buy cotton, sell cotton, drink cotton and dream cotton and—' "

Shannon laughed. "Go on."

" 'They marry cotton wives and unto them are born cotton children.' "

Her laugh was silenced, as she remembered Odalie, whose fortune, like Bruce's, came from cotton. But Mrs. Duval had forbidden Odalie to think of marrying Bruce.

"Forget about cotton," he said. "I have. Right now, I can only think of you. When you didn't send word to me that I might call on you, I tried to find you. But the only Rawlinsons I found in Mobile were a couple who own a tavern. The woman said she'd never heard of you. I wasn't surprised. I knew, the moment I saw her, that she couldn't be related to you. A fat, blowzy slattern—good-natured enough, until I started asking questions about you. Then she turned nasty."

Shannon's cheeks were hot. She couldn't allow anyone, not even Bruce, to speak that way about Aunt Kate.

"Kate Rawlinson's my aunt," she said.

"Oh, my dear, forgive me. I didn't imagine—"

"No, I'm sure you didn't. Aunt Kate raised me, after my mother died. She was kind to me."

"But she said she didn't know you."

Of course Aunt Kate had said that. Remembering Peggy, Shannon's mother, what else could she have said?

"She was trying to protect me."

"Not from me, surely," Bruce exclaimed. "But why? I don't understand."

Shannon rose. "There's no need for you to understand. Please let me go now."

She turned and started up the curving path, but Bruce followed her and overtook her. He held her arm.

"Let me go," she repeated.

"Not this way. I want to know about you, Shannon. Everything."

She twisted free of his grasp and started for the stone bridge, but her foot caught on one of the gnarled roots of the oak, and she stumbled. Bruce was beside her, drawing her down on the grass. Her bonnet had fallen back, and he undid the ribbons and took it from her head. Then he was stroking her hair.

"All right," she said. "I'll tell you everything, and after that you'll be happy to leave me—never see me again—"

"Never, my dear." He put his arms around her and she rested her head against his shoulder. At least, she would have this moment to remember: the scent of the white jessamine, the music of the windbells. The warmth of his body, close to hers.

Then she made herself draw away. Her throat was tight with the pain of unshed tears. "I told you my name, Shannon Cavanaugh," she began. "My mother's name was Cavanaugh, too. It's the only name I've any right to. My father was a planter."

She went on, her voice growing firmer, steadier. Better that he should know now, rather than later.

"My father sent me to a fine school, where I was trained to take my place in your world. But I never

can, you see. Aunt Kate was right. She wanted me to
accept myself as I am. But who am I? What am I?"

His arms went around her. "You're Shannon.
You're dear and lovely. I don't care about your family.
Only you. Nothing—no one—else matters."

His face was above hers, his lips found her mouth.
In all her sixteen years she had never been kissed by a
man. Her lips parted and his tongue explored the
moist softness.

He pressed her down on the grass, his fingers at the
buttons of her bodice. "You mustn't—"

But even as she whispered the words, her hands
sought to hold him. Timidly, at first, then with growing hunger. She caressed his hair, his shoulders.

His mouth moved to her throat. He opened her
bodice, pushed aside her camisole and kissed her
breasts. She gave a small, wordless cry. They lay
together on the grass, and his breathing had become
unsteady. She felt the hard, driving hunger in him,
saw the naked desire in his eyes.

Then, all at once, he released her. A moment
later, she heard the sound of hooves along the path-
way leading to the garden.

Swiftly, she sat up, buttoning her bodice, smoothing her hair. He was helping her to her feet as horse
and rider rounded a wall covered with white jessamine, and came into plain sight.

The rider, a stocky, deeply-tanned man, touched
the brim of his straw hat. "I'm sorry, Mr. Lathrop.
Miss Melora said you were back, but I didn't know—
you—had visitors."

"It's the overseer," Bruce told Shannon softly.

"Stay here." He went to speak to the other man. "What is it, Ferguson?"

"Beggin' your pardon sir, there's a few things I've got to know. And with your leavin' for New York tomorrow, I thought—"

"Get on with it," Bruce said impatiently.

"Will you want the north field planted or shall I leave it fallow this year? I think it should be planted because—"

"Plant it, then."

"And the stand of yellow pines on the ridge. Cory and Kincaid want to buy it. Adam Kincaid is offering a fair price."

"Sell it," Bruce said. "Cash is more important than timber right now. Anything else?"

"If you want the north field planted, we'll need at least five more prime hands."

"Out of the question right now. Make do with those you have."

"Yes, sir. Sorry I disturbed you and—the young lady."

The overseer raised his hat. Shannon moved closer to the gig, wishing she could make herself invisible. How much had Mr. Ferguson seen, or guessed? She was relieved when he turned his mount and cantered away.

Bruce came to join Shannon. "I'm sorry," he said. "Now, let's go back there to the oak tree and—"

"No, Bruce. Drive me to the landing. Please."

"You're angry with me," he said, helping her into the gig and getting in beside her.

"Not angry, but—we mustn't be alone again. I'm afraid."

"Of me? Shannon, I swear I'll never do anything to hurt you. Please believe me."

"I believe you," she said. She tried to remember Aunt Kate's warnings, but with Bruce's eyes on her, ardent, tender, there was no room in her mind for caution.

Bruce had not said he loved her, but he must love her. Otherwise, he would not have kissed her, caressed her in that intimate, frightening yet delicious way. Then she remembered what Mr. Ferguson had said.

"You're leaving for New York tomorrow."

"Mother, Melora, and I are spending the summer in Saratoga."

She felt a sense of desolation. A whole summer without Bruce.

"Mother's in delicate health. The summers down here are too much for her. Shannon, I've got to go. It isn't simply a vacation; I must see my bankers in New York City before I go on to join mother and Melora. But I'll be back in September. You'll let me call on you then, won't you."

It was not a question, but a statement. She knew that she should pretend hesitation until she had forced from him a declaration of his intentions; but for one of her forthright nature, such coquetry was impossible.

Instead, when he stopped the gig at the landing, she let him kiss her again, and she clung to him. "Come back soon, Bruce. Soon."

6

SHANNON LEANED her arms on the showroom counter, her eyes closed, as she enjoyed the late afternoon quiet. She was lost in her daydreams of Bruce, for it was the first week of September, and he would be returning from Saratoga any day now. He would come calling on her, and they would go riding together.

The shop bell tinkled, and her eyes opened, to see a dark-haired woman in gray satin standing in the doorway.

"Where is Miss Harwood?" the woman asked, walking up to the counter.

"She's upstairs, ma'am. Is there anything I can do for you?"

There was something familiar about the woman, but Shannon could not quite remember what.

"I am Mrs. Philippe Duval."

Of course. Shannon had not seen her face to face

during her last visit to the shop. A handsome woman, dark-haired, dark-eyed, like Odalie.

"Miss Harwood said that she expected a shipment of those new parasolettes from New York."

"Oh, yes, Mrs. Duval. They're in the workroom. I haven't unpacked them yet."

"Then do so. I want to see one in mauve, with black lace trimming."

"Right away, ma'am."

But before she could leave the counter, Mrs. Duval said, "One moment. I don't believe I've seen you here before."

"I'm Miss Harwood's new assistant."

"Your name?"

"Shannon Cavanaugh, ma'am."

The dark eyes were fixed on Shannon's face with disquieting intensity. "Shannon Cavanaugh," Mrs. Duval repeated. "You're Irish?"

Shannon knew that, with the flood of emigrants from Ireland, many Americans in both the North and South had developed a deep resentment against the newcomers. Perhaps Mrs. Duval shared this prejudice.

How often Shannon had heard Aunt Kate repeat the story of how, when the riverboats were being loaded with cotton, the bales rolled down a plank from the warehouse on the bluffs, the Negro hands were stationed at the top, while the Irish laborers stood at the bottom, where the bale might break through the stanchions and railings.

Shannon's grandfather, who had been hired for this work, had heard the mate of the riverboat explain to a passenger, "The niggers are worth too much to be risked here. If the paddies are knocked overboard, or get their backs broke, nobody loses anything."

Even at school in Boston, Shannon had overheard remarks about the laziness and immorality of the Irish newcomers. Now, she bristled with anger at Mrs. Duval's question, but she forced herself to answer quietly, "My mother was Irish, ma'am."

"And your father?"

"I never knew my father."

"How long have you been in Mobile?"

"Only a few months."

"And before that?"

Shannon's eyes flashed yellow; under the counter, her hands closed so that her nails bit into her palms.

"I was away at school, in Boston."

"You are a newcomer to our city, then?"

"I was born here, Mrs. Duval. But I went away to school when I was eight years old."

"What made you return? You have relatives here, perhaps?"

Maybe some of Miss Harwood's customers might take a friendly interest in a shop girl, but there was nothing friendly in the look Mrs. Duval turned on Shannon, and her voice, as she fired questions one after another, was cold.

"I have an aunt. Mrs. Rawlinson. She—"

"Rawlinson. I see."

"Now, if you wish to see the parasolettes—"

"Never mind. Come around in front of the counter. Stand over there."

Shannon told herself that Mrs. Duval was an important customer, that she must take care not to offend her.

"Yes, there, in the sunlight. Your eyes are a most unusual color." Mrs. Duval was silent for a moment, then asked, "How old are you, Miss Cavanaugh?"

"I'm sixteen."

"Sixteen." Antoinette Duval's lips tightened. "Yes, that would be about right."

Baffled, Shannon could only say, "I'll get the parasolettes now."

"Never mind." Mrs. Duval turned and left the shop without another word.

Shannon decided to say nothing to Miss Harwood about the visit; she could only hope that whatever she had done to cause Antoinette Duval's strange behavior, it would be forgotten before the woman came to the shop again.

It was two days later when Miss Harwood came into the workroom. Her eyes, behind the gold-rimmed spectacles, looked uneasy.

"I've almost finished the embroidery on these sleeves," Shannon said. "What do you want me to do next? The white silk or—"

"Put the work aside."

"Is something wrong?"

Miss Harwood did not look directly at Shannon.

"I'm afraid I will not be able to use your services any longer," she said.

"But what have I done?"

Had Melora Lathrop complained after all? But surely she would not have written a letter from New York after all this time.

"You must leave today. At once," Miss Harwood said.

Shannon pushed aside the wide, embroidered organdy sleeves and got to her feet. "I've worked hard. You've said so yourself."

"I've no fault to find with your work."

"Then what have I done, to make you want to fire me?"

"I don't want to, but I can't help myself. Shannon, please pack your things and go."

"Very well. But not until you tell me why you're sending me away. I have a right to know."

But Miss Harwood remained silent.

"You'll give me a reference, won't you?"

"It would do you no good, here in Mobile. Even if you should find work with another dressmaker, she would not be able to keep you on for long." Miss Harwood's lips trembled. "You—may keep the straw bonnet I gave you. And you may have one of those new parasolettes. Any color you choose."

Parasolettes. Mrs. Duval.

"Antoinette Duval. She's the cause of this, isn't she?"

Miss Harwood nodded. "Yes, my dear. And now, if you'll—"

"But what did I do to make her angry? I was polite to her, I answered all her questions."

"You're not to blame. But I have my business to think of." Mrs. Harwood sighed, then added, "It's lucky you have relatives here in Mobile. You can stay with them for the time being, I suppose."

"I hate the tavern, the waterfront."

"Be sensible, my dear. There's no place else for you to go, is there?"

The taproom, although close and rank-smelling, was not yet crowded. A couple of men were playing cards at a small table near the door, and a group of others were drinking whiskey and talking loudly at a round table near the bar.

Shannon heard a big, bearded man saying, "California. That's where I'd like to be heading for. If it wasn't for my old woman—"

"To hell with your old woman," another shouted, banging his glass on the table. "Plenty of juicy young trollops are heading for San Francisco. You get in on this here silver strike and they'll hop into bed with you fast enough. There's whole boatloads of French whores going out there, all the way from Marseilles."

"Damn right," said a man in a stovepipe hat. "Me, I'd like to go out there, make my pile, and spend a week in the fanciest cathouse on the Barbary Coast. Nothin' a man can't buy there. They got Chinese girls. They buy 'em up in China when they're no more'n ten or eleven, and teach 'em all the tricks."

Shannon turned and busied herself behind the bar. In the short time she had been back at the tavern, she had heard too much of such talk. With Aunt Kate's help, she had managed to avoid the taproom as much as possible, doing the heavier work instead: scrubbing the upstairs rooms and halls, carrying water and towels for overnight guests and emptying chamberpots in the backyard privy. Now, she was resting briefly before going back into the sweltering kitchen to help Aunt Kate with the cooking.

Since she had returned to the tavern, Aunt Kate had done everything possible to protect her from Jethro's evil-tempered outbursts, and from the advances of the customers; but Aunt Kate could not always watch over her. Shannon shuddered, remembering the rough hands thrust into her bodice or up under her skirts.

She finished polishing the glasses and wiped the bar. The men seated at the nearby table were no longer speculating on the talents of the Barbary Coast girls but had turned to an even more engrossing subject.

Ever since word had come through to Mobile about the discovery of the fabulous silver deposits in Nevada, every man who came to the tavern was obsessed with visions of making a fortune overnight. Shannon heard the now-familiar talk of the Washoe Range, Virginia City, Devil's Gate, the Ophir mine. She heard men's voices trembling with greed, as they spoke of "the blue stuff," "twenty-two hundred dollars a ton," "bullion bars."

Even now, Mobile Bay was crowded with ships to take prospectors to Panama's eastern coast; from there, the men would make the journey across the isthmus to Panama City, where they would fight their way aboard any hulk that could stay afloat, and take them on to California.

What fools men were, Shannon thought, to leave Alabama with its rich black soil, where planters could live like kings. Only New Orleans surpassed Mobile among the cotton ports of the world.

California and Nevada were still untamed, with settlements that were only shantytowns and makeshift mining camps. Men might be fascinated by tales of San Francisco and the Barbary Coast, but Shannon was sure that city was no place for a lady.

She closed her eyes and conjured up a vision of Jessamine, the scent of flowering shrubs, the waterlilies floating on the pool. . . .

"What does a man have to do to get a drink here?"

Adam Kincaid was standing at the bar. "I didn't expect to find you here," he said. "I thought you were working for the dressmaker."

"What do you want to drink?" Shannon asked tersely.

"Bourbon."

She poured him a drink and slid the glass across the bar with a deft motion. He gave her an impudent grin.

"You do that like a professional," he said.

She glared at him, but did not answer.

"Bring the drink to that table near the window, and the bottle, too."

She obeyed but when she turned to leave him, he took hold of her arm.

"Let me go," she said. "I have to start my cooking."

"You cook, too?"

"I'm learning."

"Then bring me some food and join me. I like company while I have my dinner."

"It will be an hour or more before——"

"Come now, Shannon. There must be some food out there."

"Cold ham and cornbread from last night, that's all."

"That'll do. And bring a plate for yourself. There's time before the evening rush. I want to hear what's been happening to you since I saw you last."

"That's none of your business, Mr. Kincaid."

His fingers tightened on her arm. "Adam," he said. "You don't need to be formal down here on the waterfront." His blue eyes moved over her body, lingering on her breasts, half-bared by the low-cut flowered cotton dress Uncle Jethro had given her to wear.

"Now Lizzie, the last barmaid, she was never standoffish. Up and down the stairs all night, I remember. One night, she took on the whole crew of a flatboat, and she—"

Shannon's fingers itched to slap the insolent smile off his face. "Take your hand off me," she said.

He laughed, but he set her free, and she hurried back to the kitchen.

"Shannon, whatever's wrong?" Aunt Kate asked, looking at her flushed face.

"It's that—it's Adam Kincaid. He wants me to join him for dinner."

"Go ahead, then. We ain't busy yet."

"But that's not all. He said that Lizzie—that she—"

"What Lizzie did was her affair. All Mr. Kincaid's asking you to do is to sit at his table. Better him than those flatboat men. There'll be a whole mob of them in here tonight. Jethro's going to have to hitch up the team and go get more whiskey before they come ashore."

Aunt Kate gave Shannon a little shake. "Get moving, girl."

Shannon cut slices from the ham end, and slapped a piece of cornbread down beside it on the plate. "Jolly the man along, dearie. That's all you got to do."

"I'll serve him his food, but I won't sit with him, and I certainly won't go upstairs with him."

"The hell you won't!" Jethro had come in from the stableyard, and had overheard Shannon's words. "You'll sit with Kincaid, and you'll bed down with him, too, if that's his pleasure."

"Jethro, no," Aunt Kate protested. "Shannon's not like Lizzie."

"That'll be enough out of you," Jethro roared. "Don't think I ain't seen how you've been keeping Shannon out of the bar."

"She ain't had no experience serving drinks, like I have."

"Time she learned, then. Those sailors'd rather have a fine-looking young piece like her waiting on them than a fat old slut like you."

Shannon felt hot fury rising inside her. "Don't you dare talk to my aunt that way."

"I'll do more'n talk. I'll fetch you a clout you won't forget. Now, get back out there and take care of Kincaid."

Shannon knew that if she protested, not only she, but her aunt would suffer. But her pride would not allow her to give in completely. "I'll sit with him," she said, starting for the door, "but that's all."

She hurried out with the food, but Jethro was right behind her. He caught up with her in the middle of the taproom. His heavy face was a mottled purple. "I'll take no backtalk from you, miss. Who the hell do you think you are?"

A few of the men turned to look at Jethro and his niece. "I'll tell you," Jethro went on, his fury growing with every word. "You're Peggy Cavanaugh's bastard brat. And don't you go forgetting it."

It was as if Jethro had stripped her naked in front of these strangers. Her will crumbled, and he saw it.

"Get about your work, slut. You're going to have a busy night of it."

Numb, shaken, she walked unsteadily to Adam's table, set down the plate and sank into a chair opposite him. Jethro turned and headed outside to hitch up the wagon.

After a moment, Shannon felt Adam's hand close over hers. "I'm sorry," he said quietly. "I didn't mean for anything like that to happen. Please believe me."

The last thing she wanted from Adam Kincaid, or anyone else, was pity. "It doesn't matter. Eat your dinner."

He looked at her closely, then shrugged, picked up a piece of cornbread and tasted it. "Did you make this stuff?"

"Yes, I did. It's the first batch I ever baked."

"You don't have to tell me that. It's like shoe leather."

"I wasn't trained to be a cook," she said sullenly.

He laughed. "From what you've told me, you weren't trained for much. Except to be the mistress of one of those plantations upriver, maybe."

"And you think that would be impossible."

"I know it," he said calmly.

"Because my mother—because of what Uncle Jethro said."

"That's only part of it."

"What else can there be? I'm no different from the girls I went to school with, back in Boston."

"And you're probably the best-looking one of the lot," Kincaid said. "But it's not enough. Don't look at me that way. I'm not trying to hurt you. Listen to me. Jethro didn't pay for your fancy education. Who did?"

"My father. He was a planter, a gentleman."

"And did he ever acknowledge that you were his daughter? Did he ever come to see you, or write to you?"

"No, but—"

"Did he provide for you in his will, then?"

"Aunt Kate said he didn't. She wouldn't even tell me his name. But I—"

"Why not?" Kincaid demanded.

"She said it would be dangerous for me to know. Dangerous for her, too. That's why I haven't even tried to see my father's lawyer, Mr. Bassett."

"Bassett?" Adam Kincaid paused for a moment, then shook his head. "There was a lawyer by that name, practicing in Mobile. He died in the fever epidemic, back in '53."

"Are you sure?"

He nodded. "In any case, another lawyer must have been handling your father's affairs after Bassett's death. If your father had left you anything, you'd have been informed, wouldn't you?"

"I—suppose so. But that doesn't mean I'll spend the rest of my life down here on the waterfront."

"Now listen," Adam said. "I know Mobile. And I know the plantation gentry. Any one of those planters would be hot to bed down with you. But marriage, that's something else. A planter wants a bride who'll bring him a dowry, and a name."

Bruce isn't like that, she told herself. *He wouldn't care about those things.*

But she felt uneasy as she though of Odalie, of the wealthy girls Bruce might be meeting in Saratoga. Pretty, too, perhaps, and showing off their charms in the kind of finery Shannon could not hope to afford.

"Don't look so miserable," Adam said. "Good Lord, Shannon, is that all you care about, snagging a rich planter?"

"It's not only the money, or a fine house I want—"

He reached out and took her hands in his, and she felt a swift, hot current move through her at his touch. "What *do* you want, Shannon?"

"You wouldn't understand."

His eyes held hers. "Tell me."

"I want to belong. To be accepted by decent, respectable people."

"Respectable people." He released her hands and she saw that he was looking past her, his eyes dark with anger.

"I was taken in by decent, respectable people, when I was a boy. Tom Sprague and his frozen-faced bitch of a wife. Church-goers, pillars of the community. Praised for their charity."

"You had no family of your own?"

Adam poured another shot of bourbon. "They died." He swallowed his drink. "Sprague owned the biggest lumberyard in Mobile. He worked me harder than if I'd been a black slave. A slave would have cost him cash. I tried to learn the work, but I made a mistake, my first week there. I damaged a piece of wooden scrollwork. It could have been fixed, but—he beat me so I couldn't walk for a couple of days. When

I was on my feet again, I ran away. He brought me back. I kept on running. Every time I did, he found me and brought me back. Until I was sixteen. Then I went off and joined the army."

"But you came back to Mobile."

"Yes," he said, his voice expressionless. "I came back. But I'm getting ready to move on again."

"Where will you go?"

"The Comstock. The silver diggings."

"That's all I've been hearing about lately," Shannon said impatiently. "Virginia City. Sun Mountain. The Ophir. I suppose you think you'll find silver and become wealthy overnight."

"Maybe. Besides, I like the country out there."

"A wilderness, without anything but Indians and— and rattlesnakes and deserts?"

"I was there with the second Frémont expedition," Adam told her. "Across the Sierra, down into California to Sutter's Fort. Back across the mountains through Tehachapi Pass and then down along the Old Spanish Trail. Yes, there were Indians, and deserts. Even rattlesnakes. But there was more."

There was an excitement in his voice and the bitterness had left his face.

"Tell me about it," Shannon urged, forgetting her earlier dislike for Adam. She had seen the hard, arrogant side of his character, but now, she sensed that there was something more, a part of his feelings that he rarely shared.

"I remember the pine forests," he said. "And the aspens, in the fall, like a sea of gold. Lakes the colors of emeralds and sapphires. And the sun coming up over the mountains, and the silence—like the dawn of creation."

"Why, Adam." Shannon was surprised and strangely moved by his words, and even more, by something that flickered in his eyes.

"It's savage country out there," he said. "Untamed. Untouched. Men find a challenge in such qualities."

She blushed and looked away. For a moment she had the feeling that he was no longer speaking only of the land that had meant so much to him. She felt a closeness to Adam, an instinctive understanding.

Like him, she had been an outcast as a child, and, in a sense, she still was. But was it only sympathy that was drawing her to him? When he had held her hands in his, she had been stirred by his touch, had felt a swift hunger coursing through her body. She would not think about it. She loved Bruce. She could never love anyone else.

"You've built a good business here," she said, shifting to safer ground. "Aunt Kate speaks well of you, and even Uncle Jethro says you're a success."

"I'm flattered," Adam said dryly. "But I'm selling out to my partner, Matt Cory, all the same. He's a family man, so he's tied down." Adam shook his head. "Married, with three children and another on the way."

"You make it sound like a terrible fate. Don't you like children?"

"I like them well enough," Adam said, "so long as they aren't mine. But we were talking about you, Shannon. What are your plans for the future?"

"I'm going to stay here in Mobile," she said un-

certainly. "I was born here. It's my home. And besides—"

"Go on."

"I've got to find out who my father was. No matter
what Aunt Kate says, I'm sure he must have made
some provision for me. So you see, I have to stay
and—"

"And go on working here. How long do you think
it'll be, before some sailor gets you on your back in
one of those beds upstairs?"

"Don't speak to me that way. I've told you—"

"What you've told me is childish nonsense, moon-
shine and fairy stories. It's time you gave up your
silly dreams about being mistress of a plantation, of
leading the Mardi Gras ball and sipping sherry in
Madame LeVert's salon." He shook his head. "It'll
never happen, Shannon. Never."

"What's left for me, then? Where do I belong?"

"Mobile isn't the world. Why not go West with
me? There are damn few women as young and
beautiful as you out there. Listen to me. Ever since
I saw you standing there on the wharf, I haven't
been able to stop thinking about you. I want you,
Shannon."

"You must be mad. We're strangers. How can you
possibly think I'd agree to marry you?"

He threw his head back and began to laugh.

She stared at him, uncomprehending.

"Marry? Who said anything about marriage?"

"But you—you said—"

"I said I wanted you. And I do. But I have no
intention of marrying you or any other woman."

He pushed away his plate. "Why not think it over? It's a rather good offer, all things considered. You can't cook. You've got a bad temper. I'm not even sure you'd be able to sew the buttons on my shirt. For all your talk about being a good seamstress, you didn't keep your job with Miss Harwood long, did you?"

"It wasn't because of my sewing," she began. Then she stopped. Her eyes widened and she put a hand to her throat. Everything was swept from her mind: Adam's indecent offer, Antoinette Duval, her dismissal from the dressmaker's shop; none of those things mattered now.

For the door of the taproom had opened and Bruce was standing there. Bruce was back in Mobile at last.

7

BRUCE CAUGHT SIGHT of Shannon and he moved swiftly through the growing crowd to the table where she sat with Adam. He bowed, saying, "Miss Cavanaugh—Shannon—I tried to find you at Miss Harwood's shop but she said you might be here."

Shannon thought he had never looked so handsome as now. He wore a dark-blue frock coat, a white satin waistcoat and light-blue trousers strapped under his shining boots. He held his tall hat in his hand, and she saw that the summer sun had tanned his face, and turned his hair to an even lighter shade of silver-blond.

"I didn't think you'd come back here but—" Then, realizing she was not alone, he turned to Adam. "Sorry, Kincaid. I didn't mean to intrude."

Adam looked from Bruce to Shannon. "No intrusion," he said. "It would seem that you and

Shannon are old friends. Shannon, get Mr. Lathrop a drink."

Shannon glared at Adam. Now Bruce would know she was working here as a barmaid.

"What will you have?" she asked, standing up.

"Brandy, please."

She went to the bar. Uncle Jethro had come back with the whisky and both he and Aunt Kate were tending bar, as more and more customers crowded the taproom.

She asked for the brandy, then returned to the table, to hear Bruce saying, "So, you're off to the Nevada territory, with the rest. Can't say I blame you, Kincaid. A tempting prospect. A mountain of silver lying there for the taking."

Shannon slipped back into her chair. Although she hated having Bruce find her here, at least he was back. And he had come looking for her.

"Everyone's talking about the silver strike in New York City and in Saratoga," Bruce was saying. "I wouldn't mind going out West myself."

"Why don't you?" Adam asked. "It's the biggest thing since '49."

"There's Jessamine," Bruce said simply.

Adam shrugged. "Ferguson's a reliable overseer, isn't he? And the land will still be there when you get back. In six months, a year, you could—"

"Bruce, no." Shannon put a hand on his arm. "You can't leave again, not now." Then, seeing the swift look of comprehension in Adam's eyes, mingled with a curious kind of pity, she went on more calmly, "There's your mother and Melora. You can't leave them."

Saratoga was one thing; a journey to Nevada was something else entirely. It might as well be China, as far as Shannon was concerned. And it was dangerous. Here in the tavern, Shannon had heard stories of men frozen to death in the mountains, trapped in cave-ins in the mines, stabbed or shot by claim jumpers, slaughtered by hostile Indians. And there were those who died of disease before they even reached the West: cholera, yellow fever, dysentery. "You mustn't think of going," she said. "It's no place for a gentleman out there."

Adam's mouth was a hard, thin line. He got to his feet. "If you'll excuse me." He strode to the bar.

Was he jealous? Shannon wondered. No matter. He did not love her, or he would never have suggested that she should go West with him without even offering marriage. But she would not think about Adam. Bruce was back and he must not leave her again.

"You weren't serious about joining the prospectors? It's madness," she began.

"Madness? I'm not so sure. Kincaid's no madman. If he's going—"

Shannon looked at him in panic. "Would you miss me if I went West?" he asked, teasingly. Then he added, "I have no intention of setting out for the Nevada territory at the moment. I only returned to Alabama yesterday. I left mother and Melora at Jessamine and then I came to see you. I didn't expect to find you here, though."

"Didn't Miss Harwood tell you? She dismissed me."

"But why?"

"I'm not sure. I was finishing Odalie Duval's ball

gown—we waited nearly all summer for the brocade to arrive from France. I was busy until all hours of the night, to have the gown ready in time for Mr. Cunningham's visit and then Mrs. Duval came in and she—"

"Cunningham?" Bruce interrupted. "Arthur Cunningham?"

Shannon nodded. "You know him?"

"Odalie spoke of him. An impossible boor, one of those millionaires from the North. Textile mills in New England. What the devil—excuse me, Shannon—you're sure he's coming to Beau Rivage?"

"Indeed, I am," she said. "To hear Mrs. Duval going on about him, you'd have thought she was expecting Queen Victoria and Prince Albert. No fabric was good enough for the ball gown. Brocade from Lyons, lace from—"

"When is he coming?" Bruce demanded. "Do you know?"

He was obviously furious, and his anger, although not directed against Shannon, nevertheless frightened her. "In a week or so, I think," she said. "Mrs. Duval ordered a whole wardrobe for the visit, back last spring."

"Damn that woman." This time Bruce was too angry to apologize to Shannon for his profanity. "Shipping Odalie off to North Carolina, and now—"

Odalie loved Bruce. She had told Shannon so. Did he love Odalie? If not, why was he so angry at the suggestion that Mrs. Duval favored a possible rival? He rose, but Shannon caught at his sleeve. "Where are you going?"

"To see Odalie," he said.

"It won't make any difference." The words came unbidden, unplanned, born of her desperation.

"What are you talking about?" Bruce demanded.

Shannon pressed her hands together in her lap to steady herself. "It's all been settled," she said.

"I don't understand."

From the moment she had mentioned Arthur Cunningham's visit, Bruce had forgotten all about her. She might as well have been a million miles away. Was he in love with Odalie? He wasn't, he couldn't be. But he might be planning to marry her all the same. Because one day she would inherit Beau Rivage, and if the two plantations were joined, they would form an empire of cotton.

Adam's words came back to mock her, to torment her.

"A planter wants a bride who'll bring him a dowry, and a name."

Shannon had nothing but herself to offer. Odalie had everything.

I won't give him up. Not without a fight.

"Bruce," she said softly, "I thought you knew. Odalie's going to marry Mr. Cunningham. The engagement is to be announced at the ball."

Bruce spoke softly, but there was a deadly edge to his voice, and his gray eyes were icy. "Odalie agreed to this engagement?"

"I heard her, in the dressmaker's shop. She sounded pleased. Mr. Cunningham's wealthy and even though he's older than she is, she said he was an important man and—and she's to have a town-house in Boston and a summer home at Saratoga."

"That's enough," Bruce said. "I don't want to hear any more."

He drank his brandy, then said, "Bring me another. No, bring the bottle."

She obeyed, trying to stifle the pangs of guilt that were already gnawing at her. When Bruce found out she had lied, he would never want to see her again.

Would he find out? Perhaps his pride would prevent him from questioning Odalie, now that he thought she had agreed to marry another man.

"Brandy, the best we have," Shannon told Aunt Kate. "It's for Mr. Lathrop."

"I'll take it to his table," Aunt Kate said. "You get behind the bar."

Unable to face Bruce after telling him that enormous lie, she obeyed without arguing. Working as quickly as she could, she served the rivermen who were swarming around the bar, a dirty, unshaven horde, in coarse cotton shirts, wide-bottomed pants and greasy, battered hats. She noticed Adam at one end of the bar, but she ignored him. Each time she had a free moment, she looked over at Bruce, who was emptying his brandy bottle rapidly. His eyes had developed a glazed look, and she noticed a slackness around his mouth.

Because she was surrounded by customers, pounding on the bar, shouting their orders, she did not see the start of the fight. Only when a tense silence spread through the taproom did she see the two flatboat men and Bruce, on his feet now, swaying slightly.

"Why don't you do your drinkin' up at the Battle

House?" one of the sailors said. He was a short, apelike man with long, muscular arms, a barrel chest and enormous hands. "This ain't no place for you. Might get them fancy duds all dirty."

"I drink where I please," Bruce said.

"Do you, now?" He pointed to the red turkey feather in the brim of his hat. "Know what this means?"

Shannon had already learned that the red turkey feather was a sign that the wearer had beaten every challenger in one or more of the towns along the river.

"I don't fight with river rats," Bruce said.

"River rat, is it? You'll keep a civil tongue in your head when you talk to Jack O'Shea, mister."

O'Shea's companion, a towering bear of a man with a flaming red beard, growled, "Leave 'im alone, Jack. He ain't worth wipin' up the floor with."

The other men moved forward, blocking Shannon's view. She tried to get out from behind the bar, but Adam pushed her back. "Get down and stay down," he ordered. Cursing, Jethro grabbed a bung starter, a heavy mallet used for opening beer barrels, and started forward. "Better not," one of the rivermen said. "I've seen O'Shea stomp a man to death." Jethro froze, obviously unable to decide whether to risk his neck or see his taproom smashed up.

Shannon saw Bruce go down, saw O'Shea draw back a booted foot and kick him in the ribs.

Bruce rolled over and somehow was on his feet again. The red-bearded man moved in and grabbed Bruce from behind, holding his arms immobile. "I don't need no help with this one," O'Shea said. But he smashed the end off a bottle and started forward.

"Adam, help him. They'll kill him."

"He was asking for trouble."

Shannon seized Adam's arm, her nails cutting into his flesh. "Please, don't let them."

He pushed her aside and waded into the fray. He seized O'Shea's wrist, brought his knee up, and, in the same moment, jerked O'Shea's arm down. O'Shea gave a hoarse cry, dropped the bottle and clutched his arm; he was doubled up with pain.

Before he could straighten up, Adam brought the edge of his hand down on O'Shea's neck, and the man dropped to the floor.

At the same time, the red-bearded man swung Bruce around and smashed a fist into his face. Jethro went to the fight, bung starter in hand, but before he could reach the center of the room, Adam and the red-bearded man were locked together, wrestling, panting.

O'Shea started to rise, but Jethro struck him on the back of the head with the bung starter and he went down again.

Adam, meanwhile, had broken free, and now swung a blow to his opponent's head. Shannon heard the sickening sound of bone shattering, saw the blood spurting from the man's nose. Adam struck again, and the red-bearded man, his face covered with blood, fell backward and did not move.

Only then did she leave the bar. She went down on her knees beside Bruce. "Adam, he's not moving."

Adam knelt beside her. "Unconscious, that's all."

"Take him upstairs," she said.

Adam lifted Bruce, and followed Shannon up the stairs to her room. There, he deposited Bruce on the bed. "Get me some water," he said. "And a towel."

"I'll take care of him," she said. Gently, she bathed Bruce's swollen face. He moaned, then was silent again. Adam pushed her aside, opened Bruce's shirt, his hands moving across the arc of the ribs, down the arms.

"Nothing broken. Let me take him over to the lumberyard. I'll see he gets back to Jessamine all right."

"I can look after him here," Shannon insisted.

"Now, Shannon, I'm more experienced with this kind of thing than you are."

"I don't care," she said stubbornly. "I want—"

"I know what you want," Adam said. "But it won't work." He looked at her, his eyes hot with anger. "Don't give me that innocent stare. You think you'll take care of him, play the angel of mercy, and when he's feeling better, you'll climb into bed with him. Go ahead, but you still won't get him to marry you."

"You think I'm not good enough to."

Adam's hands closed on her shoulders. "You're too damn good for him," he said. "He can't give you what you need. I can." He pulled her against him so that she felt the hard ridges of muscle in his chest, his thighs. He twisted his hand in her hair, forcing her head back, and then he kissed her, his mouth bruising her lips.

For a moment she resisted, then her body molded itself to his. He took his lips away and she heard him saying, "Come with me, Shannon, away from Mobile, away from—"

She heard Bruce moan and reality flooded back. Her body stiffened. "He needs me. Let me go."

Adam released her so abruptly that she staggered and had to clutch at his arm for support.

"Go to him, then. Play your little games. He may feel guilty when he finds out he's the first man you've ever had. But he won't feel guilty enough to make an Irish barmaid mistress of Jessamine."

She gave an incoherent cry of anger; drawing back her arm, she slapped him across the face with all her strength. His eyes darkened, the muscles of his shoulders tensed, and for a moment she was afraid.

Then he shrugged and said softly, "Maybe I was wrong about you, Shannon. Maybe you'll be satisfied to be a fine gentleman's whore."

Before she could answer, he turned and left the room.

Bruce called her name and she went to him. She was bathing his face, feeling only a warm tenderness, when Aunt Kate flung open the door.

"You get downstairs," she said. "Hurry now, before Jethro comes up here and drags you down. If those river men don't get their whiskey, they'll tear the place apart."

"But what about Bruce?"

"I'll see to him. Soon as I get him on his feet, Jethro'll put him in a hired carriage and send him over to the Battle House. That's where his kind belongs, in a fancy hotel, not down here, making trouble for everybody."

Shannon gave Bruce a lingering glance, filled with concern, then slowly obeyed her aunt and left the bedroom.

8

"BRUCE SHOULDN'T have left here so soon. He was hurt."

"He'll be comfortable enough over at the Battle House, where Jethro took him," Aunt Kate said unsympathetically.

It was two days after the brawl, and Shannon and Aunt Kate were in the kitchen, washing piles of greasy plates and dirty glasses. "Lucky for him that Adam Kincaid took his side, or he'd have been beaten a lot worse."

"But, Aunt Kate—"

"What was Lathrop doing, hanging around here in the first place? Better for him if he goes back and takes care of that plantation of his, before he loses the place."

"What do you mean? The Lathrops have owned Jessamine for generations. Bruce told me."

"Dearie, I've lived in Mobile a long time, and around a tavern, you hear talk from overseers, factors. Bruce ain't no different from the rest of the Lathrops. The men always gambled for higher stakes than they could afford, spent a fortune traveling to Europe and lord knows where, bringing back all kinds of fancy fixings. Statues and paintings and such. They leave the running of the place to overseers. That don't work forever, though."

"Bruce isn't poor. He can't be. Why, I've seen Jessamine. It's magnificent."

"He's been borrowing from bankers here in Mobile and down in New Orleans, until he's used up his credit. He's mortgaged next year's crop and the one after that. He's selling off slaves and timber. Adam Kincaid said he bought a big stand of yellow pine from Lathrop only last month."

Shannon bristled. "I'm not interested in anything Adam Kincaid has to say. He's jealous because Bruce is—because Bruce and I are—"

"Now you listen here," Aunt Kate said. "Adam's ten times the man Bruce Lathrop'll ever be. And if he's taken a fancy to you—"

"I don't think we'll be seeing Mr. Kincaid here again."

"Why not?" Aunt Kate demanded.

"He's leaving Mobile, going West to look for silver."

"Leaving, is he?" Aunt Kate sighed. "I'm not surprised. Never thought he'd come back to Mobile after he ran off the first time." She sighed, as she carried a pile of dirty plates to the sink. "Adam came to Mobile the first time when he was no more'n twelve. A sorry sight he was, too. Dirty. Half-starved. And the look on his face. No child should look like that."

"I don't understand—" Shannon began.

"Like he'd been to hell and back again. Nobody knew where he came from and he wouldn't talk, not at first. Some folks thought his brains were addled." Aunt Kate sighed. "We were living down by the bay, your mother and me," she said, as she immersed the plates in the hot soapy water. "And your granddad, too. Lots of us Irish were living down there then. The men had been hired to dredge the channel so them ocean-going ships could get into Mobile Bay instead of running aground on the sand bars."

"But what about Adam?" Shannon prompted her aunt.

"He hung around the shantytown settlement for awhile. Little by little, he'd started saying a few words, but he never would say anything about his people or where he came from. Folks there were sorry for him. We all gave him what we could spare, but none of us could afford to take him in. We had little enough for our own. Then Tom Sprague gave him a home. He was a church deacon, and he said it was an act of charity. That he felt it was his duty to be a good Samaritan."

"But Adam hated Mr. Sprague. He told me so."

"Shouldn't wonder. Sprague treated Adam real bad. I remember one time, Adam ran away and came back to hide in shantytown, and Sprague found him there. He was a hard man, Sprague was, for all his church-going and psalm-singing."

Shannon's hands moved automatically, drying plates and glasses, but her eyes were fixed on her aunt's face.

"What did he do to Adam?" she asked.

"Made Adam kneel down next to the wagon and take off his shirt. Then he took a mule whip to the boy. He wanted Adam to show proper humility; that's what he said. Adam wouldn't say a word, wouldn't make a sound, but the look on his face. I'll never forget that. When he finally passed out, Sprague put him in the wagon and drove off."

"Why didn't anyone try to stop him?"

"Sprague was a prosperous man, important, and mean as a snake when he was crossed." She looked at Shannon closely. "Why, dearie, you do care for Adam, don't you?"

"Not the way you mean. It's only that—"

There was a knock at the kitchen door, and Shannon went to answer it, relieved at the interruption. A small black boy said, "Please, ma'am, I got a lettah heah fuh Miss Shannon Cavanaugh."

The letter was on stationery from the Battle House, the most elegant hotel in Mobile. Shannon opened it with a delicious shiver of anticipation.

Aunt Kate fumbled in her apron pocket and handed the boy a coin, and he ran off across the stableyard.

"Oh, Aunt Kate. It's an invitation. From Bruce. He wants me to go to the Duvals' ball with him. I don't know what I have to wear to Beau Rivage, but—"

Her aunt had gone so white that Shannon thought she was about to faint. "You ain't going to Beau Rivage. Not if I have to lock you in your room."

"Of course I'm going. Don't you understand what this means? Bruce cares for me. He wants all his friends to meet me." She had a stab of guilt, remembering the lie she had told Bruce about Odalie's engagement. No matter. The lie had served its purpose. And if only he would remain at the Battle House until the night of the ball, he would not learn the truth from Odalie.

"Dearie, you got to trust me," Aunt Kate said. She put an arm around Shannon. "Promise you won't go."

She did not want to tell a second lie, and certainly not to Aunt Kate, who loved her, but there was no other way.

"I promise," she said.

"Swear it," Aunt Kate said inexorably, "on your dear mother's memory."

Shannon hesitated. "I swear it," she said, but a cold fear, a premonition of disaster touched her mind. She brushed it aside. The ball was only a few days off, and she had to make plans. She would have to get a suitable gown. And somehow, she would have to slip off to meet Bruce without Aunt Kate's knowledge.

The curving drive leading to the front of Beau Rivage was already crowded with carriages, and the windows were blazing with light when Bruce and Shannon arrived at the ball on that warm September evening. Bruce got down, then helped Shannon to alight.

For a moment, she was seized with panic. What was she doing here, before this palatial house, with its double galleries, supported by Grecian columns that glowed white in the moonlight, its beautifully designed, wrought-iron grillwork, its white marble entrance steps and portico?

Bruce had invited her, she reminded herself. He

had wanted her here tonight. She must forget her uneasiness, and prove herself a credit to him.

He gave her the warm, lazy smile she loved. "You look lovely tonight," he said. "Your gown is charming; the color suits you."

Shannon had borrowed the gown from Clarisse. "This is getting to be a habit," she had said to her friend.

Clarisse had been most generous, helping Shannon choose the gown that would best set off her coloring: an amber satin, with a full skirt billowing over a wide crinoline, and a low-cut, closely-fitting bodice. "But why're you taking off them ostrich plumes? And the jet beading?"

"I'll sew everything back exactly as it was," Shannon had promised.

"That ain't the point, honey. You want to make a splash at this party, don't you?"

Although Shannon used her own judgment in the matter of the gown, she asked Clarisse to help her to arrange her hair. Clarisse, with considerable skill, brushed soft, deep waves over Shannon's forehead from a center part, and curled the rest of her tawny hair in ringlets that fell around her face and over her shoulders. She managed to find a cluster of tea roses and fastened them into the coiffure with a black velvet band.

Now, seeing the admiration in Bruce's eyes, Shannon was glad that she had insisted on simplicity in her costume. Although she knew Antoinette Duval would not be overjoyed to see her at Beau Rivage, she would be able to find no fault with Shannon's dress and behavior. And surely, Mrs. Duval would have to be courteous to Bruce Lathrop's partner for the evening.

The dancing had already started, and Shannon was relieved that she and Bruce had avoided the receiving line. They entered the spacious hall with a few other latecomers, and Shannon heard the slave orchestra tuning their instruments.

A black butler directed Shannon to the ladies' dressing room, and Bruce to the gentlemen's cloakroom. After Shannon had tucked a few curls in place, she went to rejoin Bruce; he took her arm and together they ascended to the ballroom.

Shannon was overawed by the immense room, with mirrors, set at opposite ends, to create endless reflections of the glittering chandeliers, and of the dancers: the ladies in their full-skirted dresses of taffeta, silk and brocade, trimmed with delicate lace, in organdy or tulle, garnished with silk field flowers or velvet sprays of lilac.

The gentlemen were equally impressive, in black broadcloth, with fine ruffled shirts, satin cravats and embroidered waistcoats. But not one of them looked as handsome, as elegant, as Bruce, Shannon thought with satisfaction.

"We must pay our respects to our hostess," Bruce said. Although his words were commonplace, his tone was hard, almost defiant.

He led Shannon over to the tall French doors that opened onto the second-story gallery. Antoinette, resplendent in mauve taffeta, an amethyst and diamond necklace blazing at her throat, was talking to a burly, whiskered man in his forties. At their approach,

Antoinette turned, her eyes darkening until the iris appeared to merge with the pupil; her ivory skin drew taut over her prominent cheekbones.

"Mrs. Duval, may I present my partner of the evening, Miss Shannon Cavanaugh of Mobile?"

Shannon saw Antoinette's hand tighten on her fan.

"Miss Cavanaugh," she said. Then, looking at the burly man beside her, she said, "Allow me to present Mr. Arthur Cunningham, our visitor from Massachusetts."

Cunnningham acknowledged the introduction. "Your Southern ladies are a delight to the eye, Mrs. Duval. A galaxy of beauties."

Antoinette gave Shannon a venomous look, drew a deep breath, then turning to Cunningham, she said, "There's dear Odalie. She's promised you the first dance, I believe. Come along, won't you?"

Why does she dislike me so? Shannon thought. She wanted to ask Bruce, but he swept her into his arms and in a moment, they were moving, circling, swaying to the music of the waltz. His nearness, the triumph of this moment, blotted out all her questions, all her doubts. She would let no one, certainly not Antoinette Duval, spoil the joy of this evening.

The ballroom, banked with magnolias, jessamine blossoms and roses, was a place of enchantment. She breathed the rich, heady perfume of the flowers, and her eyes went golden, bright as the flames on the candles burning in the crystal chandeliers.

She had always known it would be this way. In spite of Miss Colter's admonitions about her future, in spite of Aunt Kate's warnings that Shannon must not aim too high, she had known that she belonged not at the tavern, or even at the dressmaker's shop, but in a ballroom like this one, in the arms of a man like Bruce Lathrop.

Hardly had the waltz finished before Antoinette made her way through the crowd. "Bruce, I want to talk to you, and to Miss Cavanaugh. Not here. Out on the gallery."

Bruce bowed, and, taking Shannon's arm, he led her out through the tall French doors. She stood close to him, her amber satin skirt brushing the iron railing; Antoinette faced them, her back to the ballroom.

"Your mother and Melora aren't here tonight," Antoinette said.

"Mother has one of her migraines. Melora wished to stay and help care for her."

"Or was it perhaps that the ladies of your family did not wish to share a carriage with this—this barmaid?"

"I must ask you to show Miss Cavanaugh the same courtesy you would extend to any other lady under your roof," Bruce said quickly. "She is—"

"She is a common trollop, and her presence here is an insult to every lady present."

Shannon, her moment of triumph slipping away, felt her anger rising. "Mrs. Duval, it's bad enough you forced Miss Harwood to fire me—"

"I thought that would be enough to convince you that your place is in your uncle's tavern, entertaining sailors. I see now that I will have to drive you out of Mobile."

"You can't do that."

"I can and I will."

"But why?" Shannon demanded. "I've never given you any reason to dislike me."

She stopped, seeing Odalie come out onto the gallery with Arthur Cunningham. Antoinette had her back to Odalie and her escort; in any case, her fury made her oblivious to everyone except Shannon.

"I wasn't sure who you were when I saw you at the dressmaker's," Antoinette said. "Although I had my suspicions. But I made it my business to find out for certain."

"I'm Shannon Cavanaugh, I told you that."

"You're the daughter of a slut who seduced my husband and held onto him even after he married me. I didn't know about Peggy Cavanaugh, not at first. Then I heard rumors. I tried to ignore them. Later, Philippe admitted the truth, and told me that Peggy Cavanaugh had given him a child. I knew that he was paying for the child's education. But he didn't provide for you in his will; I saw to that. So now, you've come here to create a scandal."

Odalie gave a little cry. "Mama. It's not true. Papa didn't— Shannon isn't—"

The two girls faced each other. Odalie did not have Shannon's coloring; she had Antoinette's black hair and dark brown eyes. But now Shannon saw that Odalie looked a little like *her,* too; that there was a similarity in the molding of the chin, in the way the eyes were set, wide-apart and slightly tilted.

Odalie is my sister. No, my half-sister. We had the same father. Philippe Duval.

The pieces began to fit together now. Antoinette, recently widowed. Shannon's father had died within this past year. Philippe Duval, master of Beau Rivage.

That was why Aunt Kate had forbidden Shannon to come here tonight, why she had refused to tell Shannon her father's name.

Even while Shannon tried to grasp the revelation, she felt sorry for Odalie, too. Her half-sister, who stood there, looking confused, shaken, and almost childlike in spite of her splendid gown of green and silver brocade, her elaborate coiffure, and the dark hair threaded with green velvet ribbons and seed pearls. "Odalie," Shannon said, "I swear I didn't know. Otherwise I never would have come here tonight."

"Bruce," Antoinette said, cutting Shannon off, "I want you to leave my home and to take Miss Cavanaugh with you. What were you thinking of, to bring a tavern girl to Beau Rivage?"

"I might ask how you could have planned to marry Odalie to this—Yankee tradesman?"

"That's enough," Cunningham said, his face red with anger. He was obviously used to giving orders. "Will you go quietly, or shall I have you thrown out?"

He put a hand on Bruce's arm, but Bruce jerked away.

"What gives you the right to order me, or anyone else, out of this house?"

"I'm going to be Odalie's husband, and soon."

"No— I won't. I never agreed to—"

But at that moment, Bruce was not listening to Odalie. He struck Cunningham across the face with his open hand. "Even a Yankee should understand that," he said. "If not, my seconds will explain."

For a moment, Shannon could not fully grasp

what had happened. She was still too stunned by the knowledge that Philippe Duval had been her father. But as the guests gathered at the open doors leading to the gallery, she heard someone say, "A duel. Lathrop and Cunningham."

Two young men in black broadcloth and ruffled shirts came to join Bruce, while a plump little gray-haired lady hurried out and put an arm around Odalie.

"Come with me, dear," the plump lady said. "This is no place for you now."

"No, Aunt Lucienne. I've got to talk to Bruce. I've got to tell him—"

"Lucienne. Take Odalie to her room, at once," Antoinette ordered.

The guests crowded forward onto the gallery, and Odalie allowed herself to be led away, crying, while Shannon stood at the iron railing, momentarily forgotten by everyone, even Bruce.

"Peter, you'll act as my second?" Bruce was asking. "And you, too, Ross?"

"No," Antoinette's voice rang out. "You can't fight. Mr. Cunningham's not experienced with pistols."

"I don't need pistols," Cunningham said. "I'll break him in two with my bare hands."

"That may be your way up North," Bruce said. "Here, in Alabama, gentlemen have other ways of settling their differences." He put an emphasis on the word "gentlemen."

"Suit yourself," Cunningham said.

"Bruce, Mr. Cunningham has never fired a pistol," Antoinette said. "He doesn't even hunt." Antoinette was obviously disturbed. *And why not?* Shannon thought bitterly. Antoinette was set on having Odalie marry Mr. Cunningham.

Ross, one of Bruce's seconds, said, "Maybe we'd better talk this over, Bruce. We all know your skill with the pistol. If Mr. Cunningham has never handled one, perhaps all this can be resolved in another way."

"Very well," Bruce said. "Let him apologize to me and to Miss Cavanaugh and agree to leave Beau Rivage tonight. That will satisfy me."

"Do you agree to those terms?" Ross asked.

"Like hell I do! I'll meet you, Lathrop, whenever you're ready."

Shannon saw the swift flicker of uneasiness in Mr. Cunningham's eyes, however. She felt a little sorry for him. He obviously did not want to lose face with Odalie.

"My seconds will make the arrangements," Bruce said. "Will one of you lend me a horse?"

"Take mine," Ross offered.

Then Bruce was leading Shannon through the crowded ballroom. She held her head high, trying to ignore the stares and the whispers. A few minutes later, he mounted the borrowed stallion, while his black driver helped Shannon into the carriage.

He leaned down from the saddle. "Cicero, you will drive Miss Cavanaugh back to Mobile."

"No, Bruce," Shannon cried. "You mustn't fight Mr. Cunningham."

"I have no choice," Bruce said. "It's a long way back to Mobile. You'd better be starting now."

Before she could say anything more, he spurred his horse and disappeared into the warm, velvety darkness.

Cicero flicked his whip and the carriage rolled forward. Shannon, turning her head, saw the lighted windows of Beau Rivage, blurred now, through the tears. Tonight was to have marked her triumph, and it had ended in disaster.

Angrily, she blinked back the tears, and straightened.

"They won't drive me away," she said.

Cicero turned on his high seat. "You say somethin', miss?"

"I want you to drive me to Jessamine."

"But Mistuh Bruce, he say—"

"Take me to Jessamine or I'll get down and walk there."

"Oh, no, miss. You can't. It's dark. You might hurt yourself."

"Then do as I say," she ordered.

"What fo' you want to go to Jessamine this time of night, miss?"

"To stop the duel."

"Once Mistuh Bruce makes up his mind, can't nobody change it fo' him."

"I can. I have to."

The black coachman sighed, and turned the carriage in the direction of Jessamine.

9

DAWN FLOODED the sky with pale yellow light, and sent shafts of gold through the Spanish moss that veiled the oak trees. Bruce, with his seconds, Ross Gilford and Peter Yates, and the doctor who had offered his services, rode in silence toward the bluffs.

Although Cunningham's behavior at the ball would have been sufficient provocation for the duel, Bruce knew that his real grudge against the mill owner stemmed from the man's claim that he would marry Odalie. How could Odalie have agreed to such a marriage?

Bruce had always planned to marry her himself. Her dowry would provide the substantial amount of money he needed to hold on to Jessamine, and one day, when she would inherit Beau Rivage, the two great plantations would become one—the largest in Alabama's Black Belt.

Not that he wanted her for her money alone. He had admired her cool, dark loveliness, her proud bearing. Her lack of physical response was also a part of her attraction for him. The few times he had kissed her, she had drawn back. Once, when his hunger had overcome him, and he had held her too tightly, she had cried out in fear, had twisted free of his embrace and gone running back to the house.

That was proper, he told himself. A Lathrop's bride must be innocent, virginal. Once he and Odalie were married, he would overcome her fears, with gentleness and patience. Perhaps she would never respond with overpowering passion, but she would give him sons. If he required an outlet for his more urgent needs, there were other girls.

Girls like Shannon. She was beautiful, hot-blooded, half-lady, half-wanton. And the daughter of Philippe Duval. He should have suspected. Shannon's eyes, amber in certain lights, pure gold in others, were Philippe's eyes. The dark, curving brows were the same, and the firm chin, the high cheekbones.

Antoinette had seen the resemblance. No doubt Lucienne had confirmed her suspicions. Lucienne, who had lived with Philippe's family before he had married Antoinette, must have known about the scandal. Perhaps she had even known the name of the pretty young Irish girl who had been Shannon's mother.

"We're nearly there," Peter Yates said. "Bruce, you're not going to shoot to kill."

"You know better than that," Bruce said. "He needs a lesson in manners, that's all. A flesh wound should do it."

The four men rode on to the top of the rise, then started down the other side. It was then that Bruce saw Shannon, sitting in the open carriage. He gestured to the others to ride on ahead, and turning his mount, he rode up to her.

"Oh, Bruce, I made Cicero bring me here. You must not blame him."

"This is no place for a woman," Bruce said with barely suppressed anger.

Shannon rose and tried to get down from the high carriage, but her full crinoline and wide satin skirt hindered her. Bruce dismounted and lifted her down. She laid a hand on his arm, her eyes feverish, urgent.

"Call off the duel," she said. "You've got to. Bruce, I—I lied to you. Odalie didn't agree to marry Arthur Cunningham. Her mother wants her to but she—"

"You said their engagement was to be announced at the ball tonight. Did you lie about that, too?"

"Yes, I did. I was afraid of losing you. Odalie has so much to offer, while I—I only have my love to give you."

Her tawny hair, disheveled now, caught the glow of the rising sun; the tangled curls gleamed like molten copper around her pale face. There were violet smudges under her eyes. "I did a terrible thing, I know, but I'm not wicked enough to let a man be killed because of it."

"No one's going to be killed, Shannon. I give you my word."

He stopped, hearing the sound of carriage wheels beyond the trees, the jingle of horses' harness.

The Duval carriage emerged from the early morning mist. In it sat Cunningham, his seconds, and Antoinette Duval.

What was she thinking of, coming here? Shannon

might not know that custom forbade the presence of a woman at a duel, but Antoinette knew. Bruce shrugged impatiently. Antoinette had always made her own rules, and now, since Philippe's death, she had become more headstrong and arrogant than ever.

Bruce wheeled his horse around and rode over to the grove of live oaks. There he dismounted. Cunningham got down from the carriage, followed by his seconds.

"It must have taken his seconds half the night to show him how to load and fire a pistol," Ross Gilford said softly.

Yates, Gilford and the doctor, along with Cunningham's seconds, stood a short distance from the two duelists. When Yates gave the word, Bruce turned his back on Cunningham and as Yates began to count slowly, Bruce and Cunningham paced off the required distance.

Then Bruce turned to face his adversary. The light was brighter now. An easy shot. A bullet through the fleshy part of the shoulder. He heard Yates say, "On the count of three, you will fire."

Bruce kept his arm bent, his long-barreled pistol pointed straight up. "One . . . two. . . ."

Cunningham lowered his arm jerkily. Bruce heard the explosion, saw the flash. The mill owner, too nervous to wait for the count of three, had fired prematurely. His shot had missed Bruce by a wide margin.

No more than Bruce might have expected. His eyes narrowed thoughtfully. He could now fire straight up into the air, showing his contempt without injuring the man physically. But he was too angry for that.

He would carry out his original plan, wound Cunning-ham slightly. First, though, he would make the Yankee wait, and sweat it out.

From the oak trees, a few birds began to call. Down below the bluffs, on the river, a boat sounded its bell.

One easy shot. But as Bruce lowered his pistol and fired, the other man lunged to the right. The bullet penetrated his chest, and he crumpled to the grass.

The doctor knelt beside him, his leather bag within reach. Yates, Gilford and the other men clustered around Cunningham, who was coughing, choking, fighting for breath. Bright blood poured from his mouth, staining the starched white ruffles of his shirt. His burly features looked pinched, his whole body somehow shrunken. He made a terrible, strangling sound. Then he was still.

The doctor rose and shook his head. "He's gone, Bruce."

Yates said, "It wasn't your fault, Bruce. If the damn fool hadn't—"

Bruce turned and walked away. He could not stop to speak to Shannon, although he felt pity, seeing the horror in her eyes. He had to get away, to be alone.

But Antoinette had gotten out of the carriage, and stood barring the path. Her voice was icy, controlled.

"You murdered him," she said.

"It wasn't murder. Even after he fired early, I'd have let him off with a scratch, no more."

"There were witnesses at the ball. They heard me tell you that Mr. Cunningham had had no experience with firearms. That will be remembered. I'll make sure it is."

"You can't—"

"I can. I will. Shannon will leave Mobile. Maybe if you're quick enough, you can leave along with her."

"Jessamine's my home. My family's here."

"Then, for their sake, you won't want to disgrace the Lathrop name. If you stay, I'll see that you're put behind bars. Dueling's illegal in Alabama, or had you forgotten?"

"No one has ever paid any attention to that law."

"In your case, the law will be enforced."

Bruce knew it was no idle threat. One of Antoinette's uncles was a judge, another, a member of Alabama's state assembly. Lawyers, bankers, men of influence and unlimited power on both sides of the family. When honor was at stake, these French families closed ranks against the enemy.

Bruce turned his back on Antoinette, and, mounting his horse, he rode over to Shannon.

"It was my fault," she began.

"That's not important now. A man is dead. I killed him." Bruce set his jaw, fighting to control himself. "Cicero, take Miss Cavanaugh back to Mobile."

"Shannon, you can't stay shut up here in your room forever," Aunt Kate said, with a worried frown.

It was late afternoon, the day after the duel. Shannon lay across her rumpled bed. The amber satin gown was on the chair, a crumpled heap; she had flung it there when she had returned to the tavern.

"I tried to warn you," Aunt Kate said. "Then, when you disappeared without a word, I was half out of my mind with worry."

"I went to the Cherokee Rose. I had Bruce meet me there to take me to the ball."

"But that's no better than a—fancy house. How come you—"

"My friend, Clarisse, works there. She lent me the ball gown. Oh, Aunt Kate, if only you'd told me who my father was, I'd never have gone."

"That's over and done with," Aunt Kate said, squaring her plump shoulders. "And as for the duel, you got to stop blaming yourself. Those Lathrop men have been fighting duels over any little trifle, since I can remember."

"But Aunt Kate—"

"Come along," her aunt said. "Get yourself dressed and I'll fix you a bit of food in the kitchen. Jethro's been asking questions. You don't want him to find out what you've been up to."

"Find out?" Jethro's harsh voice silenced Kate. He strode into the room. "You thought you could keep it from me, you stupid cow? Telling me Shannon had a touch of fever and was keeping to her bed. Lying to your own husband to protect her." He glared at Shannon. "The bitch has ruined us all."

"She didn't know about Philippe Duval," Kate protested.

"To hell with that. She's getting out of town, right now." He pushed Aunt Kate aside. Shannon reached for her wrapper to cover her half-bare breasts.

"I won't leave because Mrs. Duval wants me to. She has no right—"

Jethro grasped her shoulder. "Right? She's got the power. The Duvals run this city." His fingers tightened.

"Let go of me," Shannon cried. "You've bullied Aunt Kate until she's afraid to stand up to you. You won't do that to me."

Jethro drew back his arm, and his hand caught her across the face, so that a reddish haze blurred her sight.

He released her, unbuckled his belt and pulled it off. "Jethro, don't—" Aunt Kate grabbed his arm, but he pushed her away, slamming her against the wall. Then he turned on Shannon.

He tore her camisole to the waist. His eyes went to her bare breasts, with their small, rosy nipples. Before she could move, the belt slashed across her breasts. She screamed with pain, and twisted away. She fell face down on the bed, and the next blow caught her across the shoulders.

The flimsy camisole was shredded to ribbons. White-hot lines of fire seared her body. She fought for breath, and heard herself making whimpering animal sounds.

"Jethro, stop. You'll kill her."

"No more'n she deserves. Ruined us, she did."

"We ain't ruined yet," Kate said. "If Shannon leaves right away, that'll be enough to satisfy the Duval woman."

Shannon, her face buried in the mattress, her body curled into a ball, could make no sense of the words. How could Antoinette ruin her aunt and uncle?

She heard Jethro's belt drop to the floor, heard Aunt Kate's torrent of words. "We'll tell everybody you beat Shannon real bad and threw her out. That she's left Mobile for good. That should be enough to satisfy the Duval woman."

"It better be." Jethro was panting from his exertion; his shirt was soaked with sweat. "The Duval family controls the Merchants and Planters Bank. They can foreclose on this place any time they want to."

"It's only Shannon that Mrs. Duval's mad at. She —she don't care about us."

Jethro scratched his head thoughtfully. "Maybe. If we're lucky. Hell, I ain't even a blood relation to Shannon."

He took Shannon's arm and jerked her to her feet. "Get your clothes on and get out."

"She can't leave right away. She's hurt bad," Aunt Kate protested.

"I'm all right," Shannon said. "I'll go."

"See that you do." Jethro strode to the door. "Come with me, Kate. There'll be a mob in the taproom tonight, all wanting to get liquored up before they set off for Panama. The *Lively Bess* made port an hour ago."

"I got to take care of Shannon," Aunt Kate pleaded. But Jethro took her by the shoulders and thrust her out the door. "Let the slut take care of herself. She can drown herself in Mobile Bay for all I care."

Her aunt gave her one last agonized look, before Jethro slammed the bedroom door.

Shannon put on the first dress that came to hand, the amber satin ball gown, stuffed the rest of her clothes into her carpetbag. She could not stay here without bringing further trouble on her aunt. But where could she go without money, without friends?

Then, as she smoothed the folds of the satin skirt, she remembered Clarisse Jenkins.

The sun had not yet dropped below the waters of Mobile Bay, but the Cherokee Rose was already crowded to the doors. A group of men and a few girls were gathered around the piano singing lustily. The tune was "Pop Goes the Weasel" but the words were unfamiliar to Shannon.

> You go aboard of a leaky boat,
> And sail for San Francisco.
> You've got to pump to keep her afloat.
> Rip goes the boiler.

She climbed the stairs and knocked on Clarisse's door.

"It's me, Shannon. Let me in."

To her relief, Clarisse was alone. "What happened to you, honey?" Clarisse asked, round-eyed with horror.

"I'm afraid—your dress is ruined—" Shannon started to laugh shakily. "It dragged in the mud as I was crossing the stableyard—" Then, all at once, she was sobbing helplessly.

Clarisse forced a glass of gin into her hand. "Drink this," she said. "Lucky I didn't pack the bottle yet."

Shannon swallowed the gin, coughed, and then she saw the trunk at the foot of the bed. "Are you leaving?"

"I'm off to Panama tonight. And from there, it's on to San Francisco."

"I thought ships for Panama sailed from New York. Or New Orleans."

"Most do," Clarisse said. "But with all these men wanting to get out to the silver diggings, every old tub on the Gulf's being loaded up. You still ain't told me what happened to you."

"Jethro beat me and threw me out."

"The old devil! What made him do that?"

Briefly, between spells of weeping, Shannon told her about the ball, and all that had followed. "So you see, Mrs. Duval wants to drive me out of Mobile, and Jethro says she can."

"I wouldn't be surprised. Everyone in Mobile is scared of the Duvals. And you're Philippe Duval's daughter."

"Much good that does me," Shannon said. "There's no way I can stay in Mobile now."

"Why should you? Come to Panama with me, honey."

"I couldn't even if I wanted to. I don't have the fare."

"I wish I could lend it to you, but I only have enough to get me as far as Colón. That's a port on the eastern coast of Panama. I'll find work there and earn the rest of my passage."

"Oh, Clarisse, what am I going to do?"

"First, you're going to put a cold cloth on your cheek. It's swelling. Then you can rest up, while I finish packing. After that, you'll come down to the wharf with me. I got a friend who runs a keelboat up to Montgomery. Maybe he'll be willing to let you go along that far."

The hired carriage rattled down to the wharf. "At least I'll have somebody to see me off," Clarisse said. "But first, we got to find that keelboat man. Hope you don't mind sharing the deck with a few crates of livestock."

Shannon rose abruptly. "Clarisse. Over there. Isn't that Bruce Lathrop?"

"Looks like him," Clarisse said. "Guess maybe he's leaving Mobile, too."

Shannon ordered the driver to stop, got down, leaving her carpetbag behind, and forced her way through the crowd. "Bruce—Bruce, wait for me."

He turned and shouldered his way over to her. "Shannon. Your face. What happened to you?"

Although Shannon had changed to her flowered cotton, and put a shawl around her shoulders to hide the livid marks left by Jethro's beating, she realized that she had not been able to conceal the evidence of her ordeal completely.

"Never mind about me. Bruce, you're not leaving on the *Lively Bess,* are you?"

"It's the only way," he said. "I'd have come to say good-bye, but—"

"You would have? Then you're not angry with me anymore."

He shook his head. "I had no business taking you to the ball at Beau Rivage. No matter. I'm paying for my rashness. But you—"

"Take me along, Bruce. I have to leave Mobile, too. Uncle Jethro beat me and threw me out."

"I can't take you to Panama," he said. "It's no place for a girl like you. No, my dear, there must be another way."

"But I want to go. Bruce, I won't be any trouble, I promise."

He smiled, his gray eyes moving to the lush curves of her breasts, her small waist. "You'll always be trouble for one man or another," he said. She saw the hunger in his face. She clung to his arm.

"You're the only one I'll ever love," she said, her arms reaching for him. Her shawl fell away from her shoulders, and the marks on her skin were visible now, ugly and livid.

"Jethro did that?" Bruce went white, and he held her against him. "Shannon, my dear."

"He'll do worse, if I'm not out of Mobile by morning. Clarisse is leaving for Panama, too. There's no one who'll help me."

He pressed his face against her hair. "Don't cry, my love. You know I don't want to leave you." His voice was soft, caressing, but his tone was serious. "Listen to me. This voyage will be difficult enough for a man. The ship was already crowded when she left Savannah. There'll be men sleeping on the deck, bad food, the danger of fever. And Panama won't be any better. It's the rainy season down there. Shannon, are you listening?"

"I don't care. I'm not afraid. So long as you're with me, nothing else matters."

Shannon felt a light touch on her arm. "Honey, I'm sorry to interrupt you two, but I've got to get out to the boat. Here's your carpetbag." She made no further mention of the keelboat captain. Perhaps she sensed what Shannon's plans were, now that she had found Bruce.

"Good luck, honey," she said, and gave Shannon a

little wink. Then, putting down the carpetbag, she joined the mob pushing toward the end of the wharf.

"You see," Shannon said stubbornly, "Clarisse is going."

"She's different."

"No, she's not."

"How can you possibly compare yourself with—"

"She's my friend."

Bruce held Shannon away and looked down at her.

"You want me," she said. "I know you do."

He gave a wordless groan, and pulled her against him. "You little witch," he said, his voice unsteady. "How can I hold out against you?"

The voyage to Panama, across the Gulf of Mexico and the Caribbean, was as bad as Bruce had predicted. Shannon found herself jammed into a tiny, airless cabin with a dozen girls, Clarisse among them. Few of the girls had plans for going to the Nevada territory. San Francisco was their destination, and the gilded dives of the Barbary Coast.

During those days at sea, Shannon received an education far different from the one she had been given at Miss Colter's Academy. Here, aboard ship, the girls spoke of their past lives with a frankness that shocked Shannon, although she tried to hide her feelings. One of them, an olive-skinned brunette from a parlor house in Montgomery, found a jar of ointment and spread the stuff on Shannon's back. "It's easy to get an infection in these tropical places," she said. "Any little cut will fester."

"That's not the worst," another girl said. "They

got cholera down there, and yellow fever. And the drinking water's awful."

"I'll stick to champagne," Clarisse said.

"You won't find much champagne in Bottle Alley," the girl from Montgomery told her.

"Bottle Alley. What's that?" Shannon asked.

"That's where most of us are going to work. A friend of mine who just got back from Panama told me about it. A real lively place. Prospectors go there, and railroad men." She laughed. "They call it Bottle Alley, because it used to be all mud, but so many men threw their empty bottles down that now there's no need to pave it."

During the ten-day voyage, Shannon saw little of Bruce, who slept on the deck with the other men who had not found cabin space. With a dozen females on board, and two hundred and fifty males, the captain allowed the women to take the air only at stated intervals, guarded by the ship's officers. He was determined to avoid any outbreak of violence among the men, a hard-bitten lot armed with pistols and Bowie knives.

In a driving rain, the passengers of the *Lively Bess* got their first glimpse of Panama's eastern coast. Shannon, standing beside Bruce, saw the headland of Porto Bello, the rocky promontory gray and forbidding. The stretch of thick green trees that edged the land was equally uninviting; the dripping leaves and branches, twined with ropelike vines, looked like a jungle.

The ship turned west, following a sweep of hills, their summits veiled by low-lying clouds. It docked at last at the wharf at Colón, the eastern terminus of the Panama railroad.

Clarisse, in a low-cut dress of pale-blue organdy which was half-hidden by a waterproof cloak, joined Bruce and Shannon. She embraced Shannon, and said, "Take care of yourself." And to Bruce, she added, "You look out for her, you hear?"

Bruce nodded politely, but Shannon could sense that he did not welcome Clarisse's presence. It was natural, she told herself, that Bruce Lathrop would not want his future wife to associate with such a girl.

"See you in San Francisco," Clarisse called. Then she joined the other girls with whom she and Shannon had shared the cabin, and they started down the gangplank in the pelting rain. Bruce took Shannon's arm and she smiled up at him. Nothing could dim her joy at being here with him.

10

BECAUSE OF the heavy rain and the crowd pouring off the *Lively Bess,* even the shabbiest hired carriage was at a premium, and Shannon, trudging along beside Bruce, with water squelching through her thin slippers, was relieved to hear a man's voice shouting, "Hey there, mister, I can make room for you and the lady. If you don't mind crowding."

A mule-drawn carriage came to a halt, and a lean, sun-browned man in a shapeless, wide-brimmed hat and a waterproof poncho, leaned out. "Can't let a lady walk in all this rain."

Bruce helped Shannon into the carriage, and got in beside her, cramming their luggage into the narrow space at their feet. The carriage, although open on the sides, had a makeshift awning.

"Most generous of you, sir," Bruce said, holding out his hand. "I'm Bruce Lathrop, and this is—my wife."

Shannon heard the slight hesitation, but it didn't

matter. Bruce had called her his wife, and the vague uneasiness that had troubled her from time to time during the voyage, now disappeared completely. Bruce would marry her as soon as arrangements could be made. *"My wife."* She savored the words.

"Mark Walsh is the name," said their fellow passenger. His skin was weather-beaten and there were lines around his eyes and mouth, not because of age, but because of prolonged exposure to the blazing tropical sunlight. His hair was cut short, his face clean-shaven. "I'm a mechanic on the Panama railroad," he said. "I'm on my way back from the railroad office over there. Got to take a repair crew upriver in the morning."

"You know Colón well?" Bruce asked.

"Know it? Say, I was here when it wasn't no more than a swamp. Crocodiles, tarantulas and lizards." He glanced at Shannon. "Sorry, ma'am. I guess ladies are kind of squeamish about such things. But we're getting real civilized here now, Mrs. Lathrop."

Mrs. Lathrop. Shannon gave Mark Walsh a dazzling smile. Encouraged, he went on, "Yes, ma'am, the city's growing fast. Got hotels now, shops. Even a special refrigerator ship to bring in ice. Can't have too much ice in this climate."

"We won't be staying in Colón long. Only overnight," Bruce said. "We're taking the railroad to Panama City tomorrow morning."

"Nobody'll be taking the railroad for a few days, maybe a week," Walsh said. "A span got washed out by a freshet up near Barbacoas station."

"We're stranded here?" Bruce asked, frowning.

"That's about it, sir. Best hotels in Colón, the

City, the Howard, the Aspinwall, are full-up, with folks waiting to get across the isthmus."

"Bruce, what will we do?" Shannon asked.

"I'm staying over at the Mariposa," Walsh said. "It's not fancy, but the food's all right; it doesn't crawl away before you can eat it. Oh, sorry, Mrs. Lathrop. Fact is, I'm not used to talking to ladies these days. Not too many of them here in Colón."

The mule-drawn carriage came to a halt a few minutes later, in front of a small wood-and-stucco building with a red tile roof. Bruce helped Shannon down and carried her inside, while Walsh and the driver saw to the luggage.

"Gallego, the manager here, is a slick customer," Walsh told Bruce. "Make sure you settle on the rates before you sign in."

Shannon saw that the lobby was already crowded with prospectors. Some were stretched out on chairs, while others were unrolling their bedding, obviously preparing to make themselves as comfortable as possible on the tiled floor.

Señor Gallego, a short, fat man in a soiled white suit, listened to Bruce's request for accommodations, then said, "No rooms. None at all, señor. *Lo siento mucho.*"

"But surely—" Bruce began.

"There is nothing to be had, señor. You may find yourself a space in the lobby, one dollar a night, or out on the *galería* upstairs. We can fit in two extra cots, perhaps."

"That's out of the question," Bruce said. "My wife can't sleep among this rabble."

Señor Gallego shrugged and spread his hands. "Then perhaps you'll wish to try someplace else."

Mark Walsh, who stood near the desk, told Bruce, "Don't bother. It'll probably be about the same all over town. My own room's about the size of a broom closet, but if you and Mrs. Lathrop want it, you're welcome to it."

"That's most generous, Mr. Walsh," Bruce said, "but where will you sleep?"

"Here in the lobby. I'm heading up to San Pablo with my crew first thing tomorrow. Don't worry, I've slept in worse places."

"Mr. Walsh is so kind," Shannon said, as they entered the cubicle.

But Bruce only said, "Stranded in this hellhole. Good Lord!"

Was he remembering Jessamine, thinking that, had it not been for her, he might never had had to leave his home? She went to him, and put her arms around him. "Bruce, darling, I know this isn't what you're used to. But once we're in San Francisco, everything will be different."

"I hope so," he said doubtfully. Then, responding to her nearness, he pulled her against him and his lips brushed her cheek.

Reassured, she said, "Oh, my love, you'll never be sorry. I'll be a good wife to you, we'll make a new life."

She stopped, feeling a swift tension move through his body. He drew away, his fair-skinned face flushed, his eyes uneasy.

"I'm going downstairs to talk to Walsh. You can change and meet me in the dining room."

"Bruce, wait—"

But before she could say anymore, he had left the room.

Shannon slipped into a chair between Bruce and Mark Walsh. She was the only woman at the long table, and all masculine eyes turned in her direction, some with frank admiration, others with covert lust. Her gray dress was drying over a chair upstairs, and the flowered cotton Jethro had given her to wear in the taproom was low-cut, showing too much of her bosom. Because of the stifling heat here, she had not even put on her light shawl.

Bruce and the railroad man were deep in conversation, and although both men had risen to acknowledge her presence, they seated themselves at once and took up their discussion of the problems of crossing the isthmus during the rainy season.

"Sure, you can get across without the railroad," Walsh said. "That's how they did it back in '49. You get a native to row you as far as Cruces in a bungo, and there you hire a mule, if you're lucky. But it's no trip for a lady." Walsh poured himself a glass of wine, and went on, "Your best bet would be to wait right here until the railroad's fixed. If the rain lets up, you and your wife can do a bit of shopping on the Avenida Central. There's all kinds of stores there. Syrian, East Indian, Turkish, Chinese. They got some unusual geegaws there. Ivory, jade. . . ."

Shannon was eating her stew, a steaming, tasty

concoction of meat and vegetables. It was a welcome change from the fare aboard the *Lively Bess*. "This is delicious," she said.

"*Sancocho*, that's what they call it," Walsh said. "It's a mixture of pork, beef, sausage and—" He broke off. Shannon saw that he was looking at her left hand. She swallowed with difficulty. He must be wondering why she wore no wedding ring.

After an awkward pause, he went on hastily, "We'll have fresh fruit for dessert. Be sure and peel it. And be careful of the water. Stick with wine if you can."

Bruce, taking Walsh's advice, finished a bottle of sauterne, and half a bottle of brandy. Shannon watched him uneasily, for she knew that Bruce was hot-tempered when he had been drinking; she had not forgotten the brawl at her uncle's tavern.

"I'll be getting an early start tomorrow," Walsh said, rising from the table. "In case I don't see you both again, I'll be wishing you a safe journey west, and a mountain of silver when you get there."

Later, back in their room, Shannon looked uneasily at the wide bed. "Bruce, when we were at dinner tonight, Mr. Walsh saw that I have no wedding ring. He—he must have wondered—"

"He probably guessed the truth," Bruce said. He hung his frock coat over the chair, and began to unbutton his waistcoat.

"Don't you care what he thought of me? That I was—that we were—"

"We'll probably never see the man again." Bruce took off his waistcoat, removed his cravat and his shirt. "Now," he said, "come here, and let me—" He drew her against him, pressing her face against his bare chest.

His skin was warm and damp against her cheek. Her body began to tremble, and she longed to forget everything, to give herself up to him, without holding back.

"I thought I'd go mad wanting you," he said, his face against her tawny hair. "Every night on that damn ship, with you only a few yards away in the cabin. Oh, Shannon, my dear, I've waited so long."

He put a hand on either side of her face, tilted it upward, and covered her mouth with his. But she managed to summon the will to hold him off. "Bruce, we can't. Not yet."

"I need you."

"No. Not until after we're married."

He let her go then. "I thought surely you would understand." His eyes were tender, troubled.

"Understand? What is there to understand?"

"I can't marry you, Shannon. It's quite impossible."

"But you brought me here with you. You let me believe you loved me."

"I do love you. What man wouldn't? The way you look, the way you move, the fire in you and the sweetness."

"Then if you love me, if you want me, why won't you marry me?"

"Marriage is more than wanting. More than desire. One day, when I go back to Jessamine—"

He was silent. She became aware, all at once, of the drumming of the rain against the window, the low, distant roll of thunder, the dripping of water from the sodden palm trees in the patio below.

Her pride rose in her, strong, demanding. "Go ahead, say it. You can't bring me back to Jessamine as your wife. You called me Mrs. Lathrop down here, where no one knows us, but I'm not good enough for your plantation friends."

"Don't make me say things that can only hurt you. Maybe I was wrong to bring you here. Wrong and selfish."

"But you did bring me. You said I wasn't like Clarisse and the other girls on the ship."

"You're not. You're everything a man could want in a wife. I'd marry you tomorrow, if only—"

Anger made her throw away all caution, all reticence.

"If only I had a name. And a dowry, and a plantation like Beau Rivage. But I'm Peggy Cavanaugh's bastard brat. That's what Uncle Jethro called me. You're too much of a gentleman to say the words out loud, but you're thinking them." All the old childhood pain rose up to torment her, to tear at her. The sickness, the shame of being different.

Bruce embraced her. "Don't," he said. "Please listen to me. If there were only the two of us, I wouldn't care who your mother was. But I have to think of my own mother, my sister. The generations of Lathrops who have made Jessamine what it is."

"To hell with Jessamine." But even as the words were out, she saw in her mind's eye, the gardens, the marble statues, the little pagoda with its tinkling windbells.

She forced the memory from her. "We'll make a new start in San Francisco," she said. "Why should you go back to Jessamine at all?"

"Because I must. When I can settle my debts, and the scandal over the duel has been forgotten, I'll go home."

"Is it only Jessamine you'll be going back to?" Her voice was unsteady.

"Of course," he answered quickly, looking away.

"You're lying. You still think you can marry Odalie, don't you? You're a fool, Bruce. Her mother will never permit it."

"I think I know Mrs. Duval better than you do. When I've found silver, when I come back a wealthy man, Mrs. Duval will accept me as Odalie's suitor."

"Suppose Odalie doesn't wait for you?"

"She will. She gave me her word. Before I left Jessamine we met secretly, and she promised she wouldn't marry anyone else no matter how long I stayed away."

Shannon's legs would no longer support her. She sank down on the bed. "That night when you took me to Beau Rivage, I thought it was because you wanted to show everyone that you weren't ashamed of me. That you wanted them to accept me, too." Her mind was darting around like a frightened, caged animal. "At Jessamine, when you kissed me there in the garden, I thought—"

"Surely I'm not the only man who ever kissed you." His voice took on a hard edge. "A barmaid, in a tavern on the waterfront? There must have been others who—"

"You're the only one whose kisses ever meant anything to me. I love you so."

"Then stop putting me off. Don't waste the time we have together. Let me love you."

An aching, quivering hunger moved within her. She longed to lie naked in his arms, to give herself freely, to forget the future. But she could not.

"And afterwards?" she asked. "What will happen to me after you've gone back to Jessamine?"

He was beside her on the bed now, the weight of his body forcing her down, his voice pleading, urging.

"You'll have my protection. A little house in Mobile."

"You'll provide for me as Philippe Duval did for my mother. A house where he could come and take his pleasure with her. Only she couldn't go to Beau Rivage. And I had to be sent away to school in Boston, isolated from the other girls as if I carried the plague."

"Shannon, listen to me."

"No, you listen. Suppose we have children? Is that how it will be for them?"

He smiled. "You're looking pretty far ahead, aren't you."

"I want to know," she insisted.

He released her and got to his feet. "You say you love me." His voice was tight with anger and frustration. "Yet you sit there, making terms, bargaining. I'm sorry, Shannon. I can't give you what you want." He picked up his discarded clothing and dressed quickly. "I won't force myself on you. You needn't be afraid of that."

"You can't leave me." She reached out to him, but he moved aside. "It's better if I go now," he said. "I'm only human, and you, Shannon, are most desirable."

He took out his wallet, counted out a pile of bills, and dropped them on the bed beside her.

"I don't want your money," she said.

"Take it. And consider yourself lucky. Any other man would demand a return for his cash."

Her face went scarlet, and her eyes filled with tears of rage. Picking up the bills, she rose, and flung them at his feet. "Get out," she cried. "Get out of my sight and don't come back."

He locked his valise, picked it up and started for the door. She did not try to stop him. She flung herself face down on the bed, with its grayish, mildewed sheets, and buried her face in her arms. The door slammed behind Bruce.

She wanted to go after him, but she could not, for a series of pictures formed in her mind. Bruce and Odalie, together. Odalie, with her dark, shining hair, her soft brown eyes. Odalie would lie beside Bruce in the master bedroom at Jessamine; Odalie would walk with him in the gardens, would sit beside him in the sweet-scented twilight, sharing the beauty of the lily pond, the pagoda summerhouse, the marble statues on the sweeping lawns.

Shannon's pride would not let her accept Bruce's love on his terms. She buried her face in the pillow. "Oh, my darling," she whispered to the empty room. "What will become of me without you?"

For nearly a week after Bruce had left her, Shannon remained shut up in her hotel room. Conchita, the chambermaid, brought her meals on a tray, but she could only pick at them. The maid, a plump, motherly woman, also volunteered to clean and press Shannon's few dresses, and launder her underthings. Shannon paid for her extra services generously, with the money Bruce had left her.

It was Conchita who informed her that Bruce, with a party of other impatient *yanquis* he had rounded up in the hotel's bar, had set forth on the journey up the Changres River.

"They take bungos to Cruces, then hire mules," Conchita explained. She shrugged and shook her head. "Your *yanqui* men, always they are in a hurry."

At another time, Shannon would have laughed to hear Bruce called a Yankee. Now, she could not force a smile. He was gone, lost to her forever.

Not that she had ever really possessed him, she thought bitterly. Bruce belonged to Odalie.

Conchita said soothingly, "At least, Señor Lathrop left you well provided for. Never fear, you will find another protector."

So even the chambermaid knew the truth, Shannon thought. Her mouth closed in a hard line, and her golden eyes narrowed. She wanted no other man, not ever. She was through with love, with romantic illusions. Right now, she had to make an effort to get through the simple mechanics of living.

Then, at the end of her first week at the Mariposa, the rain tapered off, and a few shafts of sunlight came through the window overlooking the patio.

"The sunshine won't last," Conchita warned her. "You must make the most of it. Why not hire a carriage and take a drive to the Avenida Central? You cannot remain shut up here in your room like *una vieja*—an old lady."

Conchita was right. She would have to go out some-

time, to see people again, to make a few small purchases. First, however, Conchita found an ancient tin
tub and had it brought to Shannon's room, where she
filled it with buckets of warm water.

In spite of her depression, Shannon felt her healthy,
young body respond to this luxury. She scrubbed herself with a piece of scented soap, also produced by
Conchita, and washed her hair. Conchita handed her
a large, coarse towel.

"*Que hermosa!*" the woman exclaimed, as Shannon
stepped naked from the tub. "Such a fine shape you
have. And hair the color of honey. Señor Lathrop was
a fool to leave you, but never fear, there will be
others."

Shannon did not answer. How could she tell Conchita, or anyone else, what Bruce had meant to her?
She thought of her mother, who had loved only one
man, Philippe Duval, until the day she had died.
I'm like that, Shannon thought. *And I can never have
the only man I'll ever love. Never. Never."*

Still, after she had put on her freshly washed and
pressed gray cotton, and had allowed Conchita to
brush her hair until it glowed with a rich, tawny
luster, she had a new sense of well-being. The maid
arranged her hair in a high coronet of heavy braids,
then said, "What you need now is a mantilla. You'll
find one on the Avenida Central, no doubt."

But when Shannon took out the roll of bills Bruce
had left her, Conchita warned, "Do not take all the
money with you. There are many thieves in the city,
and a woman alone must be careful. Take only a
few bills. I, myself, will make certain that the carriage
driver does not overcharge you."

The streets of Colón were filled with people who had come out to enjoy the brief respite from the rain. Shannon saw dark-haired, olive-skinned girls in full pink and white cotton skirts who sold oranges, pineapples and mangos from large straw baskets. Vendors were setting up huge iron pots for spicy *sancocho*.

On the Avenida Central, Shannon found a mantilla of delicate white lace and a tortoise-shell comb to hold it in place. She draped the lace over her hair, and later bought a flame-colored flower to tuck into one side of the mantilla.

On her return to the hotel, Shannon was conscious of the admiring stares of the men, lounging about the lobby; she was completely indifferent to their attentions, and hurried upstairs to her room.

It was when she went to empty her reticule into the nightstand drawer that she discovered that the roll of bills, all that Bruce had left her, was gone.

No, it was impossible. She must have shoved the bills to the back of the drawer. She searched frantically, with mounting desperation. She pulled the drawer out of the nightstand and emptied its contents onto the bed. A few crumpled handkerchiefs. Two pairs of stockings. The handful of coins she had brought back from her shopping expedition.

She rang for Conchita, then waited, feeling sick and shaken. But it was Señor Gallego who answered her summons.

"My money's been stolen," she blurted out.

"Perhaps you misplaced it." The manager, in his soiled white suit, his thinning hair gleaming with perfumed oil, was unperturbed.

"It's gone, I tell you. Conchita saw me put it in

the drawer of the nightstand before I went shopping, and now—"

"Ah, *sí*. Conchita. She left this afternoon, disappeared. Perhaps she has taken your money. She is part Indian. They're all unreliable, thieving." He gave Shannon a look of pity. "You should have asked me to put it in the hotel safe."

"I never thought of it."

"I understand. You were distressed, confused. And no wonder. Deserted by your lover, alone in a strange city."

In spite of her agitation, Shannon clung to her pride.

"Bruce was—is—"

"A fine gentleman, surely. But he is not your husband, señorita. No need to keep up this deception. He's gone and so is your money."

"But you've got to help me get it back."

"Impossible. Conchita has, no doubt, returned to her own village by now. Who knows where that may be?"

"But that money was all I had."

"Don't trouble yourself," Señor Gallego said, patting Shannon's arm. "A young woman as beautiful as you, in this city filled with lonely men. You will not starve."

She understood, and a slow sickness began to rise inside her. "Get out," she said.

But the manager went on calmly, "Already, there are several of my guests who are interested in you. You made a charming picture, in your mantilla. Most becoming."

Had Gallego and Conchita planned this together?

Shannon wondered. The disillusionment that had begun when Bruce had walked out on her grew deeper. She considered her position with cold clarity.

Conchita had urged her to make herself attractive, had helped her to arrange her hair, had suggested that she go out shopping on the other side of the city.

"As soon as you are ready, you will tell me," the manager was saying. "I will arrange the introductions. Only men of substance, who are able to pay what you are worth. You are no common *puta,* I saw that at once."

"Get out," she said, a killing rage growing inside her.

He went on as if she had not spoken. "You may continue to occupy this room. Or perhaps I can find you something larger, more comfortable. As for the money, we will reach a suitable arrangement. I am not greedy, señorita. When a lady is so young, so lovely as you, I am inclined to be generous."

"You filthy-minded, evil— Get out of my room."

"Your room? Only so long as you are able to pay for it."

"I'll go to the authorities. I'll report this theft."

He shrugged. "You are a stranger here. A young woman traveling under an assumed name. Colón is full of loose women, adventuresses from your country."

"I'm not one of those women. I'll make the authorities believe me."

"You're not in your own country now." Gallego dropped his smooth, courteous manner abruptly. "Panama is a part of New Granada, and I am on excellent terms with the authorities here. If you make any rash accusations, you may find yourself imprisoned as a common prostitute."

"But I'm not."

"You registered here with a man who was not your husband, you tried to deceive me. *Mrs. Lathrop*." His eyes were hard, contemptuous. "It would be sad for one so young, so innocent as you, to find herself in jail with the trash from Bottle Alley."

"Get out."

"As you wish, señorita. When you have had time to think this through, you will be more reasonable."

11

AFTER SEÑOR GALLEGO had gone, Shannon paced up and down the tiny room. Her mind continued to function clearly but her emotions were numb. The change that had begun at the ball at Beau Rivage, that had grown deeper the night Bruce had left her, was now more profound than before. She would not do what Señor Gallego had suggested, every fiber of her being rebelled at the thought. Neither would she allow herself to be railroaded into jail.

I'll find work, she told herself. *Respectable work.*

She left the hotel again, but this time, she did not hire a carriage. The few coins in her reticule were all that stood between her and complete destitution. She walked through the streets, her face set, her step brisk, in spite of the humid heat.

But a few hours later, at twilight, she had to admit that she had failed. The English and American shops on the Avenida Central employed only male clerks, and the foreign shops were run by families of Syrians, East Indians, and Chinese who would not even consider hiring an American girl.

As darkness fell, Shannon began to get hungry. She caught the rich fragrance of steaming sancocho, and made her way toward a crowd of natives and Americans who were clustered around a huge, iron kettle. She exchanged a coin for a plate of the stew, carefully finishing every morsel of pork, beef and *chorizo*, a spicy Spanish sausage, every bit of squash and green bananas. She tried not to think of how she would find money for another meal.

"Shannon—Shannon—over here."

She put down her empty plate. "Clarisse. Oh, I'm so glad to see you."

Clarisse, in a full-skirted, ruffled dress of pale blue and cerise, her red hair piled into an elaborate coiffure of curls, waves and puffs, embraced Shannon.

"How've you been?" she asked. "And how's Bruce? Has he—"

"Bruce left me." The words came out hard and flat, without expression. "He's gone."

"Come on," Clarisse said. "Walk back to La Ceiba with me. That's the saloon where I'm working. You can tell me all about it on the way."

As they threaded their way through the maze of narrow streets, lined with warehouses, tile-roofed stucco pensiones, saloons and gambling houses, Shannon told Clarisse all that had happened to her since they had said good-bye at the dock. But if she had expected sympathy, she received none.

"What did you think he'd do?" Clarisse demanded. "A man pays your fare, naturally he wants something in return. And why not? You acted like you were crazy in love with him."

"I was. I am. But he's going to marry Odalie. I couldn't ever be satisfied to be his mistress and nothing more."

Clarisse shrugged. "If it had been me, I'd have climbed into bed with him and done everything I knew how to make him forget Odalie."

"You're not talking about love," Shannon protested. "Only—lust. Animal passion."

"Honey, some day you'll find out that love between a man and woman don't amount to much without that animal passion to keep it going."

Shannon could find no reply. Turning to her immediate problem, she said, "Clarisse, once you told me that I could get work in a concert saloon, remember?"

"Sure, but that was before I knew about your touch-me-not ways. I sing and dance a bit at La Ceiba, but I've got to go upstairs with any man who asks me."

"I could never do that. Oh, Clarisse, I should have stayed in Mobile."

"With that Duval bitch out for your hide? And your uncle knocking you around? Besides, Mobile's no place for you. Why, out in San Francisco, you could find lots of men who'd be fighting to marry you. It don't matter about your family out there. Nobody'd know or care who your father was."

"Adam Kincaid told me that once," Shannon said absently.

"Kincaid?" Clarisse gripped her arm. "Shannon, that's it."

"I don't understand."

"Kincaid was hot for you back in Mobile, wasn't he? And now he's right here in Colón. Got in last night. I talked to him at the saloon." Her face fell. "Oh, damn. I told him you'd come to Colón with Bruce. How was I to know that Bruce'd walked out on you?"

"It doesn't matter. He wouldn't have helped me even if you hadn't told him about Bruce. We had a fight the last time I saw him. I slapped his face and told him I never wanted to see him again."

"Maybe you can make up with him. He's got money, Shannon. He sold out his share of the lumber business and I'll bet he got a good price for it. He's staying at the Aspinwall. That's the best hotel in the city."

"I thought there were no rooms at the Aspinwall."

"There's usually a room if a man's willing to put up enough money. I kind of hoped he'd ask me to go upstairs with him last night, but he got into a poker game." Clarisse sighed. "I always liked his looks. Big in the shoulders and narrow in the flanks. And I'd bet he's hotter than a pistol between the sheets. I think he's— Oh, damn. It's starting to rain again. Come on, honey, let's make a run for it."

"Where?"

"La Ceiba. It ain't far. Hurry."

Clarisse grabbed Shannon's hand as the thunder crashed in the distance, and heavy clouds started to move in over the city. A damp wind tore at the fronds of the palm trees.

They ran swiftly, but even so, they were not yet at

the saloon when the first heavy drops began to fall. Then came the drenching downpour.

"Shannon, come on in," Clarisse urged, at the entrance of La Ceiba. "You can come upstairs and get dry."

Remembering what Clarisse had told her about the upstairs rooms, Shannon said, "I'll be all right down here."

"Suit yourself, honey. But I've got to change and— Well, will you look over there. The poker game's on again. There's Kincaid."

Shannon pushed a lock of hair from her wet forehead, and looked across the room, to where Adam Kincaid and three other men were seated around a table, under a metal-shaded oil lamp. Adam, like the others, was in his shirtsleeves, his coat over the back of his chair, his eyes fixed on his cards.

"I'd better leave, Clarisse."

"Please yourself," Clarisse said. "But if you don't at least try to get Kincaid to help you out, you're plain foolish. You ain't in that prissy girls' boarding school, now, and the sooner you—look, honey, I got to change and put some powder on. You wait for me."

Clarisse went upstairs. Shannon remained near the saloon doors. She couldn't ask Adam for help. She couldn't humble herself, admit that Bruce had deserted her.

She would have to leave. But where could she go? Back to the Mariposa, and Señor Gallego? Or should she try to get work here in the saloon?

Adam pushed his wide-brimmed hat back on his head, and laid two cards down on the table. One of the other players said something and they all laughed.

I won't ask him to give me the fare back to Mobile, she thought. *Only lend it to me. I'll pay him back, somehow.*

She smoothed her wet skirt, and fastened one of her braids more securely. Then, taking a deep breath to steady herself, she walked the length of the room, with its rough stucco walls and long mahogany bar, to the table where Adam was sitting.

Adam did not look up from his cards, but one of the others, a lean, bearded man, noticed Shannon and grinned appreciatively. "Not now, sweetheart. We got a game goin' here. Later, maybe."

It was only then that Adam turned his head, his blue eyes narrowing slightly. "Why, Shannon. This is an unexpected pleasure. But, as Seth, here, says—"

"I've got to talk to you. Right now."

His expression was cool, remote. She was painfully conscious of her wet hair, of her cotton dress, so water-logged that it outlined her body, clinging to her breasts and thighs.

Adam did not stand up, or even remove his wide-brimmed hat. She might have been any one of the saloon girls here, for all the respect he showed her. But she could not afford the luxury of hurt pride, not now. "Adam, please."

He looked at his cards, then said, "I'll finish this hand and join you at the bar."

"Now wait, Kincaid. You can't cut out when you've been winnin' right along," the bearded man protested. "You got to give us a chance to win our money back."

"You'll get your chance. My business with Miss

Cavanaugh shouldn't take long," Adam said carelessly.

The bearded man grinned, and Shannon, hot with shame as she realized what he, and the other players, must be thinking, hurried over to the bar and turned her back on them. A few minutes later, Adam joined her.

"You look like a drowned rat," he said. "Can I buy you a drink?"

The barroom was getting noisy, as prospectors, railroad men and sailors began to hurry in to escape the driving rain. Somebody started to play the piano.

"Isn't there someplace quiet, where we can talk?" she pleaded.

Adam shrugged. "There's my room at the Aspinwall. But Bruce might object. As I recall, he's handy with a pistol."

"Bruce is gone," Shannon said. "He walked out on me a week ago." She made no effort to soften the truth. Adam would have to know.

"How ungentlemanly. I'd have expected better from a Lathrop."

She might have known he would take advantage of her position, would be sarcastic and difficult. "He's gone to Panama City," she began.

"Without you? What did you do to drive him away?"

"We—had a disagreement."

"Shannon, you've got to learn to control that Irish temper, or you're sure to end up an old maid. An awful fate for a young lady from Miss Colter's Academy. All those expensive accomplishments gone to waste."

"Adam, don't—" The raw hurt in her cry caused him to fall silent. He looked at her closely. "You've been having a rotten time of it, haven't you?" There was no mockery in his voice now. He put his coat over her shoulders. "Come along," he said. "You'd better tell me all about it."

Adam's room at the Aspinwall, although not luxurious, was far more comfortable and clean than her own room back at the Mariposa. The bed was wide, with a carved headboard, the sheets were clean; a straw rug covered the tiled floor, and a massive chest of drawers stood in one corner, a rattan settee in the other. He drew her down beside him on the settee, then leaned back, crossing his long legs.

"Now, suppose you begin at the beginning. I know why Bruce had to leave Mobile, of course. The talk about the duel was all over the city. But what about you?" The sardonic note came back into his voice. "I suppose you couldn't bear to be parted from your own true love, so you came along."

"It wasn't like that," she said, her voice hard. She told him about Jethro, about how he had beaten her and thrown her out. She described the voyage briefly. Then, omitting the details of her quarrel with Bruce, she told him about the theft of her money, and Señor Gallego's offer. She did not bother to choose her words as carefully as she would have not long ago. "I can't go back to the Mariposa, and let that horrible man sell me to any of his guests who—"

"And so you want me to stake you to a room here at the Aspinwall, is that it?"

"Oh, no. I want to get out of Panama. I want to go

home. Please Adam, if you'll lend me the fare, I'll pay you back, I swear I will."

"Home? Where is that?"

"Mobile, of course." But under his steady look, she began to feel uneasy.

"When you get back to Mobile, what then? You're Philippe Duval's daughter, but you'll never be able to live at Beau Rivage. And even if Jethro takes you back, Antoinette Duval will see to it that you can't stay long."

His words, calm and reasonable, filled her with confusion. She had to have a home. Someone who would take her in, care for her. "Shannon," he went on, inexorably, "face it. You have nothing to go back to."

She got up, ignoring the weakness that made her want to hold on to the back of the settee for support. "Stop it!" she cried. "I don't want to hear any more."

He rose and stood over her. "I know you don't. But you're damn well going to listen. It takes some getting used to. I know. I was younger than you are now, when I lost my home, my family. I had no one to rely on except myself. But I managed to get along. So will you. Once you stop feeling sorry for yourself."

"I don't—"

"Yes, you do. Because Philippe Duval educated you to be a fine lady. Spoiled. Useless. And because he didn't care enough to provide for you afterwards, so that you could have the kind of life you'd been trained for." Adam shrugged. "Or, if he did, maybe that hellcat he married took pains to cover up the truth."

A swift hope stirred inside her. "Adam, is that

possible? Do you think there's a chance that my father left me a bequest, and that Antoinette—"

"Of course, it's possible. But you haven't the money or the connections to fight Antoinette Duval on her own ground. Beau Rivage belongs to her. It will go to Odalie, one day. And Bruce, being a practical man, under that façade of Southern chivalry, made the sensible choice."

Tears sprang into Shannon's eyes. "But that's— that's not fair."

"No, it isn't fair." There was not a trace of sympathy in Adam's voice. His face was cold and remote.

"My parents were decent, hard-working people. What happened to them wasn't fair, either."

"What did happen? Aunt Kate said you appeared in Mobile and no one knew where you'd come from. She said—"

"What did she say?" he demanded.

"Only that you were dazed and—and hungry. That you wouldn't talk to anyone for a long time. And then Tom Sprague took you into his home and—"

"That's right."

"But what happened to your parents?"

"They were murdered. My mother and father, and my sister, Rachel. She was no older than you are now. We were traveling down the Alabama River on our own flatboat. Pa had saved for years to get together the money to come South from Ohio, to find richer farmland. To make a better life for Rachel and me."

"But how—"

"River pirates. There were plenty of them those days, along the Mississippi, the Alabama River. Thieving degenerates. Preying on decent settlers.

We'd moored the boat for the night, and Pa sent Rachel and me to get kindling for a fire. We were a little way into the woods when we heard them screaming, my mother and father. Pa didn't want to tell where the money was hidden, you see. It was all he had in the world, all he'd been able to save over the years. But they made him tell."

"Adam, I don't want to hear—"

But he went on as if he hadn't heard her. "We hid in the brush, Rachel and me. Until they threw Ma and Pa over the side of the boat. All that was left of them. I guess I went crazy then. I made a dash for the boat. I thought if I could get my hands on Pa's rifle. They caught me then, and Rachel, too." He turned away and stood at the window. "They forced me to watch what they did to Rachel. There were six of them and they took turns with her. She was little and delicate— I think she was dead before they'd finished —I hope she was."

The look on his face. Like he'd been to hell and back again. Shannon remembered Aunt Kate's words.

"They beat me up and left me for dead, with the others. But the crew of a keelboat found me. They took me along down river to Mobile and dropped me off there. I can't remember much about the trip."

He was silent then, and Shannon became aware once more of the sound of the rain, pelting against the windows. The voices of men from the street below, laughing or swearing as they hurried for the shelter of the nearest cantina.

Shannon went to Adam, and put a hand on his arm, but he drew away. When he turned to her again, his face was composed, his voice even. "Listen to me,

Shannon. Forget Philippe Duval and Beau Rivage. Forget Bruce. He walked out on you, didn't he? And forget your idea about going back to Mobile."

"You won't lend me the money for my fare?"

"Shannon, for the love of God, hasn't anything I've said made any sense to you? Whatever daydreams you've had about Beau Rivage and your father and your right to an inheritance, you've got to put them out of your mind."

"It would only be a loan. I'd pay you back."

"No," he said. "You won't get one cent from me to take you back to Mobile." He paused and looked down at her. "But I will take you with me to San Francisco."

His voice was cold, matter-of-fact, with no trace of tenderness.

"But you must know. I've never pretended to— care for you."

"I know," he said, smiling faintly. "In fact, you slapped my face to make your feelings clear. But everything's changed, Shannon, my sweet. Right now, your feelings don't matter. You're in no position to refuse my offer, are you?"

She pressed her lips together hard, to stop their trembling. He was taking pleasure in humiliating her.

"Are you?" he repeated.

"If you think you can force me—"

"I have no intention of using force. I don't think I'll have to."

All the same, she was afraid of him. Tall, muscular, he towered over her, his broad, heavy shoulders, his massive chest outlined by his rain-soaked shirt.

"You're free to accept Gallego's offer, to entertain his guests, and the señor, too, when he gets the urge."

"I won't listen—" She turned and started for the door, but he seized her arm and swung her around to face him.

"You'll listen. Maybe you won't go back to the Mariposa. Maybe you'll end up in Bottle Alley." She tried to twist away but his fingers tightened. "Let me tell you about Bottle Alley. Each of the girls has a little stall, with a swinging door. There are barkers outside to tout the particular skills of each girl. Not the kinds of skills you learned at Miss Colter's Academy."

She gave a cry as his steely fingers bruised her flesh.

He shifted his grip, holding her by the shoulders, his face grim. "You want to go on living in your dream world, don't you? But this is one time when you're damn well going to face facts. You never have until now. You went running off with Lathrop. You were sure he was going to marry you."

"He would have, if not for Odalie. But he doesn't love her. I know he doesn't."

"You may be right. But that doesn't change anything. He's gone and he's not coming back." He drew a long breath and searched her face. "Now, will you come to San Francisco with me?"

"You still want me? Knowing I don't love you?"

"Stop talking like a schoolgirl. I haven't said anything about love. I never will. You can give me what I need, that's all."

"And what's that?"

He smiled. "Women are still scarce in the Nevada

territory. You can learn to cook my meals, I suppose. You'll improve with practice. You might even learn to make a decent cup of coffee over a campfire. You can wash my clothes. Laundresses in San Francisco are charging five dollars a dozen pieces, I'm told. And once we get into the mountains, there won't be any laundresses at all, so you see—"

His eyes glinted with amusement, and anger rose up in her. "And that's all you want me for?"

"No, that's not all. You'll share my bed, and you'll be willing and agreeable. I won't put up with your sulking or your bad temper. Not in bed or out of it."

He released her, and she took a step backward. There was still time to leave.

"And in return," Adam went on calmly, "I'll see that you get to San Francisco, and then on to Nevada and the silver diggings. You won't go hungry. And I won't walk out on you. All right, that's my proposition. Take it or leave it."

She looked past Adam at the rain-streaked window. In her mind, she saw a series of swiftly changing images. The gardens at Jessamine. The oak tree and the soft, fragrant grass beneath, where Bruce had kissed her for the first time. Bruce's face, the thin-lipped, beautifully cut mouth, the drowsy gray eyes. She felt the ache of unbearable loss, of utter desolation.

"Well, Shannon? What's your answer?"

Her hurt slowly gave way to cold, numb despair. Since Bruce was gone, what did anything else matter? She heard herself say, "I'll go with you, Adam."

"I thought you would."

She waited for him to take her in his arms. Instead,

he looked her up and down and said, "Now that's settled, you'd better get out of those wet clothes. This is an unhealthy climate. I wouldn't want you getting a fever."

She made no move to obey.

"Go ahead," he ordered. "Do as I say. Now."

Under his hard, blue eyes, she began to unbutton her bodice. Her fingers grew stiff and clumsy. Surely he would not take her now, without further preliminaries.

She wrenched at a small gilt button. The thread snapped and the button fell to the floor.

"Perhaps you need help."

"Don't touch me." She moved out of reach.

"Come now, Shannon. It isn't as if you'd never undressed for a man before."

"But I haven't."

"Don't lie to me. You came to Panama with Bruce."

"Bruce left me on our first night here. I told you we quarreled. It was because I wouldn't—not without marriage."

He drew a quick breath, and something flickered in his eyes. "I see," he said softly. "Bruce wouldn't marry you, but he was too much of a gentleman to take you against your will."

It hurt too much to talk about Bruce, to remember him. She swallowed, and tried to keep her voice steady. "I've agreed to go West with you. On your terms. You've no right to pry into—"

"Your tender feelings for Bruce? You still love him, then." She made a sound of protest and he held up his hand to forestall her. "You're a fool, Shannon."

"I think you're jealous," she began.

He shook his head. "Don't flatter yourself, sweetheart. To be jealous, a man has to be in love." He studied her dispassionately. "Now, are you going to get out of those wet clothes, or must I undress you?"

"I don't have anything else to put on," she faltered.

He laughed, went over to the massive dresser, and took out one of his shirts. "Take this," he said. "It'll have to do for a nightgown."

He put on his coat, and his wide-brimmed hat. "I'm going back to La Ceiba," he said. "I promised to give Seth and the others a chance to win back their money." He gave her a teasing smile. "I don't think they will, though. I'm feeling lucky tonight."

Although it was after midnight, and the hard, pelting rain had subsided to a light drizzle, Shannon was unable to fall asleep. When Adam's key grated in the lock, she gave a start, and her muscles went taut. She turned her face to the wall, and kept her eyes closed. But her ears strained for every small sound: the striking of a sulfur match, the lighting of the oil lamp over the dresser. His footsteps approaching the bed.

"You're not asleep," he said softly.

She turned and sat up. The sheet slid away and she was grateful for the voluminous folds of the shirt that hid her body.

"You've brought me luck, Shannon," he said. "I cleaned up at the card table tonight. When we get to San Francisco, I'll buy you a dozen nightgowns, trimmed with lace." He sat down on the bed and began to undress.

"Put out the lamp, Adam," she protested.

He shook his head. "I want to look at you. All of you." She glared at him, but he only laughed. "It's a bit late for a display of maidenly modesty, isn't it? Unless, of course, you've been having second thoughts about our bargain."

"Would it matter if I had?"

"Under the circumstance, I think it would. When I first made my offer, I didn't know you were a virgin."

"I hope you won't be disappointed," she said, her voice shaking. "Maybe you should have gone upstairs with Clarisse. She's experienced."

"Don't worry," he said. "I always get my money's worth. One way or another."

Fear swelled inside her. He put an arm around her lightly, but she twisted away, sprang from the bed. At least she would not let him have his way about the lamp. She was sure that the ordeal would be awful enough in darkness.

"Leave the lamp alone. Get back in bed." His voice was hard, commanding. "From now on, I'm giving the orders."

She backed against the wall. He got up and strode to her with a few long steps, took her by the shoulders, and pinned her against the wall, holding her there. Frantic with fear, hating him for his cold arrogance, she worked one arm free, and tried to strike at him.

He caught her wrist. "Not this time, Shannon." His fingers tightened slowly, gradually until she gave a cry of pain. Only then did he release her. With a swift movement, he slid one arm around her shoulders, the other under her knees, lifted her and carried her back to the bed. She lay where he had placed her.

He hadn't forgotten their quarrel, back in the tavern in Mobile, she realized. Of course, he hadn't. Now, he would retaliate, would pay her back for having struck him, for having turned from him to Bruce.

She tried not to think of the stories she had heard from the saloon girls, the prostitutes, during the voyage to Panama. It was no use. She turned her head away as Adam undressed. Now he was getting into bed beside her. Her eyes were squeezed shut, her hands clenched at her sides, her whole body rigid. When he put a hand on her breast, she made an involuntary, shrinking movement.

"Relax, Shannon," he said softly. He took her hands, drew her to him. "Look at me," he said. She made herself obey.

"I want this to be good for you," he said.

She searched his face. "You mean that? You'll be gentle? You'll give me time to—"

"We've got the rest of the night ahead," he said. He turned her on her side, and began to unbutton the shirt. Then he slid it off her body and tossed it on the floor. His arms went around her.

"Beautiful," he said, his voice low and husky. "You're so beautiful." Slowly his hands explored her body, caressing her shoulders, her back, stroking the base of her spine, the softly rounded curves of her buttocks. She felt the tension begin to ebb from her, under the touch of his strong, knowing fingers.

Then he took her hand and pressed it to his cheek. She saw him smile, his blue eyes glinting with gentle mockery. "Are you afraid to touch me, Shannon?"

Almost shyly, she began to caress his face, the hard line of his jaw, then his broad chest with the dark, curling hair. "Don't stop now," he said. He put his hand over hers and guided it downward, until she felt the warmth, the hardness of his throbbing manhood.

She tried to retreat, then. "Adam, I can't. I don't know how—"

"All right, love," he said. "I'll have to teach you—everything." She gave a small cry of protest as he showed her what he wanted her to do. But she submitted to his stronger will and a moment later, she heard his wordless groan of pleasure. He was breathing deeply, unevenly. "Don't stop. Oh, Shannon—sweetheart—"

She was proud, all at once, that she was able to stir his senses, inexperienced though she was. She began to know the full power of her womanhood, and she felt a warm, heady sensation.

Adam's arms tightened around her, so that her breasts and thighs were molded against him. Gently, he turned her over onto her back, and put his lips to one of her nipples, then the other, his tongue teasing, playing with her. The nipples were firm and erect now, and she felt a flurry of excitement that spread from her breasts downward into her loins, bringing warmth and tingling.

His hands were more urgent now, parting her thighs, his fingers stroking gently . . . seeking . . . finding. . . .

She was confused by her feelings. Only a little while ago, this man had been so cold, so ruthless. She had dreaded what lay ahead, her mind cringing from the thought of what he would force her to endure. But now, she thought, everything had changed. Adam had changed. No man could have been more patient with his beloved bride on their wedding night. Did Adam love her? He must, or why would he care about her feelings, why would he caress her so gently? Even now, while the intimacy of his touch startled her, she felt wave after burning wave of hunger coursing through her. She feared what she knew must follow, but she longed for it, too.

"I'm afraid," she whispered.

"Hush, love."

She began to tremble, sensing the growing urgency of his need. He raised himself and then he was kneeling between her quivering thighs. She put up her hands to delay him, but he caught her wrists, and kept her arms pinioned at her sides. She felt the hardness of the first thrust, tentative, then deeper.

She cried out, shocked by the harsh, burning pain of his entry. "Please—Oh, Adam, please—"

He lay still, but she felt the violence, the driving, inexorable hunger that possessed him; she could only guess at the restraint it took for him to hold back. He was inside her now, joined with her. She heard his murmured endearments, soothing, gentling her. Until, gradually, she shared his need, and her body began to move of its own volition. Her pain was lost in the mounting desire that engulfed all her senses. He released her hands and she gripped his shoulders, drawing him to her, surrendering herself to him, letting herself be swept on to the shattering climax.

Later, when he fell asleep, he remained close to her, his body curved around hers, one hand resting on her breast. She felt safe and cherished, no longer lonely.

She tried to understand the new emotions that had possessed her tonight. Was she in love with Adam? How could she be? She smiled drowsily, remembering how sure, how knowing she had been when she had spoken to Clarisse about the difference between love and lust. And yet, now, she was not sure of anything, except that she wanted this feeling of closeness to go on. With her back against him, she moved still closer, pressing her hips down against his lean, hard belly. He sighed, his arms tightened possessively.

"Shannon—sweet Shannon—"

Then, once again, she felt the deep, even rhythm of his breathing, as he lapsed back into sleep. She let her eyelids close. Tomorrow would be time enough to explore the mystery, the wonder of what had happened between them.

But when she awoke, the fierce, tropical sunlight was streaming through the window, and turning, she saw that she was alone. She sat up, pushed back her tangled hair. There was a full pitcher of water on the washstand, and she washed and dried herself, put on her clothes, still slightly damp from last night's rain. She was brushing her tawny golden hair when Adam came in.

Swiftly, she ran to him, but he made no move to embrace her.

"I've been at the depot," he said, his voice cool and matter-of-fact. "There'll be a train going through to Panama City at noon. We have time for breakfast, if you don't take too long with your hair."

She heard a thud and looked down to see her carpetbag lying at her feet. "I stopped to get this," he said, his mouth curving in a hard smile. "Señor Gallego was disappointed by your sudden departure. He figured he could have made a handsome profit by selling your services to his guests."

Oh, but this was all wrong. Adam should not be acting like this, talking like this, as if the thing that had happened between them last night had been unimportant, meaningless. She wanted to share her new feelings with him, but he did not give her a chance.

"I met a man downstairs in the bar. He's traveling to Panama City on the same train with us. A newspaper reporter, heading for San Francisco. He's lived here in Panama for some time, though. Might have some useful advice about getting a ship in Panama City."

"I—suppose so."

"Now, you get yourself ready, and I'll meet you downstairs." He kissed her lightly, his lips grazing her cheek, and then he was gone.

I haven't said anything about love. I never will.

His words came back to her now, with wounding force. Nothing had changed for him.

You can give me what I need, that's all.

12

THE TRAIN CLATTERED out of the depot at
Colón, and plunged into the swamp, where red, green
and yellow parrots swooped above the mangrove
bushes, and the thick tangle of ceibas and palms hung
with ropelike vines. Shannon was seated next to
Adam; facing them on the seat opposite was the reporter with whom Adam had struck up an acquaintance earlier that morning in the hotel.

Unlike Bruce, Adam had made no attempt to conceal his relationship to Shannon. "Mr. Fergus Mackenzie, Miss Shannon Cavanaugh." Mackenzie's
russet brown eyes went over Shannon in a swift appraisal. She writhed inwardly with embarrassment.
The reporter was a slight, wiry man in his thirties,
with a shock of dark red hair, a thin, shrewd face, a
cynical mouth.

Perhaps here in Panama, casual liaisons between
men and women were taken for granted. Shannon
was, nevertheless, furious with Adam. He might have

concocted a story, however flimsy, to explain their traveling together. Was he indifferent to her feelings, or was he deliberately trying to hurt her? But why? Last night he had been tender, even gentle in his lovemaking—until she was able to respond.

She was aware that Mackenzie was speaking to her.

"I'm heading for San Francisco, too," he was saying. "I've been offered a job on the *Alta California.*"

She looked at him, uncomprehending, and he hastened to explain. "That's the leading newspaper in San Francisco. Until now, I've been working for the *Panama Star & Herald*. But I'll be happy to leave the isthmus."

"You plan to settle in San Francisco permanently?" Shannon asked.

Mackenzie shrugged. "A newspaperman shouldn't settle anywhere permanently," he said. "I wouldn't be surprised if I should be sent East one of these days. I wasn't in on the Mexican War, but I'll probably get a chance to report the next one."

"I don't understand," Shannon said. "Do you think there will be another war with Mexico?"

He shook his head. "No, ma'am. This time it'll be the North against the South. Mark my words. I don't favor war, mind you. But no man in his right mind wants to see the Union torn apart by a pack of hotheaded Southerners."

"Mr. Kincaid and I are from Alabama," Shannon interrupted coldly.

"Sorry, ma'am. No offense, Kincaid. But I'm a Kansas man, born and bred, and I've seen what this kind of fighting can do, in only one state. Families torn apart, decent people burned-out, beaten, killed, because they didn't want to see slavery extended to Kansas. Bushwackers and land pirates taking up the cause of slave owners, as an excuse for looting."

"You don't have to convince me," Adam said. "And, for the record, I don't consider myself a Southerner."

"Adam, how can you say that? You grew up in Mobile." Shannon looked at him reproachfully.

"And you, my dear, were educated in Boston," Adam reminded her. "If I recall, you were quite the hot-blooded little abolitionist at our first meeting. You said—"

"I remember what I said," she snapped. "I don't think slavery is right. But all the same, I am a Southerner, and proud of it."

"And you wouldn't have minded becoming mistress of a plantation." His words stung. He hadn't forgotten about Bruce, then, or her insistence that she would one day live at Jessamine. She felt the hurt stir within her, thinking of Bruce.

"I'm afraid your politics are rather muddled, Shannon," Adam said. "You don't believe in slavery, but you wouldn't object to living on a plantation worked by slaves."

Mackenzie smiled, and said quickly, "A pretty little thing like Shannon, if I may take the liberty, doesn't have to concern herself with politics."

She glanced at Adam to see if he would object to Mackenzie's familiarity, but he did not appear to be annoyed. Yet, Shannon knew that it was highly improper for a gentleman to call a respectable lady by her first name on short acquaintance. Indeed, Miss Colter had said that many young men never called their fiancées by their first names until after the marriage ceremony.

At this moment, Shannon was painfully aware that she had passed into another world, the half-world in which her mother had lived.

I'm a kept woman, she thought. And, worse still, she had not been able to remain cold and aloof as she had hoped to do. She remembered how, last night, she had given herself to Adam, had responded with a frightening intensity.

But it was Bruce she loved. Her feelings for Adam must be of a different, a baser kind. She wished that she could talk to Clarisse, who knew so much more than she did about the relations between men and women.

She turned and tried to direct her attention to the brilliant green of the landscape, dotted with blossoms of crimson, purple and yellow. The train was emerging from the swamp now, and was passing a grassy hill, covered with countless white wooden crosses. At the same moment, the train whistle gave a long mournful wail.

"The old-timers still do that," Mackenzie explained. "It's a kind of homage to their dead. That's Mount Hope, the cemetery for the Panama Railroad."

"So many graves," Shannon said. "What did they die of?"

"Sickness, mostly. Yellow fever, cholera, dysentery."

"Were you in Panama when the railroad was being built?"

"On and off, I was. First, the American government thought about building a canal across the isthmus. But the engineering problems were insurmountable. Then, in '49, the Gold Rush was on, and a smart New York businessman, William Aspinwall, started the Panama Railroad Company. Brought in workers from all over the world. Irishmen, Englishmen, Hindustanis, Malaysians, Chinese. They say every tie on this railroad cost a man's life."

"But that's a terrible price," Shannon began.

"The cost of progress. Those workers didn't all die of fever. They were a rough bunch, the railroad men. Plenty of them were killed in brawls over cards. Or over some little *mamacita,* who was too generous with her favors."

Although Shannon was not familiar with the Spanish word, the meaning was plain enough. Was that how Mackenzie, how Adam, thought of her?

The reporter went on talking, oblivious to her feelings.

"A lot of Chinese coolies killed themselves. Ran out of opium while they were building the railroad. They couldn't get any more, and they depended on the stuff to keep them going, you see. So they strangled themselves with their own queues."

"Come on, Mackenzie," Adam interrupted, a smile twitching at the corners of his mouth. "I believe you're trying to scare Shannon with your tall tales."

Mackenzie laughed. "It makes a good story. And some of the railroad men swear it's true. The important thing is, they got the railroad built. Now it takes only four hours for the trip. We'll be in Panama City before nightfall."

"That'll give us time to get over to the shipping office," Adam said.

"Don't be too impatient," Mackenzie warned. "These mail steamers can be a week overdue, sometimes longer. And the hotels! Jammed solid with men on their way to the silver diggings. The hotelkeepers have turned the rooms into barracks, with cots jammed up against each other, and no decent sanitary facilities." He shook his head. "Don't take Shannon to one of those places."

"If the ship is delayed, I don't see that we have much choice," Adam said.

"You can stay at my place. It's a private house, small, but you'd have it all to yourselves. I've been living there since I've been working for the *Star & Herald*. I've even got a cook. Elena Rodriguez. She's handy with a skillet."

"Glad to hear it," Adam said. "Shannon has many accomplishments, but cooking's not one of them."

Shannon winced, wondering if Adam was thinking of her responses in bed last night. How humiliating. No well-brought up young lady should have such feelings; and if she did, surely she should not yield to them.

"If it's your house, Mr. Mackenzie, we don't wish to inconvenience you," Shannon said. The reporter was good-natured, but too brash and outspoken for her taste.

"You won't be," he said. "I'll be leaving on the next ship out of Panama, same as you two. And my rent's paid until the end of the month. In the meantime, there's a Spanish lady, a widow. She has a fine house near the newspaper office." Seeing Shannon's bewildered look, he added, "We have an—understanding."

While she was trying to find a suitable answer, Adam said smoothly, "I'll take you up on your offer, then. If we do have to stay in Panama for any length of time."

"We're coming into another station," Shannon said.

"That's Gatún," Mackenzie said. "And over there, that's the Changres River. From here, we'll be traveling on higher ground."

At Gatún, several passengers got on, including a man and woman who took the seats across the aisle from Shannon and her two companions. The man was tall and slender, and might have been handsome except for the haggard look of his face. His eyes were sunken, his skin oddly shriveled for a young man, and two spots of color burned on his otherwise pale cheeks. He wore a fine white ruffled shirt and a Prince Albert coat, and he leaned heavily on the woman for support. She was dark-eyed and shapely; her white cotton blouse revealed the curves of her lush breasts, and her skirt of blue, pink and yellow striped cotton billowed out around her.

The train started off again, along the base of an irregular line of mountains, then rumbled across an iron bridge and made another stop at Ahorca Lagarto. After that, the train entered a dense forest of towering trees, mahogany, lignum vitae and palms. Shannon peered into the impenetrable mass of lush, growing things, jungles of cane, gigantic lilies, huge white orchids. Flowering vines had grown around the trees, and brilliant butterflies circled in the still, humid air. Shannon was fascinated by the primitive beauty around her, but, at the same time, it made her faintly uneasy. The green of the leaves and creepers was too bright, the growth too lush. She thought of the creeping things that must inhabit such surroundings: snakes, lizards, crocodiles.

"We're a lot better riding a train through here than traveling in the open," Mackenzie said. "I've heard there are still jaguars and pumas in the back country."

It was when they were close to Matachín Station, which the reporter had said was the halfway mark on the journey, that Shannon was startled to hear a cry from the woman in the seat opposite. The man beside her had fallen forward, and now he was sprawled on the floor of the car.

Adam and Mackenzie got up and went over to help, as did several of the other male passengers. Shannon stood up but her view was quickly blocked by the growing knot of people around the fallen man. She could hear a torrent of high-pitched, hysterical Spanish from the woman. Although she still had only a slight understanding of the language, the woman's grief and terror were unmistakable.

Then Adam came back to her. "Sit down, Shannon," he ordered brusquely.

"But what's happened?"

Now Mackenzie returned to his seat. "Poor devil," he said. "Yellow fever. There's been more of it here in Panama this year than is usual."

"You're sure?" Shannon asked.

"Could be cholera, but from the look of him, I'd guess—" Then, seeing the terror in her face, he added quickly, "Try to stay calm. They'll put him off the train at Matachín Station."

"Will there be a doctor there?" she asked.

"Possibly. Not much a doctor can do for yellow fever, though."

A cold knot of fear twisted her insides. She moved closer to Adam, and he put his arm around her. She was comforted by his touch, the hard strength of his body.

She watched as the sick man was carried off the train on an improvised stretcher; the woman followed, weeping, her gaily striped skirt trailing in the mud.

It was not yet twilight when the train pulled into the depot at Panama City. Mackenzie accompanied Adam and Shannon to the shipping office where they were told that the next mail steamer for San Francisco would be delayed for at least a few days, perhaps longer. The office and the narrow street outside were crowded with men in rough clothes and heavy, mud-spattered boots, carrying knapsacks, bundles, even miners' tools strapped to their backs.

Mackenzie hired a carriage and took Shannon and Adam to his small stucco house, with a slanting tile roof, some distance from the crowded, noisy center of the city. Even now, with darkness falling, Shannon noticed the filth of the streets. Refuse decayed in stagnant puddles, the stench overpowering in spite of the heavy odors of rose and gardenia bushes that grew around some of the houses. Huge ungainly birds, turkey buzzards, Mackenzie told her, swooped down to gorge themselves on the garbage heaps.

She was relieved to find that the reporter's house was on a side street, away from the center of Panama City. The bedroom, which opened onto the *galería,* was reasonably clean, although the sheets smelled faintly of mildew. She could see that Elena Rodriguez was not a fanatical housekeeper. Tomorrow, Shannon decided, she would mend those holes in the mosquito netting, which hung around the bed in limp folds.

While Adam remained downstairs to settle the financial arrangements with Mackenzie, Shannon sank down gratefully on the edge of the bed and unbuttoned the bodice of her flowered cotton dress. The air was heavy and moisture-laden, but at least it was not raining.

Later, she and Adam dined out on the patio, Mackenzie having left, to spend the night with his mistress. The house was built around the patio, with rooms on three sides, and a high stone wall with an iron gate on the fourth. Along the wall, hibiscus and gardenia bushes grew, thick and untrimmed, and bougainvillea clung to the ancient stones.

Although Elena, the cook, a thin, dark-eyed Spanish woman, apologized for the meal, explaining that Señor Mackenzie came and went without warning, Shannon found the food delicious. In spite of the heat, she had a keen appetite, as did Adam, and between them, they demolished the high-piled platter of *empanadas,* made of spiced meat in a covering of cornmeal, the black beans and rice, the soup of milk and shredded fresh coçonuts, and the dessert of pineapples and oranges.

Later, as they sipped their *café con leche,* half coffee and half milk, she relaxed. "I don't suppose there will be any need for me to do the cooking while we're here," she said, with an edge to her voice; she remembered his remarks about her lack of skill in the kitchen.

"Plenty of time for that, my love." His blue eyes flickered with the hot light she had come to recognize.

Together, they left the patio, and went upstairs to the bedroom. A three-branched, wrought-iron candelabrum stood on the dresser. The light of the wavering candle flame turned her hair to molten bronze, and awoke the soft, golden lights in her eyes.

He drew her against him and kissed her, his mouth lingering. Although her body responded, she tried to use all her will to hold herself aloof, for she was ashamed of these strange, new feelings he aroused within her. She turned her face away.

"Shannon," he said softly, "if I hurt you last night, it was only because— It will be different this time." His lips sought hers but she evaded his kiss. "You do understand, don't you?" he demanded impatiently.

"I understand." She tried to find the words to tell him of her feelings, of the conflict within her, but he was lifting her into his arms, holding her against his chest, and she felt the warmth of his body. A slow fire stirred inside her and she dropped her head against his shoulder. Her arms went around his neck, and her lips parted to receive his kiss.

He put her down on the bed and stood looking at her.

"I suppose you want me to put out the candles." There was a glint of amusement in his eyes.

"Do as you wish," she said, anger rising swiftly. "As you told me last night, you're giving the orders."

He laughed. "You learn quickly," he said.

He stripped off his clothes and got into bed beside her. "A willingness on your part would make things more agreeable," he said.

"For you?" Her voice was hard.

"For both of us, my love." He unbuttoned her bodice and pushed her dress off her shoulders. He kissed the hollow of her throat. "Now," he said, the words muffled against her flesh, "are you going to finish undressing? Or shall I—"

"I'll do it," she said quickly.

But the laces of her stays became tangled, the knot growing tighter as she worked with her hands behind her, and at last he said, "Turn around. That's it." His fingers were swift and skillful, and she found herself wondering how many other women he had performed this service for.

"I'll lend you another of my shirts—afterwards," he said.

She did not answer. Even when his mouth began to move slowly down the length of her naked body, his tongue caressing, exploring each curve and hollow, she remained silent.

Then he parted her thighs, and she stiffened, sensing his purpose. "You can't. You mustn't." How could she, how could any woman submit to this shocking intimacy? But he was deaf to her pleading, and a moment later, she cried out in ecstasy. Her hands moved, of their own will, to press him closer, her fingers clutching at his dark hair.

And later, when he entered her, she felt only the swift excitement, the hunger, and then the shattering moment when she surrendered herself to the mounting waves of hot, savage desire.

Later, after he had fallen asleep, his face resting on the curve of her breast, his arm across her, she lay staring at the glimmering whiteness of the netting that curtained the bed.

I can't be in love with him. I won't be, she told herself. For to love Adam Kincaid would bring her only humiliation. Even while he appeased the needs of her body, her spirit would starve, her pride crumble. He did not love her, and never would. Perhaps the suffering he had endured as a child had made it impossible for him to love anyone. Somehow, even though he had possessed her body, and would, again, she would have to keep some part of her mind, her spirit inviolate.

They had been in Panama City for a week, and although Adam went down to the shipping office each day, he could get no news about the arrival of the next steamer bound for San Francisco.

On the night after they had moved into the house, Adam left Shannon immediately after dinner. "I'm meeting Fergus Mackenzie," he said. "He claims to be a good poker player. We'll see."

From that night on, she was never sure if Adam would spend the evening with her, or go down to the center of the city. Elena, the cook, retired early, and Shannon was left with long, empty hours alone.

She managed to fill a part of the time by sewing a new dress from a length of pale blue silk she found in a Chinese shop near Cathedral Plaza. Elena shook her head. "It will mildew, that fine silk. Here, everything mildews, everything rots."

Elena told Shannon that she disliked Panama, that she had come here from Madrid in the service of a titled Spanish family, who had been traveling to California.

"Why didn't you go with them?" Shannon asked.

"They died here, in this accursed place. All of them. *El conde, la condesa,* their beautiful young daughter, their fine, strong son. As the Yanquis are dying now. It is the fever, *la fiebre amarilla*—the yellow fever."

She shook her head, her narrow, lined face grim.

"Pray that you will be gone from this hellish place, before that pretty silk rots and falls apart at the seams. Before you and Señor Kincaid—"

"We will be out of Panama City in a few days," Shannon said, with more conviction than she felt. After that, she tried to avoid Elena and her doleful conversation.

Although Adam spent his evenings in the saloons and gambling houses, Shannon discovered that, when he returned home, he always had an urgent need for her. He would awaken her from a sound sleep, if necessary, and take her, sometimes gently, sometimes with a swift, violent explosion of passion.

She resented his absences, his indifference to her loneliness when he was gone, but she did not protest. What right had she to expect anything else? She was a mistress, not a wife. A convenience, nothing more.

Sometimes, she tried to hold back, to keep from responding when he took her in his arms, as if, in this way, she could retain the shreds of her pride. But always, it was useless, for under the expert caresses of his hands, the fiery touch of his mouth, she would find herself clinging to him, the sweet, hot current pulsing through her blood. Her body would mold itself to his, craving satisfaction, driven by a hunger that could not be denied.

During the days, she tried to keep busy doing chores around the house; although she disliked cleaning and scrubbing, she had become used to Miss Colter's standards of cleanliness, and later, to the tidy rooms at Miss Harwood's dressmaking shop. She had hated her brief stay in the squalor of her uncle's tavern, and she was determined to keep this house as neat and clean as she could, no matter how briefly she remained here.

She was not able to break Elena of the habit of throwing the day's refuse into the narrow alley outside the patio gate. "The buzzards, they are our street cleaners here," the cook explained calmly. Shannon came to loathe the sight of the evil-smelling, ugly birds that sometimes perched on the patio wall, or atop the iron gate.

Adam was amused by Shannon's efforts at housekeeping.

"You're quite a domestic female after all," he said, one evening, when they were dining out on the patio. "Maybe you should have found yourself a fat, respectable shopkeeper in Mobile, and settled down."

"I never wanted—"

"That's right. You wanted Bruce Lathrop."

She looked at him quickly, from under her thick lashes. Why should he speak of Bruce now? Was he troubled by the thought that she still cared for Bruce?

"I don't want to talk about him," she said coldly.

"To hell with what you want!" His anger was so completely unexpected that she drew back. He got to his feet. "You're still in love with him, aren't you? That's why you try not to respond when we're in bed." The cold fury in his eyes, the cruelty in his voice, frightened her. "You think I don't know? But you're not able to hold out long, are you? You may be faithful to Bruce in your mind, but your body has needs of its own."

She slumped forward, covering her face with her hands, humiliated to the core of her being. But he came around to her side of the table and seized her by the wrists, pulling her hands away, forcing her to look at him. "Answer me," he said. "Tell me what you're thinking, when we make love."

"Why should you care?" she cried. "We made a bargain. You're getting what you paid for. And that's all you'll ever get from me, Adam Kincaid."

For a moment, she was afraid he would strike her. Instead, he let go of her wrists. He drew a long breath, and she saw the muscles stand out along his jaw. "That's fine with me, Shannon. It's all I've ever wanted from you. Or any other woman."

He took his coat from the back of the chair and put it on. Then, turning, he started for the patio gate.

"Where are you going?" she asked.

When he did not answer, she was seized with fear. She had not forgotten how Bruce had deserted her, left her in that dingy hotel in Colón. She hurried after him. "Adam, I want to know."

"You sound like a wife," he said. "Where I spend my nights is my business." His eyes searched her face for a moment. "Don't look so scared. I won't walk out on you and leave you stranded, as your fine gentleman did. When I make a bargain, I stick to it."

He opened the iron gate and walked off down the alley to the street beyond. She hated him for having seen her fear and mocked her for it. For reminding her of her place in his life.

Slowly, she returned to her seat at the table. A light evening breeze rustled the leaves of the hibiscus and gardenia bushes, and tossed a few loose curls across Shannon's cheek. She brushed her hair back absently, her thoughts still on Adam. What had caused his outburst of rage tonight? If he wasn't jealous of Bruce, why should he try to probe into her thoughts, to share her feelings?

And where had he gone tonight? To play poker with Mackenzie? Or to spend the night with another woman? Panama City was larger than Colón, and, with the influx of young, unattached males, the plazas, the saloons would be swarming with fancy women. The kind of women with whom she had shared the cabin on her voyage from Mobile.

She was startled by a turkey buzzard swooping low over the patio and into the alley beyond to forage for carrion. A swarm of mosquitoes, drawn by the light of the candles on the table, hovered, whining, about her face and arms.

She returned to the house and tried to distract herself by sewing her new dress, the silk spread out before her on a long table. But when it was close to midnight, and Adam still had not returned, she went upstairs to bed.

She slept uneasily, for, in the short time they had been together, she had become accustomed to feeling the warmth of his body, the strength of his arms around her. And when she awoke the following morning, and reached out for him, she discovered that he had not returned. She was still alone in the wide bed.

13

IT WAS LATE afternoon when Adam came striding into the sittingroom, where Shannon was putting the finishing touches on her blue dress. He was unshaven, and his clothes were somewhat rumpled, but he was smiling.

"Put that sewing aside," he said. "Tonight, we're going out to celebrate."

She stared at him in surprise, letting the folds of blue silk fall to the table before her. A moment later, he drew her to her feet, held her against him and whirled her around. She wanted to remain cool and aloof, but her relief at seeing him again, and in such good spirits, was too much for her. "Adam, what on earth—"

"We're leaving Panama City tomorrow," he said. "That's right, Shannon. The Pacific Mail steamer's in the bay, and I have our tickets. I spent the whole night in the shipping office. For awhile, it looked as though there'd be a riot with all those men wanting space on board."

"The shipping office?" Her voice was unsteady. His eyes looked tired, but there was a boyish excitement about him. "We'll be in San Francisco before you know it, and then, on to Nevada. Mountains of silver, lying there, waiting for us."

She could not resist his mood, and she gave him an answering smile. His lips came down hard on hers; he appeared to have forgotten their quarrel of the night before, and she pushed it out of her mind.

Later, she went out to the kitchen to tell Elena the news, and to pay her the wages owed to her. "I wish you could leave here, too," Shannon said. "I know how much you dislike Panama."

"No importa," the woman said. "I save my money. Soon, I will be able to return to Madrid."

Shannon returned to the sittingroom, and spent the remaining hours of daylight finishing her dress, threading a narrow band of amber velvet ribbon through the lace that edged the bodice. When she got to San Francisco, she would buy one of those new cage hoops, but until then, her two starched petticoats would serve to hold the full skirt billowing out around her.

At twilight, she went upstairs, bathed and dressed with care. Her new gown was most becoming, she thought, as she whirled around, so that the flounces on the skirt tossed and swayed; the bodice was cut low, to emphasize the curves of her breasts, and she had tied an amber velvet ribbon around her narrow waist.

Adam nodded appreciatively as he watched her descending the stairs. She had arranged her hair as he liked it, parted in the center, with deep waves at the temples and soft curls cascading down over her shoulders.

"I've hired a victoria and a driver," he said. "There's a café I know, near the Cathedral Plaza. It's a small place, but the food's good. There's music, and a girl who dances the fandango."

He helped her into the open victoria, and the driver flapped the reins over the backs of the mules. The streets were so narrow that it was difficult for two vehicles to pass one another, and tonight, traffic moved even more slowly than usual because of the crowds of men, many wearing the red miners' shirts Shannon had come to recognize, and all of them heavily armed.

Adam, like the others, carried a gun, a double-action Navy revolver, and had a Bowie knife thrust into his boot.

"It's necessary," he explained. "Here, and even in San Francisco. As for the mining camps, in Nevada, the men have to enforce their own laws."

"But what about the police?"

He smiled at her innocence. "Those mining camps spring up overnight. There are no police, no sheriffs, no jails or courts."

"It sounds frightening," she said.

"You'll be safe enough with me," he told her quietly. There was no arrogance in his voice, only the calm certainty of a man who had confidence in his skill with a gun, a knife. She remembered that he had spent some years in the Army, that he had accompanied Frémont on one of his expeditions through

Indian territory. And she recalled the time he had come to Bruce's aid, during the brawl at the tavern.

She put a hand on his arm. "I know you'll take good care of me," she said.

Tonight, the men were in a festive mood, as word of the steamer's arrival spread. San Francisco lay ahead, and beyond, the fabulous silver mines of the Comstock. There were a number of women in the crowd that swarmed along the streets; their cheeks and lips were heavily painted, their skirts swayed around them like multi-colored flowers, and their laughter was shrill. At any other time, Shannon would have resented finding herself in such company, but tonight, it was not important to her.

The café Adam had chosen for their evening's outing was noisy and jammed to the doors, and Shannon was caught up in the excitement that throbbed in the air around her. Adam ordered an elaborate meal, starting with a pungent fish soup, and a bottle of champagne that stood chilling in a bucket of ice. "They've been getting ice down here for the last few years, all the way from Sitka, in what's called Russian America," he told her.

"I've never had champagne before," she said. "It's delicious."

"When we get to San Francisco, I'll take you to dinner at the Lick House," he promised. "Mackenzie told me that's the finest hotel in the city. And you can go shopping for those fancy nightgowns I've been promising you."

She could not resist giving him a flirtatious smile. "Only nightgowns?"

He pressed her hand. "I suppose you'll need a few

dresses, too. We won't be able to spend all our time in bed. More's the pity."

His fingers tightened around hers, and his eyes moved from her face to her bare shoulders and the soft swell of her breasts.

"Is Mr. Mackenzie going to be here tonight?" She wanted to distract him, for his words, the hot light in his eyes, embarassed her, even while she felt a rising hunger for him, a need that answered his own. As always, she was ashamed of her wanton feelings.

"What? Oh, Mackenzie? No, he's going to spend his last night in Panama City at the villa of his lady love. The Spanish widow. But we'll be seeing him on the ship."

"Adam, those things he said on the train. About maybe being sent back East to cover a war. Do you think he's right? Is there going to be a war?"

Adam shrugged. Some of the excitement, the enthusiasm he had shown earlier had drained away; he looked tired and preoccupied.

"Perhaps he's a pessimist," Shannon said. "A war between the states would be unthinkable."

Adam had only tasted his soup, but now he pushed it away, and poured a second glass of champagne for himself. He was looking past her, and there was a frown between his brows.

"I'm sorry," she said. "Perhaps, after all, you agree with Mr. Mackenzie, that women should not interest themselves in politics."

"Politics? I'm sorry, Shannon. What was it you wanted to know?"

She repeated her question about the possibility of

a war between the states. He shook his head irritably, as if trying to clear his mind.

"War? Certainly there'll be a war. The Democratic party's badly split, and if a Republican becomes President in next year's election, there'll be a lot of Southerners screaming for secession. They're not about to give up their slaves without one hell of a fight."

"But Mr. Lincoln has said that the Republicans won't oppose slavery where it already exists."

"Shannon, the country's growing fast. New territories will be applying for statehood, and each time that happens, the issue of slavery will come up again. The slave owners who move West will insist on taking their 'property' with them. And the free-soilers and abolitionists will fight them tooth and nail. And sooner or later—"

His voice trailed off. He closed his eyes and a spasm of pain crossed his face.

"Adam, what is it? What's wrong?"

"Headache. Ever since yesterday evening." He sounded baffled and annoyed, like a man used to superb health, endless energy, and who was affronted by any physical weakness.

"Maybe you shouldn't have any more champagne," she began.

"Don't fuss over me," he said irritably. "I'm thirsty and it's hot as a furnace in here."

She looked at him in surprise, for the evening was unusually clear and there was a breeze blowing in through the open windows. She fell silent, and watched, as Adam swallowed another glass of champagne. His food was still untouched.

In a small, cleared area at one end of the café, a man in an embroidered white shirt and trousers strummed a guitar, and a dark-haired girl wearing a skirt with red, blue and yellow ruffles stepped forward and began to dance. She moved with a slow and stately grace, and then, as the tempo of the music quickened, and a second musician started to play a flute and a third to beat on a wooden drum, her movements changed, her steps became faster, her lithe body dipping and swaying.

The men at the surrounding tables leaned forward to watch, but Adam kept his eyes fixed on his glass. When he had emptied it, he refilled it again at once. Shannon watched him uneasily.

When the dance was over, the men shouted their approval and pounded with their glasses on the tables. The girl tossed one of them a gardenia from her long, dark hair, and whirled into another dance.

Adam pushed back his chair. "Let's get out of here," he said.

Shannon, although bewildered, rose without protest. "Is your headache worse?" she asked.

"I'm all right," he told her, leading her out through the crowd. They paused for a moment on the narrow sidewalk.

"You said you were at the shipping office all last night. Didn't you get any sleep at all?"

"I told you to stop fussing." He took her arm and made a path for them through the horde of men that jammed the sidewalk. "I've had enough of the café, that's all. And of Panama. I'll be fine, as soon as we're out to sea."

"I'll be happy to leave here, too," Shannon said.

"Elena told me—" She broke off. "Look, isn't that a carriage for hire?"

"I'd rather walk," Adam said. They crossed the Cathedral Plaza, where a reddish moon was rising over the twin bell towers of the ancient cathedral. The dank, evil-smelling alleys and gutters were filled with piles of rubbish, rotting vegetables, dead cats and puddles of stagnant water.

"Adam, my dress will be ruined. And this is the first time I've worn it."

He stopped and looked down at her with a tired smile.

"It's pretty," he said. "Where did you get it?"

She was shaken with a swift, nameless fear. "I've been sewing on it ever since we arrived here. You went with me to the Chinese shop to buy the silk. Surely you remember."

"Oh—yes. That's right." Another empty carriage for hire was rolling past and he hailed it. "You ride home. Don't want you spoiling your dress. I'll walk. The air will clear my head."

He helped her into the carriage and as he did so, she felt a shudder pass through his body. He was trembling as if he stood in an icy gale.

She wanted to ask him what was wrong, but she did not want to make him angry. He was tired. It must have been hectic in the shipping office last night. He needed rest, that was all, she told herself firmly.

Back at the house, she waited for him in the sitting-room. The minutes crawled by, and she was seized by a mounting tension. Then, at last, she heard the gate at the back of the patio creak open. She went to the sitting-room door, and opened it.

Adam was making painful, retching sounds, gripping the iron bars of the gate for support. A moment later, he vomited, his body bent forward.

Although she had always been fastidious, she felt no disgust now, only pity, and fear. She hurried out and crossed the patio. She tried to put her arm around him, to support him, but he thrust her away.

"Leave me alone," he gasped. "Go inside." His tall, powerful body was shaking violently, uncontrollably.

Elena came to the doorway of the kitchen. "What is wrong, señorita? I did not expect you and Señor Kincaid home so early."

"It's nothing," Shannon said quickly.

"He has drunk too much *aguardiente*, perhaps?"

"He's all right," Shannon insisted, as much to reassure herself as Elena. A few glasses of champagne, or even the stronger liquor mentioned by the cook, would not cause Adam to be taken violently ill. She had seen him drink far more, with no bad effects at all.

"I'll get him upstairs," she said. "Please brew a pot of coffee, or strong tea. Adam, which would you—"

"Cold water. With ice, if we have any. So thirsty. Hot and thirsty."

Somehow, Shannon managed to get him up the stairs; she caught a glimpse of Elena's face, looking up, watching them; the woman's eyes were round with fear.

Inside the bedroom, Shannon helped Adam over to the bed. He pushed her away and sprawled on his back, breathing heavily. She lit the candles, and held the candelabrum high, to look at him; he winced and shut his eyes against the light.

He made struggling movements, trying to get out of his coat, but when she set down the candelabrum and tried to help him, he said, "Stay back. Don't touch me. I can do it."

He managed to remove the coat and let it fall to the floor, but his fingers shook as he tried to unbutton his shirt. "You're ill," she said. "You need help. Please, let me—"

With a swift, unexpected violence, he pushed her away so that she had to catch at the nightstand to keep her balance.

"Get away, damn it," he said hoarsely, but she sensed that his anger was not directed against her.

"If the steamer had arrived sooner," he said, his voice sinking to a whisper, the words slurred.

"It doesn't matter," she said soothingly. "We'll leave here tomorrow."

He grasped the railing at the head of the bed, and pulled himself into a sitting position with difficulty. His chest rose and fell as he fought for breath. His eyes were narrowed with pain, and a deep frown etched itself between his brows. "You'll leave tomorrow," he said.

"We're going together, Adam."

"Be quiet." He unfastened his broad belt, turned it over, and, from an inside compartment, he took a sheaf of bills.

"Take half of these. More, if you think you'll need it. But this time—" He managed a faint smile. "This time, don't be careless. Wrap the money in a handkerchief. Sew it into your camisole. Leave out only enough for—your immediate needs. The tickets—my inside coat pocket."

"But you're going with me. You'll take care of the money and the tickets. I know you'll feel better by tomorrow."

"No, Shannon."

"Even if you don't, I'll find a way to get you on the ship."

"Don't be foolish. No captain will carry a yellow fever case."

The words sent cold terror racing through her. "You don't have yellow fever." Her voice was high and shrill. "You can't. It's something else. The food in the café, perhaps. The fish might have been spoiled."

But even as she spoke, she realized how unlikely that was, for Adam had eaten only a little of the fish soup, while she had finished hers with no ill effects.

Still, she tried to cling to the hope that Adam was mistaken. Yellow fever spread panic wherever it appeared. Only a few years ago, so Aunt Kate had told her, there had been an epidemic of yellow fever in Mobile; hundreds of residents had fled in terror, while hundreds more had died. There was no cure, and the doctors disagreed as to the cause. Shannon remembered, too, the man and woman who had been put off the train at Matachín Station. And the story Elena had told her of the family she had worked for, all of them wiped out by fever soon after their arrival in Panama.

"Shannon, I have it. I know the symptoms," Adam was saying. "Fever, headache, chills, nausea. There've been a lot of new cases here in Panama lately. Mackenzie told me. Said it happens like this every time. Influx of newcomers—"

"But not you, Adam. Not you." Tears of fright welled up in her eyes.

"Stop that," he said. "You mustn't go to pieces now. Mustn't lie to yourself. I saw men die of yellow fever, when I was in the Army, on the Mexican border."

His voice was weaker, his eyes half-closed. He sagged against the headboard of the bed.

Adam was wrong, he had to be wrong; he could not be stricken with fever now, when they were getting ready to leave.

"A doctor," she said softly, to herself. "I'll find a doctor. He'll be able to help Adam."

She hurried down the stairs, and asked Elena where to find the nearest doctor. The cook gave her a worried look. "But Señor Kincaid will be himself by morning, if it is only the drink that has made him ill."

"Elena, I'm not sure what's wrong with him. Please, tell me at once, where I can find a doctor."

"There is Dr. Ospina," the cook said, shifting uneasily. Shannon sensed the older woman's mounting fear.

"You stay here," she said. "Go and sit with Señor Kincaid in case he needs anything."

Reluctantly, Elena gave Shannon the directions for finding the doctor's house, but she made no move to go upstairs. "I will brew a pot of coffee for him," she muttered. "That should help. If it is the *aguardiente* that has made him so ill."

The doctor's house was only a few blocks away, but Shannon found that she was trembling and drenched with perspiration by the time she found the place.

The doctor's housekeeper answered the door, and despite the woman's protests that the doctor had had a long and exhausting day, and was preparing for bed, Shannon refused to budge until she was allowed to see him.

Dr. Ospina was a small man with graying hair and a neat mustache. He was plainly fatigued, but he was moved by Shannon's frantic pleading.

"Tell Pablo to bring my carriage around," he ordered the housekeeper.

Although this was quickly done, and Shannon and the doctor were soon back at Mackenzie's house, it seemed an eternity before she was leading him upstairs where Adam lay, his half-closed eyes glazed with fever.

"The patient's name?" the doctor asked, pulling down the sheet.

"Adam Kincaid. He's an American. We both are. We're on our way to California."

"You are Señora Kincaid?"

She was too frightened to care what the doctor might think of her. "My name's Shannon Cavanaugh. Mr. Kincaid and I are traveling together."

"I see." There was no censure in the doctor's lined, weary face. He proceeded with the examination, and his movements, deft and competent, gave Shannon some reassurance. But at his touch, Adam stirred, opened his eyes, and appeared to be aware of his surroundings again. "Shannon, I told you to leave. Get out of here, while you can."

"Adam, please lie still. The doctor will help you. He'll give you something to make you feel better."

Adam shook his head, then shuddered as if even

that small movement had been painful. He lapsed back into a stupor, and the doctor completed his examination. Then he motioned Shannon out into the hall.

"The patient—Señor Kincaid—has yellow fever. There's no doubt of it. I have seen dozens of these cases during the past week. It is the disease of newcomers, strangers to Panama. Many of your countrymen have been stricken."

"But we're to sail in a few hours, on the Pacific Mail steamer. We have the tickets." It was if, by doggedly repeating the words, she could make them true.

"Impossible, señorita. Every traveler embarking from Panama City is checked by the captain, or one of the ship's officers, for signs of the fever. He would not be allowed on board. Even if he could make the trip down to the dock by tomorrow morning, which is hardly likely."

Shannon felt a mounting despair at the doctor's words.

"But what about you?" he asked. "Have you ever had yellow fever?"

Shannon shook her head. "No, never."

"Then you are in grave danger if you remain here."

"But I can't leave Adam. He must be cared for. Is there a hospital where he could be taken?"

"There is a small hospital in Colón, at the other end of the railroad line. But that's for railroad workers, and it is always filled to overflowing with yellow fever cases, with cholera and malaria and dysentery patients. Men go there only to die. I'm told the chief of staff there does a brisk business, selling cadavers to the medical schools of Europe, shipping them back in casks."

Shannon made a sound of horror. "Forgive me," the doctor said. "But you must understand that yellow fever has a high mortality. Here in Panama City, there is a fever camp. A collection of huts on Flamingo Island in the Bay. A pesthole, señorita. No staff to speak of. No supplies. The convalescents do what little they can for the dying." He looked at Shannon steadily. "I have no wish to frighten you, but it is necessary that you understand what you face, if you decide to remain and care for this man."

"I will stay. And I'll take care of him and make him well. I know I can."

"Have you ever nursed anyone through a serious illness?" the doctor demanded. "Have you any idea of what you will have to do?"

"Tell me. I can learn. I'll do whatever must be done."

He looked at her, doubt and pity mingled in his eyes, and she realized that she was still wearing her silk dress with its flounces, its trimming of lace and velvet ribbons, that her hair was still arranged in the frivolous coiffure of waves and flowing curls.

"I don't question your good intentions, señorita. Or your attachment to this man. All the same, I think that in this case, perhaps the fever camp is the only place."

"No. He can't go there. I won't let you take him there. Doctor, please tell me what to do."

He sighed, but then he outlined the instructions for Adam's care, speaking slowly, precisely. She wondered how many times he had repeated those same words since the epidemic had started.

"You have someone to help you? Servants, perhaps."

"Oh, yes. There's Elena, the cook. She knows all about yellow fever. The family she worked for—"

"Very well," the doctor said. "I will leave Señor Kincaid in your hands. But you must understand the burden you're taking on. He will have to be lifted, the bedding will have to be changed frequently. You or your servant will have to take care of all his needs. He is helpless now, you see. He will be for several days. If he survives that long. Some victims die in a matter of hours. Should he become delirious, and he probably will, you will have to restrain him, to keep him from injuring himself. He might get out of bed, and fall down the stairs. Keep the doors to the *galería* locked, and the door of his room. Tie him to the bed if you have to."

She winced at the thought of Adam, tied down like an animal. Doctor Ospina did not miss her reaction. "This is a dangerous disease, painful, ugly. If you are at all squeamish—"

"No, I'm not," Shannon said, trying to convince herself as well as the doctor. "So long as he lives, I don't care what I have to do."

"I can make no promises," the doctor said. "If the *vomito negro,* the black vomit begins, and if he slips into a coma, there will be little hope for him." He opened his leather case and gave her a few small bottles, explaining how each medication was to be given. "These will only ease some of the worst discomforts. I can offer you no cure."

He snapped his case shut, picked it up, tucked his gold-headed cane under his arm.

"You'll come back tomorrow, won't you?" Shannon asked.

"There is nothing more I can do for him, señorita. But he is a young man, and strong. Perhaps, through God's mercy, he will survive."

She paid the doctor his fee, and after she had seen him out, she turned to go back to Adam. But in the hallway, she saw Elena, a thin shawl wrapped around her head, carrying a large straw basket.

"Where are you going?" Shannon demanded. "I need you to help me."

The woman shook her head. "No, senorita. *Lo siento mucho*. I do not stay in a house with *la fiebre amarilla*. I have heard what the doctor said. Last time, I was spared, but this time, who knows?"

"But I can't manage alone. If you heard the doctor, surely you must know that Adam—Señor Kincaid—will need constant care. I don't expect you to nurse him, but surely you can help with the cooking, the laundry. I'll pay you well."

"Money? What good will money be to me, if I get the fever?" Her eyes narrowed. "Don't be foolish, señorita. Take the money for yourself, and get on board that ship. Go back to your country. Panama is a graveyard for white people. Only the Indians do not get the fever."

"I can't leave him."

"You must. You are young, and beautiful. There will be other men for you. You must not stay here and risk your life for this man."

"That's no concern of yours," Shannon snapped, her nerves stretched taut with fear.

"You are not his wife," Elena persisted. "He is not even kind to you. I heard him, that night, out on the patio. Shouting at you, abusing you, as if you were *una puta.* You owe him nothing."

"I'm staying with him," Shannon said stubbornly.

"You are mad, like all *yanquis.*" She sighed and shifted the heavy basket on her arm. "I have warned you. I can do no more." She hesitated, looking at Shannon with compassion. "You will need ice, much ice. There is only a little left in the ice chest. You will have to buy more from one of the vendors. There is enough water in the rain barrel for washing, but for drinking, you will have to buy water, too. The water seller comes each morning." Although Shannon had kept the house tidy, she had not bothered to find out about these small, but now vital details. "There is some food in the kitchen. The rest, you will have to buy from passing vendors. It will cost more than it would at the marketplace, but you will not be able to leave the house."

As the full implication of her words sank in, Shannon felt a growing terror. *I'll be a prisoner here,* she thought. *Until Adam recovers or until—but he won't die. I can't let him die.*

"*Adiós*, Señorita Cavanaugh," Elena said. She turned and hurried down the hall, the basket on her arm, and Shannon heard the heavy door close behind her.

For a moment, Shannon fought down the need to find relief in tears. Then she saw that the gray light of dawn was filtering in from the patio. She stepped out into the patio for a moment, and let the cool, fresh air blow across her face. Overhead, towering masses of clouds were edged with coral and gold. Somewhere, out in the bay, the steamer was waiting.

You are not his wife. He is not even kind to you.

She pushed away the memory of Elena's words, turned and went back into the house, back to Adam.

14

DURING THE DAYS that followed, Shannon forgot her fears for her own safety, as she fought, grimly, desperately, to keep Adam alive. Sometimes, to hold onto her self-control, she made herself remember small things out of the past.

Sitting in the stifling room, reeking with the heavy odors of sickness, she would let herself think of the neat parlor of Miss Colter's school, back in Boston. She could picture the girls, seated around the fireplace after dinner, memorizing their lessons for the following day, doing needlework, while one of them played the spinet. The scales, perhaps, or, as a special treat, Mr. Stephen Foster's new ballad, "Come Where My Love Lies Dreaming."

It was October now, and perhaps there had been an early snowfall in Boston. Shannon tried to feel the crisp, clean air, to see the white, swirling flakes.

But sooner or later, she was jerked back to reality, by the raucous screeching of a flock of parrots flying past the window, or the unearthly shrieking of one of the small howler monkeys that had found its way down from the hills beyond the city. Sometimes, the drumming of the rain against the tiled roof made her want to scream. Once, waking from a brief nap, she discovered a scorpion in her shoe, and she did scream, stifling the sound with her hand, her stomach lurching as she smashed the creature with Adam's heavy belt.

She could only take her sleep in fitful snatches, for a part of her mind was always alert for a cry from Adam, a mumbled plea for water. He could eat nothing, and sometimes, even the water she gave him to drink would not stay down. She had to hold small chips of ice between his dry lips. She was careful not to run out of ice, although she was sure the vendor was overcharging her each time he sold her a chunk. There was no running water in the house, and keeping the *tinaja,* the large water jar filled, was also expensive.

Her hands grew cracked and inflamed from washing sheets and pillowcases with harsh lye soap. Her back and shoulders ached from bending over the heavy tin tub in the kitchen. Sometimes, when she had to move Adam, to change his bedding, or to perform the other services he required, her muscles jerked and quivered in protest, for although he had lost weight, his heavy, large-boned body was still difficult to move.

Whatever fastidiousness she might have felt was gone now. In its place was only anger that, beyond the most basic nursing chores, there was nothing she could do to ease his discomforts, no way to stop the wracking pains in his head, his back, his legs. She carefully administered the medicines given by Dr. Ospina, the calomel, the laudanum, but she had no way of knowing if they eased his suffering, for he was in a stupor, scarcely aware of her presence.

The delirium began on the third day of his illness, and, although Dr. Ospina had warned her about this aspect of yellow fever, she was shaken when she heard Adam's mumbled protests, and later, his cries of terror, as he relived the incidents of his childhood. She remembered Aunt Kate's account of Adam's brutal treatment at the hands of Tom Sprague, his supposed benefactor.

In his delirium, he became steadily more restless. She did not want to tie him to the bed, for it was too cruel, too humiliating for him. But after he had lashed out at her several times, once smashing the precious jar of water and, another time, catching her arm and twisting it so that she carried the bruises for days; after he had fallen halfway off the bed, she knew that she had no choice. She bit her lip to keep back the tears as she tore strips from the sheets with the aid of Adam's knife, braided the strips together to make them stronger, and, waiting until he had lapsed into one of his frequent stupors, she had managed to tie his wrists to the ornate brass headboard.

After that, he became more violent, as he fought against his bonds, sometimes cursing, sometimes whimpering like a frightened child. She tried to soothe him, bathing his face with cool water, stroking his hair.

His skin had changed from its deep, healthy tan to

an ugly yellowish shade, and the whites of his eyes were yellow, too.

One night, when a fierce storm raged outside, when the wind flung the rain against the windows, and lightning lit up the room, he opened his eyes and looked directly at her. "We've got to stay hidden, Rachel—can't let them find us—" And a moment later, he was shouting hoarsely, "Rachel—no—I won't let them—I'll kill them—"

Then he fell back on the bed, his face twisted, his body shaken with hard, choking spasms. Shannon had never seen a man cry before.

Now, she bent over him, holding his face against her breasts. "It's all right, my love," she said. "You're safe here with me." She stroked his hair and felt some of the tension drain from his body.

On the sixth day of the fever, the dreaded black vomit began. When Adam started retching, she saw that there were traces of blood in the basin she held for him.

"I won't let you die," she said stubbornly. "I won't give you up."

And all at once she was seized with fury against the fever, against this stifling, rain-drenched city. Although she dared not give way to tears, her helpless rage found an outlet in the words she cried, words she had overheard in her uncle's tavern back in Mobile, words Adam had shouted in his delirium. She scarcely knew the meaning of some of them, but in some way, repeating them relieved her.

Until Adam opened his eyes. "Rachel, you musn't say such things. It's not fitting. You'll be punished—"

Then, as Shannon watched, she saw a corner of his fever-cracked lips lifted in a smile. She had never seen him smile that way before. His voice was teasing but affectionate. " 'S all right, Rachel," he whispered. "I won't tell on you."

Shannon fell silent, ashamed that she had lost control even for so brief a time. She had to think, to do something to help Adam. She could not stand by and watch him die.

He lapsed back into apathy, and she wiped his face, and pulled the sheet up around him. Although Dr. Ospina had said there was nothing more that he could do for Adam, Shannon had to do everything possible to keep death at bay.

She was afraid to leave him alone, but she had no choice. She checked the braided lengths of sheet that held him to the bed, then went and washed her face, brushed her hair and tucked it into a net. She put on her gray cotton, worn and faded but serviceable.

The streets were crowded, and that surprised her for it was about an hour before dawn. "What's happening?" she asked a man who had brushed against her in the crowd.

He touched his battered hat. "A steamer, ma'am. From New Orleans, bound for California."

"But the steamer left," she said, her words slurred by her growing exhaustion. She could not remember when she had slept or eaten last.

"This is another steamer," the man said. "Got in sooner than was expected. It's leaving by noon today. If you're thinking about going, you'll need to get your ticket soon."

Shannon shook her head. "I'm not going. Not this time."

The man looked at her curiously. "You all right, ma'am? You look kind of shaky, if you'll pardon my saying so."

"I'm all right," she said quickly. "Thank you."

She hurried off through the narrow twisting streets to the doctor's house. She had to wait until he had dressed and come downstairs.

"Please, if you'll only come and see him. There must be something more you can do."

"Señorita, I have told you—"

"But if you'll only come. I'll pay you well. I have money."

"It is not a question of money." He looked at her face. "Very well," he said. "But I have other patients to see first. I will come when I can." He sighed. "The black vomit, how long has that been going on?"

"Only for a few hours. But he isn't in a coma. I mean, he wasn't when I left him."

"Convulsions?"

"No. He's been delirious but he hasn't—is that a good sign? Does that mean he still has a chance?"

"Possibly. Go back to him now. Continue the cold compresses."

"Is that all?"

"I'm afraid so."

Shannon hurried back to the house, moving against the crowd now, as it surged in the direction of the shipping office and the dock. A few men glanced at her, but none tried to talk to her. Maybe it was because they were too intent on getting to the steamer, or maybe there was nothing about her now to attract a man. A little while ago, when she had been dressing and fixing her hair, she had seen her reflection in Adam's shaving mirror. Her collarbones stood out sharply, there were deep hollows in her cheeks and at her temples and dark smudges under her eyes. Her lips had been set in a hard, determined way that few men would find enticing.

Back at the house, she returned to Adam's bedside, fearful of what she might find, but when she looked down at him she saw that his chest still rose and fell with his breathing. From time to time he tugged at the bonds that held him to the bed. Was that a good sign? Did it prove that he still had the strength to fight the fever? If only Dr. Ospina would hurry.

He did not arrive until shortly before noon, his carriage driven by the same Indian boy who had been his driver on his first visit.

The doctor examined Adam, who stirred and muttered, but did not open his eyes. "His heart is still strong, and his pulse, too," the doctor said.

"Does that mean he's going to live? Oh, Doctor, surely you can tell me."

The doctor gave her a tired smile. "He has a tenacious grip on life, this man of yours. All the same, I make no promises."

Shannon swayed slightly, her legs starting to tremble. Her body was soaked with perspiration, here in this warm, humid room. The exhaustion that had been growing these past days now started to overwhelm her. She put out a hand to steady herself. The doctor took her arm and helped her to a chair. He studied her closely, put a hand to her forehead. "No, not the fever. But you cannot go on this way. You'll have to rest now. Your servant can watch Señor Kincaid."

"Servant?" she said. "Oh, yes. Elena. She left, Doctor. That first night. As soon as she found out he had yellow fever. She was afraid, you see."

"Madre de Dios!" the doctor said, staring at Shannon, his professional calm shaken. "Are you saying that you have cared for Señor Kincaid alone, all this time?"

Shannon nodded. "There was no one else."

"Listen to me," the doctor said. "I know nothing about you beyond what you have told me. But you are young and gently reared, that much is plain. What you are doing here with this man is no concern of mine. You must leave him. There is another ship in port now. Take it. Do not tempt Providence."

"I can't leave Adam."

"Even in the fever camp, he'll have a chance."

Shannon fought the weakness that was threatening to overcome her. "Do you want to stay here alone with him, until you, too, are stricken? If you get the fever, who will care for you? Do you want to die with him?"

"If I have to," she said. "But he won't. I won't let him."

"You love him that much." It was not a question but a statement of fact.

She sought for an answer. There was a thin, humming sound in her head, and she found it difficult to collect her thoughts.

Love? Love was being kissed by Bruce, so handsome, so gallant, his blond hair shining like a golden helmet in the sunlight. The garden at Jessamine, where the air was filled with the delicate scent of flowers, where lilies floated on the pool, and windbells chimed in the pagoda summerhouse. Dancing with Bruce in a satin dress, under the glittering chandeliers of Beau Rivage, looking up into his face, seeing the longing in his eyes.

She turned her head with an effort, and saw Adam, the rumpled sheet pushed back from his gaunt body, as he tossed restlessly. His face was bearded now, his eyes yellow with the disease that was consuming him, his lips cracked and bleeding. Adam, a man who had never spoken of love to her, who had taken advantage of her desperation to offer her passage out of Panama in return for the use of her body. He had shouted at her in anger, mocked her and humiliated her.

Since their first night together, she had not been able to deny that she hungered for him. But love?

"Yes," she said softly. "I love him." And her lips curved in a wondering smile. She could not see Dr. Ospina's reaction, for his face was somehow blurred before her eyes. Then Adam gave a hoarse cry. Shannon was on her feet, and moving toward the bed, but after the first few steps, the floor felt unsteady beneath her, and the walls of the room were spinning slowly at first, then faster and faster; the humming in her ears grew louder, became a roar, like the sound of a flood-swollen river.

She was lying stretched out on a narrow bed. She stirred and tried to sit up. "Adam," she whispered. "I have to go to Adam."

"Stay where you are," the doctor ordered firmly.

"Pablo, the boy who drives my carriage, he is in there with Señor Kincaid."

"Oh, but I—"

"Pablo is my housekeeper's son. I have given him his orders. He will remain with you as long as he is needed."

"Thank you," she said, her voice still shaky. "But why are you doing this for me?"

"Because you are a stubborn, headstrong young lady. Since you refuse to leave and since Señor Kincaid will have a better chance here than in the fever camp, I will make do with another driver." He smiled down at her. "My housekeeper has four other sons."

"But won't Pablo be afraid of the fever? Elena was terrified."

"She was Spanish, perhaps?"

"From Madrid," Shannon said.

"Pablo and his family are Indians, from the banks of the Changres River. They believe themselves to be immune to yellow fever, and perhaps they are right."

"I remember. Elena said something about that."

"We doctors don't understand why. But we know so little about the disease. Perhaps a mild attack, at an early age, gives permanent immunity. In any case, Pablo will stay, and do what has to be done. He is strong and trustworthy."

"I don't know what to say, how to thank you," Shannon began, but the doctor, obviously embarrassed by any display of emotion, pulled out his watch and looked at it. "I must be on my way. You are to remain in bed until evening. Don't worry. There is only a wall between you and Señor Kincaid. In case of any change, Pablo will call you at once. And, señorita, you must try to eat. Pablo will fix you a nourishing meal. You've lost weight since the first time I saw you."

"I suppose I have," she said. During the time that she had been caring for Adam alone, she had scarcely been aware of her own needs, snatching at a piece of bread or a bit of fruit as she hurried about her chores. Now she could close her eyes and let herself sink into a heavy, healing sleep.

Pablo relieved her of much of the drudgery of caring for Adam. Since they could take turns watching Adam, Shannon was able to remove the restraints that had kept him tied to the bed. Although he remained in a stupor for the next three days, toward the morning of the fourth day, Shannon saw that he was improving. The delirium had passed, and the black vomit, and he had begun to perspire heavily. By dawn, he had fallen into a quiet sleep, with Shannon at his bedside.

She was rising to put out the candles when she heard him call her by name. She hurried back to him. His eyes were open, and he knew her.

"What are you doing?" he protested, as she bent to tuck the sheet around him more securely. "We've got to get ready. The ship is leaving."

"Our ship sailed days ago," she said. "And another after that. You've been ill, Adam."

"I can't remember. The café—you wore your new silk dress. And then—"

"It's yellow fever," she said. "But you're getting better. There'll be a ship for us, Adam. Soon. Now, try to sleep."

"Yellow fever," he said. "Why—didn't you leave? You should have taken the first steamer."

She smiled. "I know. You told me to. You gave me the money and the tickets."

"But you stayed. You must have been out of your mind."

"Elena thought I was. She told me so, before she left."

"You mean you cared for me alone?" His voice trailed off, and his eyes began to close. "I don't understand," he said. "Why did you?"

"Rest now," she said. "That's right." She stroked his hair back from his forehead. He sighed and lay still, breathing evenly.

But a few days later, when she had finished feeding him the rice gruel prescribed by the doctor, he resumed his questioning. "You haven't told me why you stayed." And, when she did not answer, he reached out and took her hand. He turned it over and stared at it. "Good Lord, you must have been scrubbing floors."

Her feminine vanity reasserted itself, and she tried to pull her hand away. The skin was cracked and reddened, the nails broken. There was a barely healed blister on the back, where she had splashed boiling water while washing the sheets, a cut along the thumb from the ice pick she had used to chip ice for him.

"I'll use cucumber lotion and buttermilk on my hands as soon as we reach San Francisco."

She broke off, as Adam drew her hand to his cheek. Turning his head, he kissed her palm. The gesture, so unlike him, sent a tide of joy coursing through her.

His eyes were warm and she saw the tenderness in them. He reached out and she went into his arms. A moment later she was stretched out beside him on the bed. His cheek, now smooth and clean-shaven, was cool against hers.

The wonder, the beauty of the moment was so great that she hesitated to speak. But she must tell him she loved him. And surely, he would respond. Now, at last, he would speak of love.

"Shannon, I've been lying here, thinking," he began. "You risked your life for me. And you saved mine. No, listen. I wanted you from the first time I saw you, but I never knew you, not really, not until now. I wanted you because you were beautiful and because I sensed the warmth of you, under that prissy, ladylike manner. But I never would have expected that you'd stand by me through something like this. It must have been hell for you."

"Oh, but I—"

But he did not let her finish. "I want to repay you," he went on quickly. "And I will. You'll see. When we get to the Comstock, I'm going to make a fortune."

"Adam, I don't—"

"Yes, I know. Every man who goes out there has the same idea. But remember, I know the country. I've been out there before. Most of the others, storekeepers, clerks, schoolmasters, they'll go back home with empty pockets. Those who live to go back at all. But that won't happen to me."

This was not what Shannon had wanted to hear. This was no declaration of love. Adam still had his arm around her but he had drawn away slightly and she could see his face, the firm set to his jaw. His eyes were hard now, the tenderness she had seen there a moment ago was gone.

"I'll make a fortune and you'll share it with me. I'll give you the kind of life you've always wanted. I'll set you up in the finest hotel in San Francisco. You'll have a maid, a carriage of your own, dresses from Paris, jewels."

Pain clutched at her throat until she thought she would strangle. She must not let him know. Somehow, she managed to get the words out.

"Everything I've ever wanted. That's generous of you, Adam." She slipped from his embrace, got to her feet and walked swiftly to the window. He must not see her face for it would surely betray her.

"What's wrong?" he demanded. "You believe I can do it, don't you?"

"Yes," she said steadily. "I believe you can do anything you set your mind to."

There was only one thing he could not do, she thought, as she stared out at the patio, her eyes fixed on the brilliant colors of the hibiscus bushes, the trailing bougainvilleas. He could not give her the love she longed for; nor could he recognize her love, and accept it, when it was his for the taking.

15

ALTHOUGH IT WAS already early in November, there was still a touch of warmth in the late afternoon sunshine that lingered on the smooth lawns of Beau Rivage and struck fire from the windows of the tall house; a softness in the breeze that blew in from the winding yellow Alabama River. Cherokee roses still bloomed on the bushes that surrounded the house, their rich, heavy sweetness blending with the spicy perfume of the yellow and orange marigolds.

But Odalie Duval, dismounting from her brown mare and tossing the reins to the black boy who hurried forward, was not concerned with the lush, familiar beauty of the house and its ground. She lifted the skirt of her riding habit and hurried up the veranda steps and into the long, cool hallway.

Dinner was always served punctually at three o'clock, and she had hoped to get back to Beau Rivage in time to change and to allow Emmy, her maid, to brush her hair, so that she might appear at the table looking cool and poised, in spite of her inner turmoil. But as she drew nearer to the open doors of the diningroom, she heard the clink of china, and the sound of voices. Mama and Aunt Lucienne were already being served.

She stood still, unable to decide whether to brave Mama's displeasure by appearing at the table in her riding habit, or perhaps irritate her even more by taking the time to go upstairs to change.

She heard Aunt Lucienne saying, "Antoinette, you know I want to return to Paris. I've wanted nothing more these last years. But are you sure this is the time? With Mr. Sutherland coming to Beau Rivage?"

"I've told you, Mr. Sutherland won't be staying here at the house. He'll stay in the old overseer's cottage."

"But if he's to paint the murals in the ballroom—"

"Really, Lucienne. Since Philippe died I've had no choice but to have tradesmen come here, and factors. When I sold Tina to Mr. Kincaid, and leased those men to him for his lumberyard, I could scarcely have conducted the transaction out on the veranda."

"But Mr. Kincaid did not stay the night," Lucienne said. Then, she added quickly, "I don't mean to criticize you, Antoinette. I know it isn't easy running the place since poor, dear Phillippe passed away. But to have this young man, this artist staying here— even out in Craig Judson's old quarters, might cause talk. It was bad enough when you discarded black for half-mourning last spring, so that he could paint your portrait in a becoming gown. But at least I was in the house at the time. And Odalie."

"I've already hired him to do the ballroom murals,"

Mama said firmly. "I've agreed to his preliminary sketches. Now, Lucienne, let's hear no more about it. When you are back in Paris, you won't have time to concern yourself with affairs at Beau Rivage. Goodness knows, we've heard of nothing since you came to live here except how wonderful life in Paris was, and how you disliked this country. Uncivilized, you called it."

"I haven't changed my mind about that," Aunt Lucienne said. "Why, ever since that horrible man, John Brown, led that insurrection in Virginia, I've been living in terror. They sat that there are other uprisings planned all over the South, right here in Alabama, I've heard."

"If you're so frightened, all the more reason you'll be happier returning to France."

"But what about Odalie? She doesn't want to go."

"Odalie will do as I tell her," Mama said. "Where on earth is she? She went riding off this morning."

"I'm here, Mama," Odalie said, stepping into the doorway of the dining room. "I'm sorry I'm late."

"You will go upstairs at once, and change into a suitable dress. And hurry, we're half-finished with dinner."

But although Odalie moved toward the stairs, she lingered before starting her ascent. Had Mama definitely decided that she should go to Paris with Aunt Lucienne? Odalie's hand tightened on the newelpost at the foot of the stairs. This was one time Mama would not get her way.

She heard Mama saying, "Mr. Sutherland has chosen classical subjects for his murals. The Muses, and Apollo."

"A lot of pagan gods and goddesses, cavorting about unclothed," Aunt Lucienne protested.

"They will be suitably veiled, Lucienne."

Odalie struck at the carved wooden lion's head with her small fist. Bother the Muses and Apollo. And Mr. Edward Sutherland. If only Aunt Lucienne would refuse to accompany her to Paris. But Aunt Lucienne had been under Mama's thumb for years now; she was not likely to take a stand, particularly if it meant not being able to return to her beloved Paris.

Odalie did not dare remain downstairs any longer, for Mama was already annoyed because she was late for dinner. She hurried upstairs to her bedroom, where Emmy, the black girl who had replaced Tina, was waiting. "I bettuh brush yo' hair, Miss Odalie." She helped Odalie off with her riding habit, and into a lace-trimmed muslin wrapper. Odalie quickly managed to transfer Bruce's letter from the bosom of her camisole to the small jewel case on the dressing table.

Her hair had become somewhat tousled and untidy, in the course of the ride back from Jessamine, where the letter had been waiting for her; Bruce had sent it in care of his sister, Melora, no doubt fearing that otherwise it might have fallen into Mama's hands.

"Hurry, Emmy," Odalie said. It would not do to put Mama into a worse mood, not now. Somehow, she had to persuade Mama that she could not possibly go off to Paris, without telling her the reason.

"Ah'm hurryin'," Emmy said. But the coiffure was a complicated one and Emmy was not yet fully skilled at her tasks. She brushed Odalie's long, shining black

hair carefully, parted it in the center, and then began
to arrange the ringlets over her ears.

Although Bruce's letter, written on the stationery
of a San Francisco hotel, was now out of sight, Odalie
could still remember many of the phrases, for she had
read them over and over again. "I carry the miniature
you gave me next to my heart . . . but to have you
beside me again, my darling . . . live for the day
when you will belong to me . . . really my own, my
bride. . . . "

Suppose Bruce returned when she was far away in
France? Suppose one of the other belles in Mobile
caught his eyes? The scandal that had turned many
of the older, more sober gentry here in the county
against him had only made him a more dashing figure
in the eyes of the young ladies. Hadn't he killed a
Yankee interloper who had presumed to pay court
to Odalie Duval? These young ladies were not concerned with the details of the duel, which had already
grown vague and garbled with repetition; even their
elders were now concerned with more serious matters.
The raid on Harper's Ferry had touched off a wave of
speculation all across the South. That man Brown had
not been working alone; he was part of a great con-
spiracy to free all the slaves. Other abolitionist fanatics
would strike now. No plantation was safe, no Southern
city was immune to the terrors of insurrection. In the
face of this crisis, the talk of the duel between Bruce
Lathrop and the Yankee mill owner had almost ceased.

Odalie knew that she had to be here at Beau
Rivage, waiting, when Bruce returned. Once he
made her his wife, Mama could do nothing to oppose
the match.

Divorce was unthinkable, for no divorced woman was received in decent society in Mobile, or in any other Southern community. As for an annulment, once she and Bruce were man and wife, that would be out of the question. Man and wife. Odalie tried not to think of the implications of those words.

Marriage to Bruce would be beautiful. Not like— the memory of Craig Judson rose to torment her. He had been low, vile, an animal. Bruce's love was pure, tender; he would never demand, never expect—

"Miss Odalie, I cain' fix yo' hair pretty less you keep yo' head still," Emmy said plaintively. She was now arranging a waterfall of curls that began at the crown and fell gracefully over Odalie's shoulders.

But by the time she had finished, and Odalie, wearing her pink organdy dress with its full skirt and rose velvet sash, had descended to the dining room, she found Mama sitting at the table alone. "Your aunt's gone up to her room with one of her headaches," Mama said. She saw that Mama had finished her dinner. "I'll have a platter of chicken brought in. This is already cool. And more biscuits." She turned to the black butler. "Hosea, I want—"

"I'm not hungry, Mama," Odalie said quickly.

"That's strange, considering that you've been out riding since morning."

But she did not try to urge the food on Odalie. Instead, she said, "I'll have my coffee in the downstairs sitting room. You will join me, Odalie." It was not a question, but a command.

A few minutes later, seated opposite Mama in the high-ceilinged room at the back of the house, Odalie smoothed her billowing pink skirt nervously.

Usually Mama took her coffee alone here. Because Odalie had eaten no dinner, Hosea had brought a plate of pecan cookies, but she found she did not want even one. What was Mama planning now? She did not have to wait long to find out.

"I've told Emmy to have your trunk brought down," Mama said crisply. "There will be a good deal of packing to do. You will take the train to New Orleans. There's a ship leaving from there for France at the end of the week. You will take Emmy with you. You will stay at the home of Uncle Bertrand. He will escort you and Lucienne to the ship."

"Mama, please listen. I've told you I don't want to go to Paris."

"It's all arranged," Mama said crisply. "You won't be needing too much luggage. You'll want to look presentable during the voyage, but as soon as you arrive in Paris, you'll go to the House of Worth. He is the most fashionable designer in the city. Empress Eugénie, herself, is dressed by Worth."

"Mama, all these weeks I've been trying to explain—" Odalie was close to tears. "Don't my feelings mean anything to you? Isn't it enough that you tried to force me into a marriage with Mr. Cunningham?"

"Forget Mr. Cunningham," Mama said. "In Paris, you will meet dozens of suitable young men. Aunt Lucienne's connections will provide *entrée* into the best society. Perhaps you will even be presented to the Emperor Louis Napoleon and the Empress Eugénie."

Odalie searched her mind desperately, seeking some way to persuade Mama that the trip was out of the question. Remembering the conversation she had overheard a short time ago, she said, "Perhaps Aunt Lucienne is right. If she goes to Paris with me and you are alone here—and if Mr. Sutherland—"

"I don't need a chaperone, Odalie," Mama said.

"Don't you, Mama?"

"How dare you?"

"I'm sorry. I didn't mean—I was only thinking of what people might say. I know Mr. Sutherland will be staying in the cottage where Craig Judson—"

She swallowed hard. Even the mention of Judson's name brought a wave of sickness. After Judson had left, and Mama had returned from New Orleans, she had hired a married man to work as overseer, a taciturn, industrious Rhode Islander who, with his wife, occupied larger quarters. Mama had said that a married man might be more settled, less likely to leave his job without warning.

Odalie had never even hinted at the real reason for Craig Judson's departure, for she had been too afraid of her mother. Suppose Mama blamed her for what had happened? Although such matters were not discussed before unmarried girls, Odalie had learned from snatches of overheard conversations between Mama and Aunt Lucienne that when a girl gave herself to a man before marriage, whatever the circumstances, she was considered somehow sinful and wicked.

And Mama could be ruthless. Hadn't she driven Bruce out of Mobile after the duel? And Shannon Cavanaugh, too? Odalie had heard Mama boasting openly to Aunt Lucienne about how "that brazen creature" had gotten what she deserved.

But Odalie was beginning to realize that she had a streak of Mama's ruthlessness in her own nature. Only, where Mama could give orders, could get her own way by direct methods, Odalie would have to be devious, would have to pretend compliance.

So now, she said quietly, "I'm sorry, Mama. Naturally, I didn't mean that there was anything— wrong—about your having Mr. Sutherland here. But there's Aunt Lucienne. If she isn't willing to make the trip to Paris at her age, and in her state of health—"

"There's nothing wrong with your aunt's health," Mama interrupted. "She's been wanting to return to Paris ever since I can remember. She never would have come to Alabama, except that her father was killed fighting for Bonaparte, and her mother died soon after. Now, I'm giving her a chance to return home."

"But, Mama—"

"And as for you, miss, once you're in Paris you'll forget all about Bruce Lathrop. Your aunt has excellent connections in France. And Louis Napoleon is favoring anyone who served his uncle. He wants to establish his right to the throne, as an heir to Bonaparte."

"I don't care about Louis Napoleon or Paris," Odalie cried.

"You will," Mama said calmly, sipping her strong, black coffee and nibbling at a pecan cookie. "Why, any other girl would jump at the chance I'm offering you. If I had been given such a chance when I was your age—"

"When you were my age, you married Papa."

"It was an arranged marriage. Oh, I was attracted

by his looks, his charm. Any girl would have been. But after the first few months—" Mama broke off, but Odalie caught her meaning.

After the first few months Mama had learned about the pretty young Irish girl, Peggy Cavanaugh. Papa's mistress. And later, she found out that Peggy had given Papa a daughter.

Odalie remembered the look on Shannon's face that night outside the ballroom, when she had learned who her father was. If it had come as a shock to Odalie, how much worse for Shannon! Those ugly words Mama had used.

Even in her own distress, that night, Odalie had felt sorry for Shannon. Her half-sister.

Now she protested, "But Mama, if you were so unhappy in your own marriage, surely you want me to have a better life. Bruce is the only man I can ever love."

Mama rose, smoothing her skirt, and saying, "That will be all. You are leaving Beau Rivage on the day after tomorrow. I had planned to remain here. I have a great many things to do. It's not easy, running a plantation without a man. But I think now that I'd better go along to New Orleans with you and Aunt Lucienne. If necessary, I will see you aboard the ship."

And she would do it, too. Mama always got her way.

Odalie lowered her eyes. Always? No, not really. Papa had not broken off his liason with Peggy Cavanaugh. And he had paid for Shannon's education, Mama had said so. Papa, soft-spoken and courteous to Mama, had nevertheless kept one part of his life free from Mama's interference. Without raising her eyes to look at Mama, Odalie said softly, "I can't marry anyone but Bruce because—because I already belong to him."

Mama's dark eyes widened. She came to Odalie's side so swiftly that her full skirt brushed against the small table, causing the tiny china cups to rattle.

"Do you know what you're saying? Odalie, did Bruce—compromise you?"

Odalie began to tremble but stronger than fear, deeper than shame, was her need to remain here at Beau Rivage until Bruce returned to marry her. Otherwise, what would prevent Mama from concocting some dreadful lie that would cause her to lose Bruce forever? If Mama were to make it known that she was betrothed to one of those Frenchmen—even lie and say that she was married—

"Answer me," Mama demanded.

"It's true," Odalie said. "It happened the night before Bruce left. He wanted to marry me, but he couldn't take me along to California, and then to some mining camp. He said—" She searched her mind, trying to remember the words Bruce had written to her, to twist them to her own purpose. "He said he wanted me to belong to him, to be really his bride before he went away."

Mama's face had gone white. "Oh, you fool," she said. "You've ruined everything."

But Odalie felt a surge of triumph. Mama was beaten now. She had won. "So you see, I'll have to marry Bruce now. There's no use your sending me to Paris because—"

"Be still," Mama said. She gave Odalie a long,

appraising look. "How do I know you're telling the truth?" Odalie gave a small, startled cry. "There are ways of finding out. I don't suppose you know that." She turned and walked to the door.

"What are you going to do?"

"I'm going to send for Jincey," Mama said. "Jincey will know."

Jincey was a stooped, old black woman who was the midwife to the field and house workers alike. Even white ladies had sometimes called for her services, in difficult confinements. Fear clogged Odalie's throat. "Mama, you couldn't shame me so."

"You've shamed our family, haven't you?" She turned and gave Odalie a long, level look. "That's what you told me."

Odalie thought she was going to be sick. There was still time to deny her lie. But she would not. Jincey would confirm the story, and neither the old midwife nor Mama could know that not Bruce, but Craig Judson, had been responsible.

"Call Jincey, Mama."

"It is true, then," Mama said slowly. For the first time since she could remember, she saw her mother's shoulders slump forward slightly, saw the cold arrogance drain from her face.

"Are you going to have a baby?" she asked Odalie.

"No, Mama."

"You're sure?" And when Odalie remained silent, she asked her a few blunt questions, not bothering to choose her words with delicacy. Odalie answered in a low voice.

"No," her mother said. "You're not carrying Bruce's child." She began to pace the floor of the sittingroom, her full taffeta skirt rustling around her. The silence grew between them, until Odalie thought she would scream. Then her mother turned and faced her.

"Nothing has changed, then," she said. "You'll go to Paris as I planned. And you'll find a husband there. Lucienne will use her connections. If you haven't found one by spring, if you're still not engaged, I will come over and join you, and arrange matters. In the meantime, you will behave with discretion. Do you understand me?"

Odalie pressed her lips together. She had lied, had humiliated herself and slandered Bruce, and still Mama had not been swayed.

But she could not give in, not this time. Looking at her mother coldly, dispassionately, Odalie saw her for what she was: an unscrupulous woman, bent on gaining her own ends no matter who got hurt in the process. Right now, she wanted to get Odalie out of the house and far away from Beau Rivage at all costs so that she could be with the handsome, young artist, Edward Sutherland.

She would not marry him. She would never forget her background and breeding to that degree. But she would have a fling with him, and she did not want her daughter's glowing, youthful beauty to form an unwelcome contrast with her own maturity.

Maybe I should feel sorry for her, Odalie thought. *Papa didn't make her happy, and now she's reaching out for what she can get.* But Odalie could feel little compassion for a woman who would push her own daughter into a loveless marriage. If only Bruce would come back quickly.

"Why must Aunt Lucienne and I go to New Orleans to get a ship?" Odalie asked. "Why can't we wait here in Mobile?"

"New Orleans is a larger port. More ships sail from there, bound all over the world," Mama said impatiently. "You and your aunt will have excellent accommodations."

Odalie remained silent, her mind working feverishly. Ships bound all over the world. Not only to France but to California. To San Francisco, itself.

Bruce had probably left San Francisco for the Comstock shortly after he had written her the letter she had received today, but he had added a postscript, telling her that if she could manage to write to him, she was to address her mail to the hotel where he had been staying. If she could get out to San Francisco, she could find Bruce through the forwarding address he had left at the hotel.

California was so far away, and it frightened Odalie to think of making such a journey alone. Or would she be alone? Emmy was going along to New Orleans as her personal maid. Would the girl agree to go with her to California, instead of to Paris? California was a free state. There was no slavery out there, and surely that should be an inducement.

Then her heart sank, as she thought of how difficult it would be to give Mama the slip, to somehow get hold of her ticket and cash it in for a ticket to California.

"You're very quiet, Odalie. I hope you're beginning to realize what a wicked thing you have done. Surely, you should feel some shame. You, a Duval, behaving like some fancy girl down on the Mobile waterfront."

Odalie spoke softly, her eyes fixed on her folded hands. "I'm ashamed, Mama. And I'm—sorry. I don't know how I could have done such a dreadful thing. It was only that Bruce was going away." She fumbled for a tiny, lace-trimmed handkerchief, and turning her head away, she dabbed at her eyes.

"Now, Odalie, it's no use your crying. You're fortunate, all things considered. If he had left you with—in an embarassing condition—you'd be far worse off."

Odalie noticed that Mama was no longer speaking in the blunt, forthright way she had, only a little while ago. She had regained her poise, sure that Odalie would submit, however unwillingly. And Odalie would do all she could to build on that assumption, for Mama did not really want to go to New Orleans. She wanted to remain right here at Beau Rivage, so that she could send for Mr. Sutherland at once.

"Mama, even if I do meet a gentleman in Paris, one who is attracted to me—"

"You'll meet dozens," Mama said quickly. "You cannot imagine the kind of social life that you will find in Paris now, with Louis Napoleon and Eugénie setting the pace. There will be costume balls, visits to the opera, the theater, rides around the lake in the Bois de Boulogne. You will be seen and admired."

"But even so, if a gentleman should become interested, I mean, if he should want to marry me, how could I—" Odalie drew a deep breath and held it, forcing a blush to her cheeks; it was a trick she had used before, and most effectively.

"What is it you're trying to ask me?" her mother demanded impatiently.

"If I were to marry someone else, wouldn't he know, or guess that I'm not—"

Mama smiled faintly. "Not if you're clever. I will tell you what to do. After all, you're not the first girl who has made one foolish mistake."

During the next two days, Odalie did everything possible to convey the impression that although she still loved Bruce, she was resigned to her mother's plans for her. She even asked a few questions about Paris, and both Mama and Aunt Lucienne painted glowing pictures of the city.

"Octavia LeVert went there recently," Mama said. "She told me that the fashionable Parisian women now change their clothes five or six times a day, that the dresses are all quite splendid. Brocades from Lyons. Court gowns of satin and velvet, trimmed with Brussels lace. And the great new department stores— we have nothing like them here in the South. Le Louvre. Au Bon Marché. Everything under one roof, with the prices marked. Even a shopgirl can be smartly dressed in Paris."

"And the fine new restaurants," Aunt Lucienne said wistfully. "How I have missed the cuisine of France."

Odalie pretended to listen, and to be fascinated. So that, when it was time to leave, Mama conceded that Odalie and Aunt Lucienne might travel to New Orleans without her.

"I've a great deal to see to right here," Mama said. "The repairs on the old overseer's cottage—"

Her mind was already on providing a comfortable place for Edward Sutherland to stay, while he was at Beau Rivage. And although Odalie could not plan too far ahead, although she knew she would have to seize her opportunity to escape from Aunt Lucienne whenever she could, still, she was looking forward to the trip to New Orleans.

Somewhere in that port city, she would find a ship traveling to California. She might have to go by way of Panama or Nicaragua, or around Cape Horn, but she would get there. And when she did, Bruce would be waiting for her.

16

THE HIRED CARRIAGE drew away from the wharf, but although Shannon peered eagerly through the window, to get her first look at San Francisco, the swirling fog dimmed her view, so that she could get only a confused impression of warehouses, saloons, and crowds of people, mostly men. Here and there, the flare of a gaslamp picked out the gilt lettering on a board sign: the Bella Union, the Arcade Saloon, the El Dorado.

The voyage had taken only a little over two weeks, aboard the fast Pacific Mail steamer, and the cabin that Shannon had shared with Adam, although small, had been far more comfortable than her squalid, crowded quarters aboard the *Lively Bess*. Nevertheless, although she had made the voyage from Mobile to Colón without a single bout of seasickness, on this last trip, she had suffered from spells of queasiness early each morning, and on toward afternoon she had become so drowsy that she often retired to the cabin for a nap. The queasy spells always passed after a walk on deck and by breakfast time she found that she had worked up an unusually sharp appetite. Adam, watching her get dressed before their departure from the steamer, had said, "You're going to get as plump as your Aunt Kate if you're not careful."

Although she had glared at him, she had been forced to admit privately that she had filled out. She laced her stays with some difficulty, even with Adam's assistance, her blue silk dress, donned in honor of her landing in San Francisco, felt tight around the waist and it pulled across the breasts. She wrapped her light shawl around her, hoping that it would help to conceal her opulent new curves.

"You'll need a warm cloak," Adam said. "The city gets damp and chilly this time of year."

Now, although she was inside the closed carriage, she shivered slightly, and moved closer to Adam. He put an arm around her shoulders. She felt the hard swell of his muscles through the sleeve of his dark broadcloth coat. During the voyage, he had recovered his strength completely. His face was a deep, healthy tan again, his blue eyes clear and alert.

Adam had directed the driver to take them to the Lick House at the corner of Montgomery and Sutter Streets.

"The place is named for the man who built it, James Lick," he explained. "He used to be a cabinetmaker, until he came to San Francisco and piled up a fortune speculating in real estate."

During the voyage, while Shannon had been resting in their cabin, Adam had spent his afternoons in the bar, playing poker and drinking with the other male passengers, and there he had picked up a wealth of information about present conditions in San Francisco.

"I think you'll find the hotel comfortable," Adam was saying now. "We'll have a good dinner, and then, tomorrow, we'll go out and have a look at the city. The last time I saw it, it was only a sleepy little Spanish settlement, Yerba Beuna, they called it. Now, it's—"

He broke off, as they heard the frantic tolling of bells. Shannon, peering through the fog, saw a reddish haze toward the direction of the waterfront, and caught the smell of burning timber.

A moment later, the driver forced the carriage to one side of the narrow street, as a team of three horses came pounding toward them at full speed.

"Another damn fire," the man shouted furiously. The heavy, cumbersome fire engine scraped against the side of their carriage, so that it swayed and tilted dangerously and Shannon was thrown against Adam.

The reddish haze grew brighter, until it lit up the misty sky. The cab driver got down to quiet the nervous horse.

"Wait here," Adam said, and when he opened the door, the sharp, acrid smell of smoke and charred wood was stronger. The street was crowded now, with men running in the direction of the waterfront, dark shapes in the fog, their boots pounding on the board sidewalks.

Shannon pressed her handkerchief to her face, coughing. The firebells continued to clang furiously. A few moments later, Adam climbed back into the carriage and the driver started off again. Gas lamps made wavering blurs in the fog.

"The driver says it isn't a bad fire, as they go," Adam told her. "They have a good many of them here."

"I don't wonder," Shannon said. "If the city's growing as fast as you say, and the buildings are still jerry-built, many of them—"

"That's part of it, but not all," Adam said. "The driver told me these fires don't start by accident in every case."

"But who would set a fire on purpose?" Shannon asked.

"There's profit in it," Adam explained. "San Francisco's had more than its share of lawlessness since gold was discovered back in '49. Criminals who were transported from England to the penal colonies in Australia. True, some of them are rehabilitated and become solid citizens out there. But a lot of them escape, or break their parole, and come back across the Pacific. San Francisco's the first big port of call, so they settle down here, and go right back to their old trades."

"But what reason do they have for setting fires? I don't see—"

"A fire can cover up a robbery. A warehouse catches fire, everyone runs to watch, and in the meantime, the Sidney Ducks loot every other warehouse in the vicinity." She looked at him anxiously and he said, "Nothing for you to worry about, sweetheart. We won't be staying here long."

"You intend to leave for the Comstock right away?"

"That's the idea. It'll be rough going this time of

year but we'll make it. I've crossed the Sierras before. I know what route to take."

The cab drew up before the hotel, and Adam helped Shannon down. When they entered the hotel lobby, she was impressed by the marble floors, the polished mahogany woodwork, the fine plush sofas and sparkling crystal chandeliers.

"It isn't very crowded for such a large hotel, is it?" she remarked to Adam, as he was signing the register. The high-ceilinged lobby had a deserted look.

The desk clerk, overhearing her, said, "That's only because so many of the gentlemen have gone off to see the fire. Nothing for you to worry about, ma'am. There's not much wind tonight. The fire won't spread this far." He stroked his mustache with a complacent look. "Now, back in '49 and '51, we had some really bad fires. In '51, we had twenty-two blocks burned out. Fire went on for two days. That was in May, as I recall. Then, in June of that same year, we had another blaze. A bad one. The authorities arrested a suspect—one of that Sydney-Town bunch—but they let him go on a technicality, if you can call it that."

"I don't understand," Shannon said.

"Politicians, judges working hand in glove with the worst element in the city. That was when the decent citizens got together and formed the Vigilante Committee." Then, he added, "We've had lots of fires since, though. Only last year—"

"You sound proud of those fires," Adam interrupted, with a trace of a smile.

"Oh, no indeed, sir. Not of the fires. But let me tell you, as fast as San Francisco burns, why, we build it right up again, bigger and better than before. Lots of new buildings going up all the time."

Shannon, tired and hungry, wished that the desk clerk would cut his talk short, but Adam was leaning on the desk, his blue eyes alert, obviously deeply interested.

"This is no mining town, not any more. Men are bringing out their wives, making fortunes in the Comstock, building fine new houses. If you and your wife take a drive out to Fern Hill—Nob Hill, some are starting to call it—you'll see mansions as elegant as any in the East."

He broke off. "Sorry to be going on this way. You and your wife will be wanting to go upstairs and rest before dinner, no doubt."

Adam had signed the register Mr. and Mrs. Kincaid, but although she was grateful to him for sparing her embarrassment, she also suspected that perhaps he had done it for the sake of expediency, since they were to share one suite.

"I'm sure you'll find our meals to your liking," the clerk added, motioning to the bell captain. "Our dining room's an exact replica of the dining hall of the Palace of Versailles."

As Shannon passed the entrance to the dining room, which was flanked by pillars of Italian marble, she caught a glimpse of colorful murals, inlaid wood floor of intricate design, and great mirrors with carved rosewood frames.

Although many of the hotel's guests had gone off to see the fire, there were still a number of diners for whom a good meal was more interesting. The men outnumbered the women, but Shannon noticed that those members of her own sex who sat at the tables were wearing skirts of taffeta and velvet over enormous crinolines; and she was aware that her pale blue silk, which had looked so elegant back in Panama City, was somewhat inappropriate for San Francisco in December.

The bell captain led Adam and Shannon up the broad, winding staircase, and, when they were settled in their two-room suite, and he had left them, Shannon sank down on a magnificent sofa of purple plush, enchanted by the luxury around her. "Adam, it's beautiful, but isn't it expensive?"

He did not answer, and she saw that he made no move to take off his coat, to go into the bedroom to get ready for dinner. Instead, he opened one of the tall windows and stood looking out. Cool, damp air filled the room.

"I'm hungry," Shannon said. "Can we go down to dinner soon?"

He did not answer, but remained standing at the window, his back to her, his hands thrust into the pockets of his coat. He did not seem to be aware of her presence.

"I hope the blue silk will be suitable. It's the only decent dress I have left. The ladies in the diningroom all looked so splendid. Those enormous crinolines—"

Still, he paid no attention to her and, irritated by his indifference, she rose and went into the bedroom.

"At least I can have hot water for washing," she said. "I'll do my hair the way you like it."

It was a relief to take off the blue silk, for it really was too tight; her breasts tingled and felt slightly swollen. She would have appreciated Adam's help in undoing her stays, but since he was so remote and silent, she decided, with some annoyance, to manage by herself.

But after she had washed with the scented soap and dried herself on the huge, soft towel, after she had put on her wrapper, she could not keep from calling to him.

"What a wonderful place." She flung herself down on the wide, soft bed, reveling in the sheer physical comfort of her new surroundings. If the dining room had been modeled on that in the Palace of Versailles, she thought, the rest of the hotel was no less palatial. Deep, heavy rugs, a full-length mirror, spotless, freshly ironed linen on the bed.

She stood up, went to the mirror, and opened her wrapper. Not only had she gained back the weight that she had lost while caring for Adam in Panama City, but there were lush new curves to her body.

Adam came striding into the bedroom, looked at her appreciatively, then, coming up behind her, he put his arms around her and cupped her breasts, his fingers tightening, caressing. He pushed aside the heavy, tawny-gold masses of her hair, and pressed his mouth to the side of her throat. She felt the familiar warmth in her loins, the aching need that still made her feel ashamed. But stronger than shame was her desire for Adam.

Back in Panama City, after he had recovered from the fever, and then later, in their cabin aboard the steamer, he had taken her fiercely, passionately, as if he could never get enough of her. Now she began to tremble with anticipation. The bed was so wide and inviting. But all at once, he released her and moved away. "You'll have to restrain yourself for awhile, my love," he said, and there was mockery in his eyes. Had she been too bold, too quickly responsive? She turned away, not wanting him to see the disappointment, the hurt that must be showing in her face.

"I'd better dress for dinner," she said, trying to sound cool and remote, and not succeeding too well. "I should be wearing velvet or taffeta, but the silk—"

"We're not going down to the dining room, so there's no need for you to dress."

"But what are you—"

"I'm going out. Don't worry, sweetheart, you won't starve. I'll have a tray sent up."

"I'm not hungry."

"Don't sulk," he said briskly. "I'll be back as soon as I can."

"But on our first night here?"

"I have to find Fergus Mackenzie. I'll try the newspaper office first."

She turned away abruptly. Nothing had changed since Panama City. No doubt he'd spend half the night in a saloon playing poker with Mackenzie. He could not even spare the time to have dinner with her. After the heavy, uninspired food aboard the steamer, she had been looking forward to the fine cuisine of San Francisco.

But Adam was strapping on his gun belt, checking the Navy colt, loading it. She thought of what he had told her about the Sydney Ducks, the criminal element that infested the city. "Adam, please stay here with me." And, when he did not answer, her voice took on an edge of sarcasm. "I'm sure they have a bar here in the hotel, and at least one poker game going on."

She stopped short, remembering their violent quarrel that night in Panama City, when she had complained about being left alone. "You sound like a wife," he had said. As if reminding her of her place in his life.

Now, however, he did not seem angry. He kissed her lightly, and added, "Don't wait up, Shannon."

Then, before she realized it, he was out the door.

The tray was sent up, as he had promised, and in spite of her disappointment at being left alone, her uneasiness over Adam's safety in this lawless, unfamiliar city, she found that she had a sharp appetite. The onion soup, laced with Burgundy, smelled delicious, and her mouth watered at the sight of the crisp roasted duck with cherry sauce, the small silver dishes of baked mushrooms and potatoes in cream.

Adam had warned her that she would become as plump as Aunt Kate if she continued to eat so heartily. But she was always hungry lately. She put down her spoon with a clattering sound.

During those days when she had been sharing the cabin on the *Lively Bess* with Clarisse and those other girls, she had learned a great deal about matters that had been hidden from her before. She pushed away the soup dish. No, it wasn't possible. But her unusual appetite, her queasiness early in the morning, her drowsiness in the middle of the afternoon. The changes in her body. She made a few swift calculations. And she knew. Maybe she had known for some time but had hidden the truth from herself.

I'm going to have a baby. Adam's baby.

At first she felt a warm joy coursing through her. She loved Adam, and now she was carrying his child.

But her happiness ebbed away. Adam did not want a child, or a wife. Not now, not ever. He had told her so on more than one occasion. He wanted to be free to come and go as he pleased.

He had promised to stay with her, to share with her the fortune in silver that he was sure he would find here in the West. But he had never promised to marry her. She went to the window, and stood looking down at the busy intersection of Montgomery and Sutter Streets. But her mind was not on the view.

Like all the other men who had joined the stampede to the Comstock, Adam planned to leave for Nevada as soon as possible. Even under ordinary conditions, the journey across the Sierras would be difficult for a woman. For her, in her present condition, it would be impossible. And, if she could not go, Adam would leave her behind. Knowing the ruthless determination that was a part of him, she had no illusions that he would give up his chance at a fortune to remain with her.

She pushed aside the heavy, plum-colored velvet draperies and stared down at the street, where carriages rumbled past and men jostled one another in their hurry to get to see the fire, or perhaps, she thought bitterly, only to find a convenient saloon. Or a parlor house. Was Adam making the rounds of the saloons with Mackenzie, and would they later go to one of those dreadful places?

Aunt Kate used to say that any man, married or single, craved variety, and she had admitted that Jethro often went out to find a girl in one of Mobile's concert saloons. But, Shannon told herself, she had done everything to please Adam. Maybe her willingness had become cloying to him.

And, with advancing pregnancy, she would become less attractive. He might not want her at all.

There were ways of ending a pregnancy. Clarisse and the other girls aboard the *Lively Bess* had spared her none of the details. It was a painful, dangerous process, getting rid of an unwanted child.

But I want Adam's baby, Shannon told herself. *Even if he doesn't.* She shivered and folded her arms across her body in a protective gesture.

Then, returning to the small table where her dinner was growing cool, she forced herself to eat, but she might as well have been eating Aunt Kate's fatty ham and coarse cornbread.

The noise from the street did not lessen; indeed, the uproar in San Francisco got louder and more boisterous as the night wore on. At last, she went to the wide bed and lay down across it, burying her face in the soft pillow, longing to have Adam lying beside her.

Adam did not come back that night and when Shannon awoke the following morning, he still had not returned. But the fog had cleared and sunlight streamed in through the windows. December in San Francisco was like fall back in Boston, she thought; a crisp nip in the air, but no bone-chilling cold.

She dressed and went downstairs to the lobby. Each time the door opened, she felt the air, cool and bracing, delightful after the cloying heat of Panama. She wanted to go out for a walk, to explore the city by daylight, but from the interested and openly admiring glances of the men in the lobby, she decided that it might not be wise for her to go strolling about alone. Instead, she went to the desk, bought a copy of the *Alta California,* and found a chair in an inconspicuous corner. She put the newspaper up in front of her to ward off the unwanted attentions of the men who were strolling around the lobby or moving toward the dining room.

Then she tried to concentrate on the news. She read a long and disturbing article about the execution of John Brown. With a small band of men, he had raided the arsenal at Harper's Ferry in Virginia, hoping to capture the building and use it as a base for starting a slave insurrection. He had been tried, found guilty of murder, insurrection and treason against the Commonwealth of Virginia, and, on December second, he had been hanged.

Shannon remembered Adam's talk of a coming war. Mackenzie, too, had said that a war was likely. She knew that the Southern planters had always feared a mass uprising among their slaves, and now they were denouncing Brown's raid as part of a widespread plot, fomented by the Republicans in the North. Northern moderates had deplored the raid as a rash, lawless action. But many distinguished men— Emerson, Thoreau, Longfellow—had hailed John Brown as a martyr to the cause of abolition.

Shannon understood little of politics, but all at once, she found herself thinking of what a war between the North and the South would mean to those she knew. Odalie Duval, safe and comfortable at Beau Rivage. Odalie, waiting for Bruce to return and marry her. Antoinette Duval, who had driven her from

Mobile. And what about Aunt Kate? She and Jethro owned no slaves, but a war would touch their lives, and change them, all the same. Back in the tavern, Shannon had heard many Southerners who did not own slaves speaking out fiercely against the abolitionist movement.

Although she kept the paper up in front of her, her eyes wandered from one item to the other, and she was unable to concentrate.

If Adam left her when he learned about the baby, Aunt Kate would be her only refuge. But how could Aunt Kate protect her from Uncle Jethro? Although the marks of the beating had long since disappeared, she would never forget the horror of it. She remembered how she had crouched on the bed, half-naked, trying to burrow into the mattress as the heavy belt had descended. How she had screamed like a tortured animal. No, she could not go back to the tavern.

I could leave Adam, she thought, *I could find work as a seamstress here in San Francisco. It's such a big city, I'm sure there are positions open. And I could pass myself off as a widow. I could—*

"Why, Shannon, how flattering."

The voice was familiar, and when she lowered the newspaper, she recognized the speaker, Fergus Mackenzie. "Perhaps you're so engrossed in something I've written for the paper. . . . " he was saying, but she hardly listened. For Adam was with him. Freshly shaven and barbered, his blue eyes alert, he did not look like a man who had spent the night carousing. He carried a large shiny box under his arm. It was tied with a wide, pink satin ribbon.

Even if she had had the courage to tell Adam about

her news at once, it would have been impossible with
Mackenzie there. She felt herself go hot, then cold,
felt her palms beginning to perspire. She found it
difficult to look at Adam, much less to speak to him,
but he did not seem to notice her confusion for he
had news of his own.

In the huge diningroom, over a breakfast of ham,
eggs, wheatcakes, coffee and pastries, Adam made
his startling announcement. "We won't be going to
Nevada, Shannon. Not for a long time."

"But all along you've been saying—"

"I've changed my mind. I've bought a lumberyard
here in San Francisco. There are living quarters over
the offices. We'll be moving there tonight, so you'd
better enjoy all this luxury while you can."

She looked at him in bewilderment. He laughed and
Mackenzie grinned. "Once he makes up his mind
Adam doesn't waste any time going after what he
wants," the reporter said.

"But you— Are you telling me you came all the
way from Mobile, to buy a lumberyard here?"

"That's right," Adam said calmly, attacking his
breakfast with relish. "It took nearly every cent I had,
but it was a bargain at that. The fellow who owned it
couldn't wait to start out for the Comstock."

"But all the way from Panama, you were talking
about the Comstock, too. About making a fortune in
silver."

"True enough. But last night, that fire, and then
our talk with the desk clerk gave me other ideas."

"I don't understand. If there have been so many
fires here, surely a lumberyard is a risky investment. It
could go up like a torch, the next time a fire breaks

out, by accident, or if those—those Sydney Ducks, those convicts you told me about were to—"

"It's risky," Adam said. He poured a cup of coffee, and gave her a reassuring smile. "I think I can take care of my property. Even if it means hiring a few extra watchmen who are handy with guns. It's a sound investment, Shannon. Remember what the clerk said. No matter how often this city burns, the people start rebuilding at once, bigger and better than before."

"And that's not all," Mackenzie said. There were a few lines around his eyes, a little puffiness, but although he lacked Adam's boundless energy, he apparently had caught some of his enthusiasm. "Adam kept me up all night, pumping me for every bit of information about lumbering and lumberyards around the city. It's a sound idea, Shannon, believe me. Think of the expansion that's going on here. New sidewalks, new buildings, new wharfs. And then, in the mining country, they're screaming for lumber for timbering shafts and tunnels, for building dams, flumes, sluices. Adam'll be needing his own sawmill later on, and maybe a few ships to carry the wood from the redwood country down here to the city, but he'll make a fortune. He knows the business, been at it since he was a boy, from what he's told me."

She could scarcely take it all in, except for one fact: Adam would not be leaving for the Comstock. He would be staying right here in San Francisco. She would not have to tell him that she was pregnant, not right away, because he would not be setting out across the Sierras. But sooner or later, she reminded herself, he would have to know.

"Try these wheatcakes," he urged. He piled a few on her plate. "And the syrup. You wouldn't think it, Mackenzie, but Shannon has an appetite like a lumberjack's."

"I don't want anything. Only coffee."

He shook his head. "Women," he said to Mackenzie. "All the way up the coast, she was looking forward to the restaurants here. Now, she's getting finicky. I suppose at that fancy girl's school, they taught her that a hearty appetite is unladylike."

Mackenzie gave Shannon a swift, appraising look, his shrewd brown eyes speculative. "That's enough," he said quietly. Then, "Shannon, are you feeling all right?"

"Yes—no—oh, leave me alone." She stood up so quickly that her chair tipped over, lifted the skirt of her blue silk dress and fled upstairs to the suite. But Adam caught up with her outside the door.

"What the devil's wrong with you?" he demanded. She would not answer and they went inside. He closed the door behind them. He still carried the beribboned box.

"I think you'd better explain. Running out of the dining room like a scalded cat."

"Get out," she said. She wasn't ready to tell him about the baby, not yet. Not like this.

"Is it because I bought the lumberyard without asking your advice? What do you know about business —you, or any female? If you're afraid you won't get your half, you needn't be. Silver mining's not the only way to make a fortune out here. Don't worry, you'll be able to go back to Mobile in style. That's what you want, isn't it?"

"You don't know anything about me, or what I want."

"I know you were complaining last night, because you didn't have a fashionable wardrobe to go sashaying around the city in." He thrust the box into her hands. "Here. This should do for now."

She took the box automatically. "But how did you know the size—and—"

"I didn't. Miss Delphine said it would be right. One of her girls is about your size. Don't worry, it's never been worn."

Shannon looked at him, an ugly suspicion forming in her mind. "Who is Miss Delphine? What kind of girls—"

"What kind do you think? Miss Delphine runs a parlor house over on Pike Street. Mackenzie wasn't at the newspaper office so I had to go there to track him down."

She felt her face begin to burn.

"Damn it, half the business in San Francisco is transacted in places like Delphine's. She's a friend of Mackenzie's."

He went over to the plush sofa and sat down. "Now, why don't you try it on and then come back downstairs? We don't have much time today. I want to go over to the lumberyard. Go on, what are you waiting for?"

He had bought a dress for her from a parlor-house girl. She would not let herself speculate on what else he had done there last night. Anger welled up in her, and she threw the box at him, as hard as she could. But he moved aside quickly and it struck the wall, then rebounded onto the carpet, the ribbons slipping off, the lid falling open, so that she saw the billowing skirt of honey-colored velvet, the lace and velvet bodice. Even a glance told her that the dress was expensive, that it was new and fashionable. But she did not care. Tears of hurt and rage streamed down her cheeks.

"Stop it," he said harshly. "I told you when we first got together that I wouldn't put up with your sulking and your tantrums. I meant it."

"Then get out," she sobbed. "Go to your lumberyard—or your—your—Miss Delphine."

He laughed. "You needn't be jealous of her. She's old enough to be my mother. And as for the girls, what would I want with them when—"

"Go on, why don't you say it? You don't need to go to one of those places because you've got me right here, any time you want me."

"Good Lord, Shannon, I didn't mean— I could never think of you that way. Now calm down, and get hold of yourself. And try to listen to reason. You may not like the idea of living over a lumberyard office. The rooms there aren't much. Nothing like this. But you'll be a hell of a lot better off here in San Francisco this winter, than in some shack in a mining camp." When she did not answer, he lost control of his temper once more. "All right, then. If you won't listen to reason, if you've got this Comstock fever, I'm sure you'll be able to find yourself some man who'll be glad to take you along with him."

"Not now," she said.

"Why not?"

"Because I'm going to have a baby."

He got to his feet. "You're sure?"

She nodded. "I guess I suspected it for the last few weeks, but now I'm sure."

Adam thrust his hands into his pockets. There was a long silence. Her heart began to beat in an odd, irregular way, and she was afraid to look at Adam's face.

Then he said quietly, "Pick up the dress. Now."

Although he did not raise his voice, there was something in the tone that made it impossible for her to refuse. She dropped to her knees and gathered up the voluminous folds of velvet and lace. "Now, put it on." When she hesitated, he came to her and took her in his arms, crushing the dress between them. "It's not the right color for a wedding dress, but it'll have to do. You're not used to the San Francisco climate, and I don't relish the idea of your catching cold on our wedding night."

She thought of what it would mean to be married to Adam. She loved him. She had known it since that terrible day in Panama City, when he had been close to death and the doctor had tried to persuade her to leave Adam, to send him to the fever camp.

She could be Adam's wife now, Mrs. Kincaid, safe, respectable. And her baby would be safe, too; it would never know the shame that she had known.

"You're going to marry me, Shannon," Adam said.

"I can't, not this way. I can't let you marry me out of pity. Or a feeling of obligation."

"Pity? I don't pity you. Pity is for fools and weaklings, and you're neither. As for my sense of obligation, nothing can change that." He released her, and added, "Now, go and get ready. Mackenzie should know where we can get married without delay."

"I haven't said I'd marry you."

"No, but you will. You've still got a head filled with romantic nonsense, but when the chips are down, you do what you have to. You did, back in Colón, the night you agreed to stay with me. And you will this time." He cupped her face in his hands, and his mouth covered hers, lightly at first, then harder, forcing her lips apart. A swift, hot hunger rose inside her, sweeping away her doubts. She moaned softly as his tongue explored her mouth. A moment later, he let her go. "I'll wait for you downstairs," he said. "Don't be long."

After he had left her, she stood staring first at the door through which he'd gone, then down at the dress. A dress bought from the madam of a fancy house.

"My wedding dress," she said. She knew that she should be outraged, but her lips were still warm from Adam's kiss. Her cheeks still felt the touch of his fingers.

She tried to tell herself that she was going through with the marriage only for the sake of the child she carried within her, but she knew better. She wanted to be Adam's wife, and if he offered only passion, not love, she would take him on his terms.

17

IT WAS LATE on a sunny afternoon in May, and Shannon, seated in the parlor of the living quarters over the lumberyard office, was scarcely aware of the now-familiar sounds from below: the teamsters, shouting to one another, the rattling of the wagon wheels, as cargoes of planks and shingles were brought into the yard and set down, with a loud clatter. During the five months that she and Adam had been here, she had become used to these noises; indeed, she had begun to find them homelike and comforting.

She looked around at the small, low-ceilinged parlor with satisfaction, pleased that she had been able to make it look inviting and respectable, if not luxurious. Not that she had done it all. Adam had forbidden her to do any heavy work, and had sent up a couple of men from the yard to clear out the collection of junk left by the previous owner: rusted tools, kegs of nails, oily rags. He had also ordered his workmen to wax the floors and wash the windows, and to carry in and arrange the inexpensive furniture, at Shannon's direction. However, she had busied herself by sewing curtains of turkey-red calico, and cushions covered with the same bright fabric, for the sofa and chairs. For the baby, she sewed high-necked, long-sleeved dresses of nainsook and cambric, decorating them with delicate embroidery.

Adam, coming upstairs from the lumberyard one evening, and seeing her at work on one of these small dresses, had asked, "How many of those things can one baby wear?" But his voice was gentle, affectionate, and she thought that she caught a look of pleasure in his eyes.

During the early months of their marriage, Shannon knew that he was working hard to make a success of the new business. And his work was paying off handsomely, for, as Mackenzie had told him, lumber was in great demand in San Francisco, and in the mining country as well. One sunny afternoon, he took her out to the North Beach section, a district about a mile north and west of the city. "I'm buying land here for a sawmill," he told her. "And after that, I'm going to buy a wharf."

Although the money began to come in quickly, he was putting much of it back into the business. "I want a schooner of my own, to bring the lumber down from Mendocino County. Shannon, you never saw such trees. One of them is enough to provide lumber for six houses. And there are thousands of redwoods up there. And beyond them, in Oregon, there's fir and pine."

But although he was engrossed in his new business, and worked long hours, making frequent trips up to the timber country, he managed to spend some time with Shannon. She discovered that he was tireless, that he could return from a trip to Mendocino, changing from his rough red flannel shirt and jeans to a starched shirt and a broadcloth suit, and take her off to a good restaurant, or to the theater.

One evening, to her delight, he took her to Tom Maguire's Opera House to hear the celebrated singer, Elisa Biscaccianti, who had recently returned from a triumphant tour of Europe. Although Shannon had no way of knowing if Adam really liked the performance of the coloratura, who sang the arias from Italian operas, then finished her performance with a rendition of "Home Sweet Home," she was pleased that he had thought to take her to the performance. Never once had he made a sarcastic remark about Shannon's finishing-school education, which had enabled her to appreciate such performances to the fullest.

Shannon suspected that the minstrel shows, an important part of San Francisco's entertainment, were more to Adam's liking; and she enjoyed those, too. And the sensational melodramas of Boucicault, which caused Shannon to fumble in her reticule for her handkerchief, to Adam's amusement.

But although Adam took her to the theater, when he could spare the time from business, he drew the line at the melodeons. "They're not too different from the Cherokee Rose, back in Mobile," he told her firmly.

"Fergus Mackenzie told me that the Bella Union offered a performance of a drama based on *Dombey and Son,* by Mr. Dickens," she reminded him.

"It has a lot of other entertainment that's a far cry

from anything of Mr. Dickens'," Adam retorted. "It's no place for a lady."

She was moved by his protective attitude, but she could not resist saying, "Adam, you used to tease me about wanting to be respectable, remember. That day at the tavern, you said—"

"Never mind what I said," he told her. "You weren't my wife, then."

As her pregnancy advanced, and Adam became increasingly obsessed by his expanding business, he was often away, and she felt a growing sense of isolation. True, whenever he had to go up to the lumber camps, he asked Mackenzie to drop in to make sure that she was all right, and to find out if she needed anything, but although she came to enjoy the reporter's lively, if cynical, conversation, she sometimes wished that she had a woman friend to talk to. She was not afraid of having a baby, Adam's baby, but she would have liked to discuss her condition with an older, more experienced member of her own sex.

If only Aunt Kate could be with her. She had written to her aunt, telling her of the marriage, and her pregnancy, and her aunt had replied in a short, badly spelled but welcome letter, full of congratulations and affection. But Kate was back in Mobile, still living in the tavern with Jethro, and Shannon was often lonely.

As her pregnancy progressed, Adam's lovemaking became infrequent and constrained. Was he afraid of hurting her, she wondered, or was he simply uninterested? *I can't blame him for not wanting me now,* she thought ruefully.

Now, sitting at the parlor window, she was surprised

to hear footsteps on the flight of wooden stairs that ran up the side of the building to the rooms on the second story. Adam had left the previous afternoon, saying that he would be back this evening. His foreman had been having trouble with the equipment in the sawmill, and he wanted to be sure it was properly repaired. It wasn't Mackenzie climbing the stairs. These were the light, tapping steps of a woman, and, as she rose and leaned out the window to get a better look, she caught a flash of purple taffeta and green ostrich plumes.

"Clarisse!" Shannon exclaimed, opening the door. "How long have you been in San Francisco? How did you find me? Oh, it's so good to see you."

Clarisse kissed Shannon warmly, then took a seat.

"I've been here for the last couple of months," Clarisse said. "I saw Adam last night at the Bella Union. I'm working there now. He came backstage and told me where you two were living. He couldn't stay long, though. He was on his way down to the waterfront, looking for some kind of machinery."

"But he did have time to stop at the Bella Union," Shannon said, feeling a twinge of uneasiness.

"Oh, honey, he saw my name on the bill outside, and dropped in to say hello. I'm a headliner now, Shannon. Songs, dances, dramatic skits."

"I'll make some tea," Shannon said. "Or would you rather have coffee?"

"Coffee, but wait a minute. Did I say something wrong?"

"No. I'm pleased for you, Clarisse, truly I am. Only—I didn't expect Adam to be at a melodeon last night."

"Now look here," Clarisse said. "You ought to know that you can't keep too tight a rein on a man like Adam. Tell you the truth, I never thought he'd marry at all. Not the type."

"I know," Shannon said quietly. "When we got to San Francisco—that was back last December, and he found out about the baby—he felt he had to marry me because of Panama City, and my taking care of him when he had the fever, and so—"

"You'll have to fill me in," Clarisse said, cutting off her words. "The last I saw of you, you were getting ready to leave La Ceiba and run out into the pouring rain, rather than face him. Honey, you looked like you were scared of him."

"I was." Shannon smiled. "I guess I still am, sometimes. But I had no choice."

"What happened?" Clarisse demanded. "Tell me everything."

Shannon went first to the kitchen to prepare coffee, then, over steaming cups of the rich, dark brew, she told Clarisse something of the events leading to their present meeting. Some of the details were far too personal to share, even with Clarisse. And some were too painful. She still hated to remember those terrible days when Adam had lain close to death in Panama City.

Clarisse listened avidly, the plumes on her purple taffeta bonnet nodding from time to time, her eyes warm with interest. And, when Shannon had finished, she said,

"So now you have a rich, handsome husband and a baby on the way."

Rich, Shannon thought. *Yes, I suppose he is.*

"Most of his profits are going into expanding the business, but we're quite comfortable," she added quickly. "Adam's been generous with me."

"Aren't you glad you went over and talked to him that day at La Ceiba, instead of running off like a scared rabbit?"

"Yes, I am. Only—"

"You don't sound awfully sure." Clarisse poured cream into her coffee and added two teaspoons of sugar, stirring the hot brew. "Shannon, you're not still in love with Bruce, are you?"

"Bruce? Oh, no. It's Adam I love. There'll never be anyone else for me. Only—I never know what he's thinking. He gets moody, sometimes, and draws away, into himself."

"I guess I know what you mean," Clarisse said. "When he was talking to me backstage he started telling me how you'd fixed this place up. He said it was the first real home he'd had since he'd lived with his folks back in Ohio. So, I asked him about his family. Where in Ohio they'd had their farm and— he shut up, just like that. And he looked—his eyes were like ice and—I don't know—it was like I'd asked something terrible. Right after that, he left."

"His parents are dead," Shannon said. "They died when he was a boy."

"How did it happen?"

Shannon told her briefly, then added, "When Adam was so ill back in Panama City, he talked about it. He was delirious, but I—I think it must have been horrible for him."

Clarisse nodded sympathetically. "Maybe if you

could get him to talk about it, when he wasn't out of his senses, I mean, it might help."

"No," Shannon said slowly. "I don't think he wants to talk about it. Not to anyone."

"You're his wife."

"I've told you, Clarisse, he only married me out of a feeling of obligation."

"I don't believe that. And even if it's true, men have been known to change. After the baby comes—"

"He doesn't care about the baby. He's never wanted anyone or anything that would tie him down."

"He hasn't said that, about not wanting the baby, has he?"

"No. He's kind and thoughtful, when he's here. He's gentle with me, but—I want something more, Clarisse."

"Now you listen to me, honey. A girl's got to make the best of what she gets. And it looks to me like you're going to get more than you ever hoped for. With his drive and ambition, Adam could end up rich as any of those Alabama cotton planters. You could have a house as fine as that place—what's it called— Beau Rivage."

"I suppose so," Shannon said. She told Clarisse about the wharf Adam had bought, the lumber schooner, the sawmill. "He's buying parcels of real estate out in the North Beach section, too. And he's been talking about buying a brickyard, because he says that one of these days, the people of San Francisco are going to decide that with all these fires, brick buildings are more practical than wooden ones. But there'll still be a demand for lumber, because they use so much of it out in the Comstock, and in the mines here in California, too."

She broke off. Then, abruptly she asked, "Clarisse, does Adam go to the Bella Union often?"

"How should I know? I've only been working there a few weeks. Suppose he does? Half the men in San Francisco drop into the Bella Union for a few drinks and a little entertainment."

"What kind of entertainment? He wouldn't take me there. He said—"

"Go on," Clarisse urged.

"He said it was no place for a lady." Shannon flushed, hoping that she had not offended Clarisse. But Clarisse gave her an impish grin. "He's right, honey. A melodeon ain't no Sunday school, that's for sure. The girls are expected to sell drinks between the acts, and there are little curtained boxes where a man can— But the Bella Union's got some of the top talent out here."

"Including you?" Shannon asked, unable to repress an answering smile.

"That's right. And I ain't going to stop with working in the melodeons. I'm taking singing lessons, and learning new dance steps and one of these days, I'm going to be in a show in a real theater here. Maguire's Opera House, maybe." She laughed. "Then you can come to see me perform."

"I'd love to," Shannon said. "You always said you'd make your fortune in San Francisco, and I'm sure you will. You look quite splendid already."

Clarisse smoothed the enormous skirt of her purple taffeta with a complacent look. Although newspapers had alternately ridiculed and condemned the new style, with its hoop-shaped whalebone framework, the hoop skirts had taken hold. They were somewhat impractical for the windy streets of San Francisco, where a sudden gust might tilt the hoop at an angle, giving the delighted male spectators a glimpse of embroidered petticoats and pantalettes.

Shannon sighed, and wondered how long it would be before she, too, could resume wearing fashionable dresses instead of those loose, flowing wrappers she had made for the last months of her pregnancy.

"I've got to be going now, honey," Clarisse said. "I've got a performance to give tonight."

"You'll come to see me again, though, won't you?"

"Every chance I get." She patted Shannon's shoulder. "And you remember what I told you. Give that man of yours a loose rein."

Clarisse kept her word, and she and Shannon spent many long afternoons together, sipping coffee, while Clarisse regaled her with the gossip of the theater. "San Francisco's a great theater town," she was saying, late one afternoon in July. "It ain't all melodeons and minstrel shows. Edwin Booth played here, in *Hamlet* and *Romeo and Juliet* and Laura Keene, and Lola Montez—not that Lola Montez did much acting, but her Spider Dance was sensational. They still talk about it, over at the Bella Union and one old-timer told me—" Clarisse stopped, and looked closely at Shannon. "Anything wrong, honey?"

"I'm not sure, but I think—" She caught her breath, as pain clutched at her, then ebbed away. She managed a shaky smile. "Clarisse, I think it might be the baby."

"Oh, Lord," Clarisse said. "I thought it wasn't due for a couple of weeks."

"So did I," Shannon said. "But the midwife, Mrs. Fogarty, said she couldn't be sure."

"And Adam's off, goodness knows where."

"He's up in Sacramento. There's a man up there who wants to sell a brickyard and Adam— He wasn't sure he should go, but I couldn't keep him here waiting."

"I'll have one of the workmen down there get word to him. What hotel's he staying at?"

"No, Clarisse. I don't want—he'll be back in a couple of days. Just get the midwife. She's over on Sutter Street."

Shannon gave Clarisse Mrs. Fogarty's address, and Clarisse hurried downstairs to the lumberyard, where Adam's foreman dispatched an apprentice to get the woman at once. Then she returned to help Shannon change into a plain muslin nightgown, and got her to bed.

It was twilight before the midwife arrived, a stocky, florid woman who wore a neat black bonnet and carried a small leather bag. "You can go on to the Bella Union now," Shannon told Clarisse.

"Not on your life," Clarisse said. "They'll have to carry on without me tonight."

Mrs. Fogarty looked Clarisse up and down, somewhat scornfully. "This ain't no place for the likes of you," she said.

In spite of her pains, which were starting to come closer together, Shannon could not help being amused. She decided that the midwife might be excused for her doubts about Clarisse's usefulness in this situation.

Clarisse looked as if she had stepped from the pages of *Madame Demorest's Mirror of Fashions,* the newest of the fashion magazines from the East. She wore a dress of apple green silk, with a wide flounced skirt that billowed over an enormous hoop; the flounces were edged with black lace and dark green velvet bows; the bodice was cut daringly low for daytime wear, so that the black lace bertha emphasized rather than concealed the curves of her ample breasts. Her dark green velvet bonnet was edged with marabou of a lighter green, and her red hair fell from beneath the bonnet in a mass of ringlets.

But she gave Mrs. Fogarty an impudent grin and said, "Don't you worry about me. I helped my mother when three of my sisters were born. We lived in a dogtrot cabin in the Alabama hills. My pa was never sober enough to go get a midwife in time."

"Guess you can stay then," Mrs. Fogarty said grudgingly.

"But Clarisse, your show! You can't disappoint all those gentlemen. It might cause a riot."

"It might at that," Clarisse said, with a complacent smile. "All the same, I'll stay as long as I can. And I'll be right back after I finish my last number." Then she asked gently, "You sure you don't want me to get word to Adam?"

"I don't want him here." Shannon did want him, desperately, but he was in Sacramento on important business and she had no right to hamper him. It might be different if he loved her, she thought wistfully. If he hadn't married her only out of a sense of obligation.

"Mrs. Kincaid's right," the midwife said, as she

put on a spotless, starched white apron over her poplin skirt. "At a time like this, a man's about as useful as tits on a boar hog."

"That's for sure," Clarisse agreed.

A hard pain gripped Shannon, and she sank her teeth into her lower lip to hold back a cry. She held onto Clarisse's hand while the midwife made a swift examination. "Everything's going fine," she said.

Darkness fell and a soft fog drifted in from the bay. The noises from the lumberyard lessened as the men stopped work for the day. "You'd better start now," Shannon told Clarisse. "Adam's foreman will find you a hansom. The streets aren't safe for—"

A viselike pain gripped her, held her fast.

"Sure you want me to go, honey?" Clarisse asked.

Shannon nodded, unable to speak.

"Breath deep and slow," the midwife said. "Save your strength. You'll need it in a little while."

"I'll be back as soon as I can," Clarisse assured her. "I won't even stop to take off my makeup."

But before Clarisse could return, at two the following morning, Adam's son had been born, a healthy boy who cried lustily from his cradle beside the bed.

It was a day later, early in the afternoon, when Adam returned. Shannon heard his footsteps on the wooden staircase outside. Then, through the flimsy door that separated the bedroom from the parlor, she heard Clarisse saying, "Everything's under control. The baby—"

"Why the hell didn't somebody send word? I told Shannon where I'd be staying. Is she all right?"

"She's fine," Clarisse said. "Here, have a drink."

"I want to see Shannon."

"Keep your voice down. She's sleeping."

"But why didn't you send for me? Why didn't you or Mackenzie—"

"Your friend, Mackenzie, dropped by a few hours ago. Said he'd be back. Adam, Shannon didn't want you here."

"She told you that?" Shannon had to strain to catch the words.

"Adam, come here," Shannon called.

"You woke her," Clarisse said accusingly.

But he was inside the bedroom in a moment. He hesitated on the threshold, looking ill at ease, unsure of himself. Then Shannon held out her arms to him and he came to embrace her, gently, as if he was afraid she would break. "You look so pale. Are you all right?"

She raised her lips to his and felt the warmth of his mouth, tender yet urgent. Then she asked, "Don't you want to see your son?"

He turned to look into the cradle beside the bed. "He's small, isn't he?"

"He certainly is not," Shannon said indignantly. "He's nearly nine pounds." She added, "He's got quite an appetite, too."

"He's a fine boy," Adam conceded.

"He looks like you."

"He'd better," Adam said. He came and sat beside the bed, and took her hand in his.

"I haven't decided what to call him," Shannon began.

"I have. We'll call him Colin." His fingers tightened on hers. "Colin Kincaid."

"Colin. Yes, I like that," she said.

"Colin was my father's name," Adam told her.

She felt warm with pleasure, knowing that Adam wanted to name the baby for his own father; their son would carry on the name, he would be part of a family. He would belong.

"What was he like, your father?" she asked.

"He was a good man. Strong, hard-working. He had to be to get a bare living out of our farm. It was mostly rocks and the soil was poor. But he kept us fed and clothed and he saw to it that I got as much schooling as possible, even when it meant he had to do without my helping with the chores." His face darkened. "He wanted a better life for us all, that was why he took us South. He had great plans. I was to go off to school to study law, when I was old enough. And Rachel was to have pretty dresses, a fine dowry."

He fell silent and Shannon said hesitantly, "You called for Rachel when you were delirious with fever, back in Panama. You thought I was Rachel."

His eyes hardened, and she saw the old bitterness in them. "You? You're nothing like Rachel," he said. "She was shy, delicate. As fragile as a porcelain statuette. She had black hair and soft brown eyes."

"You must have loved her very much," Shannon said gently.

"I loved her, but when she needed me, I couldn't save her. I couldn't do anything at all." He looked down at Shannon, his face filled with self-loathing. "Don't ever speak of my sister again, or of any of my family."

She leaned over and tried to take his hand but he moved away. "I didn't mean to pry," she said. "It's

only that I never had a family of my own, except for
Aunt Kate. I don't even remember my mother, and if
I ever saw my father, I was too young to recall him,
either. I've never even seen his picture. Odalie's my
sister, but we scarcely know each other."

"You can be thankful for that," he said harshly.
"You have nothing to lose. It's better that way."

"I have a son, now," she reminded him. *And I have
you. I love you.* But she could not speak to Adam of
her love for him. He wanted her body, yielding and
filled with passion, but that was all.

She started when a heavy wagon, loaded with
lumber, came rumbling into the yard down below.
There was a deafening crash as heavy planks fell to
the ground. The foreman swore at the driver, shouting at the man for his clumsiness.

The baby stirred and began to wail fretfully.

Before Shannon could get to the cradle, Adam had
picked up the child, and was holding him carefully,
and peering down into his face. "Shannon, he's turning red."

She smiled, touched by his concern for his son.

"Bring him to me," she said. She took the baby in
her arms. "He's hungry, that's all." She put the baby
to her breast and he began to suck greedily. A few
minutes later, he was asleep in her arms, well-fed and
contented.

"You see," she said. "He's a big boy. He's got a
tremendous appetite."

"All the same, I don't want him scared out of his
wits by that racket down there."

"He'll get used to it," Shannon assured him.

"He won't have to get used to it," Adam said.

"We've got money now. There's no need for my wife and son to live this way."

He leaned over the bed. "Look here, Shannon, the lumberyard, the wharf, the rest of my properties are paying off handsomely. And now, I have a brick works up in Sacramento."

"You bought it then?"

"I did. And not only that. I'm going to buy a mine as soon as I can get a good deal on one. I'll have to go out and see it first, though."

"But, Adam, I won't be able to go with you to Virginia City. Not right away, and not with the baby."

"I don't expect you to," he said. "I'll go alone, and as soon as possible."

He had only returned less than an hour ago, and now he was already planning to leave her again. She felt the hurt welling up in her, and although she tried to conceal her feelings, they must have shown in her face.

"I'm not leaving this minute, sweetheart," he said, seating himself on a chair next to the bed and putting an arm around her. "I'll get you and young Colin settled in your new home, first."

She longed to tell him that she did not care where she lived, that her home was with him, wherever he went. She wanted to hear him say that he would wait until she and Colin could go out to Virginia City with him. "What's wrong?" he asked. "I thought you always wanted a home of your own, a fine house where you could entertain those respectable people you used to talk about."

Then, when she did not reply, he went on quickly, "I have a place in mind. It's the finest section of San

Francisco. There are seventeen houses, all brick, at the foot of Rincon Hill. The man who built it got the idea from one of those stylish London mews. He's an Englishman, himself. George Gordon's his name. He designed the residential blocks to center around a floral park. The whole area will be enclosed by a locked iron fence, and only residents will have the keys."

"It sounds pretty, but a little like a fortress."

"No different from Gramercy Park, in New York City," he told her. "I want you to be protected, and my son, too." His arm tightened around her and their sleeping child. Understanding his need to assure himself of their safety, she did not protest again, but said, "I'm sure I'll love the new house, Adam."

"I'd be surprised if you didn't," he said, and went on to tell her of the shopping district near Market Street, and the horse-car line that would enable the residents to ride into town and home again. "But you won't be needing that. We'll have our own carriage and team."

"Oh, Adam, it all sounds so lavish."

"I told you back in Panama City that I'd give you a fortune, everything you ever wanted. This is only the beginning."

18

ODALIE TUCKED her dark hair under her plain straw bonnet, and wrapped her long gray cloak more closely around her, for the September evening was raw and damp. A heavy fog had drifted in from the Golden Gate, across the bay, to shroud the streets of San Francisco. As she turned into Clay Street, she caught the strong sulfur smell as a lamplighter kindled his taper to light the gas lamps; there were other smells, too, which had become familiar to her during her months in San Francisco: salt and kelp, fish and spices, and, as she moved into the more crowded section of the city, where Clay Street intersected with Montgomery, she caught the mingled scents of heavy perfumes: patchouli, heliotrope and jasmine, worn by the women who were walking slowly along the street, trailing their wide skirts over the board sidewalks, their eyes moving quickly, appraisingly, from one passing male to the next.

Perhaps she should have hired a cab to take her

from her boarding house at the foot of Telegraph Hill to Mr. Gelber's pawnshop, near Portsmouth Square. She still had a few coins left in her reticule, but she had decided to save them, and walk, instead. She had no idea of how much money she would be able to raise on the small collection of jewelry she was bringing to the shop. And she would need every penny to tide her over until Bruce returned.

He would have been furious to know that she was abroad on the streets after dark, and unescorted, but she had little choice, for she had spent all the money he had left her when he had departed for Nevada, nearly two months ago.

Although she would have been bitterly humiliated to have had to ask any of her fellow boarders for the name of a pawnshop, she had listened carefully to the chatter at the boarding-house table, and had managed to pick up the needed information. Pride also forbade her going to the shop during the daylight hours, for there was always the possibility that one of the boarders might see her and spread the word that the "high-toned Mrs. Lathrop"—she had heard one of them call her that—was in desperate straits. The other ladies at the boarding house disliked her, because she kept to herself, because she refused to join in their gossip or accompany them on their shopping expeditions. Once, she had heard a thin, long-faced Yankee woman mimicking her accent, to the amusement of several of the other ladies in the parlor.

Now, as she lifted her skirts to dodge an oncoming carriage, its lamps blurred by the fog, she wished that Bruce had been able to settle her in a boarding house with a Southern clientele. But at least, she reminded herself, as she reached the board sidewalk opposite, the boarding house was respectable, which was more than one could say of many San Francisco lodgings.

She jumped back as a dray, loaded with beer barrels, splashed mud on the hem of her grey organdy dress. The dress, like the straw bonnet, was not suited to the season here in San Francisco, but when she had managed to give Aunt Lucienne the slip, back in New Orleans, she had had little time to think about which clothes to bring along; it had been difficult enough to get away with her maid, Emmy, carrying her carpetbag.

She sighed. Emmy had left her, some months before, to better herself working as a laundress. No matter. If she had kept a personal maid in a boarding house, it would only have been cause for further ridicule, and besides, there was no money to pay the girl's salary.

If only Bruce was successful, this time, in raising the funds to develop his mine, out there in the Comstock. She had thought that finding silver would be enough, but she had soon learned that Bruce would need a great deal of money to keep the Silver Vixen operating. The mine, Bruce had explained, had reached a depth where a windlass and bucket could no longer be used to operate it. Then water had come flooding in, and the engineers Bruce had called in to consult with had told him that a steam engine would be needed for pumping, an engine of fifteen horsepower at least. Unless he could find a backer, Bruce would have to abandon the mine.

Odalie sighed as she moved down the crowded

street. Thank goodness that pawnshops here were open so late. They had to be, to accommodate the patrons of San Francisco's many gambling houses, who might find themselves in need of ready cash on short notice.

Now, she stopped before the small frame shop with the three brass balls hanging over the entrance, and she hesitated, feeling a sinking sensation in the pit of her stomach. How could she, Odalie Lathrop, Philippe Duval's daughter, have come to this?

She longed to turn and retrace her steps back to the boardinghouse, but she knew that she could not. With Bruce away in Nevada, and the highest mountain passes soon to be closed in by the first snows, she had no way of knowing how long it would be before she saw him again. If he had already crossed the Sierras and was on his way down to the California side, it could be a matter of weeks; otherwise, she might not see him until early spring. She needed money for rent at the boardinghouse, for warm clothes.

She hated this raw, savage land that had promised so much and had given her only hardship, fear and loneliness. She could remember how, on her arrival in Virginia City, she had been sure that all her dreams were about to become reality. Bruce was there, to welcome her. And he was promising her not only his love, but a life of ease, of luxury. He had found his silver mine, where so many others had failed to do so. It was only a question of working the claim, of bringing the precious blue ore up from the depths of the mountain.

She would not have the wedding she had dreamed of, with a gown of white silk, and a lace veil, with her friends as bridesmaids, but no matter. All through the brief ceremony in the office of a Virginia City judge, she had floated along on a tide of happiness. Until the darkness closed in over the towering heights of the mountains, and she was alone with Bruce in the flimsy, one-room shack and he was pushing her down on the narrow cot. . . .

"Bruce, wait—please." She had forced the words out with difficulty, for her breath was being crushed out of her by the arms that encircled her. "I can't. Not yet."

"You're my wife, Odalie," he said, his voice hoarse, unsteady. The voice of a stranger. The body of a stranger, pressing her down on the thin mattress. Hard, alien hands exploring her body through her thin cambric nightdress.

She looked up at his face, but the features blurred, shifted, changed. She saw the face of Craig Judson, felt the weight of Judson's muscular, perspiring body on top of hers.

That was insane. Bruce was her husband. He loved her. He would be patient, would wait, if only she could make him understand.

But there was no way to tell him of her terror, without telling him about the overseer, and all that had happened in his cottage on that long-ago night.

"I need time to—to—"

"Time? You've had time. All those months we've been apart. Odalie, I need you. Now—"

Standing before the pawnbroker's shop, she forced away the memories of the pain, the revulsion of her wedding night. She made her way into the shop, where the pawnbroker, a thin, stooping old man, examined the chatelaine watch, a gift from Papa, a garnet brooch, a cameo that had belonged to Papa's mother.

The pawnbroker studied each piece carefully. "Interesting workmanship," he remarked, turning the delicate cameo in his hand.

"It came from France. It's old and quite valuable, I believe."

"Yes, my dear lady, but unfortunately, there is little demand for such pieces at present. If you had a diamond ring, perhaps something of that sort—"

She stroked the tiny, hard square of her engagement ring, given to her by Bruce the day before their wedding. She could not part with that, not yet. She shook her head.

The pawnbroker sighed and counted out five silver dollars. "I can't do any better than this," he said, as she gave a little cry of protest.

"Oh, but surely—"

"I'm sorry, ma'am. Not many would give you even this much." He began to write out the ticket, and before she could say anything more, she heard the tinkling of the shop bell. A pale, dark-haired man in a well-cut black broadcloth suit and a satin cravat, entered the shop.

"Ah, Mr. Gelber," he said, with the familiarity of a regular customer. "A chilly night, and no mistake."

Odalie gathered up the coins and waited impatiently while the pawnbroker finished writing out the ticket and entered a record of the transaction in a ledger; even if she had been disposed to haggle, she could not do so in the presence of a third party.

"Not too chilly to keep the crowd from going over

to Portsmouth Square," Mr. Gelber remarked. "Are you headed that way?"

"To hear Asbury Harpending's speech? No, indeed. I've already heard him talk. Eloquent enough, I'll say that, but imprudent. He and those followers of his are likely to land in jail one of these days. Or worse."

Odalie took the ticket from the pawnbroker and put it into her reticule, along with the coins, but she made no move to go. She, too, had heard the rumors about Harpending, the brash young Kentuckian, who had run away from home to join William Walker's filibustering army in Nicaragua. Harpending had narrowly escaped joining his leader in front of a firing squad, after the revolution had failed.

Now, Asbury Harpending was the leader of those forces here in California who sympathized with the cause of the South, transplanted Southerners who were urging the overthrow of the California state government, and the formation of a new republic, to be called the Republic of the Pacific.

Odalie remembered the night, shortly before Bruce had departed for Nevada, when she had overheard one of his friends, a young man from Savannah, somewhat the worse for drink, speaking of the "Knights of the Golden Circle."

She had been in the other room, sewing, and had heard Bruce say harshly, "Be quiet, you damn fool. You know what the penalty is for even mentioning the name."

Later, she had questioned Bruce anxiously, but he had disclaimed any connection with Harpending's group. Still, she could not be sure he had been telling her the truth. Bruce was hot-headed and passionately devoted to the Southern cause. Hadn't he said that if Mr. Lincoln were elected, the South would have no choice but to leave the Union?

But was Bruce a member of the secret organization? Had he taken the oath? She had never been interested in politics, a matter for men. But now, all at once, she had to know how far Mr. Harpending and his followers were really prepared to go. And Portsmouth Square was close by.

"When will Mr. Harpending be speaking?" she asked the gentleman in the black broadcloth suit.

He looked at her with interest, his eyes coolly appraising her. She was thankful for the drab gray cloak and the plain, straw bonnet, a sedate, almost matronly costume.

"He should be starting shortly," the gentleman said. "If you wish to hear his speech, you should go over now, so as to get a place near the front of the crowd."

"That would be most unwise," Mr. Gelber said, shaking his head. "Begging your pardon, ma'am—but tempers are running high on both sides. There could be trouble."

Odalie nodded, and left the shop, but although she recognized the wisdom of the pawnbroker's advice, she was determined to hear at least a little of the speech. So far, she had heard only rumors about the movement. Now, perhaps, she would be able to discover the facts for herself.

As soon as she was out on the street, she found herself caught up in the tide moving in the direction of the square.

She sighed, realizing that, although her marriage to Bruce had turned out to be completely different from her daydreams; although he was not at all the man she had fallen in love with, she loved him still, and always would. And the thought that he might be risking his life by throwing in his lot with a dangerous secret organization terrified her.

Adam helped Shannon into their carriage, a large, dark gray vehicle with highly polished brass trimming, and seats upholstered in soft, deep plush of a lighter gray. She arranged her full skirt around her, and watched Adam as he got in beside her.

How fine he looked in his new evening clothes: the perfectly-tailored black suit, the white brocade vest and white kid gloves. He had little in common with the brash, carelessly dressed man who had lifted her from the dock in Mobile that evening, nearly two years ago, and had swung her up onto the seat of his lumber wagon. He had worn a coarse cotton shirt open at the throat, heavy workman's boots, and his jacket had been slung over his shoulder.

But even then, she had found his face arresting, and now, as she studied the planes and angles she had come to know so well, she felt her pulses quicken, her breathing deepen. How familiar that face had become: the wide, sensual mouth, whose kisses still sent a swift hot current through her body; the eyes, startlingly blue against the deep mahogany tan of his skin; the hard, arrogant line of the jaw.

In a few hours, they would be together in their huge, silk-curtained bed in the new house. Her hands would cling to him, her thighs part for the swift, fiercely-sweet thrust that would join them. . . .

She lowered her eyes, sure that he could see the

hunger in them, ashamed of the urgency of her need. Surely such thoughts, such feelings were improper for a respectable married woman.

She asked quickly, "Do you like my new dress?"

"You look elegant," he said, with a half-smile. "Though I must say, that—what do you call it—"

"If you mean my cage hoop," she said primly, "every fashionable lady at the theater tonight was wearing one."

"It's an instrument of torture."

"I don't find it uncomfortable."

"I do," he said. "How am I supposed to get close to you?" But a moment later, his arm was around her, and his hand slid under her amber velvet cloak to cup her breast.

"Adam, not here."

His fingers moved caressingly. "Why not? It's my carriage, and you're my wife." She turned her face to him, leaning her head back, her lips parting to receive his kiss. Now he pushed aside the lace and taffeta bodice, to find her warm, smooth skin. Her nipples were taut and hard under his knowing fingers. He bent her back on the seat and the hoop tilted upward. Adam swore softly, then laughed. "Never mind, we'll be home soon enough. And then you'd better be out of that contraption fast. Otherwise I'm liable to tear the damn thing off you."

"Adam—the coachman will hear you."

"He's having all he can do, getting through this mob." But he released her and she smoothed her honey-colored taffeta skirt, with its flounces of black lace. "All right, Shannon," he said, "we'll stick to polite conversation, until we get back to Rincon Hill. Shall we talk about the play?"

"It was wonderful, wasn't it?" she said sighing. "So moving."

"Too moving, if you ask me. With the temper of the people here in the city right now, I don't think that a play about the evils of slavery was a wise choice."

"And since Mr. Boucicault is Irish, you think he should only write plays like *Colleen Bawn*."

"You enjoyed seeing it, as I remember," Adam said.

"Certainly I did," she agreed. "Mr. Boucicault is a gifted playwright. But that is all the more reason why he should deal with topics of current importance, as he did tonight."

He smiled at her, a little indulgently, she thought.

"Shannon, a play like *The Octoroon* doesn't change anyone's basic ideas. Those who are already abolitionists will be more convinced than ever that all slave owners are black-hearted villains, while Southern sympathizers will reject it as unfair and untrue."

"And which are you?" she demanded. "You said you don't think of yourself as a Southerner. Are you in favor of abolition, then? If war comes, which side will you be on?"

"I'll be on the side of Adam Kincaid," he said coolly.

"As you've always been."

"And why not? I'm certainly not about to take up arms to defend the rights of the slave owners. I leave that to men like Bruce Lathrop."

She ignored the reference to Bruce. "You're sure there'll be a war? But that would be a terrible thing."

"More terrible than you can imagine. All the same, it's coming." He shrugged. "Don't look so worried, Shannon. It won't hurt us. In fact, there'll be fortunes to be made, right out here in California."

"I don't understand."

"Wars have to be financed, my dear. Both sides will need gold, and silver. We'll be rich, Shannon. You'll have all those things you dreamed about, when you were back in your uncle's tavern, tending bar."

"We have enough now, and besides—Oh, Adam, how can you be so unfeeling? To speak of building a fortune through a war—to profit from suffering and death."

"Your father built his fortune on the labor of slaves," he told her calmly. "So did the Lathrops."

"That's not the same. It's not—" But Shannon could not find the words to refute Adam's argument.

Abruptly, the carriage jolted to a halt. Shannon forgot her discussion with Adam, as she realized that something unusual was happening. The streets leading to Portsmouth Square were often congested, even late at night, but not like this. Men were pushing toward the center of the square, some carrying torches, and others holding placards.

Adam stood up, opened the carriage door, and shouted to the coachman, "Try one of the other routes, Jerry."

"Can't, sir," the man called down from his perch on the box. "They're all mobbed tonight—Clay, Kearny, Washington."

Adam took his seat again, beside Shannon. "It's that young fool, Harpending, trying to stir up a following for his cause. He's made plenty of soapbox speeches before, but he's never drawn a crowd like this one."

Their carriage was stopped at the side of the square where the improvised platform, hung with gaudy bunting, had been erected. Here, the glare of the torches dispelled the softness of the swirling fog.

"No slavery in California!" someone shouted.

"Independence for California," came from another part of the crowd. "Down with the Union. States' Rights!"

The mob was pressing so close to the carriage that Shannon could feel it begin to sway. She looked over at Adam, and took some reassurance from his calm, set face. Fists were flying now, stones hurtling through the air, and although Harpending was still shouting his message from the platform, it was lost in the uproar from the crowd.

Then, only a few feet from the carriage, a woman, caught in the mob, was knocked against a lamppost. Shannon saw her clutch at the post for support, saw her bonnet pushed awry, and then she cried out, "Adam, over there!"

He looked in the direction in which she was pointing.

"Good Lord!" he said. He rose, and before Shannon knew what he was going to do, he was out of the carriage, shouldering his way to the place where the woman still clung, crushed by the struggling men. She saw Adam swing on one man, knocking him down, saw him strike another with the full weight of his shoulder.

Shannon had only seen the woman's face for a moment, in the full glare of the torchlight, but even before Adam had returned to the carriage with the woman in his arms, Shannon was sure that she had not been mistaken. Odalie Duval.

19

SHANNON SWUNG the carriage door wide, long enough for Adam to get back inside. He was carrying Odalie, who struggled fiercely but ineffectually, and Shannon saw the look of blind panic on her face.

Adam shouted up to the coachman. "Get us out of here, Jerry. Fast. Use the whip if you have to, but get us through."

The heavy-set coachman swung his long whip now on one side and now on the other, so that closely packed men moved away, to escape the sting of the lash. The horses reared and whinnied, striking out with their hooves, forcing the men in front of them to dodge out of the way. Shannon slammed the door shut and locked it and the carriage lurched forward, away from Portsmouth Square and onto Kearny Street.

Adam held Odalie on his knees, one arm around her to steady her, but she struck at his chest and tried to claw his face. "Let me go! Please, let me out of here!"

Adam caught her wrists. "Stop it, Miss Duval. I'm not going to hurt you. Don't you know me?"

Shannon realized how frightening it must have been for Odalie, first to be caught in a mob of battling men, then to be picked up and carried off, pushed into a carriage.

"It's all right," she said quickly. "Odalie, you're safe now."

Only then did Odalie cease her struggle. She turned her head and gave a little cry of surprise. "Why—it's —Miss Cavanaugh."

"I'm Mrs. Kincaid now," Shannon said.

Odalie's slender body relaxed against Adam's supporting arm. "Kincaid?" She looked up into his face. "Adam Kincaid. Yes, I remember. Mobile. The lumberyard. I met you that day on board the *Amaranth*." She was still trembling violently, and her face was white, but she tried to regain control. "I'm sorry. Those men out there— I was so frightened and when you picked me up I—"

"I understand," Adam said. "Portsmouth Square is no place for an unescorted lady at night. Especially when Asbury Harpending is stirring up the mob with his talk of insurrection." He helped her over to the seat opposite where she slumped against Shannon. "I should have introduced myself, but under the circumstances, there wasn't time."

"I'm most grateful, Mr. Kincaid."

"My pleasure. Now, if you'll tell me where you're staying, I'll see you get home safely."

"The other end of Kearny Street. At the foot of Telegraph Hill. It's a boardinghouse."

He gave her a sharp, swift look, his blue eyes

narrowing. Then he nodded and directed the coachman to get them to Telegraph Hill as quickly as
possible. Shannon knew that although the place was
not really a part of the Barbary Coast, it was close
enough to that infamous section. Starting with Sydney-
Town, the gathering place for Australian convicts
who had managed to make their way back across the
Pacific, and had no wish to return to England, the
area had spread like a blight, had become known
halfway around the world as a pest-hole where
prostitutes, thieves, murderers and arsonists lived and
plied their various trades. What was Odalie doing anywhere near such a place? Shannon wondered.

"Do you have friends who can look after you?"
Adam asked.

"No. I'm alone right now. Bruce is in Nevada, you
see. Unless he's already crossed the Sierras and is on
his way home." She swallowed, plainly on the edge
of tears.

"I hope he is, because otherwise, once the mountain passes are blocked with snow, he could be
trapped there for the winter." She stopped, seeing
Adam's curious look. "Bruce and I are married," she
explained quickly.

"My best wishes to both of you," Adam began.

"Oh, but I thought you'd be waiting for him at
Beau Rivage, until he found silver and could—" Shannon stopped herself, hoping that she had not said too
much. Odalie must not know the circumstances under
which she had heard this, from Bruce. Shannon remembered the night at the Mariposa Hotel in Colón,
the night Bruce had tried to make her his mistress.

"I believe what my wife means is that San Francisco is a bad place for a lady to be alone. That you might have been safer at Beau Rivage."

"I hate San Francisco," Odalie cried. "It's raw and ugly. Nothing but fires and robberies and saloons. Street brawls and shootings. Yankees, everywhere, even at the boardinghouse. But Bruce won't go back to Alabama, now that he's found the Silver Vixen."

"The what?" Adam's eyes were alert, and he leaned forward a little in his seat.

"The Silver Vixen," she repeated. "It's a mine on Sun Mountain. Near Virginia City. Bruce went back there on business. And I'm all alone in this awful place, and I'm afraid."

"About the mine, exactly where is it?" Adam asked. "And what sort of yield has it had so far?"

"I don't know, and I don't care. Why did Bruce have to come here? Why did I follow him? Even if I wanted to go back home and wait for him, Mama would never let me, not after I disobeyed her. She wanted me to go to France, but I—"

Adam made an impatient gesture. "Forget all that," he said. "You're here, and you're not alone. Nothing's going to happen to you. Even if your husband's delayed in Virginia City until spring, you'll be all right. Unless you run around to political rallies late at night," he added. "What were you doing at Portsmouth Square tonight?"

"I wanted to hear Mr. Harpending. I wanted to find out what he intends—"

"I had no idea you were so interested in politics, Mrs. Lathrop," Adam said.

"I'm not. It's Bruce I'm worried about. You must have heard the rumors about Mr. Harpending. Suppose Bruce has joined his Knights of the—oh!" She pressed her hand to her lips and stared over at Adam, and Shannon felt the tension in her body, under the shabby gray cloak.

"Be calm," Adam said. "You haven't said anything you shouldn't. Bruce's politics are his own business. And California's not about to secede and form a separate republic, not now."

But it was plain that Odalie was far too shaken to listen to his words. Had it been only the riot tonight that had made her this way? Shannon wondered. Or was there something more?

The carriage drew up in front of the two-story frame boardinghouse, and Shannon could see the dark shape of Telegraph Hill looming up behind it, swathed in fog.

"Shannon, go inside with Mrs. Lathrop. She's in no condition to be alone yet. Get her to bed. I'll drive over to the lumberyard and come back in half an hour to get you."

"The lumberyard? But it's so late. And perhaps—" Shannon hesitated. "Perhaps she would rather be alone."

But Odalie shook her head. "Oh, no. Please do come with me."

Most of the guests in the boardinghouse had retired, but Shannon was conscious of the stares she received from the few who had lingered in the parlor. Her splendid honey-colored taffeta dress, her velvet cloak, the diamond and topaz earrings she wore, were obviously out of place in this shabby establishment. And so, she thought, was Odalie.

If Bruce owned a silver mine, why did he allow

Odalie to live this way? She reminded herself quickly that it was none of her business. She had been a little surprised when Adam had urged her to accompany Odalie to her room in the boardinghouse, and even more surprised when Odalie had agreed.

She was sure that Bruce had said nothing to Odalie about his relationship with Shannon; that he had never mentioned their voyage on the *Lively Bess* or that night at the Mariposa in Colón. No, a man like Bruce would not be likely to discuss such things with his bride. Besides, Shannon thought with a touch of irony, the whole affair had not shown Bruce in a particularly favorable light.

She turned her attention to Odalie, who was standing helplessly in the middle of a small, dreary room, the parlor of the two-room suite. Her dark eyes were a little dazed, her face drained of color. And she was shivering.

"You'd better get to bed," Shannon said gently. "Come along, I'll help you take your things off."

The reticule slipped from Odalie's nerveless hand, and the strings came undone; a small shower of silver dollars fell to the floor. "Here, I'll get them," Shannon said.

"Oh, no. Let me," Odalie cried. She sank to her knees and began to gather them up, but her fingers were trembling. The coins eluded her and all at once she buried her face in her hands, her shoulders shaking.

"Odalie, my dear—"

"It doesn't matter." She was sobbing uncontrollably. "I didn't want you to—to see the—pawn ticket. I was so ashamed. That's where—I went tonight—

before the rally in Portsmouth Square. To a pawn shop, because the money Bruce left me had run out, and I don't know when—"

Shannon helped Odalie gather up the money and the ticket and put them back into her reticule. "But that's nothing to be ashamed of. Please, don't cry. You'll make yourself ill." She drew Odalie to her feet, and put an arm around her. "I've been without money, too. And I didn't have anything to pawn."

She tried to imagine what Odalie would have done if she had been left stranded in Colón.

"How—did you manage?"

"Things worked out better than I would have hoped. Listen to me, Odalie. You're not alone. Adam told you that. We can help you, and when Bruce gets back, why, everything will be all right again."

"But it won't. Shannon, you don't understand. Bruce has the mine, but unless he can find a backer with money enough for a steam engine and oh, all sorts of machinery—without capital, the mine's no use to him."

Shannon said, "I understand. But right now, you've got to get hold of yourself. Is there anything to drink here?"

"No wine. Only brandy. And Mama always said strong spirits aren't suitable for a lady. Aunt Lucienne drinks more apricot brandy than she should and she—"

"Never mind Aunt Lucienne. Where's the brandy?"

"There, in the cabinet. But I really don't think—"

Shannon found the bottle and a clean glass, and poured the brandy. "Now you sit down and drink this. It'll steady you."

She lifted the glass to Odalie's lips, and Odalie swallowed and coughed. "It burns," she said. But the color came back to her cheeks.

Shannon led the way into the bedroom, put the glass down on the nightstand, and helped Odalie to undress and get into a thin cambric nightgown. Like her dress, it had once been pretty, embroidered and trimmed with fine lace; now it was worn and frayed. Odalie allowed herself to be put to bed like a child, and when Shannon held the brandy to her lips again, she swallowed obediently. "That day in the dress shop. You helped me then, too. Only I didn't know you were my sister."

Odalie took another sip of brandy. "That night at Beau Rivage, I was shocked, of course. But I was so sorry for you. Mama had no right to blame you. It wasn't your fault." Her speech was becoming a little slurred. "Besides, it was your mother that Papa loved. Did you know Papa?"

Shannon shook her head. "No, Odalie. I went away to school when I was eight. Your—father gave me a fine education, in a school up in Boston. I think he must have cared about me, a little."

"Oh, yes. I'm sure he did. You know, one night, Aunt Lucienne started to say something about some sort of provision that Papa had made for you. Mama told her to be still. Aunt Lucienne was always afraid of Mama, everyone was, even me. But I'm not any more."

"What kind of provision?" Shannon asked.

"I don't know. Mama wouldn't let her say any more about it. Besides, it's not important now, is it?

I mean, you and Mr. Kincaid must be wealthy. Your dress, and that cape, and the carriage—"

"Adam's done well," Shannon said. How could she explain to this young woman, who had always known that she belonged, who had always had the security of a proud name and a great house, what it meant to be illegitimate? The knowledge that her father had remembered her, had made some provision for her, that was what mattered. But Odalie was asking, "Are you in love with Mr. Kincaid? That night when I saw you with Bruce at Beau Rivage I thought perhaps—"

"I love Adam," Shannon said simply. "I didn't know it at first, but now I do. And we have a son, a beautiful little boy. You must come and see him one day. That is, if you—"

"I'd like to see him," Odalie said. Then a shadow crossed her face. She rested her head against the pillows.

"Shannon, tell me. Is it really awful—having a baby, I mean?"

"Well, there's pain, but it doesn't matter because— Odalie, are you and Bruce—"

"Oh, no!" She lifted her head and a look of fear came into her eyes. Shannon was startled. "But some day maybe we will, and Shannon, I dread it so."

"But Bruce is your husband. You came all the way out here to marry him. I know all this isn't what you're used to, and it isn't easy, being without him, but surely, if you love a man you want his children."

"I do love him," Odalie said. "Only I hate being married. I thought being married to Bruce would be so wonderful. I thought he'd be—different. He was always so gentle before we were married. Kind, chivalrous. But he's no different from— He wants— he expects—"

The brandy had loosened her tongue, and Shannon was sure that Odalie was expressing her true feelings. "I think Bruce goes to other women. You know the kind I mean. San Francisco's full of them. I should hate him for that, but sometimes I wish—I wish that he would be satisfied with them, that he wouldn't ask me to—"

"Hush, now," Shannon said, feeling her cheeks grow warm. "You mustn't say such things. You're tired and overwrought. Try to sleep."

Odalie closed her eyes, but went on speaking, her voice a drowsy monotone. "I still love him. Strange, isn't it? And I miss him."

"Bruce will be back soon, I'm sure," Shannon said soothingly. "Maybe he's made it across the Sierras by now. And even if he hasn't, Adam says there are places where men can cross, even in winter."

Bruce did return from Nevada early, the first week in October. When Shannon gave Adam the news, he startled her by saying, "We'll have him and Odalie to the dinner party on Saturday. Send Jerry over with an invitation."

"Adam, no."

Shannon was seated on the rosewood and velvet chaise in the bedroom of their new house. Now she started up, pulling her wrapper around her.

"You mustn't do that," she cried.

Adam looked down at her curiously. "Why not? You told me you wanted to see Odalie again. What better opportunity could there be? The party was your idea," he reminded her. "To celebrate Clarisse's debut at Maguire's Opera House."

"That's the trouble," Shannon said quickly. "I don't think that Odalie would care to sit down to dinner with Clarisse, even though she's created such a stir in the new show."

"Your sister's in no position to dwell on her elegant background, not now," Adam said. His voice was hard, and Shannon flinched under the brutal directness of his words. "She's on her uppers, that's what you told me. And since Bruce wasn't able to find a backer for that mine of his, he must be close to bankruptcy."

"I shouldn't have told you," Shannon said. "Do you want to have Bruce and Odalie here so that you can flaunt your success?"

"My reasons are more practical," Adam interrupted. "Bruce has a mine. I want to invest in one. Or buy it outright. I'd have to go out and see it, first."

"You'd go into partnership with Bruce, after—after—"

"Go on," Adam said. He smiled but his eyes were cold.

"Adam, I'm your wife. Don't you ever care that Bruce and I were—that we—"

"Bruce wanted you to be his mistress, but you didn't accept his offer, back there in Colón." His eyes searched her face. "Why didn't you, Shannon?"

"He'd promised to marry Odalie, my sister."

"Your family loyalty does you credit. Does Odalie regard you with equal affection?"

"We hardly know each other. But I'd like to get to

know her better. I think she needs me, Adam. She's never had to fend for herself, you see, and she's so helpless here."

"Her husband's back now," Adam reminded her dryly. "Can't he take care of her?"

"They haven't been getting along well." She stopped herself, for Odalie's marital problems were too intimate to share, even with Adam.

"I don't wonder," Adam said. "Bruce was set on marrying an heiress. Now that Odalie's defied her mother and run away, she may find herself cut out of Antoinette's will."

"Oh, Adam, that night I was with Odalie at the boardinghouse she told me that there was a chance that my father left me some sort of bequest. Aunt Lucienne started to tell her about it, but Antoinette interrupted and—" She put a hand on his arm. "Is it possible, do you think?"

A look of irritation crossed his face. "Still daydreaming about Mobile, Shannon? Don't you have enough right here to satisfy you? The house, a closet full of fancy clothes. A staff of servants."

"You've been generous, Adam." Why couldn't he understand her feelings? It wasn't her father's money she wanted, if, indeed, he had left her any. She wanted a link with Philippe Duval, wanted reassurance that he had loved her enough to make provisions for her future. That he had truly thought of her as his daughter.

Adam was saying, "Bruce will jump at the chance to have me invest in that mine of his. From what you've told me, he can't keep it going without a backer. And if the mine pays off, you'll have more than you ever dreamed of." He put his arm around her and held her against him for a moment. Then he released her, saying, "Now, you go and write that invitation to Bruce and Odalie."

Odalie took off the gown of green and silver brocade and hung it away carefully. "Do you think Shannon recognized my dress?" she asked Bruce. "Oh, she must have. She worked on it, back in Miss Harwood's shop in Mobile. She didn't say a word about it this evening, but I'm sure she—it was humiliating."

Bruce stood in front of the small, wavy mirror in the bedroom of their suite at the boardinghouse. "Why did you wear the dress, then?" he asked, unfastening his cravat.

She sighed and began to struggle out of her petticoats. She would never get used to dressing and undressing herself. "Because it's the only dress I own that's suitable for the kind of dinner party Shannon gave tonight. That house! Those mirrors and the carpets. And a brand-new rosewood spinet, all the way from New York. And Shannon's dress—"

"You'll have a dozen just as fine," Bruce said. "As soon as the Silver Vixen's operating again."

"And when will that be?"

Odalie heard the shrewish tone in her own voice and she hated herself for it. Somehow, during the months of her marriage, she had begun to lose her soft-spoken, charming ways, her carefully practiced habit of deferring to gentlemen, of being sweet and flattering no matter what her feelings might be. "Is Adam really interested in investing in the mine?"

"More than that. He wants to go and look at it right away."

"Right away? But you can't leave for the Comstock again until spring. You said the first snows were blocking some of the passes already."

"They are. But Adam's willing to take the chance and so am I. Odalie, I can't afford to miss this opportunity."

She stepped out of her petticoats and put on a wrapper.

"You can't go. I won't let you. It's too dangerous."

"Adam crossed the Sierras with Frémont, and his party, when he was in the army. He's told me all about it. There are places where men can get through, even in winter. Not with wagons, but on horseback."

"Bruce, listen to me. I've been alone for so long and now, after you've just returned, you're planning to leave me again. Don't you care about me?"

He drew her into his arms, and stroked her long, dark hair. "Of course I care. But we need the money, Odalie. And we need it right away."

"Forget the mine," she begged. "Let it go. Sell it outright to Adam, if he wants it. Let him make the trip alone."

"He won't buy it without seeing it. And if he goes, I go. Do you think I'm less of a man than he is?" Bruce's gray eyes flashed with barely concealed anger.

"You haven't had his experience. And besides, I'm tired of California. I hate it out here. I want to go back to Mobile. Bruce, take me back. I don't belong here and neither do you."

"We'll go back to Jessamine one day," he told her.

"But not until I have enough to pay up my debts, to put in a new crop. You remember Melora's last letter. If we don't get hold of a substantial sum of money, and soon, we'll lose Jessamine."

"There's Beau Rivage."

"Don't talk like a fool," Bruce said, stripping off his shirt and tossing it over a chair. "You don't think your mother's going to welcome us with open arms, do you? If you'd only waited until I had enough money to come back for you, instead of running off as you did."

"I came because I loved you and I didn't want to lose you. I was afraid that if I let Mama send me off to France—"

"I know," he said impatiently. "But now you're here, you've done nothing but whine and complain. What did you think San Francisco would be like? Mobile? Or New Orleans?"

"Don't be angry with me," she said, her voice unsteady. Tears gathered in her dark eyes and sparkled on her lashes.

He drew her into his arms. "Odalie, don't cry." He held her against him and she clung to him. "We'll go home, my dear. As soon as we can. Everything will be just as it was. You'll see. I know you don't belong here, anymore than I do. But, in the meantime, you'll have to be brave, and not worry about me."

"I'll try, but, Bruce, I love you so much. When I think of the dangers up there in those mountains—avalanches, and blizzards—"

"Don't," he said tenderly. "I haven't left yet. Let's make the most of the time we're together." His arms tightened around her and she felt the hardness of him, pressing urgently against her, felt the swift, now-familiar change from tenderness to fierce hunger. Even now, after these months of marriage, she was still afraid, and her body turned rigid in his embrace. He took no notice, as his hands explored her softness, curving around her buttocks to draw her still closer. His breath was hot against her cheek.

He lifted her and swiftly carried her to the bed and she heard the springs creak as he set her down and stretched out beside her. He cupped one hand around her breast, his fingers seeking the warm flesh under her camisole, stroking, kneading. He stripped off her remaining garments, and then moved to position himself above her.

"Bruce, not yet. Please wait."

"For what?" His voice was harsh in the darkened room. She winced at the bitterness in his tone. "You're as ready as you'll ever be."

She tried to fight off the deepening waves of panic, as he lowered himself and thrust into her. *It shouldn't hurt,* she told herself. *Not after all this time.* But it did, for the deepest part of her was closed against his invasion, as if it had a will of its own. She cried out.

He hesitated for a moment, and she lay still, half-hoping that he would withdraw from her, that he would not force her to undergo this painful, frightening ritual yet again. But her lack of response, her stiff, unyielding body, seemed to arouse a ruthless anger in him, a need to force her to show some feeling. His thrusts became harder, deeper, more brutal; all trace of tenderness was gone, and she felt sure he was trying to hurt her, to punish her for her coldness.

But she couldn't help it. If only he would understand. She must make him understand. But she could only wait for the shudder that came at last, shaking his body; the explosion of passion that left him lying heavy and spent with his full weight upon her.

Then he rolled away from her and she thought he was asleep, until she heard him say, "Don't despair, Odalie, my dear. I'll be leaving by the end of next week. You can have your bed to yourself. That ought to please you."

"Bruce, no. I love you. You have to believe me. It's only that I—"

He turned to her, raising himself on one arm. "Only that you hate sharing a bed with me, having me touch you." His voice was hard, and she flinched at the cruelty of it. "Didn't your mother ever tell you about a husband's rights?"

"I've never denied you your rights," Odalie reminded him. "But you expect me to behave like a trollop. I suppose there are women who take pleasure in satisfying a man's lust. That actress we met at Shannon's house tonight. Clarisse Jenkins. Maybe she'd know how to please you. Or maybe Shannon, herself."

"Shannon," Bruce said softly. "Yes, Shannon would know. She's a loving, passionate woman. And if I had been able to follow my instincts, to forget my promise to you, my duty to my family, that night in Colón, if I'd offered to marry her, I might be better off now."

"Colón? She was with you in Colón?"

"I took her with me to Panama. There was no place else for her to go. She couldn't stay in Mobile."

"You never told me."

"There was nothing to tell. Nothing happened between us."

"You're lying," Odalie cried, sick with jealousy. "Shannon was your mistress."

"I wish she had been. But she refused me, she sent me away."

"I don't believe you."

"Believe what you like." Bruce turned away from her and a little while later, his even breathing told her he was asleep.

She closed her eyes but for her, sleep would not come. She was tormented by the memory of Shannon, as she had looked that evening, presiding over the table in her fine, new house. Shannon, who knew how to love a man, how to give him pleasure and take pleasure in return. Bruce had loved Shannon, she was sure of it. Did he love her still?

20

WHEN THE NOTE from Odalie was brought to her by Mrs. Beal, the housekeeper, Shannon was surprised and faintly annoyed. She had not heard from Odalie since that evening in October, shortly before Adam and Bruce had left San Francisco for Virginia City. She had tried hard to establish some sort of relationship with Odalie, had invited her to the house at the foot of Rincon Hill, had gone to call on her at the boardinghouse. But Odalie had met Shannon's attempts at friendship with coolness, and a kind of nervous uneasiness, and at last, Shannon had decided that there was little point in trying to force herself upon her sister.

True, Odalie had been cordial enough that night when Adam had rescued her from the mob in Portsmouth Square; she had communicated her fears, her unhappiness about her marriage, to Shannon, with an almost childlike frankness. But since then. . . .

Shannon became aware that the housekeeper was

watching her. Mrs. Beal, hired by Adam before he had left, was a quiet, efficient New England woman who had been left a widow during the long voyage around Cape Horn, and who had been grateful for her job; she kept the house running smoothly and supervised the other servants with firmness and unruffled calm.

Now, she stood waiting patiently while Shannon read the untidy scrawl on the cheap notepaper.

Shannon,
    Please come to see me right away. I am ill and there is no one else I can ask to help me. Please.

The second *Please* was underlined. Shannon sighed and put the note down on the polished rosewood table beside the dark red velvet sofa. Adam would be returning tomorrow night. Jerry, the coachman, had already started for Sacramento to meet him with the carriage.

In anticipation of Adam's return, Shannon had been trying on a succession of new dresses, unable to make up her mind which would be most suitable for tomorrow night. She had settled at last on a taffeta dress in the flattering new color, Eugénie blue, named for the Empress of France; the basque fitted smoothly, clinging to the curves of her breasts and the skirt billowed out over her wide hoop. At her throat, she had fastened the brooch Adam had given her, a sapphire set with diamonds.

They would have a long, leisurely dinner here in the house and then, if he complained about the width of her hoop, she would take it off. Upstairs, in their bedroom, she would strip herself of her new finery and lie naked in his arms.

How she had missed him, all through the fall and winter. She had filled the time with caring for Colin, playing with him, cuddling him, until Mollie, the little English nursemaid, had protested that she would spoil him. But she did not care, for when she held the baby against her, pressing her face into the dark ringlets, she felt closer to Adam. The boy looked like his father, even now. The same blue eyes, the same mouth. Adam might never give her his love, but Colin would.

Still, she saw some wisdom in Mollie's words, and she made herself spend time away from the baby, going on shopping expeditions with Clarisse, whose wardrobe grew more lavish as her fame spread. Occasionally she accompanied Clarisse and Fergus Mackenzie to one of the city's many fine restaurants. To Shannon's surprise, Mackenzie had become smitten with Clarisse at their first meeting. He had too much worldly wisdom not to know the kind of woman Clarisse was, and to guess at what her experiences had been before their meeting, but he did not appear to care. Or so Adam had said.

"You won't tell Mackenzie about the Cherokee Rose, and that time she was working at La Ceiba."

"Of course not," Adam had told her, the night after the dinner party, when she had first sensed that Mackenzie had been attracted by Clarisse. "And even if he finds out, I doubt he'll care. Clarisse is a good sort, generous, big-hearted. And damn good-looking, too. What would a man like Mackenzie do with some milk-and-water miss whose idea of love is simpering over a fan? Some girl out of a finishing school who thinks she has to slap a man's face if he kisses her?"

"I was like that when you met me," Shannon reminded him.

"I remember," Adam had said, laughing and catching her to him. "But even then, I sensed the possibilities. Something in your face, and the way you moved."

He had tightened his embrace, and had said, "Lord, but I'm going to miss you, sweetheart."

And she had hungered for him, lying alone in their bed after he had gone. Her body had ached to feel the touch of his hands, the weight of him against her.

And now, when he was coming home, she had been summoned by Odalie. She would not bother to change, she decided. If Odalie was really ill, and alone, she needed someone. She said quickly, "Please find me a hansom cab, the first one that's passing by. And send Mollie upstairs to get me a cloak and bonnet. It doesn't matter which ones."

"I hope it's not bad news I've brought you, ma'am."

"My sister's ill. I have to go to her."

She was a little startled when Mollie brought a heavy cloak of blue velvet, trimmed with bands of sable, more appropriate for a visit to the theater than for her present errand. The matching velvet bonnet was trimmed with the same rich, dark fur. No matter. No one would see her in the hansom cab, and Odalie needed her urgently, or she would not have sent such a note.

"If I'm not back by five, give Colin his supper. And be sure to leave a night light in his room. And—"

"My goodness, ma'am, ain't I been takin' good care of the little fella all this time?"

"Certainly you have," Shannon said. "You've been doing a fine job."

The English girl turned pink with pleasure at Shannon's words. Smiling at her, Shannon hurried out into the late afternoon sunlight. There was a hint of spring in the air, and the sky was a clear, hard blue with only a few wisps of cloud. She turned for a moment to look at the house, with its fine red brick facade, its tall chimneys at either end, and the brass gaslamps on either side of the doorway. She shivered as a cool, damp breeze fluttered the ribbons on her bonnet. She was baffled by a sudden impulse to return to the house, to stay here and wait for Adam. But he would not be home until tomorrow night. And Colin was safe enough in Mollie's capable and loving care.

She noticed the cab driver's look of surprise when she give him Odalie's address, and she could understand the reason for it. Telegraph Hill was too close to the Barbary Coast for comfort. With the influx of new wealth from Nevada, more and more men were pouring into San Francisco, and the collection of shanties, gambling houses, thieves' dens and brothels was spreading.

Only the other day, Shannon had read one of Mackenzie's articles, denouncing the new wave of crime on the Barbary Coast, and especially around the Sydney-Town settlement.

"How long will we continue to receive the refuse of the Australian penal colonies?" the article had demanded. "How long will decent citizens walk in fear, at the mercy of organized gangs of criminals? Our police force is not adequate to deal with this growing menace. . . . Let us hope that the respectable element of our city will not once again be driven to take up arms against these malefactors . . . that our elected officials will take action. . . ."

But privately, over dinner at the Lick House, he had admitted to Shannon and Clarisse that there was little to hope for, since many of the elected officials were working hand in hand with the criminals; that ballot boxes were being tampered with; that men in the city's government were making a profit from the wave of crime.

"The police, most of them, are fairly honest," Mackenzie had said, "but they're afraid to go into the worst parts of Sydney-Town even in pairs. Can't say I blame them."

Now, as the hired cab stopped before the boarding-house Shannon saw that the air was becoming hazy, that the mist was exploring the streets with silver-gray fingers. Shannon had grown used to the fog, used to the city, and had decided that, in spite of its faults, she liked it as Adam did. There was a pulsating vitality in the air, a sense of growth and change, that she had not found in Mobile.

Adam would be home soon. How good to feel his warmth beside her again, his arms around her, his mouth exploring her body. She smiled, thinking of his return, and, under the heavy flounces of her blue taffeta dress, under the silk and lace of her petticoats, she felt her body start to tingle, as if anticipating his touch.

But first, she would have to see to Odalie. Why had Odalie sent for her? That first night when Adam had rescued Odalie from the mob in Portsmouth Square, she had been more than friendly to Shannon, had shared her intimate feelings about her marriage, her doubts and fears. She had called Shannon her sister. Then, abruptly, she had changed.

Maybe I shouldn't have asked her and Bruce to the dinner party after all, Shannon thought, as she mounted the boardinghouse steps. Back in Mobile, respectable married ladies did not sit down to dine with actresses—except for the irrepressible Madame LeVert who kept her salon open to theater people, artists, musicians, anyone who amused and entertained her. But Odalie might be more rigid in her standards.

Shannon rang the bell, and the landlady, a thin, graying woman with sharp eyes came to admit her. As the landlady examined Shannon's costume, she wished that she had taken the time to change. Quickly, she asked to see Mrs. Lathrop. "She wrote that she is ill," Shannon said.

"She's been draggin' around these last couple of months," the landlady said indifferently. "Not comin' down to meals half the time. You'd think she was the only female to find herself in the family way."

Then, seeing Shannon's surprise, she added, "Didn't you know? Five months gone, I'd guess. And puking up her guts half the time. And that man of hers. Back one day and off he goes. Ain't been home for three nights."

"That's no concern of yours," Shannon said, feeling pity for Odalie. It couldn't be pleasant to have this old harridan for a landlady, poking and prying.

Shannon lifted her rustling skirt. "I'm going up to see Mrs. Lathrop now."

Odalie was lying on the bed, and Shannon saw at a glance the thickening of her once-trim waistline, the greenish pallor of her face, her swollen eyes.

"Shannon. You did come."

"You sent for me," Shannon said. "Are you really ill? Or is it only your pregnancy that's making you feel badly?"

"I don't know. My head aches so."

"You've been crying, that's why." The bedroom was untidy, and Odalie's wrapper was crumpled, her long black hair tangled around her face. "Where did Bruce go?"

"You know about that?"

"Your landlady takes quite an interest in your affairs," Shannon said dryly.

"I don't know where Bruce went. A bar, maybe, or a—a—" She lowered her voice, and two spots of color burned in her cheeks. "A sporting house," she whispered.

"Now, you don't know that," Shannon said, taking off her velvet cloak and laying it across a chair.

"I wouldn't blame him, I guess. Oh, it was so awful. His first night back and I—got sick— I couldn't help it. I was so humiliated and—and—"

"You don't mean he walked out simply because you—"

"I told him that I hated the idea of having a baby, here in this dreadful place. And he said I'd hate having a baby anywhere, that I wasn't a normal woman and that he'd prefer a—one of those women—to me, that at least they knew how to treat a man and—"

Odalie dissolved into hard, wracking sobs, and Shannon sat down beside her on the rumpled bed, drawing her into her arms. "Don't," she said, stroking Odalie's tousled hair. "Odalie, men get angry and say things they don't mean. But they get over it. Why I remember one night, back in Panama City, when Adam got furious and went off. I was so scared."

"Was that after Bruce left you in Colón?" Odalie asked, her body stiffening under Shannon's hands.

"You know about that? He told you?"

Odalie nodded miserably.

Shannon took her by the shoulders and looked at her steadily. "Bruce and I never slept together," she said.

"But you were in love with him, weren't you? That night when he brought you to the ball at Beau Rivage, I thought you might have been."

"I— Odalie, try to understand. I knew nothing about men, or about my own feelings, when I came home from school in Boston. And Bruce was so handsome and gallant, I thought, but I didn't know what love was, not then. And not for a long time afterward. Not until Adam was so ill in Panama and I took care of him. And then, all at once, I knew." She took Odalie's hands in hers. "Love has nothing to do with waltzes and moonlight and pretty words."

"But Bruce changed after we married. He's cruel, Shannon. He doesn't care about my feelings. He—"

"He's a man," Shannon said quietly. "He has needs, like all men."

"He's a gentleman. At least, I thought he was."

Shannon could not repress a smile. "He's a man,

first, and don't you forget it. Not if you want to keep him home nights."

Odalie jerked her hands out of Shannon's. "I shouldn't have expected you to understand. You worked in your uncle's tavern, and your mother——"

Shannon's temper flared. "My mother was the woman your father loved, remember? He couldn't marry her because of his family. When he had to make a choice, he chose your mother, but——"

"Just as Bruce chose me, is that what you mean? For land and wealth and a name."

"I didn't say that."

"You didn't have to," Odalie cried, and her body began to shake as if with a chill. "He told me, the night of your dinner party. A loving, passionate woman, that's what he called you."

"That's why you've been avoiding me all these months," Shannon said, understanding now the reason for Odalie's behavior. "You've no reason to be jealous. Any woman can be loving and passionate if she cares for a man. You do care for him. You told me so."

"What does it matter?" Odalie began to cry again. "He's gone now."

"He'll be back," Shannon said. "And if he isn't, I'll ask Adam to try to find him. Adam and his friend, Mackenzie, must know every bar, and sporting house, in San Francisco. At least by reputation," she added quickly.

"But he may be hurt. The Barbary Coast is a horrible place."

"He's probably too fastidious for the Coast," Shannon said with a wry smile. "I should think one of the better houses, on Pike Street, would be more to his taste. Madame Delphine's place, maybe."

Shocked out of her hysteria, Odalie stared at Shannon round-eyed, her mouth half-open. "How do you know about such places?"

Shannon remembered her wedding dress, bought from one of the girls at Delphine's place, so Adam had said. "It doesn't matter. If Bruce isn't back by tomorrow, Adam may be able to find him."

"Has Adam returned from Sacramento? Bruce said he was staying behind for a few days to take care of some business."

"He'll be home tomorrow night. I was trying to decide what to wear to welcome him home, when your note came."

"Is that why you're all dressed up? Shannon, you look so elegant. The color of that dress suits you, and the brooch—"

"Adam bought it for me, right after Colin was born."

Odalie wiped her eyes and sat back against the pillows.

"He must have been pleased about having a son."

"Yes, I think he was."

"Don't you know?"

"Adam doesn't show his feelings. But most men want sons. I'm sure Bruce does, and maybe this baby will be a boy, and then everything will change. And even if it's a girl, I'm sure Bruce will be pleased. Now tell me, are you really ill or only scared and worn out with crying?"

"I guess I'm scared, mostly."

"Don't be. I'll be here if you need me."

"Even after the way I talked to you? Oh, Shannon—"

"Do you have a midwife picked out yet?"

Odalie shook her head.

"Mrs. Fogarty's experienced and she's kind." Shannon stood up and reached for her cloak. "I'll stop by her house on the way home, if you like, and I'll tell her to call on you. She may be able to give you some medicine to keep you from being sick to your stomach so often. She has all sorts of cordials and nostrums."

"Then ask her to come over, please. As soon as she can."

Shannon put on her cloak, smoothing the soft velvet over her full-skirted dress. The dark, thick trimming of sable framed her face in a high, standing collar. She adjusted her bonnet and prepared to leave. "Now that Bruce has sold Adam half-interest in the mine, you won't have any more money problems, at least," she said.

"And I'll have you to stand by me when the baby comes," Odalie said. "I need someone now, Shannon."

"I understand," Shannon said. "I'll be here. Don't shut me out again, Odalie. Like it or not, we are sisters."

Odalie smiled, then, rising from the bed, she went to the dresser and after rummaging about, drew out a small, satin-covered box. "I want you to have this," she told Shannon, reaching into the box, and holding out a gold locket on a chain.

"There's no need," Shannon began, but Odalie pressed the locket into her hand. "Open it," she said.

Puzzled, Shannon obeyed. She looked wide-eyed at the painted miniature inside. Her heart began to speed up, and there was a thickness in her throat. "Odalie, is it—"

"Papa," Odalie said. "You look like him. His hair was black, like mine, but he had hazel eyes. Sometimes they looked amber-gold, like yours. I had him with me all those years I was growing up. But you never knew him, did you? Take it, Shannon."

What a contradictory, unpredictable person Odalie was, Shannon mused. Childishly self-centered one moment, and warm and generous the next. "You do understand what this means to me," Shannon said softly, as she fastened the locket around her neck. It contrasted oddly with the expensive diamond and sapphire brooch that blazed at her throat, but it was equally precious to her.

"Now, I'll go and see Mrs. Fogarty," Shannon promised. She was sure that even talking to the midwife would calm and reassure Odalie.

She hurried down the stairs, feeling warm and happy. She had something that had belonged to her father, a token that she, too, was Philippe Duval's daughter. And in a little while, Adam would be home.

When she came out of the boardinghouse, she saw that the mist had thickened, so that a heavy gray blanket of fog shrouded the streets and the lower slopes of Telegraph Hill. She was glad that she had worn the warm, fur-trimmed cloak after all.

She must find a cab, or a horse car and quickly, for it was evening now, but she could not see more than a few feet ahead. The fog played strange tricks, so that people loomed up suddenly, without warning, and a moment later, disappeared. The air was still and the fog pressed damply against her face. The gas-lamps had been lit, but in this part of the city they were few and far-between, and she could only make out a few vague blurs of light.

Once, she heard the sound of horses' hooves ahead, and called out, but at the same moment there was a burst of music from a tavern nearby, and it drowned out her voice. The cab rolled by and disappeared into the fog.

She was becoming confused, as she moved slowly through the fog, for she was not at all familiar with this part of the city. She started slightly at the sound of ships' bells from the Inner Bay. Was she, then, so close to the waterfront, or was the fog playing tricks with sound as well as sight? If only she could find a cab.

She heard music and raucous laughter, and a woman's shrill scream, cut off abruptly. A man in a striped jersey, a cap pulled low on his forehead, stumbled by; she saw that he was drunk, and she dared not stop him to ask directions.

A moment later, she gave a gasp of fright at the sight of a pair of tattooed Maoris, from New Zealand; harmless, Adam had told her, but nevertheless she shrank back into the mouth of an alley, as they passed, with no more than a glance in her direction. There were men from every corner of the earth here in San Francisco: Chinese, Hindus, Kanakas from the Sandwich Islands, bearded Russians from Sitka. This feature of San Francisco life, the mixture of races and nationalities, had fascinated her, but now she longed to find someone who could speak English, and who was sober enough to get a cab for her. There were plenty of American ships in port, and it was only a matter of time before she would get help. But this was apparently a street lined with taverns, melodeons and dancehalls.

Then she sighed with relief as she heard footsteps again, heard a man speaking with an English accent. "Hell of a night to be out, Bert. Let's find ourselves someplace to get warm and have a few."

"I want more'n a drink to warm me up," the other said.

A moment later, she saw them. One was tall and thin, with sharp features; he wore a shabby frock coat that might have been elegant when new; the other, stocky and broad-shouldered, with small, red-rimmed eyes and a nose that looked as if it had been broken and improperly mended. He wore a filthy jersey shirt that strained over the massive width of his chest, and a pair of equally dirty woolen trousers.

Although she felt uneasy, she forced herself to say, "Please, can you help me? I seem to have lost my way, and I need a hansom at once. The fog's so thick."

"Nasty weather for a fine lady like yerself to be out, that's sure," said the stocky man in the jersey. As he moved closer, she caught the smell of sweat and gin. He turned to his companion, who lifted his lip away from his teeth in the semblance of a smile that showed broken, blackened teeth.

"And down here on Pacific Street, too. No place for a lady in any sort of weather."

Their speech was vaguely reminiscent of Mollie's

Cockney accent. Pacific Street. She must have walked farther than she realized.

"Can you find me a cab?" she asked, her voice unsteady, as she looked from one to the other.

"What's the hurry?" the tall, thin man asked. "Bert and I were going to have us a drink. Maybe you could use one, too."

She clenched her hands on her reticule and looked around, hoping that someone would come along, but the street appeared to be empty.

"Let me by," she said. "I'll find a cab for myself."

"Not so fast." Bert put a huge, callused hand on her arm while his companion moved in closer. "Fine lady like you, maybe you could spare us a few dollars." With a swift movement, he pulled her close to him, so that she gagged at the smell of his unwashed body. "Why, this here cloak of yours is fit for a queen. Ain't it, Clyde?"

His fingers stroked the soft fur at her throat, and a moment later, his huge hand tightened, cutting off her breath. With one swift motion, he jerked her reticule out of her hand. "Nice 'n' heavy. We got us a real haul, Clyde. Think of that. Only a week in this city and we're on the road to fortune."

Shannon sagged forward, motes of light dancing before her eyes. "Let her go," Clyde said. "Don't choke the life out of her. Not yet." He caught Shannon as Bert released her, and he opened her cloak with quick, skilled fingers. "Look at this, will you?" His hand gripped the brooch. "Can't see in this damn fog, but looks to me like—"

"Take your hands off me," Shannon cried. "Don't touch me!"

Clyde tossed the cloak to Bert, and then his hand went to the brooch and she heard the sound of ripping taffeta as he tore it free. She fought, striking out blindly, clawing, kicking, until she saw something in Bert's face that paralyzed her momentarily. He was staring at her breasts, half-exposed now. "Will you look at that?" He hooked his huge hands into either side of her camisole, and ripped it open to the waist. He pushed her against a board fence, and leaned his weight on her. She screamed, and he slapped her so hard that for a moment, everything was blotted out. "You just quit carryin' on, and we'll do fine, the three of us. Let's get her into the alley here."

"Not her," Clyde said, his voice soft and silky. "A fancy piece like her doesn't belong in an alley. We'll take her to the shack with us. Plenty of time then, and no one to interrupt us. You've got to take your time with her kind. A real beauty, she is."

Bert made a growling noise in his throat, like an animal. "To hell with that. They're all the same, lyin', cheatin' bitches." His hands closed on Shannon's bare breasts, his powerful fingers tightening until she gave a strangled cry. She tried to claw at his face, until he took one of her nipples between thumb and forefinger and squeezed it viciously. Pain lanced through her from her breast deep into her loins, and tears of agony filled her eyes and spilled down over her cheeks. She heard herself whimpering, "Don't— please—"

"That's better," Bert said. "Stay quiet or you'll get worse than that."

"Better do what he says," Clyde warned. "Bert's

got a bad temper when he gets mad. That's how he got himself shipped off to Sydney."

"Stow that," Bert said, his red-rimmed eyes glaring at his companion. "To hell with Sydney. I got me a fine piece now. I'm goin' to make up for lost time."

Convicts, Shannon thought, her mind working dazedly, stunned as she was with pain and terror. *Escaped from one of the Australian penal colonies.*

"Let me go. My husband will find me. He'll kill you both."

"By the time we're finished with you, your husband won't want you. He won't even recognize you. If you've got a husband."

Bert twisted her arm behind her, bringing her wrist up so hard that she was sure the bone would snap.

She screamed again, and this time he hit her, not with his open hand, but with his closed fist, so that the fog turned reddish, then black, and she slumped against him, consciousness blotted out.

21

THE SHACK was set among a cluster of others, rickety, unpainted warrens close to the bay. Shannon, who had recovered consciousness as she was being carried inside, caught the mingled odors of salt water, rotting fish and kelp. Clyde lit an oil lamp that hung on a nail, and she saw that the only furnishings were a filthy mattress lying in one corner of the room, and several upended packing crates. High in one wall was a small, grimy window, the broken places stuffed with rags.

Bert pushed Shannon down on the mattress, his huge hands tearing at her clothes. She cried out in terror. "You can't. You don't know who I am."

"Who are you then, luv? Queen Victoria, herself, out for a stroll on Pacific Street? Or maybe the Empress of France?"

"I'm Shannon Kincaid!"

Bert laughed harshly. "That supposed to mean

something special around here?" The two men were obviously newcomers.

"You can ask anyone. You can—"

"Not now, luv. We got better things to do with you."

She cried out again, and saw Bert draw back his arm. A moment later, his fist smashed into her jaw, and her brain reeled under the impact. She was limp, unable to speak or to struggle as Bert stripped her dress off, then her frilled undergarments. She cowered away from him, paralyzed with fear and revulsion, watching as he tilted a bottle of gin to his mouth, then passed it to Clyde. Instinctively, she clutched at a tattered blanket that lay at the foot of the mattress, and tried to draw it over her body, but Bert tore it away.

"Modest, ain't she? Here, Clyde, pass me that bottle. A sip of gin'll loosen her up."

"Adam will kill you for this," she panted.

"Adam? Who's he? Your fancy man?"

"My husband. He's—"

"No respectable woman with a husband would be wandering around on Pacific Street at night. We may be new here, but we know that much."

"Now wait," Clyde interrupted. "Her clothes. That brooch—"

"A high-priced whore from one of them fancy parlor houses. I've been wantin' to get my hands on one of them ever since we landed here. Looks like now's my chance," Bert said. He twisted his hand in Shannon's hair, loosened from its pins now and tumbled about her naked shoulders. He forced her head back and pushed the bottle between her lips, laughing as she gagged on the burning liquor. "Maybe there's something you'd like better," he said.

He straddled her body, his powerful thighs pressing against her shoulders and she sensed his purpose even before he grasped her jaw, his fingers locking like steel pincers on either side. With his other hand, he fumbled at his trousers. This was a man who took some twisted pleasure in degrading women; she saw it in his small, slitted eyes.

"I can't. Don't make me." Better to be beaten, killed than to submit to this. Then she thought of Adam, and their child. She had to survive, to return to them. If she could satisfy this monster she would be spared, for a little while. She closed her eyes, and did what was required of her, nausea churning inside her. Until she heard Bert whispering hoarsely, "That's enough." He pushed her backward on the mattress, moving down, forcing her legs apart; his huge, callused hands gripping her shoulders. "What's this?" she heard him say, and a moment later, he had grasped the chain of the locket Odalie had given her; had ripped it from her neck so that her flesh was torn and bleeding.

She gave a dazed cry of protest as he flung the locket into a corner. Then she screamed more frantically as he thrust himself into her again and again.

Later, she saw Clyde's face above her, and felt a rag being pushed into her mouth. "Can't stand a screaming woman," he said. "Like things nice and quiet. Easy, now, luv. Clyde knows how to treat a high-class piece like you. I ain't rough like Bert." He fondled her breasts, and she writhed, unable to cry out now. Then, sensing that her struggles only excited him, she lay still, tears wetting her face.—

In the hours that followed, Shannon was pushed inexorably to the brink of sanity, and beyond. She knew that there were other men in the shack. She heard the heavy tread of their booted feet, heard Clyde haggling over money and the clink of coins. She was an object without feeling, a receptacle for the varying lusts, hitherto unknown obscenities inflicted on her by men who had spent long years in the penal colonies, deprived of contact with women. She no longer wished for escape, only for unconsciousness, which came at last.

When she opened her eyes again, she could not remember where she was, until, staring upward, she saw the warped, unpainted beams overhead, and a crimson glow outside the window. Dawn? Sunset? She could not be sure. The gag had been removed from her mouth, but her lips and tongue were bruised and swollen, her throat ached from the pressure of her throttled cries.

She turned her head and saw Bert sprawled beside her. He reeked of gin and stale sweat, and there was an empty bottle beside him. He wore only his boots and trousers.

Cautiously, she looked around the room. Clyde was gone. And her clothes, which had been tossed on top of one of the crates, were gone, too.

A tattered blanket covered her, and under it, her muscles throbbed with agony. But she had to get away now, while Clyde was out of the shack. Slowly, she inched away from Bert, holding onto the blanket, drawing it with her; she could not run out into the street stark-naked, not even here in Sydney-Town.

She forced herself to her feet, clutching at the blanket, and she saw that the crimson glow was fading into darkness. Evening, then. She had been unconscious all day. She was still weak and dizzy, but she knew that she must not let herself faint. Somehow, she would get back to Adam and her child. She swayed but kept on her feet, wrapped the blanket around her bruised body, and tied the ends into a clumsy knot between her breasts.

The rays of the setting sun caught the glint of metal on the floor. The locket. She moved stealthily across the floor, knelt to pick up the little golden oval.

"Hold it right there, slut," Bert bellowed.

Shannon made a run for the door but her legs were unsteady, and he was right behind her, grabbing her hand as she struggled with the bolt. "Sneakin' out, were you?"

"Let me go. I won't tell anyone. Not ever. I swear—"

"Lying bitch. Same as all the rest of 'em." He twisted her arm behind her. "Fifteen years in that damn prison stockade in Australia. Fifteen bloody years, and you know why?"

She did not answer, until he twisted harder, so that a searing pain shot up her arm and into her shoulder. "I don't know," she gasped.

"Because of a slut like you, with a soft, pretty face like yours. My wife. Tried to run off and leave me, she did." He shook her. "Know what I did?"

"No."

"Took a knife to that face of hers. I'll bet no man wanted her after that."

"But I'm not your wife."

"You're all alike. Sly, sneaky. Only waitin' for a chance to get away."

He dragged her back and threw her down on the mattress. Dear God, he was mad!

"I'm going to fix you like I fixed her." He picked up the empty gin bottle, smashed it against a crate.

Shannon tried to scream but no sound would come. She tried to cover her face with her arm.

"Drop it, Bert."

The bottle crashed to the floor, and Shannon saw Clyde standing just inside the door, a pistol pointed at Bert's chest.

"But she was tryin' to—"

"I don't care what she was trying to do. I don't want her scarred. Got a customer outside. He's in the market for women. Going to take her over to one of the cribs on Pacific Street."

The customer was nothing like the men who had been brought to her last night; he was slender, though wiry, and wore a canary-colored silk shirt, diamond studs, and a diamond pin in his satin cravat. There was a brisk, businesslike air about him, as he strode over to the mattress.

"Pretty battered, isn't she?"

"Bruises fade," Clyde said. "She's young and she's got a fine shape. Too good for one of them cribs, but what the hell. Me and my mate here, we need ready cash."

The customer shrugged. "Stand up," he said to Shannon. "Turn around."

She had no more will of her own. She was too shaken, too badly hurt in body and spirit. She obeyed.

"She'll do," the customer said. "Fifty dollars."

"Fifty dollars? For a prime piece like her? I could get more for her myself."

"I got the connections. Get her off your hands right now, smooth and easy."

Clyde and the man in the silk shirt argued briefly, while Shannon struggled into the flimsy stained cotton wrapper the man had tossed to her. It smelled of stale perfume and sour wine.

"Better gag her again," Bert said when the transaction had been completed to the satisfaction of the three men.

"She'll behave," the man said. "Leave it to Charlie Watkins. I know my business. You ain't going to make no trouble, are you, honey?"

"No. No trouble," Shannon mumbled.

He had to lift her into the shabby hansom that waited at the end of the narrow street, its shades drawn. The cab started off, and she heard Watkins saying, "That Clyde, he was right. You're too good for a crib. Forty men a night." He lifted her hair, ran it through his fingers, and she whimpered, fearing another assault. "Girl like you won't last long there. If it wasn't for those marks on you, you'd do for a fancy parlor house over on Pike Street."

Something stirred at the back of Shannon's numbed mind. A parlor house. On Pike Street. Miss Delphine's, where Adam had gotten her wedding gown.

"Mr. Watkins, listen. Why couldn't you—"

He looked at her sharply.

"You'd get more money that way, wouldn't you? And Bert and Clyde, they wouldn't have to know. A fancy parlor house. Miss Delphine's."

He smiled thoughtfully. "She might. She just might, at that. How do you know about Miss Delphine?"

"Everybody knows Delphine's, don't they?" Mackenzie had said that once.

Charlie Watkins gave the driver the new instructions. His face wavered before Shannon's eyes and she slumped against him. By the time they reached the rear entrance of the tall, narrow house on Pike Street, he had to half-drag, half-carry her up the steps.

They were admitted by a dark-skinned woman in a neat maid's uniform, who told them to wait. From a room somewhere on the same floor, Shannon heard the sound of shrill, feminine laughter, the deep voices of men, the music of a piano and a girl's voice singing "Open Thy Lattice, Love."

Then Shannon caught the strong smell of patchouli perfume, and saw a stout, well-corseted woman in a dark red velvet dress, with dyed blond hair piled on her head in an elaborate coiffure of ringlets, puffs and braids, interwoven with red silk flowers.

"Heard you were short a couple of girls. This one's a real beauty."

The woman looked Shannon up and down, her eyes sharp and observant. "What's wrong with her? She drunk or drugged?"

"She just got in from Virginia City. A rugged trip over those mountains. But she's a prize, Delphine. I wouldn't bring you anything except top-quality stuff, you know that. Now, about the money—"

"Not so fast," Miss Delphine said. "Can't she talk for herself. What's your name, honey?"

"Sha—"

"Charlotte," Watkins said quickly. He gave Shannon's arm a warning squeeze. If he did not sell her here, would he take her to Pacific Street?

"Charlotte," she repeated automatically. If only her brain would clear. A thin gauze veil seemed to drift before her, blurring her vision.

"Who beat her up like that?"

"A customer. Drunk. You know how it is."

"My girls don't get beat up, Charlie. And my customers don't want damaged goods. Or girls who drink too much."

"I'm not drunk." Shannon wrenched her arm away from Watkins' firm grip. "Miss Delphine—" She clutched at the woman's velvet sleeve. "Please, you've got to help me. I'm Shannon Kincaid, Adam Kincaid's wife. You know Adam."

"What kind of a line are you trying to give me?"

"Oh, but it's true. Believe me. Adam, I want Adam."

"Like I thought. Drunk. Or sick in the head. Get her out of here, Charlie."

"No—please—" Shannon was hysterical now, clinging to Delphine. The singing had stopped in the parlor, and some of the girls and their customers were crowding into the hall, attracted by the commotion.

"I don't want any trouble in my place," Delphine said. "Get her out of here, before I have you both thrown out."

Shannon quailed under the cold fury of Charlie Watkins' eyes. He reached for her, but she evaded his

outstretched arm and ran blindly, like a hunted, terrified animal, down the hallway, and through the
velvet-draped entrance to the parlor. She stumbled
against a small, marble-topped table, heard the crash
of glasses, and then she fell to her knees. A man's
hand gripped her shoulder and she screamed like a
mad woman.

"Shannon, what in God's name—"

She looked up. Bruce was staring down at her. He
drew her to her feet and held her against him.

"They hurt me," she whispered. "Don't let them
hurt me any more."

The darkness was closing in, thick, stifling. From
what seemed like a long way off, she heard Delphine
asking, "You know this girl, mister?"

"Damn right I do. She's Adam Kincaid's wife."

"She tried to tell me, but I thought—how was I
supposed to know? Look at her."

Then Shannon could no longer hear Delphine's
voice, or anything else.

22

SHANNON floated in a dark sea, then slowly surfaced into the light. She was afraid to open her eyes at first, but she forced herself to do so, and saw the familiar surroundings of her own bedroom: the round, painted globe of the lamp on the small table beside her bed, the pale yellow silk curtains that hung in soft folds looped back to the bedposts with tasseled cords. And Bruce's face, white and strained. He slid his arm around her shoulders and raised her against the soft pillows. "Drink this," he said. He held a steaming china mug to her lips.

Even with the support of his arm, Shannon found it difficult to comply, for the slightest movement brought pain. Her lips were cut and swollen, her jaw throbbed, and her breasts and thighs were so badly bruised and abraded that even the soft muslin nightgown, brushing against her skin, made her bite back a gasp. She was cold, shivering, but she felt a harsh burning sensation in the secret, hidden places of her body, reminding her of the indignities that had been inflicted on her. She moaned and Bruce held her closer. "Just take a few sips, please, dear. It'll help."

She swallowed obediently. The pungent mixture of hot water, rum and spices made the chill recede, helped her taut muscles to relax.

"Who did this to you?"

"Bruce, I feel so— I feel as if I'll never be clean again. Never."

"Who did it, Shannon?"

She turned her face to him, and he stroked her heavy, tawny hair as she began to tell the nightmare story of the past hours. She would not tell him all of it. She would never tell a living soul. But she said enough to bring cold fury to his eyes.

"I didn't know there were men like those. I wanted to die. And when Delphine told that—that man to take me away—" She clutched at his coat. "If you hadn't been at Delphine's tonight—"

She stopped short, tensing at the sound of footsteps in the hall. She cried out, for even here, in her own bed, with Bruce beside her, the nightmare would not go away.

She heard Mrs. Beal saying, "Oh, Mr. Kincaid, thank goodness you're home. When she didn't come home last night, I notified the police. But they didn't find her. Mr. Lathrop did."

The bedroom door was flung open, and Adam came striding into the room, then stopped short, seeing Bruce there, his arm around Shannon. She tried to rise, then fell back against the pillows. How often, during the past months, she had imagined the first moments of Adam's return. And now— She gripped

Bruce's hand so hard that her nails bit into his flesh. "Don't tell Adam. Bruce, he mustn't know." She spoke in a feverish whisper.

"What the hell's going on here? Mrs. Beal wasn't making any sense." He caught his breath. "Shannon, your face."

"An accident." She forced the words out. "I had an accident. I'm all right now. Bruce, tell him I'm all right."

"He has to know sooner or later, Shannon," Bruce said.

"No. You don't understand."

Gently, Bruce disengaged her frantic, clinging hands and stood up. "You're not to blame. Those men—not men, animals."

"What men?" Adam demanded of Bruce. There was a driving fear in his eyes.

"That Sydney-Town bunch. That filth from the penal colonies."

"What was Shannon doing in Sydney-Town?"

"She went to Telegraph Hill, to the boardinghouse. Odalie and I had quarreled, you see. Odalie's—she's pregnant, and scared. From the time I came home she was at me, blaming me. I couldn't take it so I walked out. She sent for Shannon. I was making the rounds of the taverns and the—"

"To hell with that," Adam interrupted, his face dark with anger. "What about Shannon?"

"She was trying to find a hansom, after she left the boardinghouse. She lost her way in the fog."

Shannon gave a wordless cry, but Adam did not go to her. His eyes were fixed on Bruce. "And then?"

Bruce put a hand on Adam's arm. "Over here," he

said, leading Adam to the far end of the room. Shannon could not hear what he said, only the rise and fall of his voice, interrupted, from time to time, by Adam's questions. She had forgotten her own sufferings for the moment, and could think only of Adam. If he learned what had happened, no power in heaven or hell would stop him from plunging into the dark cesspool of Sydney-Town. He would find the men who had raped her, and he would try to kill them. But he was one against many. And Mackenzie had said that even the police feared the gangs in Sydney-Town. The human vultures who lived there might battle among themselves, but they would close ranks against any attempt at vengeance by an outsider.

She heard Bruce saying, "The man who brought her to Delphine's got away in the uproar. I'd have killed him otherwise."

"The man will die. He, and the rest of them." He went to the dresser and Shannon's eyes caught the dull glint of metal, as the lamplight moved on the long barrel of the Navy Colt. Adam did not raise his voice, but his words made Shannon's blood freeze.

"How will you find them?" Bruce asked.

"I'll find them." Adam strapped on his gunbelt. It contrasted oddly with his fine dark-blue suit, his satin waistcoat and fashionable cravat. "Delphine can describe the man who brought Shannon to her. She may know his name. I'll go to her place first."

"Adam, wait!" She tried to rise from her bed, and Adam went to her swiftly, sat down beside her and drew her into his arms. He held her carefully, as if she might break. "They'll pay for what they did. This time."

"This time?" Bruce repeated. "I don't understand."

But Shannon understood. Shocked and dazed though she was, she understood. Adam was thinking of his sister, the river pirates, the terror and shame of that far-off day. He had been a boy then, too young, too powerless to defend Rachel. The guilt of it must have tortured Adam all these years. That was why she had feared to let him know the truth. He would go into Sydney-Town, not only to avenge his wife, but his dead sister. He had to prove something to himself, and Shannon, clinging to him, knew she was powerless to stop him.

Still the words came. "Adam, don't leave me. Oh, my love, I need you."

Her nightgown slipped from her shoulder, and he saw the bruises, livid and ugly. He drew a harsh breath. For a moment, the icy composure dropped from his face; he looked shaken, vulnerable.

He got up and turned away.

"Adam—please," she begged.

When he turned back to her, the moment had passed; his face was immobile. His hand touched her cheek, lightly. Then he pulled her nightgown back in place. He brushed the side of her throat, and she winced as the fingers touched her lacerated flesh. Remembering how Bert had torn the locket off, after he had forced her to submit to his twisted lust, she felt icy sickness engulf her mind, so that her thoughts were confused. "The locket," she said. She was finding it difficult to form the words. "He tore off the locket. I tried to get it back. But he woke up angry. Said he'd cut my face."

"What's she talking about?" Adam demanded of Bruce.

"She kept saying something about a locket, when I was bringing her home. But I couldn't make any sense out of it."

"The locket—my father's miniature—Odalie wanted me to have it."

Adam was leaning over her, his voice harsh with urgency. "Where's the locket now, Shannon?"

"The shack. Bert and Clyde. Sydney-Town. Men kept coming in and going out all night—paying to—to—"

"The street," Adam demanded. "Do you know where the street was?"

"The fog was so thick, I couldn't see. I heard a ship's bell. And I smelled salt-water and—fish. Kelp."

"I'll find the place." He took her hand and held it against his cheek. "I'll bring the locket back. After I've finished with them."

"There are too many. If you go alone you'll be killed."

"He isn't going alone," Bruce said. "I'm going with him."

She tried to tell Bruce that he must not go, for Odalie was alone and frightened. Odalie was going to have a baby, and she needed him. As Shannon needed Adam. Her lips moved but the words did not come. The lighted globe of the lamp flickered and receded.

"They'll be killed."

Mrs. Beal wiped the perspiration from Shannon's face. "No, Mrs. Kincaid. It will be all right. Rest now."

"I'll never see Adam again."

"Try to sleep. The doctor said you must sleep."

Throughout the rest of the night and the following day, Shannon drifted in and out of darkness. But sleep brought terrifying dreams, and she woke with a cry.

Once, hearing the clanging of bells, she sat up and said, "Fire. There's a fire."

"It's on the other side of town," Mrs. Beal said. "Nothing to worry you." And she covered Shannon and soothed her back to sleep.

It was late the next evening when Shannon, fully conscious now, and propped up on pillows, heard a carriage turning into the drive below her windows. "Please let it be Adam," she whispered.

But it was Fergus Mackenzie who came upstairs to stand in the doorway of the bedroom, with Mrs. Beal. Shannon cried out when she saw the bandage on his face. Like the rest of him, it was black with soot and he moved stiffly to the side of her bed, as if it hurt him to walk.

"Is Adam with you?"

Mackenzie shook his head. "He's all right, though. He told me to come here as soon as I could. I didn't stop to get cleaned up."

"Shall I get you a drink, sir?" Mrs. Beal asked.

"I could use one," Mackenzie said. Then, unexpectedly, he grinned. "That was one hell of a fight." He accepted the decanter and glass Mrs. Beal put down for him. "I'll pour it myself," he said.

"As you wish, sir." She rustled out of the room.

"You're sure Adam's safe. You aren't just saying that to—"

"I give you my word." He drained the brandy in his glass and poured himself another stiff drink. "They were ready for us by the time we got to Sydney-Town. Ready and waiting."

"You went too?" Unexpectedly, Shannon felt her eyes sting with tears. "Oh, Fergus."

"Always wanted a chance to cover a real war. And this was war, Shannon."

He went on to tell her of Adam's arrival at Delphine's place. Mackenzie had been summoned by Delphine, who was afraid of what Adam might do when he discovered her part in the affair of that night. She pleaded with Mackenzie to make Adam understand that she had had nothing to do with Shannon's being brought there. She had described Charlie Watkins in detail, and had told Adam where the man could be found. "There were the three of us, Adam, Bruce and me, but there were a lot of other men at Delphine's who know Adam and respect him. They insisted on going along. Others joined us on the way across the city. Adam's logging crew, the men who were down from Mendocino."

But it had been Adam who had found the shack, who had broken in on Clyde and Bert. "Clyde put a bullet through Adam's shoulder before Adam killed him," Mackenzie said. Ignoring Shannon's startled cry, he went on to describe the fighting that had spread through Sydney-Town. Bert had tried to make a break for it, but Adam had caught up with him in a burning warehouse. "Half of Sydney-Town was ablaze by that time."

"But Adam was wounded."

"I don't think he even felt the pain, not until later. I tried to hold him back. It looked as though the roof was going to give way. But Adam wouldn't let anyone or anything stop him." Mackenzie rubbed his hand across the dirty bandage on his forehead.

"Adam hit you?"

"He didn't know what he was doing. I never saw Adam look that way. He went in and dragged Bert out. Bert was badly burned, but Adam forced a confession out of him. Before Bert died he told us—"

Adam's men had run Charlie Watkins to earth, and the crowd wanted a lynching on the spot, but Adam had prevented it. He had regained his control by that time.

"It wasn't easy. He wanted that man dead, like the others. He still does. But he told the men that they had to take Watkins to jail, and have him held over for trial. That's where Adam is now, over at the county jail on Broadway near Dupont Street. The city marshall's with him, and the police. But Adam and his men are going to make sure that none of Watkins' friends get him out."

"Adam's men, vigilantes?"

"Call them what you like. The fact is, plenty of solid citizens here in San Francisco are fed up with the way the politicians are protecting men like Watkins, accepting bribes."

"But the vigilantes. An undisciplined mob."

"They did a necessary job back in '51 and again in '56. Only this time, there'll be no lynching. I don't know if you realize what an influential man Adam's become here in this city. They're talking about running him for political office in the next election. A complete clean-up."

"I don't care about that. Adam's hurt. I want him here with me."

"He'll be here as soon as he can."

"And Bruce?"

"He's gone home to his wife. And, Shannon— Adam said to give you this." He pressed something into her hand. The locket.

"Don't cry, Shannon. Don't." He gave her a helpless look. "Mrs. Beal, come in here, will you?"

In the weeks that followed, as the air grew warm and sweet with the scent of the spring flowers in her garden, and sunlight bathed Rincon Hill, Shannon tried to shake off her lingering fears, to blot out the memory of her recurrent nightmares. She could not force herself to go into the streets of the city, not even in the carriage, but spent her time in the house or in the walled garden behind it.

Adam's bullet wound had been a clean one, and it had mended quickly. He spent many of his evenings out, and when he was at home, he was often occupied with visitors. There were committees demanding that he run for political office. Later, when he had made it clear that he did not wish to go into politics, that his expanding business enterprises, which now included the development of the Silver Vixen, would keep him too busy to devote himself wholeheartedly to city government, other citizens' groups, made up of businessmen whose interests were similar to his own, requested his support. They wanted to clean up the city, not for moral reasons, but because they did not see any future for San Francisco until order had been established. Adam agreed to give his financial support to several of these groups, and to use his growing influence to further their ends—and his own.

Then, gradually, the furor over local issues was eclipsed by the increasingly disturbing news from the East. On April 12, Fort Sumter was fired upon. Nine days later, the news exploded in San Francisco. Shortly afterward, the word came that President Lincoln had declared that a state of insurrection now existed, and issued the first call for volunteer troops. Southern ports were to be blockaded to prevent the importing of war materials for the Confederacy.

Even Shannon, still shaken by her own personal fears, had not been unmoved. It was difficult for her to realize that since last January, Alabama was no longer a part of the Union, but had banded together with other Southern states to form a new nation. The Confederate States of America. How strange, how alien that sounded.

She tried to shut out the realization of what was happening in the world around her, to remain secluded in her garden, playing with Colin, doing needlework, reading Mr. Dickens' enthralling new novel, *A Tale of Two Cities*.

She was engrossed in its pages one afternoon, toward the end of April, when Adam came from the house into the garden, and shook her out of her detachment with a piece of startling news.

"Fergus Mackenzie's leaving for the East," he told her. "He's going to cover the war for his newspaper."

She put down the book. "He told us he wanted to cover a war. Back in Panama, remember?"

Adam nodded. "But that's not all." He held out his arms to Colin, who had been toddling among the flower beds. He picked up the little boy, swung him in the air and made him crow with delight. After he had set Colin down again, he went on, "I didn't think I'd see the day when Mackenzie would be willing to give up his freedom."

Shannon looked at Adam blankly.

"Clarisse. He's asked her to marry him and go East with him. And she said yes."

"I'll miss her. And Fergus, too."

"The thing is, she lives in that hotel, and Fergus has a room in a boardinghouse, and so I offered them our home for the wedding. And the reception."

"Oh, no. You shouldn't have done that. Not without asking me."

"Clarisse is your friend. You've always told me how much she's done for you. That time in Mobile, and then, when the baby was on the way—"

"I want Clarisse to have a beautiful wedding. But not here. I can't face a crowd of people."

"You can't stay in hiding for the rest of your life," Adam said.

"I didn't expect you to understand. No man could."

"Maybe not. But you're going to be the hostess at this wedding. And then you're going to start acting like a woman, not a scared rabbit. I've come to the point where I have to do some entertaining, for businessmen and politicians. I need my wife to help me."

"I know. But not yet. Not this soon." In spite of

the warmth of the sunlight in the garden, she began to tremble.

"The wedding will be held in this house, a week from now. It's short notice, I know, but Fergus has to leave as soon as possible. I've already spoken to Mrs. Beal, and she'll be able to cope with the details. All you have to do is to buy a suitable gown."

Now, late on the afternoon of the wedding, Shannon had finished dressing. Her hair had been carefully arranged by Lottie, the maid Adam had hired for her.

The gown was suitable enough, Shannon assured herself, although far more subdued than the dresses she usually wore. It was a soft shade of brown, with a high rounded collar and full, wrist-length sleeves. Although it was becoming, the dressmaker, who had come to the house to do the fittings, had tactfully suggested something more low-cut.

"It is perfectly correct to bare the shoulders since this is to be an evening wedding. And perhaps a less matronly color. You'd look beautiful in a topaz satin, or one of the watered silks, in blue or green."

The bruises on Shannon's body had healed long since, and her shoulders and bosom were smooth and white. But there were other scars, inflicted on her spirit, that were slower to heal. "The bride will be the center of attention," Shannon reminded the dressmaker. "No one will notice me."

Now she smiled faintly, thinking of Clarisse in one of the other rooms down the hall. Lottie would be helping her now, slipping on her bridal gown of white brocade, trimmed with Brussels lace, adjusting her veil. Shannon knew that she should be with Clarisse, too, but she could not bring herself to leave the bedroom.

Even when Adam entered the room, she stood frozen.

"Come along," he said. "You're ready, aren't you?"

"Not—not yet."

"You look fine to me." He put his hand on her arm and for one brief moment, she felt a stirring of desire. Adam had not shared her bed since before he had gone away to Virginia City with Bruce, to examine the Silver Vixen. He had moved into one of the other bedrooms, and she had lain awake, night after night, hearing him walk past her closed door, fearing that he would come to her, hoping that he would.

"The minister's downstairs, and Fergus is in the library, fortifying himself with whiskey for the occasion. The first of the guests should be arriving soon."

"Adam, I can't do it. Make some excuse. Say I'm ill."

He shook his head. "If you don't care about your own future here in San Francisco, you might think about mine. Yes, and our son's, too. If you don't come down it will be harder for you the next time." He looked down at her steadily. "You're not a coward, Shannon. I know you won't fail me tonight."

He held out his arm and she took it, drawing reassurance from the feel of the hard muscles beneath her fingers. Miss Colter's training helped, too, for she found that she was able to raise her head and straighten her spine, saying, "I'm ready, Adam."

Adam stayed at her side on the receiving line, and later, during the reception that followed the ceremony. He introduced her to those guests she had not yet met, and she felt the knot of tension inside her loosening.› She was impressed by the number of prominent citizens who had accepted invitations. William Stewart, who had been California's Attorney-General, with his wife, Annie, daughter of ex-Senator Foote of Mississippi. Jim Fair and his wife, Teresa, who had been the daughter of an Irish tavernkeeper. Mrs. Fair cut a dashing figure in a gown of jade green satin, and there were diamond and emerald earrings, and an emerald necklace to add majesty to her appearance, for Fair had struck it rich in Nevada.

Congressman Jonas Meade and his silver-haired wife greeted Shannon warmly, as did the army officers in their dashing blue uniforms. Their commander, General Edwin Sumner, and his lady, had come to the reception, as well. Like the other guests, the couple were pleasant and cordial, and it was the general who danced the first waltz with Shannon.

Although everyone present must have known the reason for Adam's raid on Sydney-Town and its aftermath, Shannon was relieved that no one made a mention of the affair. Still, she was sure that they were speculating on her feelings, particularly the women. She pushed the thought from her mind, as she saw Clarisse, moving gracefully in the arms of her new husband, her eyes shining, her flaming hair covered with a lace veil.

Bruce and Odalie had attended the reception, but Odalie was too far along in her pregnancy to join in the dancing. Back in Mobile, it would have been unthinkable even for her to appear at a social function in her condition. But this was San Francisco, still raw and untamed, not bound by the rigid conventions of the older cities on the East Coast.

It was close to midnight when Clarisse embraced Shannon in farewell. "We'll be seeing each other again, honey," she said, tears sparkling on her lashes. Fergus bent to kiss Shannon warmly, then shook Adam's hand before setting off for the dock where their ship was waiting, to take them down the coast to Panama.

It was after the departure of the bride and groom, as Shannon was sitting in one corner of the flower-banked, candle-lit ballroom, talking with Odalie, that she became aware of a disturbance nearby.

"That's your last word, then?" Bruce demanded of Adam. Bruce's face was flushed, and Shannon was sure that he had had too much champagne. His gray eyes were dark with anger.

"Yes, it is," Adam answered. "And keep your voice down." He jerked his head in the direction of a group of blue-uniformed Army officers who were preparing to leave with their wives.

"Why the devil did you invite them? You're a Southerner. Or have you forgotten?"

Shannon rose swiftly and stepped between Bruce and Adam. Odalie came to join them, moving a little awkwardly, her swollen body covered with a lace shawl. Her face was troubled. "Bruce, dear, I'd like to go home now. I'm a little tired."

"As you wish," Bruce said, but it was plain that he was annoyed by the interruption. "It's time you decided where you stand," he said to Adam. "Or are you so eager to make a fortune that you've forgotten where your loyalties lie?"

"That's enough," Adam said. "This isn't the time or place for such talk. Come, Shannon. I think Mr. and Mrs. Fair are getting ready to leave. And the Mackays."

He took Shannon's arm and led her away firmly, but even as she was bidding her guests good-night, she was painfully aware of the clash between Bruce and Adam. Although she did not understand the immediate cause, she felt the dark shadow of the war, far away in the East, moving across a continent to threaten her and those whose lives were linked with hers.

23

ALTHOUGH IT WOULD be dawn in a few hours, Shannon sat on the cushioned chair before her dressing table, in her nightgown, a sheath of pale golden satin over which she wore her topaz velvet wrapper. Her tawny hair had been unpinned and brushed by Lottie, her maid. The house was quiet, for the last of the guests had long since departed and even the servants had finished their chores and retired. But for Shannon, there could be no sleep. Not yet.

She started slightly as she heard Adam's footsteps, passing her door. She knew that she had pleased him tonight, acting as a gracious hostess to their guests. Even the brief clash between Adam and Bruce had not caused a stir; Odalie had kissed her before leaving, agreeing to visit her for tea, and soon.

But there were too many unanswered questions in Shannon's mind to permit her to retire with any hope of sleeping. Beneath its yellow silk canopy, the bed looked large and empty. And lonely.

Drawing the belt of her wrapper more tightly around her, she rose and went out into the silent, dimly-lit hallway to the room that Adam had been using ever since his return from Sydney-Town. He had begun to undress, and wore only his trousers. She felt a stirring within her as she looked at him in the lamplight. High on his shoulder, clearly visible against his deeply tanned skin, was the raised white scar left by the bullet wound.

He looked at her in surprise. "What's wrong?" he demanded. "Colin's all right, isn't he?"

"He's sleeping like an angel. I went in to kiss him good night a little while ago. Adam, we've got to talk."

"Right now? Can't it wait until morning?"

"I can't sleep until I know what happened between you and Bruce. He's in some sort of danger, isn't he?"

"He could be, if he doesn't start using common sense." Adam put an arm around Shannon's shoulders. She felt the warmth of his body through her wrapper, and caught the comforting and familiar odors of bay rum, bourbon and Havana tobacco. "I don't want you worrying over Bruce."

"We both owe him so much," Shannon reminded Adam. "And I'm concerned for Odalie, too. She's in no condition to deal with any outside problems. She needs rest and freedom from worries."

"I realize that," Adam said. "Too bad Bruce doesn't. Damn fool. Getting himself mixed-up in this harebrained scheme."

"Adam, tell me, please."

"All right. I know you'll keep your mouth shut about it. The fact is, he's got himself involved with those Southern hotheads who've been carried away by those speeches of Asbury Harpending."

"Oh, no. I thought Harpending had agreed to disband his Knights of the Golden Circle. Fergus said that Harpending was called in for questioning by General Johnston, a few months ago, and that Harpending gave his word to—"

"Harpending's an opportunist. A mercenary and a rabble-rouser. His word counts for nothing. But I couldn't get Bruce to believe that. He wanted me to join the secret society. To help finance the movement with profits from the Silver Vixen."

"You wouldn't do that, would you?" she asked fearfully.

"Don't worry, sweetheart. It'll be a cold day in hell before I get caught up in anything like that. The Knights want to overthrow the state government. They're even talking about taking over the Comstock and getting shipments of silver and gold back East to fill the Confederate treasury. If they go ahead with their schemes they'll land in prison. Or up against a wall in front of a firing squad."

"Oh, no! It couldn't come to that. Why, Southern gentlemen have always had their secret societies. In Mobile and New Orleans they—"

He took his arm from her shoulders and turned to face her. "Oh, for God's sake, Shannon. This is no Mardi Gras they're mixed up in. It's war. You think the Union forces are going to look the other way, if those Southern gentlemen try to finance the Confederacy by smuggling silver and gold across the continent. Or sailing up and down the Pacific Coast, on privateering expeditions, seizing Pacific Mail steamers and shipping their cargoes of precious metals to the South?"

"Oh, but surely Bruce isn't—He wouldn't."

"He is. And he will."

"You've got to talk to him again," Shannon insisted. "You've got to convince him to leave the Knights."

"Bruce is a grown man. I saved his neck in that scrap back there in your uncle's tavern. He's on his own now."

"Have you forgotten what he did for me?" Shannon asked, her voice unsteady. Even now, she cringed from the memories of those hours in Sydney-Town.

Adam shook his head impatiently. "I haven't forgotten. I tried to talk to him tonight. He accused me of being a renegade to the Southern cause. And a few other things, none of them flattering. To hell with that. He was drunk. Probably didn't know what he was saying. All the same, he's going to have to take the responsibility for his own decisions. I won't interfere again."

"But suppose something happens to him? What will become of Odalie?"

"Are you sure you're concerned for Odalie? Maybe it's only Bruce you're worried about." He looked down at her, his eyes narrowing. "I wonder if you've ever gotten over your infatuation for the man. Have you, Shannon?"

Hurt and anger coursed through her. "Why should you care? You don't love me. You don't even want me to share your bed since—"

"That's a lie. If I haven't touched you since then,

it was only because I thought you'd wanted it that way. I thought it would disgust you, frighten you, to have any man touch you."

"You're not any man. You're my husband. Maybe it would have been difficult at first, but now—now I need you."

She reached out to him, and then she was in his arms. He lifted her, carried her to the bed, and undressed her, his hands swift and expert. He moved away to turn off the lamp and take off the rest of his own clothing, and she heard him saying, "So many nights I went past your bedroom door. I wanted to come to you. I thought I'd go crazy with wanting you. But I had to wait until you were ready."

"I'm ready now," she said. "Love me, Adam."

Then he was beside her and the mounting tension in his body communicated itself to her own. She turned on her side and he held her against him, gently at first, then more tightly. His naked flesh was warm against hers, his hands caressing, soothing. He bent his head and took one nipple between his lips; it grew hard and erect under his tongue, and a shiver of desire passed down her length, warming her loins, so that the soft tingling deepened, became a swift, fierce pulsing. His hardness was pressed against her, and he was turning her over onto her back. His mouth moved downward from her breasts to the taut, silken skin of her belly and the tawny golden triangle below.

Her thighs parted, and he explored the smooth, moist folds.

She cried out and he knelt over her, while she held him with her arms and her long, quivering thighs, raising her hips for his entry. He moved within her slowly at first, stopping from time to time to kiss her throat, her shoulders, her breasts, delaying his fulfillment until her own urgency could not be denied. Until she pleaded for release with her mouth and her hands and her whole straining body. His thrusts became quicker, deeper, and she clung to him in frenzied abandon, until he took her with him to the explosive, ultimate release.

Spring moved into summer, and although the war raged on the other side of the continent, in San Francisco, men were absorbed in more mundane matters. The Silver Vixen had begun producing again, and a river of silver flowed from Virginia City across the mountains, to enrich Adam and Bruce.

Although they were forced to meet on business matters nearly every day, Bruce did not come to the house again. Odalie did, however, for Shannon sent the carriage to bring her across the city. Together, the two young women sat during the long afternoons, and Odalie appeared to relax a little in Shannon's company.

Nevertheless, her face grew haggard and pale, and her dark brown eyes were sometimes shadowed with apprehension as she waited for the birth of her child.

Late one afternoon in midsummer, when Shannon was seated with Odalie in the walled garden, sipping China tea and nibbling thin slices of pound cake, Shannon saw Odalie go white. A moment later, the thin delicate teacup slipped from Odalie's fingers and shattered on the flagstones at her feet. Odalie cried out, and Shannon asked, "Did you burn yourself? I'll get a bit of butter."

Then, looking into Odalie's face, Shannon knew. Quickly she rose and ran to the house to call for Mrs. Beal. Between them, they got Odalie into the house and up the stairs. Odalie clutched at Shannon's arm. "I'm frightened. I want Bruce."

"He'll be here soon," Shannon said. "I'll have the coachman go and get him. Where is he, down at the mine offices?"

"I don't know. He never tells me where he's going anymore. He never tells me anything."

"Right now, we'd better send for the midwife," Mrs. Beal said. And so the carriage was dispatched, instead, to Mrs. Fogarty's house. Shannon, seeing the terror in Odalie's face, prayed silently that Mrs. Fogarty had not gone out on another case.

When Adam came home, shortly after sunset, he was startled by a high-pitched scream from the second floor. Without removing his coat, he ran up the stairs, to see Shannon emerging from one of the guest bedrooms.

"What's wrong?" he demanded.

"It's Odalie. The baby's coming. She doesn't know where Bruce is, and she's been calling for him."

"I haven't seen him for the last few days," Adam said. "I wish I'd never gone into partnership with him on the Silver Vixen."

Odalie cried out again. Adam winced at the sound.

"She's only been in labor for a few hours," Shannon told him. "Mrs. Beal says the baby may not arrive until tomorrow."

"Good Lord," he said. "How can she stand that much pain?"

"I don't know if she's really in extreme pain yet—

but she is frightened. She's always been afraid of childbirth."

From the bedroom, Odalie cried out, "Shannon—come here. Don't leave me."

"Where's the midwife?" Adam asked. "Why isn't she here?"

"I sent for her some time ago. But she may be with another woman. Her services are much in demand."

Shannon hurried into the bedroom, and Adam followed her. Mrs. Beal tried to block his way. "You'd best go downstairs, sir. I'll tell Cook to fix you a pot of coffee, and some cold roast beef."

"Not now," Adam said tersely.

"Mr. Kincaid," Odalie called. "Don't go. I must speak to you."

Adam looked surprised and uneasy as he approached the bed. Shannon had gone to light the lamp on the dresser.

"Mr. Kincaid—Adam—where's Bruce? I want him."

"You don't need Bruce right now," Adam said. "You need the midwife. Damn the woman, what's taking her so long?"

Odalie tensed before the onslaught of another pain. She cried out and tears streamed down her face. She reached out blindly to Adam, who took her hand between his. "I'm sorry," she whispered when the pain had abated. "I didn't know it would be—this bad."

"She needs help," Adam said. "I know the military surgeon out at Fort Point. I'll ride out there and get him."

Odalie rallied, and raised herself against the pillows. "A man—at a time like this. I don't think it would be proper—"

"To hell with propriety," Adam said. "You're not at Beau Rivage now." Then, more gently, he added, "I'll saddle a horse and ride out to the fort. I'll be back with the doctor as soon as possible. Don't be afraid, Odalie. You're going to have a fine baby for Bruce."

He motioned to Shannon to follow him outside. "I'm going to send the surgeon back here, and try to find Bruce myself."

"Where will you look? Odalie says he's been out every night for the past week." Then, remembering what Adam had told her about Bruce's connection with the Knights of the Golden Circle, she asked uneasily, "Do you think he's in some sort of trouble?"

"It wouldn't surprise me. I have a number of friends among the Union officers. I've heard rumors. Harpending may be getting ready to make a move."

"Oh, Adam, if anything should happen to Bruce, what would Odalie do?"

"She might be better off without him."

"She loves him," Shannon said.

Adam shrugged. "That's her misfortune."

Odalie cried out again. "Go to her," Adam said. He kissed her lightly and hurried downstairs, and around to the stables.

Before the night was out, Shannon had cause to be grateful for the arrival of Major Bixby, the military surgeon, for it soon became evident that this was not to be a normal delivery.

"The baby's turned," the major told Shannon, after

a brief examination. Odalie lay writhing on the bed, beyond shame now, indifferent to the presence of the surgeon. "I'm going to die—I know I'm going to die—"

"Nonsense, my dear," the stocky, tanned surgeon said comfortingly. "All women feel the same the first time, all expecting the worst. When you have your second, and your third—" But his eyes were worried.

Toward morning, he drew Shannon aside. "She can't go on much longer. I'd hoped the baby might turn by itself, but so far it hasn't happened."

"You can't let her die."

"I'm going to try to turn the baby myself. I won't lie to you, Mrs. Kincaid. It's a dangerous procedure, and painful. It might be best if you remained outside. Go and lie down. Your housekeeper's a calm, sensible woman. She can give me what assistance I need."

"No, Major Bixby," Shannon said firmly. "Odalie's my sister. I'll stay with her until—" She clenched her hands at her sides, willing herself to remain steady. "Until the baby's born."

Eugénie Lathrop was born shortly after sunrise. It was not until mid-morning, however, that Adam returned with Bruce. Even in her exhaustion, Shannon sensed a coolness between the two men. But it was not until Bruce had gone in to see his wife and his new daughter that Adam exploded.

"If it wasn't that I had to get him back here to Odalie in one piece, I'd have broken his neck."

"Adam, keep your voice down. Odalie's had a terrible time. Mrs. Fogarty was off in Placerville, delivering twins. By the time she got here—"

"Never mind Mrs. Fogarty," Adam said. Shannon did not remember when she had seen him so furious. Nevertheless, he lowered his voice, and followed Shannon into the dining room. He swallowed two cups of black coffee, laced with brandy, and then he told Shannon what had happened last night.

"It's a good thing for Bruce I went out to the fort. Otherwise, he'd be in jail this morning, with the rest of them. Harpending's bunch."

"What did they do?"

"They got hold of a schooner. They were going to be the first of Harpending's privateers. The plan was to capture a mail steamer that was leaving for the East with a cargo of gold bullion. They were going to run the captured steamer through the blockade, with their own crew aboard, and turn over the gold to Jefferson Davis."

"But how did you find out?"

"I have friends at the fort. I was an Army man myself, remember. The authorities had gotten wind of Harpending's plan some time ago. They were waiting for him to make his move. I wouldn't have cared if Bruce had ended up in the Disciplinary Barracks at Alcatraz, along with his friends. But I know how you feel about Odalie. And I couldn't help feeling sorry for her myself. It isn't her fault she's married to an irresponsible fool."

"Aren't you being unfair? Bruce is a Southerner. He believes in the Confederate cause."

"That's his right. But when he drags me into it— Shannon, that schooner was to be heavily armed. She'd have to be, to capture the mail steamer. Bruce let his friends store their weapons in one of our warehouses, along with the new machinery for the Silver Vixen. Rifles, Colt revolvers, cases of shells. Two brass twelve-pound cannons. If I hadn't gotten to him before the authorities did, the warehouse might have been confiscated, along with the rest of my property. Even the Silver Vixen."

"The mine belongs to Bruce, too."

"Not any longer. He's agreed to sell me his share, and take Odalie back East."

"To Alabama? But if he does that he'll want to join the Confederate army."

"No doubt he will," Adam said.

"What will happen to Odalie and the baby?"

"They can stay at Beau Rivage, or Jessamine."

"And you?"

"I have plans of my own. First, I've got to go back to Virginia City. I have to make certain arrangements about the mine."

Her heart sank. "Don't leave me alone. I need you, Adam."

He turned and took her in his arms, and held her so tightly that she could scarcely breathe. "I won't leave you. Not this time. I need you, too. Wherever I go."

This was no ardent declaration of love. But, Shannon thought, with a small, wry smile, it was the closest Adam Kincaid would ever come in admitting his feelings for her. And as she reached up, her hands pressing against the hard muscles of his shoulders, she knew that it was enough, more than enough.

24

ADAM AND SHANNON took the boat up the Sacramento River, late in August. Although Odalie had not fully recovered from her ordeal, Bruce was eager to go back to Alabama and offer his services to the Confederacy, and Odalie, too, was filled with patriotic fervor. Shannon was still heavy-hearted, remembering how she had parted from her sister, the strain and tension of their last good-byes.

While Shannon was waiting with Adam at Placerville for the stagecoach that would take them on from California to the Nevada Territory, he became aware of her low-spirited mood. In the tavern, where they were eating flapjacks and bacon amid a crowd of other travelers, he leaned over toward her. "What's wrong? Not worried about Colin, are you? Mollie and Mrs. Beal will take good care of him."

Shannon shook her head. "It's Odalie. Things will never be the same between us again."

Adam drank his scalding coffee out of a heavy tin mug.

"I suppose she thinks I'm a renegade, as Bruce does."

Shannon hesitated. "She knows that if it hadn't been for you, Bruce might be in that terrible prison. I don't think she could have stood that. She's grateful to you."

"She needn't be. I didn't get Bruce out of danger for his sake, or for hers. I did it for you, Shannon. And I offered him a good price for his share of the Silver Vixen to get rid of him. He's far too unstable to make a suitable business partner."

"Whatever your reasons, Odalie was so pleased to be going home. She told me that Bruce is going to use the money for Jessamine, to pay off his debts and put in a new crop. It will be a showplace again, as it was before he—"

"Before he squandered his money on gambling and— The devil with Bruce. Why did you quarrel with Odalie?"

"She couldn't understand why you weren't going back to Alabama, like Bruce, to join the Confederate army. She said she knew you weren't afraid to fight, so it must be because you were more interested in making money than in proving your loyalty to the South."

"She's right," Adam said calmly. There was a scramble for the tavern door, and a hoarse shout from the driver of the arriving stage. "Come along," Adam said. And although Shannon said no more about Bruce and Odalie, she could not shake off the lingering sadness she felt, remembering that last meeting with her sister.

The stage followed the Washoe trail, over the Sierra to Dayton and Gold Canyon, a journey of some hundred and fifty miles. It was an arduous trip, but an exciting one for Shannon. The trail was jammed with other travelers, mostly men. Some traveled by coach, others, mostly gamblers and confidence men, Adam told her, rode fine horses. A few used covered wagons, and many traveled on foot.

They ascended the tree-covered foothills of the Sierra, in the golden warmth of late summer, raising clouds of red dust around them. The slopes were bright with wildflowers: the red and yellow paintbrush, the blue gentian and the pink blossoms called shooting stars. She caught sight of tanagers, and heard their song as they swooped and darted against the sky. Here and there, she saw a quail, scurrying for cover.

"You told me once that you love this country," she said to Adam. "Back in the tavern in Mobile, remember? I didn't understand then, but now I do."

From the heights of the Sierra, Adam pointed out the silver ribbon of the American River, winding on its course five hundred feet below them, on its way to the ocean.

The coach made its tortuous way, swaying and creaking, toward the rocky summit. Early one morning, when they stopped to rest the horses, Adam lifted Shannon down and led her to a bend in the trail, from which she could see, far below, the emerald-and-sapphire glitter of Lake Tahoe. "It's so beautiful, this part of the country. It makes me feel a little giddy."

"It's not all like this," he said. "Virginia City's fascinating, but it can't be called beautiful. Hot and dusty in summer, and freezing cold in winter. Clouds of smoke and alkali all year round."

"Odalie told me a little about it—she spent her honeymoon there with Bruce, you know. She hated it."

Adam raised an eyebrow. "Virginia City, or her honeymoon?"

Shannon flushed and looked away. "Both, I think. She—doesn't like— I think she's afraid, even now."

"That's rough on Bruce," Adam said, without much sympathy. "I'm glad I found myself a shameless wench like you."

Shannon chose to ignore his last words. "Maybe things will be better for Odalie now. She belongs in a fine mansion like Jessamine."

"You thought the same about yourself once," Adam reminded her. "Odalie's living in a dream if she thinks Jessamine or Beau Rivage, any of those Black Belt plantations, will remain untouched by this war. When the South is defeated—"

"You think it will be?"

"Yes, I do."

"How can you be so sure? Bruce told Odalie that the war would be over by Christmas."

"Don't bet on it," Adam said. "I think that this war will be a long and bloody one. And when it's over, Odalie's world will have been destroyed. I wonder whether she and Bruce will have the strength and the courage to make a new one for themselves."

"Bruce is not a coward," Shannon said, her amber eyes hot with anger. "You should know that. Didn't he go with you to Sydney-Town?"

"There are different kinds of courage. I know that Bruce isn't afraid to face a loaded pistol—or a cannon. He can ride and shoot, and I've no doubt he'll distinguish himself in a cavalry charge. But he'll need more than that if he's to survive what's ahead."

It was not difficult for Shannon to understand Odalie's dislike for Virginia City. She, herself, was overwhelmed, dazed by the frenzy of activity in this boomtown that had grown up on the side of Sun Mountain. During their stay, she never ceased to hear the clattering of the stamping mills, the thunder of hoists, the shriek of whistles. Stages came and departed constantly; pack trains moved across the Sierra, laden with wine and cards, salt and flour for the miners, along with the finest satins, laces and perfumes for the more successful of the prostitutes who had followed on the trail of the silver-seekers. Copper and mercury were brought over the mountain passes, too, to be used in the mills, and machinery for mines.

"Those three streets are called 'A,' 'B,' and 'C,'" Adam told her pointing up at the winding thoroughfares that straggled up the mountain.

He called her attention to men from every part of the world, who crowded the streets. Chinese coolies in pigtails, balancing baskets on shoulder yokes. Mexican *vaqueros*, dark and dashing, riding fine horses with silver-mounted saddles. She saw miners in blue jeans, Frenchmen in modish, imported suits. And Paiute Indians, the first inhabitants of the region.

"Over there's the Wells Fargo office," Adam said, as they passed an impressive, iron-faced building with heavy doors and shutters. Crowded along the streets were countless saloons and restaurants, including a "Café de Paris" and a German *bier-keller*.

The International Hotel, where Adam had taken rooms for himself and Shannon, was equipped with iron balconies, billiard parlors, smoking rooms and a magnificent bar, where Adam spent a good deal of time, talking business with engineers, dealers in mining equipment, shareholders in other large mines, with politicians and judges and army officers. He went to inspect the Silver Vixen, and told Shannon that he was satisfied with the progress being made in the development of the mine.

Since Virginia City had its share of Confederate sympathizers as well as Union men, there were frequent clashes, sometimes settled with fists, other times with Colt revolvers or Bowie knives. Adam refused to be drawn into any such conflict.

One evening, when he had hired an open carriage to take Shannon to the theater, their progress down C Street was interrupted by the beating of drums, and then, by a column of marching men. "Lincoln's called for volunteers," Adam said. "Looks like Virginia City's going to contribute her share."

Shannon looked after the straggling line of recruits, many of them wearing their miners' jeans. Angry shouts of protest arose from the secessionists who crowded the sidewalk; one of them sprang down with a shout to wrest the drum from the boy who led the procession. A moment later, a blue-uniformed recruiting sergeant charged into the fray. Now C Street erupted into violence. Adam swore, as he held onto the reins of the open carriage, and fought to keep the team from bolting. Knives flashed and Shannon heard the crack of a pistol.

"Get down and stay down," Adam shouted, and she obeyed, crouching on the floor of the carriage, clutching at the seat, her face pressed against the smooth leather.

"We licked them at Bull Run and we'll do the same in Virginia City," a secessionist yelled from somewhere in the crowd. But the fight ended abruptly with the arrival of Union reinforcements, armed and mounted. Another drum was brought and the parade formed again, heading in the direction of City Hall. One of the recruits began to sing and the others joined in lustily.

> John Brown's body lies a mouldering in the grave.
> His soul is marching on.

Shannon remained trembling on the floor of the carriage, until Adam reached out a hand to help her up. "It's all right now," he said. "We'll get along to the theater."

"No, Adam," she said shakily. "Please, take me back to the hotel."

Adam nodded, and turned the carriage around. But even back at the hotel, Shannon was aware of the tension. As the Union recruits marched passed the open doors of the lobby, still singing, a group of Confederate sympathizers charged out of the bar, and took up the opening lines of a song Shannon was to hear again in the weeks to come.

> Hurrah! Hurrah! For the Southern Rights, Hurrah!
>   Hurrah for the Bonnie Blue Flag,
> That bears a single star!

The tune was stirring; it thrilled her and even upstairs in the hotel suite, she could still hear the men singing the words from below. She sank down on the end of the bed and realized that her face was wet with tears.

"Easy there, sweetheart," Adam said, misunderstanding. "You're safe here with me."

"It's not that. Oh, Adam, we've got to go home, as Bruce and Odalie did. You can get a commission in the Confederate army. Why, with your experience with Frémont, you could—"

"Shannon, I've told you before, I'm not about to rush to the defense of the Confederacy." He stripped off his coat and poured a shot of bourbon. "However," he went on, "we will be leaving for the East. And soon."

"Leave California? But you just said you weren't going to join the Confederate army."

"That's right. I came here to Virginia City to hire a competent manager to take over the running of the Silver Vixen. And an engineer to handle the installation of the new equipment. I've had a number of talks with Congressman Meade. You met him at Mackenzie's wedding, remember? He's made me an offer. With the approval of certain officials in Washington. The government is concerned about the possibility of trouble from secessionists in this part of the country. They could waylay shipments of gold and silver. They need a man in Washington, who knows this part of the country well, who can anticipate where and when such action might take place."

"Not you, Adam!"

"I don't want to leave California, and turn my business interests over to management by other men. We've made a good life for ourselves out here, and I had hoped to stay clear of this war."

"Then why don't you? You're not an abolitionist."

"There's more at stake than the slavery question. There's the Union."

"You're going to join the Union army?" Shannon stared at him in disbelief. "You can't! Adam, you're a Southerner."

"I'm going to Washington, but not to join the Union army. I'll be working for the War Department. I'm told I'll be most useful there."

"Useful? To the Yankees?"

"To the Union. Shannon, this country can be great, powerful. But not if sections are allowed to split away at will. Suppose California decided to leave the Union and form an independent empire? Or if the New England states joined in their own confederacy?"

"I don't care about all that," Shannon cried. "I'm a Southerner. Philippe Duval—"

"Forget about Philippe Duval. You're Peggy Cavanaugh's daughter. It was your father's people who cast you out. Or have you forgotten? You don't even have a right to his name." Then, seeing her stricken look, he said more gently, "You have no stake in preserving the plantation system. Besides, I think the time has come when slavery is no longer practical. Perhaps it never really was."

"How could plantations like Jessamine and Beau Rivage go on producing without slaves?"

"That's no concern of mine," Adam said harshly. "Or yours. Tell me, Shannon, if you had a claim to Beau Rivage, would you be able to live on the forced labor of other human beings?" His laugh was hard and mocking. "I remember how you took on the day we met, because you had to ride in a wagon with those slaves."

Her amber eyes narrowed with anger. "Your slaves, Adam. Yes, I know you'd only leased the men to work in the mill. But you bought Tina outright. You showed the captain of the *Amaranth* a bill of sale."

"Good Lord, you're not still angry over Tina after all this time, are you?"

To her surprise, Shannon realized that she was. Loving Adam as she did, she was jealous of every other woman he had ever had.

"Antoinette would have sold Tina in any case," he was saying. "She hated the girl. The overseer told me so."

"What reason would Antoinette Duval have to hate a slave? Her own property?"

"Are you sure you want to know?" Adam asked. And when Shannon nodded, he went on, "Philippe Duval had an eye for a pretty female. White or black."

Shannon sprang from the edge of the bed, where she had been sitting. "Are you saying that my father and Tina—"

"He never bedded down with her. He was too ill, after that first heart attack, to do anything more than look at her. But that was enough to arouse Antoinette's jealousy. And you should know what Antoinette Duval's like when she thinks she has cause for revenge." His face grew hard. "I know what a flogging feels like, Shannon. I should, after those years with Tom Sprague. It's not only the pain. It strips away every shred of dignity, of humanity."

"So you bought Tina out of pure kindness. An act of charity, was it?" The moment the words were out Shannon wanted to call them back. For the first time, Adam had tried, however briefly, to share with her his feelings about the past, about the experiences that had shaped, and, in some ways, twisted his character. She reached out her hand to him, but he had turned away. His glass was empty, and now he poured himself another drink.

"No need to be ladylike with me, sweetheart. If you want to know about Tina and me, you've only to ask."

"It doesn't matter. Truly, it doesn't."

"Don't lie," he said softly. "Obviously, it does matter or you wouldn't be making such an issue of it." He sipped his drink, then put down the glass on the dresser. "Yes, I slept with Tina. It wasn't rape, if that's what you're thinking. She was scared at first, but in a little while, she was willing enough."

"I don't want to hear about it. Not now, or ever again."

"That's fine with me," Adam said. "Next time, don't pry into things that don't concern you. Right now, we've other matters to discuss. Our trip to Washington. I can either lease our house in San Francisco or sell it."

"No, you can't. Because I'm staying in San Francisco, with Colin. You can go to Washington alone."

Adam shook his head. "Not a chance, my sweet. You're my wife and you're coming with me."

Infuriated by the quiet, arrogant certainty in his voice, she said, "You can't force me to go. I'm not your property."

He reached out, and turned her around so that her back was against the wall, then put an arm on either side of her. She recognized the hot hunger in his eyes. "I'm not—I won't—"

"Be still," he said. She tried to protest but his mouth came down on hers, in a long, searching kiss. The weight of his body held her immobile, pinning her against the wall. Through her light organdy dress, her thin silk undergarments, all that she had worn on this scorching hot night, she felt the hard muscles of his thighs. His hands fondled her breasts. He was taking his time, caressing her in a slow, leisurely way, unmindful of her attempts to free herself. He took his lips from hers, but only to start unbuttoning her bodice, her eyes never wavering as he looked down into her face. Her dress lay crumpled into a soft cloud of pale blue organdy, her camisole was down around her waist, and he was stroking her breasts.

I won't give in, she thought, *not like this. I won't respond. . . .*

But her body had a will of its own, and as he pressed against her once more, his fingers exploring her body, probing, withdrawing, she felt the first tremulous stirrings that grew more fierce, until she moaned and let her head fall back. He kissed her again, and then his hands moved up under her flounced petticoat, quickly pushing aside the last flimsy barrier of silk that kept her flesh from his touch. Her knees went weak and she leaned against him.

He put an arm around her and she thought he was about to carry her to the bed, but instead, he drew her down with him onto the thick, soft carpet.

Quickly, he began to strip off his own clothing.

Pride would not let her give in at once, but she knew, even as she writhed in his grasp that he had conquered. His tongue touched her ear, the hollow of her throat, the softness between her breasts. Then he was naked, too.

"Adam, I don't—"

But her protest trailed away and she moaned softly as he parted her thighs, and slid his hands under her to raise her to receive him. And she was weeping, first with shame because she had submitted, then, later, with joy as they became one, sharing the fierce, sweet ecstasy.

Later, when she lay still, relaxed and drowsy, her tawny hair spread across his chest, her face pressed against the hardness of his shoulder, she heard him speak, as if from a long way off. "You're coming with me." It was not a question, not even a command, but a simple recognition of the bond between them.

She raised her head and kissed him on the mouth, knowing that she had given him his answer.

25

SHANNON HAD FINISHED dressing, with the help of Lottie, and with the imperturbable Mrs. Beal hovering in the background, her calm somewhat shaken, for once, by the momentous occasion. Tonight, Shannon was to attend her first White House reception.

She smiled a little, thinking of her girlish daydreams when she had been a student at Miss Colter's Academy. Then, she had imagined a ball at the home of a prominent Boston manufacturer or shipbuilder as the height of her aspirations. And later, in Mobile, she had dreamed of leading the Mardi Gras ball at the Battle House, or of taking tea in Madame LeVert's drawing room. Never had she expected to be the guest of the President and his First Lady.

If only it could have come to her under different circumstances, she thought wistfully; for now Washington was the capital of a divided nation, where every social occasion was darkened by the universal awareness of the struggle over the survival of the Union. Where an endless procession of boxcars crowded with wounded soldiers waited for ambulances at the Maryland Avenue depot, the terminus of the trains from Virginia, or at the Sixth and Seventh Street wharves where the hospital ships docked. Where makeshift hospitals cared for the survivors without enough competent nurses, without enough supplies, where inefficient, underpaid "contract surgeons," lopped off arms and legs until the limbs lay in piles around their blood-soaked operating tables.

Washington was a city crowded not only with staff officers and their wives, and with politicians, but with speculators, profiteers and the inevitable camp followers, "the painted Jezebels with which the city is stocked," as the *Star* had complained in one of its editorials. Elegant courtesans in satins and plumes promenaded with officers, or went riding about in carriages, displaying their charms to the male population, and ambitious madams took over the handsome brick mansions on tree-shaded residential streets, side by side with decent families.

Nevertheless, Shannon had found Washington an exciting place in this winter of 1862. As soon as she and Adam had arrived in the city, he had rented on H Street a fine house which had formerly been occupied by a Mississippi congressman and his family. Shannon had been busy going to the well-stocked shops to find those small items that would give the house a personal touch. In addition to the necessary furniture, which the congressman's lady had left in the house, Shannon had put up her own topaz velvet drapes, and had made a skirt for her dressing table, a dainty flounced affair of silk trimmed with satin bows.

She had bought a silver tea set for the massive sideboard in the dining room, armchairs of laminated rosewood for the parlor. Adam had told her to buy whatever she wished, and she had taken him at his word.

Because of his position with the War Department, Shannon had been invited to the endless round of receptions, balls and teas that kept the ladies of the capital occupied while their men were engaged in the more serious business of trying to bring the Union together. Shannon was grateful that Mrs. Beal, Mollie and her personal maid, Lottie, had been willing to accompany her to Washington.

But although she had enjoyed her social activities, tonight's event eclipsed all that had gone before. She had read the effusive account of one of Mrs. Lincoln's parties in *Leslie's Weekly* recently.

"No European court or capital can compare with the Presidential circle and the society in Washington this winter," the article had said. "The dingy, sprawling city on the Potomac is bright with the blue of Northern eyes, and the fresh, rosy glow of Northern complexions."

Since Shannon's clash with Adam, back in Virginia City, she had tried to make no further criticism of his decision to support the Union. But she could not help thinking of herself as a Southerner and she found herself drawn to those ladies who, although now on the Union side, had come from the South.

"You look beautiful, ma'am," Mrs. Beal was saying.

"Even that uppity Miss Chase won't outshine you tonight."

Kate Chase, the daughter of Salmon P. Chase, the Secretary of the Treasury, was one of Washington's most popular belles, and had even crossed swords with Mary Lincoln, whom she had sought to undermine at every opportunity.

"Miss Chase wanted her father to be President," General McClellan's wife had confided to Shannon over tea one afternoon. "She has always wanted to be the White House hostess, and Mr. Chase is a widower. Mr. Lincoln was elected instead, but she still has her eye on the next election."

Now, as the door opened and Adam came into the bedroom, Shannon forgot about the gossip that was a staple of Washington society, forgot about her faint resentment of his position in Lincoln's cabinet. No matter what their differences, his nearness always stirred the same response within her. Tenderness, excitement, and pride in this handsome, distinguished-looking husband of hers. Yes, she decided, he was distinguished-looking now. Time had changed him from the carelessly dressed rake who had taken her, rain-soaked and bedraggled, to his hotel room in Colón and who has said coldly, "You're no position to refuse my offer, are you?"

"Why are you smiling?" he asked her. "And your eyes, like a cat's—"

Lottie giggled and Mrs. Beal hushed her with a stern look as they both withdrew from the room.

"Now," he said, "tell me."

"I was only thinking how fine you look tonight," she said, evading the question.

"It's not every night we get to meet the President and his lady," Adam said. "Stand up and let me look at you."

She rose and he took her hands, his blue eyes sparkling with undisguised admiration. "I'll be the envy of every man at the reception tonight. That's quite a costume. What's it going to cost me?"

"You said to spend as much as I liked."

"I'm not serious, sweetheart. Why, with the profits that have been rolling in from the Silver Vixen these past months, you can wear one of those hoops made out of solid silver, if you want to." He kissed her lightly. "I'm so proud of you, Shannon."

The delicate fabrics of the pre-war years, the fragile gowns of tulle, gauze and organdy, decorated with artificial field flowers, grasses or sprays of lilac, had given way to stiff, heavy materials in glowing jewel tones. Shannon's gown of turquoise and silver brocade was cut daringly low to reveal her smooth white shoulders and the curves of her bosom; the skirt flared out like a bell. A tiara of diamonds and sapphires glittered on her head, while her tawny hair, thick and glowing in the soft lamplight, was drawn back to reveal her sapphire and diamond earrings.

"Ready, Shannon?"

"I want to go to the nursery."

"Colin's been asleep for hours," he chided her.

"I think he knows when I'm there, even though he's sleeping," she said.

"You'll spoil that boy," Adam said.

"I want to spoil him. I want him to feel cherished and protected always." The seriousness in her voice caused Adam to look at her in faint surprise.

She could not tell him that because Colin so reminded her of him, she showered the child with the love that she longed to give Adam, but did not, because she feared that he would not respond. Colin, she thought, was Adam, as he had been once, before life had hurt and twisted him.

After she had gone to the nursery and returned to Adam, who was waiting at the head of the stairs, she said impulsively, "I'm so glad we're rich."

"So am I," he said, laughing. "But I didn't realize that you were so mercenary, my love."

"I'm not. It's only that I want Colin to be safe from anything that might threaten him, or hurt him. Money can do that, Adam."

"Sometimes," he said slowly. "But neither money nor position can guarantee a child's safety." His eyes clouded. "The President's son, Willie, is dangerously ill. I heard about it this afternoon. It could be typhoid fever."

Shannon looked at Adam in surprise. "And the Lincolns are still going ahead with this ball?"

"It's an official function. The invitations were sent out days ago."

She preceded him down the stairs, her full skirts swaying. Outside, he helped her into the carriage.

"Mr. Stanton will be there tonight. And his wife, Ellen," Adam was saying. "I don't believe you've met them yet."

"I don't think I care to meet Mr. Stanton," Shannon said coldly.

"Oh, now, Shannon, I thought we'd settled all that. The man's my superior, he—"

"He's a hard, tyrannical man. I've been hearing

about some of the things he's done since he was appointed Secretary of War. He's had people arrested on the slightest suspicion of treason. They've been locked up in the old Capitol building. That dreadful place."

"It's not Willard's Hotel," Adam said dryly. "But many of those prisoners have been arrested with good reason."

"Even so," Shannon retorted, "they've been denied legal advice. Carried off secretly at night, their homes searched. Not even told what charges have been made against them. It's barbaric. Mrs. Greenhow is a prisoner in that jail. With her little daughter. There are lice in the cells and the food isn't fit to eat."

"How do you know so much about Mrs. Greenhow?" Adam demanded.

"She's written letters to her niece. Addie Douglas."

"Addie Douglas is loyal to the Union, so far as I know, but her relationship to Mrs. Greenhow could make her suspect. Is she a close friend of yours?"

"I've met her several times. I like her."

"That's as may be. But as long as I'm connected with the War Department, you'll have to choose your friends more carefully."

"Are you forbidding me to see Mrs. Douglas?"

"Hardly. She'll probably be at the reception tonight. But there are a great many Confederate sympathizers here in the capital, women whose first loyalty is to the South. Don't get mixed up with them."

"Are you afraid Mr. Stanton will have me arrested, too?"

"It's no laughing matter," Adam told her sternly. "Look here, Shannon, I'll admit, between the two of us, that Stanton can be high-handed at times. Even something of a fanatic."

"He's becoming one of the most hated men in Washington," Shannon said.

"He knows what he's doing."

"Do you approve of the fact that he's denying the writ of habeas corpus to American citizens, going against the Bill of Rights?"

"Only in certain cases."

"All prisoners are entitled to legal counsel and a speedy trial," Shannon reminded him.

"As they should be. Under ordinary conditions. But this war has changed everything."

"Even you, Adam?"

He gave her a warning look. "Don't meddle in matters you don't understand. Be careful of your associates. You could endanger my work here otherwise."

"I won't do that. I want to be a good wife to you, Adam. I've always tried to be."

His face softened a little. "I know you have," he said. "But you're inclined to let your feelings interfere with your judgment. Like most women."

Shannon saw that they had reached the White House, and she sighed with relief, as their carriage joined the long line of others, and Adam began to speak of lighter matters. "I'm told Mrs. Lincoln is going to wear half-mourning tonight, to impress Lord Lyons, the British Ambassador. A mark of respect for Queen Victoria's dear departed consort, Prince Albert."

"They say the British will still come to the aid of

the Confederacy," Shannon said. "The British mills need Southern cotton."

"Perhaps. But the British also have a knack for choosing the winning side."

Inside the executive mansion, Shannon was overwhelmed by the splendor of the occasion. Chase was there, and his daughter, Kate, who was in her element, chattering effusively in French with the Comte de-Paris and the Duc de Chartres, the two young princes of the House of Orleans, who, exiled from their native country, had offered their services to the Union Army.

Adam introduced Shannon to General Frémont, and the two men spoke of the expedition across the Sierra. "Good thing this husband of yours joined the expedition," the general told Shannon. "He wasn't much for drilling and marching. No parade-ground soldier. But he took to that country out West as if he'd been born there." Frémont's small, delicate but vivacious wife, Jessie, chatted cordially with Shannon, and complimented her on her gown. "You're lovely, my dear. Mr. Kincaid is most fortunate."

Shannon met General McClellan's wife, an imposing woman in a white tunic dress with bands of cherry velvet and a headdress of white illusion. Then, holding her head high and forcing herself to show a cordiality she did not feel, Shannon permitted Adam to introduce her to Mr. Stanton. The Secretary of War, with his round body and short legs, his mottled complexion and cold eyes, was not a prepossessing individual, and Shannon felt sorry for his pretty wife, Ellen, who dressed simply, almost severely, in contrast with the other ladies present. She wore her shining hair parted in the center, and her brows slanted upward over her dark eyes. Shannon decided that she was a shy, retiring person, and made an attempt to draw her out.

When Shannon spoke of Colin, Ellen Stanton's face lit up in a rare smile, as she told Shannon that she, too, had a little son, James. As the two women spoke of their children, a warmth sprang up between them. Before they parted, Ellen Stanton had accepted an invitation to tea the following week, and Shannon could see that Adam was pleased.

But the high point of the evening for Shannon was the moment on the reception line when she was introduced to the President and his wife. Mary Lincoln was a plump, short, and not particularly pretty woman, but her white satin gown with its train of black Chantilly lace, and her wreath of black and white crepe myrtle lent her a certain air of melancholy dignity.

Remembering what Adam had told her earlier that evening, Shannon felt pity for Mrs. Lincoln, who had been the target of so much brutal criticism since she had come to Washington. She was accused of extravagance, an uncontrollable temper. And, because of her Kentucky background, she was said to be a Confederate sympathizer. How could she help that, Shannon thought, when she had two brothers in the Rebel army? There were even rumors that she was acting as a spy, passing on the secrets of the Union generals to the Confederate authorities.

As Shannon accompanied Adam to the table, she was remembering his warning. Perhaps he was right.

If even Mrs. Lincoln was not above suspicion, how could she, herself, hope to avoid it, unless she was careful of every word, every move she made.

"Don't look so serious," Adam said. "You're supposed to be enjoying yourself, remember?"

Shannon tried to get back into the spirit of the party, and dutifully exclaimed over the lavish feast. On one table was a sugar model of Fort Sumter, a masterpiece of the pastry cook's art. The frigate *Union* was in full sail on a stand supported by cherubs and draped in the Stars and Stripes. Water nymphs made of nougat cavorted around a fountain, and sugar beehives foamed with charlotte russe.

"A vulgar display," she heard one lady whisper to another.

"What else can one expect?" said her companion, who was piling her plate with turkey and pheasant.

Then Shannon saw that Mr. Stanton, standing in a corner of the room, was motioning to Adam with a brusque gesture, and Shannon found herself alone at the elaborately spread tables. But not for long.

A few moments later, Shannon was speaking French with the Prince de Joinville, the uncle of the two young princes of the House of Orléans. He drew her to the bowl filled with champagne punch and after she had been served, he questioned her with great interest about the West. "Your husband was a part of the Frémont expedition, I am told," he began. "I should so like to see the western part of your country."

His interest was genuine enough, and Shannon, after a few moments of shyness, found herself talking easily, describing San Francisco, the Sierra, and Virginia City. His nephews, the two young princes in their blue army uniforms, detached themselves from Miss Chase, and came to join in the conversation around the punchbowl.

"And you crossed the Isthmus of Panama with your husband?" the Comte de Paris said, his dark eyes gleaming with admiration. "So adventurous, you American ladies. And," he added with a gallant bow, "so charming, too."

Shannon blushed, remembering that when she had crossed the Isthmus with Adam, she had not been his wife, but his mistress.

"And now Mr. Kincaid is one of the silver kings," the Duc de Chartres said.

"Hardly," Shannon replied. "Although the Silver Vixen is producing well, now that the miners are getting down to the deeper ledges."

"And is it true that in Virginia City men drive about in coaches encrusted with gold, that the horses are shod with silver?"

"I've heard stories to that effect," Shannon said. "A few of the lucky ones, who've become millionaires overnight." And she went on to tell them of the silver magnate who, on his wedding night, had put champagne into the water-tank so that, at his bridal feast, the taps ran with Mumm's, Pommery, Veuve Cliquot.

By the time Adam returned to her, Shannon was surrounded by a group of gentlemen, some in blue uniforms, others in formal black evening dress, as well as members of the diplomatic corps: Lord Lyons, Señor Tassara, Chevalier Bertinatti. Adam drew her aside and said, "I'm sorry, Shannon. I won't be able to drive home with you."

"What's wrong? What were you talking about with Mr. Stanton?"

"Government business. I have to go over to the old Capitol building at once."

"At this hour? Adam, it's nearly two in the morning."

"I know the time," he said curtly. Then he added, "I'm sure one of these gentlemen would be pleased to escort you."

They were more than pleased; they vied for the privilege. Shannon should have felt flattered and triumphant, but instead she was depressed. What sort of business could Adam have at the dark, gloomy jail? She tried not to think about it, as she flashed a dazzling smile upon Lord Lyons, and agreed that he might escort her home.

The joy, the excitement had gone out of the evening. She had counted on driving home with Adam, and having him praise her for her social triumph. She forced herself to make polite conversation with the British ambassador, as he accompanied her through the promenading that went on for another hour, while the Marine Band played the popular tune, "The Girl I Left Behind Me," and she laughed at his sharp, witty remarks, all the while feeling resentment at Mr. Stanton for calling Adam away from this glittering occasion to carry out his duties. And what duties could Adam have at the jail? she wondered uneasily.

She guessed that she was not the only troubled lady here tonight, for Mrs. Lincoln looked tense and unhappy. Both the President and his wife had left the festivities several times to look in on their ailing son. The splendid, newly decorated East Room was filled with music and laughter. The gaslight gleamed on the crimson, garnet and gold patterned cloth velvet wallpaper, on the French crimson brocatelle draperies, trimmed with heavy gold fringe and tassel work, hung from massive gilt cornices. But Shannon could see the anguished look on Mary Lincoln's face, and knew what she must be feeling. The President's eyes were somber and brooding as he bid good night to his departing guests.

It was early morning when Adam returned home from the Old Capitol. Shannon stirred in bed and opened her eyes.

"Sorry I woke you," Adam said, taking off his coat. "You must be tired after last night's revelry. You're a belle now, my love. I saw Miss Chase glaring at you when Lord Lyons offered to take you home." He sat down on the side of the bed, and drawing her to him, he kissed her. "Go back to sleep. Mrs. Beal will see to my breakfast."

"Adam, why did you have to go to the jail last night?" Shannon asked.

"Official business," he answered. "Nothing that need concern you."

He took off his vest and shirt and tossed them on a chair.

"What sort of official business has to be carried on in the middle of the night?"

"An interrogation," he said.

In spite of the warm comforter that covered her, Shannon felt a chill. "Surely, that's not a part of your duties," she said shakily. Even in the short time she had been here in Washington, she had heard whispers about the secret examinations of prisoners in the solitary cells of Carroll Prison, the Old Capitol annex. These were usually conducted by William Wood, the prison superintendent, a loyal Stanton man.

"You're not a jailer," Shannon protested. "What do you have to do with—interrogations?"

"Don't let your imagination run away with you," he said, seeing the look she gave him. "Nobody used physical force on the prisoner. It's true, though, that a man awakened during the night and brought to one of the solitary cells for questioning is likely to be thrown off balance. That makes it easier to get information."

She had known, from the first, that Adam had a streak of ruthlessness in his nature, but his cold, matter-of-fact tone brought it home to her now as nothing else could have done.

"What was the man—the prisoner accused of?" she asked.

"He was trying to run the blockade out of Richmond, and was headed for San Francisco. He was carrying certain seditious letters. And a commission in the Confederate army, from Jefferson Davis. The Rebels still haven't given up the idea of getting control of California and the resources of Virginia City. That's why Stanton wanted me to be present. I knew what questions to ask, and I had a fairly good idea of the truth of the man's answers."

"And you forced the answers from him."

Adam's eyes were icy. "Force wasn't necessary. If it had been, I wouldn't have hesitated. I don't expect you to understand. I know well enough where your loyalty lies."

"My first loyalty is to you," Shannon said indignantly. "I thought I proved that last night."

"You were charming, I must agree. Even to Mr. Stanton. You made an excellent impression. But I won't have you questioning me about my duties, even here, in the privacy of our home. I'll do what I must, just as I would if I were in the Union army."

"Don't be angry with me, please," she begged, frightened by his coldness, the barely suppressed anger in his voice. "It's only that—I don't want to see you changed by the war."

He shifted on the edge of the bed, moving closer to her. He put an arm around her. "War changes everyone, Shannon," he said. "But it can't change the way we feel about each other. Unless you let it."

"I'll never do that, only—" But he took her face between his hands and kissed her, silencing any further questions.

26

ODALIE SAT in a wicker chair in the garden of her mother's Creole cottage, the two-story townhouse of rosy brick, and watched the late afternoon sunlight filtering through the latticework of the scuppernong arbor, to make intricate patterns on the grass. It was September but the air was still heavy with the sweet scent of the Cherokee roses and the orange trees.

Much had changed in southern Alabama, but Mobile had changed less than Odalie would have thought possible; the cottage and its garden were exactly as she had remembered them during those months of exile in San Francisco.

It was different upriver on the great plantations, she thought sadly. Beau Rivage and Jessamine, where the season of the cotton harvest should have been at its busiest, were deserted, the fields lying fallow. The field hands had been deserting steadily, first a few at a time, then whole groups. The news of the proclamation that had set them free, had spread swiftly, and the former slaves had left the fields to go straggling off to Washington, or to the Union army lines. Many crowded into squalid settlements on the fringes of captured Southern cities.

Odalie sighed as she remember the last time she had seen the gardens of Jessamine. Bruce had been gone for months then, serving as a captain in the Confederate Army. Melora and Bruce's mother were already packed, and preparing to leave for Texas. For Melora, who had been headed for spinsterhood, had surprised everyone by snaring a fellow officer in Bruce's regiment, a loud-voiced, brawny Texan who had accompanied Bruce home to Jessamine when the regiment had been given a short leave.

The Texan had lost an arm at the Battle of Shiloh, and had been honorably discharged. Melora and her mother had announced their plans to go to live with Melora's husband and his family in Texas.

"Of course, you're welcome to come along," Melora had told Odalie sweetly. But Odalie had refused. She had realized, as soon as Bruce had brought her and Eugénie home to Jessamine that neither she nor her child was really wanted there. She could not entirely blame Bruce's mother and sister for their feelings. Hadn't Antoinette Duval driven Bruce out of Alabama, as if he had been a criminal? Melora had never quite believed that Odalie had not been betrothed to the unfortunate Arthur Cunningham and so had been partially responsible for the duel and its aftermath.

In any case, Odalie had no desire to go to live in Texas among strangers. The Texans might be Southerners and loyal Confederates, but they lacked the

cultural tradition of Mobile and the Alabama plantation country.

She could not stay at Jessamine, either, even had
she wanted to. Only a few loyal house servants had
stayed on and they were departing with Melora and
the elder Mrs. Lathrop. The gardens were neglected.
The small bridge over the lily pool had cracked and
there had been no one to mend it; the flowers, the
white jessamine, the petunias and the snowball bushes
had gone untended, and even the windbells on the
pagoda summerhouse had sounded melancholy to
Odalie as they chimed out their delicate music. Perhaps when Bruce returned, the plantation could be
made a showplace once again. But now, Odalie could
not bear to be there alone, even had it not been for
the practical problems of running the depleted house-
hold.

And so, with Aunt Lucienne acting as intermedi-
ary, Odalie had taken Eugénie and come to Mobile
to live with Mama.

Odalie no longer cherished any illusions about her
mother. She knew that Mama had been willing to
welcome her errant daughter home only because of
the money, in Federal treasury notes, that lay on deposit in the bank. Antoinette Duval owned Beau
Rivage, but it brought her no income, now; it had
become a liability.

Aunt Lucienne, however, was delighted to see
Odalie once more, and she adored little Eugénie, ex-
claiming constantly over "dear Philippe's first grandchild." Eugénie had inherited Philippe's dark,
blue-black hair and his amber eyes. She was, Aunt Lucienne said, a true Duval. Mama, however, was some-

what resentful of being a grandmother, although she took pains to conceal her feelings.

Now, Odalie rose at the sound of carriage wheels on the shell road. Mama had returned from the center of the city, where she had been off on a shopping expedition. After leaving her purchases in the house, Mama came sweeping out into the garden, looking regal and handsome in her dress of richly printed silk challis. "My dear, it's lucky I went down to the shops today," Mama said, putting a few parcels on a cushioned, wrought-iron bench and seating herself. "Those ladies were swooping down like vultures. There won't be a thing left that's worth buying by the end of the week."

"I think it's shameful," Odalie said. "Stocking the blockade-running ships with luxury goods when our men need cloth for their uniforms, shoes, medicines."

"Oh, now, Odalie, you must not feel that way. It's our duty to inspire our men by looking attractive and well-dressed. You should have come along with me. Goodness knows, you need some new clothing yourself."

"What for?" Odalie said, feeling the familiar choking sensation rising in her throat, the hard ache in her chest. Only a few weeks ago, she had gotten word that Bruce had been captured and shipped off to a prison camp in Ohio.

"My word, Odalie," Mama reminded her, "you're not a widow yet."

"How do I know that? Bruce was wounded."

"A flesh wound, nothing more."

"He's lying in some horrible Yankee prison camp, and winter is coming."

"Johnson's Island is a camp for officers," Mama said. "I've no doubt that Bruce will be treated with the respect befitting his rank."

"How can you be sure? The Yankees need food, blankets, medical supplies for their own troops. I doubt they'll have much to spare for our men."

"Odalie, my dear," said Aunt Lucienne, who had come out into the garden carrying a stack of back issues of the fashionable *Leslie's Weekly*. Her gray curls bobbed under her lace cap as she shook her head. "Oh, I'm sure that Bruce will come home, safe and sound. And even those dreadful Yankees can recognize a gentleman when they see one. You must not allow yourself to lose heart."

"Oh, hush," Mama interrupted. "Have you told Callie to bring out the lemonade for us? I'm quite parched."

"I've told her, Antoinette," said Lucienne, seating herself in one of the wicker chairs. She opened one of the fashion journals and studied it eagerly. Like all the ladies of Mobile, Lucienne was starved for news of the latest Paris fashions, the glittering social events that were taking place in New York, Saratoga and Newport. She sighed. "I declare, I believe some of these styles must already be passé in Paris. Perhaps even in New York."

"You're lucky to have these old copies of *Leslie's*," Mama reminded her. "Think of the ladies in occupied cities like New Orleans. They have more to bear with than the late arrival of the fashion news."

"I wasn't complaining," Lucienne said with an injured expression, her plump, round face reproachful. "I'm most grateful to you for bringing the magazines, and the length of satin for me."

"And the apricot brandy," Mama added with a cold, malicious smile.

"Now, Antoinette, you know I only drink that for my neuralgia. I declare, you make it sound as if—"

"Oh, for heaven's sake stop it, both of you," Odalie cried, her taut nerves strained to the breaking point by the endless bickering between her mother and Aunt Lucienne.

"You will not take that tone with me," Mama said. "Remember you're still my daughter. Even if you did disgrace yourself by running off and eloping like some common Yankee servant girl."

Aunt Lucienne's soft little mouth tightened, and her hazel eyes were sharp, accusing. "If anyone's disgraced the name of Duval, it's not been Odalie. She went away to marry the man she loved, the man you should have allowed her to marry. It was you who stayed on at Beau Rivage and brought shame on dear Philippe's memory by taking up with—"

"Lucienne. That's enough," Mama warned. Aunt Lucienne subsided. For years she had been subservient to her nephew's wife, and it was not easy to change even in her present circumstance. But Odalie sensed that Aunt Lucienne no longer stood in awe of Mama.

"Just because I'm not as young as I used to be doesn't mean I'm deaf and blind. You and that artist, that Mr. Sutherland, in Philippe's own house—"

But Aunt Lucienne's eyes dropped before Mama's hard stare, and she went back to the pages of *Leslie's Weekly*.

The arrival of Callie, the golden-skinned quadroon maid, in her starched white apron, carrying a pitcher of frosty lemonade, glasses and a plate of pecan cookies, brought a momentary cessation of hostilities.

"Even though you refused to join me on my little shopping trip," Mama said, "I brought you something. A length of rose moiré antique. It's a lovely shade, and so becoming to you, Odalie."

"Mama, why can't you understand? I don't need material for a new wardrobe. I haven't the slightest desire to take tea with Madame LeVert, or to attend your social evenings here. And if you're ashamed of the way I look, I'll be more than happy to remain upstairs with Eugénie while you entertain your friends."

"Don't be foolish," Mama snapped. "It's not natural for a girl your age to hide herself away. Odalie, you're only nineteen."

"I'm a married woman. My husband is wounded. Perhaps—" She found it difficult to go on, for the thought of Bruce in a Yankee prison camp brought stinging of unshed tears to her eyes. "If I lose Bruce, I don't care what becomes of me."

"I lost your papa, and I found it possible to go on living."

There was a faint snort from Aunt Lucienne, but she said nothing.

"If you should lose Bruce," Mama went on coolly, "you'll still have many good years ahead and you'll have to make the best of them. A beautiful young widow, from one of the finest families in Alabama, and well provided for, will have plenty of chances to—"

"Stop it!" Odalie cried, sickened by Mama's callousness. "I won't listen to another word."

"You should. If you had listened to me when I wanted to send you to Paris, things might be different for you now. A titled husband, a place at the court of Louis Napoleon and his empress, a fine chateau."

Odalie's dark eyes narrowed. "Perhaps you should go to Paris, Mama," she said sweetly. "You might be able to find a titled husband for yourself. You're not unattractive. For a lady of your age."

Antoinette went scarlet, then dead white. For a moment, Odalie thought that her mother might strike her. She remembered that day—how long ago it seemed—when Mama had slapped her in the dressing room of Miss Harwood's shop. But Mama was no fool. She did not need to be reminded that it was Odalie's money that paid for the imported wines, the *pâté de foie gras*, the fine silks and laces and the bonnets from Paris, the perfumes and creams that helped to preserve Mama's slightly fading allure.

Mama took as deep a breath as was permitted by her tightly-laced stays. She tossed her head and said, "I'll consider the idea. There are many Southern families in Paris even now, and should we lose the war, there will be many more."

"We won't lose the war! We can't!" Odalie said indignantly. "How can you even—"

"Oh, my goodness!" Aunt Lucienne cried. "Will you look at this?" She held out her copy of *Leslie's Weekly*, round-eyed with excitement.

"Hush, Lucienne," Mama said impatiently. "We're not discussing fashions at the moment."

"This isn't about fashions. It's—here, read it for yourself."

Sighing impatiently, Mama took the magazine and started to read the column that Aunt Lucienne had pointed out. Mama's thin nostrils flared and her brows drew together. "I'm not surprised," she said. "What else would one expect of the society in Washington? With an uncouth, backwoods clod for a President, and his hysterical frump of a wife. I've heard that she's lost her mind since the death of her son."

"It's not unusual for a mother to be grief-stricken over the loss of a child," Lucienne said. "Besides, you know perfectly well that it wasn't the references to the President and his wife that caught my eye. It's the mention of Shannon Cavanaugh. Shannon Kincaid, I should say."

"What about Shannon?" Odalie asked eagerly.

"Her husband is attached to the War Department in an advisory capacity," Aunt Lucienne said. "And she was one of the leading belles of the Washington season last winter. 'The beautiful and gracious Mrs. Adam Kincaid,' that's what the article calls her."

"Odalie can read it for herself," Mama said, thrusting the copy of *Leslie's* at Odalie as if the paper had scorched her fingers. "I haven't the slightest interest in the social life of the Union capital." She gave a sharp little laugh. "I wonder if the writer of this article knows that the 'beautiful and gracious Mrs. Adam Kincaid' used to serve whiskey to the sailors at Rawlinson's tavern."

"Shannon might have been spared that, if she had received her rightful inheritance when she returned from that boarding school in Boston," Aunt Lucienne said.

"What inheritance? You said something about it once before, but Mama silenced you. What did Papa leave to Shannon?"

"That's not your concern, Odalie," Mama said.

"But it is." Odalie faced her mother with a cold stare that matched Antoinette's own. "Shannon was kind to me when I was out in San Francisco. When I was frightened and miserable and there was no one else to turn to, Shannon came to me. When Eugénie was being born, she stayed right there with me. And Adam brought an army surgeon to help with the birth. I'm not defending what he's done since. Abandoning our cause to go over to the Union side. But he always behaved like a gentleman with me."

Mama put down her empty lemonade glass. "I refuse to stay here and listen to you singing the praises of that trollop and her husband. As for you, Lucienne, I advise you to watch what you say, unless you're prepared to back it up with facts."

Mama turned and left the garden. "Oh, dear," Aunt Lucienne said nervously. "She's furious with me."

"Don't worry about that," Odalie said. "She won't do anything to hurt you. I'll see to that."

"Why, Odalie, you're—you've changed."

"I suppose that I have," Odalie said slowly. "I used to be afraid of so many things. Of Mama. Of being married and having babies and—Now only one thing frightens me. Losing Bruce." She forced the thought from her mind and went on briskly, "You were speaking of Shannon's inheritance."

"Philippe was a good man. He had his faults, his weaknesses, as all men do. But he was determined to take the responsibility for his mistakes. When he was dying, I heard him speak of a bequest, for Shannon. He said to me that it was safe, over in England, on deposit with his bankers there. Philippe did a good deal of business in England, you see. He was afraid to keep the money here, because he knew what Antoinette was capable of. I don't know how your mother cheated Shannon, what scheme she worked out with that new lawyer, the one who took over Philippe's affairs after Mr. Bassett died. Perhaps it's too late to find out now, with this dreadful war going on."

"Adam Kincaid has influence in the Capitol. And he's wealthy in his own right. I'm sure he could find a way," Odalie said.

"It's not likely that Shannon Kincaid needs Philippe's legacy now," Aunt Lucienne reminded her.

"That's not the point. I want her to know that Papa remembered her at the end. That he thought of her as his daughter."

"Perhaps you could get word to her," Aunt Lucienne suggested.

Odalie smiled sadly. "I doubt that Shannon would wish to hear from me now."

"But you said you were on such good terms back in San Francisco."

"We had a falling-out before Bruce and I left. I couldn't understand why Adam was siding with the Union. I still can't. I said some harsh things to her."

"If you don't want to write to her, perhaps you could get her Aunt Kate to do it for you."

Odalie smiled. "That's what I'll do. I'll go down to the tavern tomorrow."

Lucienne pressed her small, plump hand to her lips in dismay. "Oh, my dear, that would be most unseemly. You can't go to a sailors' tavern. Suppose someone saw you."

Dear Aunt Lucienne. Still a stickler for the proprieties. What would she say if she knew about the shabby boardinghouse on Telegraph Hill, where Odalie had lived back in San Francisco? About the riot in Portsmouth Square, from which Adam had rescued her? The nation might be torn apart by war, Beau Rivage might be abandoned and falling into ruins, but Aunt Lucienne still clung to the code by which she had always lived.

"I'll be most discreet," she assured her aunt. "I'll have Caleb drive me down in the closed carriage. I'll go there in the middle of the morning. There shouldn't be any drunken sailors about at that hour."

But in spite of her precautions, Odalie found Aunt Lucienne waiting for her anxiously, when she returned from Rawlinson's tavern the following day, after her brief and unproductive visit there.

"Kate Rawlinson isn't at the tavern," Odalie told Aunt Lucienne. "In fact, she's left Mobile."

"Where has she gone?"

"To Washington. Mr. Rawlinson told me. He was furious. A dreadful man. I'm so glad Shannon was able to get away from him." Odalie removed her deep-brimmed bonnet and handed it to Callie. "He went on about his wife's deserting him to go and live in high style. That's what he said. Only he used the most awful language." She sank down into a chair. "It seems that Shannon sent for her aunt, and Mr. Kincaid made the necessary arrangements. He's got all kinds of influence now, and so he was able—"

Odalie broke off. Her dark eyes grew thoughtful.

"What is it, dear?" Aunt Lucienne asked. "What's wrong?"

Odalie did not answer. She was scarcely aware that Aunt Lucienne had spoken to her. She rose. and, lifting her wide skirts, she hurried up the stairs to her room. Eugénie lay napping in a small bed in the corner.

Odalie tried to collect her thoughts but her heart had begun to pound so hard that it became difficult to breathe. She went to the window, and stood looking down at the sunny, high-walled garden, breathing the scents of the Cherokee roses, the orange trees.

Then she turned away to pace the floor, back and forth, and her thoughts began to take shape. Adam Kincaid. He was a man of influence now, working for Mr. Stanton, the Secretary of War. He had made arrangements for his wife's aunt to get to Washington.

"I'll go to Washington, too. I don't know how, but I'll get there. Maybe I can find a ship to take me as far as Richmond, or Wilmington, North Carolina. I have plenty of money. That's no problem. I'll go to Adam and ask him to use his influence to help get Bruce out of the prison camp on Johnson's Island. Adam can do it. I'm sure he can."

Prisoners were still being exchanged. Not as often or as easily as they had been during the early days of the war. But it was still possible. It had to be.

She clenched her hands so that the nails cut into the palms. She felt a steely determination begin to grow within her.

Then, an uneasy memory stirred to life at the back of her mind. Adam had been furious with Bruce when he had learned that Bruce was involved with the Knights of the Golden Circle. "Bruce had no right to use the mining company's warehouse to store the arms and ammunition for Harpending's men," Shannon had said at their last meeting. "Adam can't forgive him for that."

And Odalie had replied coldly, "Adam is a Southerner. He should have helped Bruce and the others. He should have been proud to risk everything for the Cause."

"I will not allow anyone to criticize my husband. Not even you, Odalie."

How could she go to Adam Kincaid now and plead for his help? He was a renegade, a traitor who had chosen to ally himself with the side he thought would win. A hard, ruthless man who had fought his way upward ever since the day he had first appeared in Mobile, and had gone wandering around shantytown, begging for scraps of food. Shannon had never told Odalie anything about Adam's life, before his arrival in the city. She had admitted that she knew, but had refused to discuss the matter.

But Adam could be kind, too, Odalie reminded herself, seeking desperately to bolster her courage. He had come to her aid that night in Portsmouth Square, had fought his way through the crowd of brawling men to her side, had lifted her and carried her back to the carriage. And the night of pain and terror when Eugénie was born, she had reached out to him, and he had taken her hand and tried to comfort her. Then he had gone for the military surgeon who had saved her life, and the baby's, too.

But maybe he had only done those things for Shannon's sake. And what reason did Shannon have to want to help her now? Maybe Shannon would take pleasure in seeing Odalie before her as a supplicant, begging for help.

No, Odalie thought. *Shannon's not like that.* But Shannon had made it plain that her loyalty was to her husband. If he refused to help, would she even try to make him change his mind?

Adam must not refuse. She would have to find some way to convince him. She would appeal to his vanity, perhaps, now that he was so influential. And if that failed she would throw herself on his mercy. Her pride was strong, but she knew now that her love for Bruce was stronger still.

She had failed Bruce as a wife, during the few years of their marriage, right up until that last night when he had gone back to his regiment. Each time he had taken her in his arms, her body had turned cold and unresponsive.

Odalie's eyes filled with tears, as she remembered her flight from New Orleans to San Francisco. She had thought herself so brave, so daring, but she had been a foolish young girl, filled with romantic illusions. To her, Bruce had been a handsome, gallant cavalier who would marry her, yet continue to worship her from a distance, who would give in to all her wishes.

On her wedding night there in the cabin on Sun Mountain, she had been shocked into an awareness of what marriage really meant to Bruce. She had discovered that he was possessed by the same frightening lusts, the same animal urges as any other male. That he would not be put off or denied his rights.

I failed him, she thought sadly. *Not only that first night. I think he might have understood that. The way I fought him, the way I struggled, he never guessed I wasn't a virgin. But all those other nights, when I turned away from him. And then he started going to places like Delphine's. Oh, but it wasn't my fault. After that time with Craig Judson, how could I let any man—even Bruce—use me that way?*

The afternoon sunlight flooded the room from between the flounced curtains. Even now, in autumn, she could feel the warmth of the sun. But in Ohio, it would be growing colder. Soon it would be winter. Snow and sleet. Bone-chilling cold and biting winds. She thought of the stories that had been trickling into Mobile from the North about the conditions in the Yankee prison camps. Accounts of the spoiled, scanty food the prisoners were forced to eat. And Bruce had always been so fastidious, refusing to eat a slice of meat that was too fatty, or biscuits that were less than fluffy perfection.

There were not enough blankets in those camps, and the few they had were filthy and infested with lice. Confederate soldiers wore the rags of their uniforms and often went barefoot.

She had heard whispered stories about the brutality of some of the Yankee prison guards. Of Confederate soldiers shot while trying to escape. Soldiers dying of dysentery, pneumonia, typhus. Of neglected wounds that turned gangrenous and limbs that were amputated without anesthetic.

"Not Bruce," she whispered. "Oh, please God, not Bruce."

At dinner, a few hours later, Odalie sat in silence, not noticing the food that was placed before her. Her mind raced feverishly, making plans.

"Odalie, I wish you would do me the courtesy of answering when I speak to you."

"I'm sorry, Mama. What did you say?"

"I said that I've been thinking of giving a small musicale here in a few weeks. I would like you to play and sing a few simple selections. And you will need something suitable to wear. That rose moiré should be charming."

"I won't be here, Mama," Odalie said quietly.

"Then you are going to hide yourself away in your room. Now, Odalie, really. You can be provoking."

"I won't be in Mobile," Odalie said, still speaking softly but with determination. "I am leaving for Washington as soon as possible."

"Have you lost your senses? What possible reason could you have for going to Washington?"

"I'm going to see Adam Kincaid. Perhaps he will be able to arrange for Bruce's release."

"You would humiliate yourself, all of us, by going to Shannon's husband for help?"

"I'd go to the devil himself, if it would help Bruce."

"Your fears have unsettled your mind. You can't go to that woman to ask for—"

"Ask? I'll beg. I'll—"

"I won't allow it," Mama said.

"Oh, Mama. You couldn't stop me from going to California. How do you think you can stop me now?"

"It's difficult enough to get to Washington from Mobile now. It means running the blockade, if you plan to go by water, or crossing through the battle lines of both armies, if you——"

"I'll find a way."

"You'd go off and leave your own child?"

"I'm taking Eugénie with me."

"You can't travel alone."

"I can," Odalie said, her face hard, her voice steady. "And I will, if I have to."

"You won't have to." Odalie turned to stare at the speaker: Aunt Lucienne. "If you think I will allow Philippe's daughter, and his grandchild, to go off alone, you're mistaken. You are a Duval, even though you are married now. You will travel as a respectable lady should."

"Now look here, Lucienne," Mama began, "you're far too old to undertake such a trip. You're not strong."

"You were willing enough to send me off to Paris with Odalie, only two years ago," Aunt Lucienne said. "That was different, wasn't it? Then you wanted us out of the way so that you could carry on with your Mr. Sutherland. I would have walked out then and there, but I felt that I owed it to Philippe to remain at Beau Rivage. But you didn't care about dishonoring your husband's memory. You sent me away to New Orleans and you only allowed me to come back after Odalie had gone off to join Bruce. You made it quite clear that you didn't welcome my presence even then. But you couldn't turn me out by force, and I was too afraid of you to protest even when your behavior had become quite shameless."

Aunt Lucienne's plump bosom was heaving under her lace and taffeta bodice; her cheeks were flushed with long-suppressed anger. "I'm not afraid of you any longer," she said. She rose and left the table, moving with dignity in spite of her short, round body and bobbing gray curls.

27

ALTHOUGH WASHINGTON'S social season would not be in full swing for at least another month, Shannon had already ordered her new wardrobe, and parcels were arriving daily from Madame Hermantine du Riez of the Place Vendôme in Paris, others from Arnold Constable and Company and A. T. Stewart in New York City. The social life in the wartime capital was complex and elaborate, and every kind of affair required a particular costume. This season's gowns were made of rich velvets, of tarletans, of heavy moirés and stiff brocades, to be worn at balls and levees; rustling, jewel-colored taffetas and velvet mantles for afternoons at the National Race-Course; bonnets bloomed with whole gardens of silk and velvet flowers, and fashionable ladies lifted their skirts to the ankle to reveal a glimpse of scarlet petticoats or a brightly colored walking shoe in blue, green, violet or crimson.

On an afternoon late in October, Shannon was in

her bedroom with Aunt Kate. Her aunt was staring wide-eyed at a dress of wine-colored velvet with a lace collar and heavy braid trimming. "Oh, dearie. It's much too fine for me."

"Nonsense," Adam said, coming into the room. Shannon whirled around to look at him in surprise. "You'll be going shopping, and to the theater. You'll need it."

"Adam, I didn't expect you home so early," Shannon said, somewhat surprised, for he had been spending long hours at the War Department for the past few weeks.

"I thought I'd surprise you," he said, but there was something in his voice that made Shannon uneasy. Aunt Kate, too, was quick to catch the tension in the air.

"I'll take the dress to my room, and try it on," she said. "You're both far too generous to me."

Adam put an arm around her shoulders. "No more than you deserve, Kate."

After her aunt had left the bedroom, Adam closed the door. "Aunt Kate's so fond of you," Shannon said. "It was good of you to let me have her here."

"After all those years with that evil-tempered skinflint, Rawlinson, she deserves a little security and comfort," Adam said. "But I wasn't being entirely unselfish in sending for her."

"What do you mean?"

"I have to leave Washington. I didn't want to tell you before, because I knew you'd worry. I'll be gone for some time. A few months, perhaps longer. I'll feel better knowing Kate's here with you and Colin."

"Where are you going?"

"I can't tell you that," he said.

"Adam, I'm your wife. Surely I have a right to know."

"It's a confidential mission. For Stanton. I'll be leaving day after tomorrow."

Shannon put a hand on his arm. "Take me with you. Please. Aunt Kate can look after Colin, and there's Mrs. Beal and Mollie."

He put his arms around her. "Not a chance, sweetheart. You don't want to miss the season here in Washington. Didn't you tell me you've ordered a fine new dress for Miss Chase's wedding?"

"Adam, stop it. I'm serious. I don't want you to leave me." She clung to him, raising her eyes to his. "Back in San Francisco you promised to take me wherever you went."

"This is different," he said impatiently.

"There'll be danger, then?"

"Sweetheart, I didn't join Stanton's department to spend my time at White House levees and official dinners."

"You're going out to California, or Nevada, aren't you?" When he did not answer she went on, feeling her chest tighten with fear. "You told me that you were needed because of your knowledge of the country out west, the routes through the mountains. You said the Confederate sympathizers would try again to get shipments of gold through to Richmond. Now it's about to happen, isn't it? They need gold for the Treasury, if they're going to go on with the war and you—"

"Be still," he ordered. "No matter what you suspect, I want you to promise me you won't discuss this with anyone. Not Kate, not your Southern friends here. Give me your word."

"I'll say nothing, I swear it. But I'm frightened, Adam."

His face changed to gentleness. "I know you are," he said. He forced a smile and said lightly, "I'll be back before you know it. In the meantime, you'll find plenty to keep you busy. From the number of dresses that have been arriving these last few weeks, I'd guess you have a full social calendar. And there's no shortage of unattached men to squire you around. The Prince de Joinville, Lord Lyons. Or that young journalist, Whitlaw Reid."

"I won't go to parties. Not while you're away, risking your life."

"There are a great many men risking their lives right now, on both sides. If there's to be a speedy end to the war, the Confederate resources must be wiped out. Without gold to buy guns and supplies from abroad, that will happen all the sooner. Now, so long as I'm still here, I want you to put on one of those elegant new dresses. Tell Kate to do herself up in her finery. I'm taking you both to Ford's Theater tonight."

"I couldn't possibly go to the theater. I couldn't keep my mind on some foolish play when you're—"

"Be still," he said quietly but firmly. "After I've gone, I want you to continue to behave as if I were away on routine government business. Don't show your concern. Go to teas and dances. Your volunteer work at the hospital. The relief committees."

"But I don't care about all that. I want—"

"It doesn't matter what you want right now," he said, his eyes somber. "Or what I want." His arms tightened around her. "Do you think I want to leave you? I'm under orders, and so are you, my love."

The hours had gone swiftly, and before Shannon had been able to grasp the fact of Adam's departure fully, he was gone. She could not share her fears with anyone, not even Kate.

Remembering Adam's instructions, she forced herself to go about to afternoon teas at the homes of Addie Douglas and Ellen Stanton, to a splendid reception in honor of Miss Chase, who was soon to wed the wealthy former governor of Rhode Island. Those who disliked the beautiful but haughty daughter of Salmon P. Chase whispered that she was marrying the "Boy Governor" to secure his family's financial backing for her father, who hoped to be the next President.

Shannon went to dinners, levees and *matinées dansantes*, escorted by members of the diplomatic corps, by high-ranking, blue-uniformed army officers. Two mornings a week she did volunteer work in the hospital, where, thanks to her experience in Panama, she was of more use than many of the well-meaning but weak-stomached ladies who fled at the terrible sights, the sickening smells and the cries of the wounded men; although hospital conditions were improving since the start of the war, thanks to the efforts of the Sanitary Commission, and such dedicated women as Clara Barton and Dorothea Dix.

On a gray afternoon, late in October, Shannon returned from her duties at the hospital to find Aunt Kate waiting for her in the downstairs hallway, obviously agitated.

"Dearie, you have a visitor. It's that Miss Duval—Mrs. Lathrop, Bruce Lathrop's wife—I wouldn't have let her in, but she's traveled all the way from Mobile, and she looks so worn-out. She's in the parlor."

Odalie, here in Washington? Swiftly, Shannon handed her mantle to Aunt Kate and hurried down the hall.

She found Odalie seated on the horsehair sofa, her slender body drooping with exhaustion, her face white and drawn. But she straightened her shoulders as she saw Shannon. And she rose to her feet, saying quickly, "I know I should have sent you a note, but I was so afraid you wouldn't see me."

For a moment, Shannon hesitated, remembering how she and Odalie had parted, recalling Odalie's criticism of Adam and the painful coolness that had marked their last hours together. But Shannon's reservations were swept aside, as she saw the look of grief in Odalie's dark eyes.

"Please, do sit down," Shannon said. "I hope you haven't been waiting long. Shall I ring for tea?"

Odalie shook her head. "I have to speak with Adam," Odalie said. "As quickly as possible."

"Sit down here with me," Shannon said, drawing Odalie down on the wide sofa. "Adam's away."

"But he'll be back soon, won't he? I know he can help me, if only he will."

"Why do you want to see Adam? What's happened?" Then, remembering the accounts she had been reading of the fierce fighting of the past months, she shuddered. "Bruce isn't—he hasn't—"

"He's alive, so far as I know," Odalie said, with

a calm directness that surprised Shannon. "He's been captured. He's in a prison camp called Johnson's Island, somewhere in Ohio."

"I believe I've heard of it."

"Adam can help him, if he wants to. I know he and Bruce quarreled over that business of the Knights of the Golden Circle. Bruce said some dreadful things to Adam, but—oh, Shannon, he's always been hot-tempered. You know that."

"I know," Shannon said softly. "And I'm sure Adam would be willing to help, but he's away. I don't know when he'll be back."

"You can write to him, surely."

Shannon chose her words carefully. "I'm afraid not. He's traveling, on government business."

"Union business," Odalie said, unable to keep the bitterness out of her voice.

"Adam did what he thought was right, just as Bruce did. I couldn't understand why he chose the Union side, not at first. But now, I think I'm beginning to."

"Papa never should have sent you to school in Boston," Odalie said.

"Slavery would have been repugnant to me no matter where I'd been educated. But you're not here to argue about politics, are you?"

"Hardly. I've come to ask—to plead for Adam's help. Prisoners are still being exchanged. Adam's with the War Department. Oh, yes, we manage to keep up with the news from Washington, even back in Mobile. There was mention of you and Adam in a back issue of *Leslie's Weekly*. Adam's an important man now. He can use his influence—"

"Adam doesn't approve of the exchange of prisoners. He believes, as General Grant does, that such exchanges only serve to prolong the war."

"And you, Shannon? Have you become so cold and heartless that you can bear to think of Bruce in that camp up North? Oh, Shannon, he's wounded. He needs care and decent food. Winter's coming. He may be sleeping on the ground, without blankets. He may have typhus by now, or gangrene may have set in."

"I've just come from one of our own hospitals, Odalie. The men there are suffering, too." But she could not ignore Odalie's misery, or her own concern for Bruce.

And when Odalie said, "Suppose it were Adam, there in that camp," Shannon could not hold herself aloof any longer. She knew that, in Odalie's place, she would move heaven and earth to try to free her husband.

"I do understand," Shannon began, her voice warm with sympathy, but Odalie interrupted.

"Do you? How can you understand? Adam's not in the Union army. He's safe enough, working for the War Department, taking you to White House receptions, to the theater and the races."

Shannon looked away, fearful that her eyes would betray her. She was frantic with worry over Adam, off in the West, for she knew that the Confederates there would stop at nothing to get their gold shipments through to Richmond. But she could not share her fears with anyone, not even Odalie.

She felt Odalie's small hand on her arm. "Don't be angry, Shannon. It's only that I'm so worried about Bruce. I didn't mean to criticize you or Adam."

"It's perfectly natural," Shannon said. She was thankful that Odalie was too preoccupied with her own worries to ask exactly where Adam had gone and why.

"Surely there's something you can do," Odalie went on. "You know so many government officials— Mr. Stanton, himself. Surely, you could plead my case to him. He'd listen to you."

"It isn't that simple. Adam doesn't wish me to meddle in government business. We quarreled about that, soon after we arrived here," Shannon explained. Briefly, she told Odalie about the night when Adam had gone to the Old Capitol to assist in the interrogation of a prisoner. Although she did not give Odalie any of the details, she tried to show her the difficulty of interfering now in anything having to do with Mr. Stanton's department.

"But this is different," Odalie said. "It's Bruce we're talking about." Her dark eyes held Shannon's. "You loved Bruce once. I know you did. And he loved you."

"Did he? A little, perhaps. But he left me stranded in Panama. Because he had promised to marry you."

"You haven't forgiven him for that, have you? That's why you don't want to help him now."

"I forgave him long ago. And I suppose I still have a—kind of affection for him. But I don't think I can help him now. Not without going against Adam's wishes."

"You can smooth things over with Adam when he comes home."

She was completely single-minded in her driving need to get Bruce out of prison, and Shannon sensed the change in her sister. Odalie did not weep, her voice was steady, although Shannon could well imagine her inner turmoil. *She's come a long way from that spoiled, flirtatious girl who came to the landng at Cypress Bend to meet Bruce that day,* Shannon thought.

War changes everyone, Shannon. Adam's words came back to her with new meaning now.

"You've got to go to Mr. Stanton. They say that he's loyal to the men who serve him well. I'm sure Adam has. If you ask him for a favor, he won't refuse you, surely."

"Mr. Stanton's not an easy man to understand. He's arrogant and fanatical. Even those who support the Union cause have come to dislike him."

"But surely, in your case, he would be willing to make concessions," Odalie said.

"I'm not sure. Every morning, in the reception room of the War Department, he gives exactly one hour to the public. Not a minute longer, Adam has told me. He sees all sorts of people. Politicians, contractors, wounded soldiers, prostitutes, wives and parents of men who have been accused of disloyalty to the government. They are forced to state their requests before everyone. And at the end of the hour, the provost guard clears the room."

"Are you afraid of him?" Odalie asked.

"Perhaps I am," Shannon admitted. "He's a ruthless man. I think it would give him more pleasure to refuse a request than to grant it."

"I'll go to him myself," Odalie said. "I'll make him listen."

Shannon shook her head sadly. "That would be worse than useless. The wife of a Confederate officer

—no, Odalie. I'm afraid there's nothing either of us can do. Perhaps when Adam returns."

"You said it might be a matter of months. Bruce might be dead by then."

Shannon looked at her helplessly, unable to deny the truth of her words. Even in the military hospitals here in Washington, men were dying every day of gangrene, dysentery, typhus. *How much worse it must be for Confederate prisoners,* she reflected.

"I see you are still wearing the locket I gave you," Odalie said quietly. She was reminding Shannon of the bond between them.

"I'm probably foolish to do so," Shannon said. "Philippe Duval cared nothing for me. I've tried all my life to believe he did because I needed to. But I'm not a Duval. I never can be."

"You're wrong. He couldn't give you his name, and I know how much that must have·hurt you but—"

"It did once, but no more. I am what I've always been. Peggy Cavanaugh's bastard."

"You must not say that." Odalie's face flushed deeply.

"Why not? It's true, isn't it? Bruce refused to marry me because of what I was. If not for Adam, I'd have ended up in one of the cribs in Bottle Alley, back there in Panama. Philippe Duval provided me with a fine education at a finishing school for young ladies. Then he turned his back on me and left me to fend for myself."

"That isn't true," Odalie said. "I told you once that I had reason to believe Papa had left you provided for. I was right, Shannon."

"I don't believe you."

"There's money on deposit with his English bankers. It's been there all this time. Mama schemed with a lawyer to hide the fact. She's always hated you."

"You would make up any story, invent any lie, to get Bruce free," Shannon said, unable to keep the bitterness out of her voice.

"Maybe I would. But I'm not lying about this. Don't you remember when I first told you about it, back in San Francisco. I had no reason to lie to you then. I said I wasn't sure, but now I am."

Shannon found herself wavering, longing to believe, yet afraid to. Odalie went on quickly, "Aunt Lucienne's here in Washington. I can take you over to the Willard Hotel and she'll back up my story. I know you have no need of Papa's money, not now." Odalie looked around the luxuriously furnished parlor with its fine carpets, marble fireplace and velvet draperies. "But I want you to know that Papa cared about you, and was concerned about your future. He didn't leave you to struggle on alone. He had no way of knowing how far Mama would go to take revenge on you."

In spite of the tension between them, in spite of her ever-present fears for Adam's safety, Shannon felt a swift surge of joy. Her father had not abandoned her, then. He had cared enough to provide for her.

"Thank you, Odalie," she said. "I do believe you. And I'm more grateful than I can say. I know it wasn't easy for you to tell me this."

"Then you'll help me. Say you will, Shannon. If not for Bruce's sake, then for mine. And Papa's."

"All right," Shannon said. "I can't promise you anything, you know that. But Ellen Stanton and I are friends. She's a kind and generous woman. Perhaps, if she's willing to intercede, Mr. Stanton will listen to her."

"I'll never forget this, never. And you will act quickly, won't you? I want Bruce with me. I need him so."

"There's something else," Shannon said. "Bruce will have to take an oath to do nothing to help the Confederate cause again. He may have to take an oath of allegiance to the Union. It's possible he'll refuse to accept his freedom on those terms."

"Oh, he can't! He mustn't! For my sake, and Eugénie's."

Shannon rose and went to ring for tea. "Did you leave Eugénie back at Beau Rivage?" she asked.

"She's here with me. Aunt Lucienne's looking after her. We're quite comfortable at the hotel." She smiled at Shannon, a sad smile. "No one lives at Beau Rivage now. Or at Jessamine."

"But why not?"

"Melora's married a Texan and gone off to live with him there. And Bruce's mother went with her. The people all ran off, except for a few house servants who accompanied Melora and Bruce's mother. Everything's changed since Mr. Lincoln issued his proclamation. Bruce always wanted Jessamine to be a showplace. He had such plans. And now even the gardens—they were so lovely, the gardens. There was a little summerhouse, with white wisteria growing up the sides."

"Don't," Shannon said, surprised by the pain she felt at Odalie's words. "It's no good looking back. It hurts too much." She must not let Odalie see how deeply moved she was, and so she spoke briskly.

"Now, what we both need is some good strong tea. And sandwiches. You probably haven't eaten all day."

"I don't remember," Odalie admitted.

"I thought so. Remember, you have a baby to care for. And you don't want Bruce to come back and find you ill." She hesitated. "I would ask you to come and stay here with me, you and Eugénie and your aunt. It's only that—"

"I know," Odalie said, and now her smile was genuine. "Mrs. Rawlinson wouldn't be happy with that arrangement, would she?"

"I'm afraid not. But I know I could talk her around. It's Adam's position with the War Department. It would do him no good if people were to learn that he's related, even by marriage, to—"

"Don't be embarrassed to say it. To the family of a Confederate officer. There's no need for anyone to know of our relationship, not even Mrs. Stanton. You can say I'm an old friend. And we're all perfectly comfortable at the hotel."

"You do understand then. Even Mrs. Lincoln has been accused of being a traitor because she has two brothers in the Confederate army. I've heard that the Senate members of the Committee on the Conduct of the War met in secret session to consider reports about her treasonable conduct."

"I can't believe that. The President's wife?"

"It's true enough. But Mr. Lincoln appeared in the committee room when the meeting was about to begin. He told them that he positively knew that no member of his family was involved in any kind of treasonable plot. All the same, it hasn't stopped the gossip. So you see—"

Odalie nodded. "I don't want to make trouble for you, or for Adam. I only want Bruce back here with me. I—haven't been a good wife to him, and I do so want to make it up to him."

28

"I DON'T understand you, dearie," Aunt Kate said, shaking her head. "You don't owe anything to Odalie or any of those Duvals. And as for Bruce Lathrop, what's he ever done except make trouble for you? How can you forget? Why if he hadn't taken you to that ball at Beau Rivage, you never would have had to leave Mobile. Then, walking out on you in Colón— Lord only knows what might have happened to you, if Adam hadn't come along."

"Oh, Aunt Kate, it was all so long ago. And besides, Odalie is my sister. She loves Bruce as I love Adam. When I told her that Bruce would be coming home, you should have seen her face. I couldn't have done it without Ellen Stanton's help, of course, and there's still a lot of red tape. But in a few months he'll be here in Washington with Odalie and their baby."

"And what will Adam say when he gets back and finds out what you did?"

"Adam and Bruce have had their differences,"

Shannon admitted. "But I know that Adam would not want Bruce to remain in that dreadful place."

"Maybe not. But he might think that you got Bruce out because you—still care about him. Men can be mighty jealous, dearie."

Shannon smiled a little sadly. "Adam once told me that a man has to be in love to be jealous."

"Adam loves you," Aunt Kate protested.

"You don't understand. He married me because he felt obligated to me for saving his life back there in Panama City. And when he found out I was pregnant, he believed he owed me the protection of his name."

"And look at all he's done for you. You always wanted to be a lady. Now you are. You have this fine house, a regular mansion it is. And your gowns and jewels, and your own carriage. And he's been good to me for your sake."

"But he never once said he loved me. I don't believe Adam can love anyone."

"Shannon, that's a terrible thing to say."

"Yes," Shannon said slowly, "I suppose it is. But, Aunt Kate, you know the life he had back in Mobile, with Tom Sprague."

"What on earth has that got to do with his feelings for you?"

"I'm not sure, but it wasn't only what Mr. Sprague did to him. He told me once how he came to Mobile, alone, and what happened to him before that."

Aunt Kate leaned forward in her chair, and Shannon told her briefly about how Adam had lost his parents, and his sister, Rachel. About what had been done to Rachel before her death. "He was only twelve. And he saw it all. I think it destroyed something inside him."

"It was a terrible thing, surely. But I've seen him with you, Shannon, and I can't believe he doesn't have some feeling toward you. The way he looks at you sometimes——"

"He wants me. I satisfy his needs. And he's proud of me, I know. He enjoys buying me fine clothes and jewels, and parading me around the city. But that isn't love, or tenderness. I don't think he has those things to give, not to me or to any other woman."

"A man can change. But you've got to give him time. And you mustn't do anything to provoke him. When he finds out about Bruce——"

"I couldn't let Bruce rot in a prison camp, and besides, there's Odalie."

"Philippe Duval married that cold-hearted she-devil, and Odalie grew up a fine lady at Beau Rivage. She wasn't sent off to Boston, to keep her out of sight. She was well provided for, Miss Odalie was."

"Odalie told me that my father provided for me, too. In his will. But Antoinette schemed with his lawyer, the one who took Mr. Bassett's place. There's money for me in a bank, in England."

"I didn't know that," Aunt Kate said slowly. "All the same, those Duvals have brought us nothing but trouble. First, it was my poor sister Peggy. Head over heels in love with Philippe Duval, even when she knew from the first that he'd never marry her. And now you."

"There'll be no trouble for me," Shannon reassured her. "No one knows that Odalie and I are related. I told Ellen Stanton that I was asking for help for a school friend, a girl who'd attended Miss Colter's Academy with me. And thank heavens Bruce has agreed to take the oath of allegiance. I was afraid he might not."

"All the same, I don't like it. Not one bit. It's Adam you should be thinking about. Where's he been all this time, anyhow? When's he coming home?"

"I've told you, I'm not sure. The mails are slow and uncertain these days. When he's completed his business for the War Department, he'll be back."

"And you gallivanting about with all those men. That fancy Lord Lyons. Those Frenchmen. Russians, even."

"All the ladies in Washington were eager to attend Mr. Seward's party for the officers of the Russian fleet," Shannon said, smiling. "I happened to be fortunate enough to be invited. And you know perfectly well you went on that excursion from the Seventh Street wharf for a sight-seeing tour of the fleet."

"And a strange-looking lot they are, them Russians, with their beards and that funny kind of lettering on their caps. I noticed that Mrs. Lincoln didn't give a ball for the Russian officers, though."

"She's still going out very infrequently," Shannon said. "I don't believe she's gotten over losing her son."

"That's as may be. It's you I'm worried about, not Mrs. Lincoln, poor woman. It doesn't look right, your going around with other men when your husband's away."

"Adam told me he wanted me to," Shannon said, then closed her lips firmly, fearful of revealing anything more.

"I wish Adam'd come home. This house ain't the same without him. I miss him."

Shannon laughed. "Why, Aunt Kate, if you were a few years younger, I'd be afraid to have you under the same roof with my husband."

"And you'd be right," Aunt Kate said. "I know a real man when I meet one, let me tell you. A fine, lusty devil who knows how to keep a woman happy where it matters. Between the sheets."

"Oh, Aunt Kate, really!"

"Spare me your ladylike airs, dearie. I've taken care of you since you were in diapers. Nothing wrong with a wife enjoying that part of marriage, is there?"

"I don't know. Sometimes I miss him so much I could cry."

"And I'll bet he's missing you right now. Even if he don't use a lot of fancy love-talk, he needs you, girl. You've got a good marriage, Shannon. Don't do anything to spoil it."

"I won't," Shannon said, putting her arm around her aunt and giving her a little hug. But she found herself wondering what Adam would say when he returned and discovered her part in getting Bruce freed.

One slushy, gray afternoon, late in January, Shannon went to visit Odalie in her small, rented cottage near the Navy Yard on the Eastern Branch. The war still dragged on through that winter, and the trains of government wagons blocked the streets; the wounded still died in the overcrowded army hospitals, and dishonest contractors and quartermasters lined their pockets at the expense of the army.

But while the blockade was growing tighter off the Southern waters and the Confederacy was struggling for its existence, the social season in Washington had been a brilliant one for those fortunate enough to be accepted in the highest government circles.

In this, the third year of the war, Washington had never been so lively, with its constant round of balls, theatricals, tableaus, musicales and levees. Odalie had remained in seclusion, not wanting to cause Shannon any embarrassment; she understood the delicacy of the situation, with Adam working for the War Department. Besides, as she had explained to Shannon, she had little desire to go about and see the sights. She could only think of Bruce and pray for his return.

But this afternoon, Shannon was determined to take Odalie out for a drive. It would distract both of them from their worries, Shannon decided. If only she would get some word from Adam.

The carriage drew to a stop on the road in front of the small wooden cottage and the coachman helped Shannon to get down, then handed her the basket of hothouse grapes and peaches, and a bottle of wine. She drew her mantle of sable-lined, ruby-red velvet more closely around her, for the wind from the Eastern Branch was damp and chilly.

It was Reba, Odalie's newly-hired octoroon maid, who came to the door. The petite, golden-skinned girl was smiling, her dark eyes shining with pleasure.

The maid took Shannon's mantle and the basket. "Come in, Miz Kincaid, ma'am. Miz Lathrop's in the parlor. They all are."

Shannon was puzzled until she heard the deep, familiar masculine voice from inside the small parlor, and even before she had followed Reba into the room, she felt her heart lift with pleasure and relief. Bruce was seated on the sofa near the fireplace, his arm around Odalie.

Odalie's face was raised to her husband's, and there was such burning joy in her huge, dark eyes that Shannon could not repress a tiny stab of envy. *I'll look at Adam that way,* she thought, *when he comes home.*

Bruce caught sight of Shannon then, and, rising swiftly, he came to greet her. He took her hand in his, and as he stood looking at her, she saw that he had changed: his face was lean and drawn, so that his cheekbones jutted out sharply. *He has gone hungry, then,* she thought. There was a pale scar on his forehead, from the temple to the place where his silver-blond hair fell across his brow. His gray uniform was faded, the gold braid tarnished and frayed, and he wore a pair of boots so shabby that he would not have offered them to one of the house servants back at Jessamine. Faint lines etched the skin around his eyes and mouth. But the months of imprisonment had not changed his proud, erect bearing, and his gray eyes were warm.

"Shannon. Oh, my dear. This makes the joy of my homecoming complete." Her fingers tightened around his, and then, with a swift, impetuous movement, he drew her against his chest, and held her close.

Although she no longer felt even the memory of desire, it was good to have his arms around her. He was a friend, home from the war. That he and her husband were now on opposing sides no longer mattered. "Welcome home, Bruce," she whispered.

Then, all at once, she felt his lean, hard arms

tighten around her, so that the buttons of his uniform cut into the soft curves of her breasts. She could not help but sense the hunger in him. She told herself that it was only natural: a man like Bruce, confined in a prison camp all these months, deprived of a woman's embrace. Nevertheless, she put her hands against his shoulders and drew away.

"I've—brought a bottle of wine," she said. "Now we have something to celebrate. If you will tell Reba to bring glasses, we can all drink a toast. Miss Lucienne, too. Where is she?"

"Upstairs in her room, quite overcome with the excitement of having Bruce home again," Odalie said. "But I'm sure she can be persuaded to join us."

Bruce had released Shannon, but she saw a flicker of the lingering hunger in his eyes. She remembered Odalie's stammered confession about her distaste for the marital relationship; but surely now, after Bruce had been away for so long, after Odalie had fought so hard to secure his release, that would all be changed.

"I only arrived less than an hour ago," Bruce was saying. "Shannon, I have no words to thank you. I'm grateful to you. And to Adam, of course."

"It was Shannon who helped you," Odalie said quietly. "Adam's been away on business for the War Department for some time."

"I see," Bruce said. "I must confess, I had been wondering why Adam would have gone out of his way to help me after our differences. But no matter. Let me look at you, my dear. You're positively blooming."

Shannon stood still, as Bruce's eyes moved from her gray velvet bonnet with its curling, dark-red plumes, to her tawny hair, cascading down over her shoulders in the fashionable new waterfall curls. Her dress was pale gray velvet, topped with a jaunty red velvet jacket.

Aunt Lucienne, who had recovered herself enough to come downstairs, hurried into the parlor. "I declare, Bruce, Mrs. Kincaid must be chilled. It's so raw outside. Reba's bringing the wine. Please, do sit near the fire, my dear."

"Of course," Bruce said. "I'm forgetting my manners. Forgive me, Shannon. It's been so long since I've had the pleasure of being with three lovely ladies all at the same time."

Shannon was grateful to Lucienne for putting an end to the tension she had begun to feel, with Bruce's eyes upon her. Although Odalie urged Shannon to stay for dinner, she refused, pleading a previous engagement. Odalie would surely want to have Bruce all to herself, tonight of all nights.

On the carriage ride home, Shannon thought with envy that Odalie would not have to sleep alone any longer. She realized, more strongly than ever, how lonely she had been in that wide bed, without Adam at her side. Sometimes, unable to sleep for wanting him, she had tossed restlessly, until dawn. *Oh, my love,* she thought, as she gazed out at the muddy, crowded streets of the city, with unseeing eyes. *Come home to me soon. Soon.*

Shannon saw little of Bruce and Odalie in the weeks that followed, and it was probably just as well, she thought, remembering how tightly Bruce had held her in his arms on the day of his homecoming.

The season's activities went on, building up to a feverish pace. Mrs. Lincoln had come out of her self-imposed seclusion at last, and at her New Year's Day reception, in a splendid costume of purple silk, trimmed with black velvet and lace, she had received callers. But Shannon had seen the unquenchable grief in Mary Lincoln's eyes.

Still, President Lincoln and his wife had begun to attend the theater again, and Shannon had seen them at their box at Ford's, an elegant enclosure papered in dark red, carpeted and hung with Nottingham lace curtains. The box had been decorated with flags and flowers, and the President had sat in his upholstered rocking chair.

On another occasion, Shannon had been a guest of the Lincolns', when the slender young Adelina Patti had moved her audience to tears with her rendition of "The Last Rose of Summer."

All of Washington was caught up in a whirl of pleasure that winter. The citizens of the capital felt secure, with the Army of the Potomac stretched along the Rappahannock, between Washington and the forces of the Confederacy.

Then, as winter gave way to spring, the Union troops were on the move again, the pace of the war quickened, and everyone knew that the drive on Richmond was to be resumed. In March, General Grant was named commander-in-chief of the Union armies, and a month later, Shannon felt a stir of apprehension, when she saw the flatcars beginning to move out of Washington, loaded with blue-coated soldiers on their way to Virginia.

The trees in her garden were in bloom now, and

the flowerbeds were bright with daffodils and tulips. Along Rock Creek, the redbuds were bursting into blossom, and there was a new warmth and softness in the air.

But she had little heart for the beauties of spring, when, late in April, she stood in the crowd, watching General Burnside's men, the Ninth Corps, moving down Fourteenth Street: infantry, cavalry, artillery. Among them were five new regiments of black troops.

Then, early in May, she waited, with the rest of the city, to hear the latest news from Virginia, where heavy fighting had broken out. The newspapers were filled with the latest accounts of the Wilderness campaign, and Shannon was saddened by the terrible suffering on both sides. When the wounded began pouring back into the city, she went down to the wharves with hundreds of other women to pass out desperately needed food and hot coffee, to pour water on dressings which had dried and stiffened during the agonizing journey back from Virginia.

And then, one night when the flaring torches made splotches of brightness on the black waters of the Potomac, and the ambulances moved into line Shannon saw a familiar face on a blanket-covered stretcher.

She gave a little cry and ran forward. "Fergus. Oh, Fergus!"

His face was white in the torchlight, and his eyes were sunken, but he managed a faint smile as he reached out to clasp Shannon's hand. She quickened her steps to keep pace with the stretcher-bearers. Then they stopped so that other wounded men might be loaded onto the waiting ambulances, and she blinked back the tears. "You shouldn't be here. You're a reporter."

"A correspondent, registered with the War Department. I always told you, I wanted to—cover a battle, first-hand."

"Don't try to talk. I'll find out where you're being taken. I'll come to you as soon as I can."

"It's my leg," he said. "Hurt like hell at first—now—don't feel anything."

She put a hand to his forehead and felt that he was burning with fever. His eyes closed, and she thought he had lapsed into unconsciousness, until she felt his fingers grip hers. "Clarisse," he muttered.

"Where is she? I'll get word to her."

He shook his head. "No. Doesn't need me now. Doesn't need a crippled husband. She's up in New York—on the stage there—"

She glanced down at the blanket that covered him, then turned to one of the stretcher-bearers.

"His leg?"

The man nodded grimly. "Amputated at one of the field hospitals. He'll make it all right though, ma'am. I've seen them a lot worse than this. You a relative of his?"

"A friend." She bent and kissed his forehead, before he was lifted onto the ambulance. She got the name of the hospital from the stretcher-bearer, and left, determined to locate Clarisse and get word to her. Generous, warm-hearted Clarisse would want to be with her husband now. His injury would not change anything, she knew.

After endless inquiries, she was able to learn the name of the theater where Clarisse was performing, and a few days after she sent a telegram, she received word that Clarisse had left the show, and was on her way down to Washington. Each day, Shannon went to see Fergus at the hospital, laden with fruit and other small comforts.

Early one sweltering afternoon, Shannon arrived home to find Mrs. Beal waiting for her in the hallway. The housekeeper's stolid calm had given way to a fluttering excitement.

"He's back, ma'am. Mr. Kincaid. I fixed him a nice, hot bath and he's—"

"Adam!" Shannon cried. She turned and ran up the stairs, then burst into the bedroom to find Adam, just out of the tub, his hair clinging damply to his forehead, a loose robe wrapped around him.

"Oh, my darling—" The rest was smothered into silence as he crushed her in his arms, his mouth coming down over hers. Her lips parted to receive his kiss and she clung to him hungrily. A few minutes later, she was beside him on the bed. She trembled with eagerness as he undressed her and threw off his robe. His lips caressed one soft, rounded breast.

He was not gentle, and she did not want him to be. She drew him to her with a fierce, hot need that matched his own, a need born of endless nights of longing. She raised herself to receive the swift, hard thrust that joined them, her hands caressing the heavy muscles of his shoulders and back.

Later, as they lay close together, her eyes moved over his body and she gave a little cry. A scar ran from his lower ribs, cutting diagonally across his hard, lean abdomen ending only a few inches above the groin. "Oh, Adam, how—what—"

"Souvenir from a determined rebel with a Bowie knife. It was rough out there for awhile. But old Jeff Davis won't be getting his gold, and that's the important thing."

"But you might have been killed," she said.

She touched the scar with her fingertips.

"Damn good thing for me that knife stopped where it did. Otherwise—" He grinned at her and she could not resist an answering smile. She ran her fingers down along the scar.

"You keep doing that and we'll have to spend the rest of the day in bed."

She moved down and bent her face over him so that it was hidden by her heavy, tawny hair. She let her tongue trace the line where her fingers had been exploring. Adam moaned and drew a long, harsh breath. "Shameless," he said huskily. "You're positively shameless. Insatiable—beautiful—" His hands tangled in her hair. She heard him whisper, "Don't stop. Please, don't stop—"

The late afternoon sunlight was fading when Adam moved away from Shannon and got out of bed. "I don't want to leave you, even for a few hours. But I'm late as it is."

Shannon sat up in bed and reached for her wrapper, drawing it around her. "Surely you don't have to report to Mr. Stanton's office, not your first day home."

"Only a preliminary report. I'll be back in time for a late supper. Just the two of us. Oh, by the way, I didn't see Kate when I got in this afternoon."

"She's at the hospital. That's where I've been every day this week. With Fergus Mackenzie."

"Fergus? What's happened to him?"

"He was wounded in Virginia. He's lost a leg."

Adam swore, his face tight with pity and anger. "He's not a soldier, damn it."

"He says the Confederate artillery makes no distinctions between soldiers and war correspondents. I've sent for Clarisse. She'll be here soon, maybe tomorrow."

He nodded. "She'll stand by him. She's a good woman, in every way that matters." He started to put his clothes on. "Maybe now that you've seen the results of war, you understand why I've said we have to bring it to a successful end as quickly as possible. I saw the ambulances myself, as I was coming across the city. And the coffins."

"It will be over soon, won't it?" Shannon asked.

"I think so, now that Grant's in command. There's no more exchange of prisoners now, the blockade's even tighter than before. The Rebels are good fighters, but even they can't hold out without men or weapons."

"You won't be sent on another mission, will you?" she asked anxiously.

"Not as long as this one," he said. "But there may be some shorter trips South." He smiled down at her. "Don't worry about it now. You see to it that there's a good dinner waiting for me when I get home. And afterwards—"

He glanced at the rumpled bed. Shannon smiled at him, her eyes provocative. "And you called me shameless," she said.

Kate had sent a message telling Shannon that she would spend the night at the hospital. She had done it before, snatching a little sleep when she could. Because she was used to hard work, and was not squeamish, like some of the other volunteers, her services were in demand.

Shannon gave instructions to Mrs. Beal for a special dinner, with all of Adam's favorite foods. "And champagne," she said. "We must have champagne. Get out the silver vases and the new candelabra. I'll cut the flowers myself."

Later, Shannon went upstairs and got into a new gown, a simple but becoming white silk that was enhanced by her own vivid coloring. She wore no elaborate jewelry, only the locket Odalie had given her.

Eager with anticipation, she ran to the window at least a dozen times before she heard the carriage drive up. She was seated in the bedroom, and Lottie was finishing her coiffure. "Perhaps a few flowers, ma'am. I could fasten them here, and here. With a velvet ribbon."

Lottie stopped her work as Adam entered the bedroom.

"Dinner's been ready for nearly an hour," Shannon said, "but Mrs. Beal's having it kept warm. All your favorite dishes. Roast duck with that sauce you like and—"

Something in Adam's eyes silenced Shannon. Lottie put down the comb and brush and twisted her apron between her fingers.

"Get out," Adam said to Lottie. The girl scurried off, closing the door behind her.

"Adam, you shouldn't talk to Lottie that way. It's not like you."

He looked at Shannon, his eyes cold with anger.

"Why did you do it?" he demanded.

"I don't understand. What have I done?"

He strode to her side and grasped her shoulders in a hard, punishing grip. "Why did you pull wires to have Lathrop released from Johnson's Island while I was away? Did you think you could hide the truth from me?"

"No, of course not. I was going to tell you."

"When? After we'd had our cozy little dinner? After you'd let me make love to you again?"

She cringed before the implication. "How can you possible believe that of me?"

"You've lovely, Shannon. Seductive, passionate. You were counting on your charms to leave me so besotted that I would overlook what you did." He released her and pushed her from him so that she had to grasp the bedpost for support.

"That's not true. All those months without you. I wanted you as much as you wanted me."

"Did you, my dear? I should not have thought you'd have been so starved for a man's love, with Bruce back here. I'm sure he was most grateful to you for getting him out of prison and since Odalie—how did you put it? Since she doesn't enjoy that side of marriage, you had a clear field."

"That's a lie," Shannon cried, her eyes glittering with angry tears. Then, struggling to maintain her control, she asked, "How did you find out about Bruce?"

"From Peter Watson. Stanton's Assistant Secretary. I warned you not to interfere in government matters."

"This had nothing to do with government matters," she said. "Odalie came to me and begged me to help her."

"And so you used my name, my influence with the War Department, to get Bruce out of Ohio, to bring him here."

"What else could I have done? You were away. I had no way of reaching you."

"You might have at least waited until I came home, and asked me."

"While Bruce was lying wounded, freezing, without decent food, exposed to disease."

"I'm told there are many Union soldiers at Andersonville who are suffering equally severe hardships. Worse, perhaps. Would you like me to tell you about Andersonville, Shannon?"

She shook her head. "I've heard. And it's horrible. But I don't know those men. Bruce is my sister's husband."

"He's more than that to you. I haven't forgotten that you followed him to Colón, that you would have followed him to the ends of the earth if he'd been willing to marry you. You were in love with him once. You can't deny it."

"I did love him. Adam, try to understand. Until I came to Mobile, I'd never been near a young man. When Bruce was so kind to me, that day at Jessamine —Adam, no man had ever kissed me before. He was tender and gentle and I—"

"Spare me the details," Adam said.

"But I've got to make you understand. After that first night with you, everything changed for me."

"Come now, you're not going to tell me that you gave yourself to me because you loved me. We made a bargain, that's all. I kept my part. I even married you."

"Because you felt obligated to me. You said as much at the time."

"Whatever the reasons, you are my wife. You owe me your undivided loyalty. I warned you months ago, before I went away, to be discreet, to stay clear of Confederate-sympathizers. Washington's a hotbed of espionage right now."

"So that's it. You're not jealous of Bruce at all. No, of course you aren't. A man has to be in love to be jealous. That's what you told me, wasn't it?" She turned her face away to hide the tears that threatened to spill over. "You needn't worry," she said. "It's true that Bruce was involved in plotting against the Union back in San Francisco, but he won't do anything like that again. He's taken an oath of allegiance to the Federal government. He's on parole."

"And how long do you suppose he'll honor his oath, now he's free. Parole, hell! There are too damn many paroled Rebel officers swaggering around the city in full uniform these days."

"I suppose you'd rather they were dying in Yankee prison camps."

"You know me better than that, or you should. I only want to see an end to this war."

"Are you suggesting that Bruce can carry on the Confederate side of the war single-handedly?"

"Every Confederate who's free to fight for the

South, or plot to undermine the Union is helping to keep the war dragging on. Grant knows that. That's why he's forbidden any further exchange of prisoners. And Stanton's doing all he can, working day and night, to save the Union."

"By establishing a secret service. A network of spies and informers."

"It's necessary." Adam glared down at her. "Probably it's too much to expect a woman to understand these matters. But I do expect you to know your duty to your husband. And from now on, I intend to make sure you don't forget."

"What is it you want me to do?"

"To begin with, you'll stay away from Bruce and Odalie."

"I can't hurt Odalie that way."

"Be quiet. You will attend official functions with me, you will entertain those people I choose to invite into this house. No one else."

She raised her chin, and her eyes narrowed with anger and humiliation. "And when we're alone here in our bedroom?"

"I've never had any cause to find fault with you on that score," he said. "I've no doubt you'll go on pleasing me. Now," he said, taking her arm, "shall we go downstairs and have our dinner?"

"You may go down if you wish. I've lost my appetite."

"Too bad, sweetheart. No matter, you may keep me company."

29

ALTHOUGH SHANNON made no further protests, inwardly she seethed with resentment over Adam's high-handed treatment, his complete lack of understanding. Because she had helped Odalie, he looked on her as a traitor. He demanded her utter, unquestioning loyalty, and what did he offer in return? If he had spoken one word of love, of tenderness she might have tried to accept the restrictions he had placed upon her.

When, early in August, the news came to Washington that Admiral Farragut had closed off Mobile Bay, after a bitter naval battle, Shannon, disregarding Adam's orders, slipped out of the house and went to see Odalie. Their meeting was strained and uneasy. "I can understand Adam's feelings," Odalie said carefully. "And I do not want you to go against his wishes again."

"He's not my jailer," Shannon said, her voice tight with anger. "I'm free to come and go as I please."

"All the same, it might be better for all of us if you did not come here again," Odalie said, her eyes not meeting Shannon's. Then changing the subject quickly, she went on to tell Shannon that Antoinette had left Mobile, on one of the last blockade-runners to make it through the bay, before Farragut's attack. "She's in Paris now. Many of the French aristocrats have espoused the Confederate cause. She's in her glory, Shannon. I think she plans to make her home there permanently. She's met a man, a wealthy widower, with a title, and I shouldn't be at all surprised if she marries him."

"Heaven help him," Shannon said, and Odalie nodded ruefully.

Shannon had taken a hired carriage to Odalie's home and back again; although she had wanted to see her sister, she did not wish to provoke another quarrel with Adam. Since the night of his return from the West, when he had confronted her with cold fury, their relationship had settled down to a kind of distant politeness. Whether he was escorting her to some social function, or dining with her at home, he treated her with courtesy, but remained withdrawn.

The tension between them increased as summer advanced and Washington sweltered in a stifling heat wave, as Confederate artillery moved so close to the capital that some said the Rebel forces were planning to capture the city.

"Not a chance," Adam assured her. "We're safe enough here."

All the same, the heat and the sound of the guns, which could now be heard inside the city, put an added strain on Shannon's nerves. She might have fought with Adam except that he was away from the house so often. His trips were brief, and he pointedly refused to discuss them with Shannon.

He still treated Kate with warmth and friendliness, and when he was with Colin, he relaxed and gave the boy the same affection he had always shown. On Colin's fourth birthday, Adam brought home a present, a St. Bernard puppy, and for a few brief hours, Shannon was able to forget her bitterness, her hurt feelings.

"Couldn't you have chosen a smaller dog?" she asked.

"For a big boy of four?" Adam asked, ruffling the child's dark, curly hair. "Colin will be able to handle him." He held the boy close to him. "Won't you, son?"

"Sure I will," Colin said confidently. He wriggled free and soon he was rolling around with the puppy on the parched grass of the back garden. Shannon could not help smiling. She felt Adam's hand on her arm. "He's a fine boy, Shannon," Adam said proudly. Then, more softly, he added, "Thank you, my dear, for giving me a son."

Then, as if embarrassed by his show of feelings, he took his hand away, and went over to Colin, and soon the two of them were discussing plans for building a dog house, since Mrs. Beal would not appreciate having to clean muddy pawprints from the carpets, or the plush and velvet furniture.

The moment of closeness had passed, and Shannon was relieved when Aunt Kate came to join them, carrying a plate of frosted cakes and a pitcher of lemonade.

The nights were the worst, Shannon decided. If Adam did not come home, as often happened, she tossed restlessly, her damp nightgown clinging to her body. Was he at work at the War Department offices? It was well-known that Edwin Stanton often worked through the night, and that he did not hesitate to keep his staff working with him.

Worse yet, was Adam with another woman? She did not think so, because, in spite of their quarrel, he still reached for her often, taking her without tenderness, without making any effort to arouse her. He was never brutal with her, but she thought he used her only to ease his needs. *As he would take a girl in one of those parlor houses,* she thought.

On one such night, when he had taken her, then turned away, she could not repress her tears. Adam usually fell asleep immediately after he possessed her, and she thought he was asleep now. Her body shook with long-repressed sobs, and she jammed her fist against her mouth so that she would make no sound.

A moment later, Adam turned and reached for her.

"Don't cry, Shannon. Here, let me—" He tried to draw her into his arms. She longed to yield, to find comfort in his warmth and closeness, to fall asleep with his body curved around hers. But her pride was too strong, and she remembered his angry question, on the night of their quarrel. "I married you, didn't I?" As if, having done so, he had fulfilled his obligation to her.

"It's stifling in here. Not a breath of air." She pulled away and went to sit by the window. He made no attempt to bring her back, and she remained in the chair, looking down at the moonlit garden, listening to the far-off crack of gunfire.

When they went out together, they continued to maintain a truce, hiding their estrangement from the rest of the world. But they were not always successful.

One afternoon, they went to the hospital for a last visit with Fergus Mackenzie. Clarisse was in Washington, and now that the doctors had given their permission, she was preparing to take Fergus back to New York.

"Will you be returning to the stage?" Adam asked.

"Only for a little while," she said. "I'm starting to show already, and there aren't many parts for a pregnant leading lady." But Clarisse was obviously pleased by her condition, and Fergus was beaming with pride. Somehow, Clarisse had been able to restore his confidence in himself, to ease the bitterness that had been his first reaction to the loss of his leg.

"We'll miss both of you," Shannon said.

"I think we'll be seeing each other again," Fergus told her. "As soon as the baby gets here, and we're both able to travel that far, we're heading back to California. I've been offered my old job on the newspaper. And I guess you and Adam will be turning up in San Francisco once the war's over. Right, Adam?"

"I'm not sure," Adam said slowly. He turned to Shannon. "How do you feel about going back to San Francisco?"

"Does it matter to you how I feel?"

The words had come out before she had been able to stop them. Clarisse smoothed over the awkward moment saying, "Adam's always had a mind of his own, that's for sure."

But later, while Adam remained beside the bed, talking to Fergus, Clarisse drew Shannon aside. "All right," she said with her usual frankness. "Tell me about it."

"I don't know what you mean."

"The hell you don't. Honey, I've known you and Adam too long for either of you to pull the wool over my eyes. Whatever's wrong, make it up with him. Don't wait too long."

"He won't forgive me," Shannon said. "I used his name, his influence, to get Bruce Lathrop out of a Yankee prison camp." Quickly, she told Clarisse the details.

"Can't say I blame him for being jealous."

"He's not jealous. He's only angry because I went against his wishes, and meddled in his business."

"Maybe that's what he told you. He may even believe it. But he's a man, Shannon. He can't forget the way you went mooning after Bruce, back in Mobile. The way you went off to Colón with him. Adam's got his pride, honey. Same as Fergus. Thank goodness Fergus got me pregnant last time we were together in New York. Even so, it took a lot of persuasion to convince him that he's still the man I married. That I'm still as much in love with him as I ever was."

"How did you manage it?" Shannon asked.

"How do you think? I bribed one of those horse-faced nurses to let us have a room to ourselves for a few hours."

"Oh, Clarisse, I didn't mean to pry."

Clarisse gave her a rakish little grin. "Don't start sounding like that prissy little schoolgirl you were when I first met you on board the *Amaranth*. You know as well as I do what it takes to make a man happy. And, Shannon, don't let your pride get in the way. Adam's the kind of man a woman goes after. If you don't give him what he needs, if you don't make him believe he's the only man in your life, some other woman will." She fell silent as Adam rose and came over to join them.

"Promise you'll remember what I said," Clarisse insisted.

"I'll try," Shannon said.

Later, as Adam and Shannon were driving away from the hospital, through the hot, dusty streets where ambulances still rattled by, and soldiers went about their business, some with bandages on their heads or arms, others limping on makeshift crutches, Shannon asked, "Will we be going back to San Francisco soon, do you think?"

Adam shrugged. "The war can't last much longer. With Mobile Bay bottled up, there are only a few ports through which the South can get supplies. The Confederacy's strangling now."

"And we'll leave Washington as soon as the war's over?"

"I will," he said.

She flinched at the coldness of his words. "We're a family," she said, forcing herself to speak in a conciliating way. "You and I. And Colin."

"Are we? I trusted you, Shannon. And you betrayed my trust."

"Can't you forgive me for that? Must you go on punishing me?" she asked.

"I don't know what you're talking about."

"Don't you?" Her sense of injustice was too strong to be repressed. "You've forbidden me to see my sister. You've—"

"You went to see her in spite of what I said."

"How—did you know?"

And when Adam remained silent she demanded, "Are you using one of those paid informers who works for the War Department to spy on your own wife?"

"No one was set to spy on you. But Odalie's home is under surveillance. You were seen going in there."

"Odalie can't be under suspicion. She cares nothing about politics or—"

"No, but Bruce does. I told you he'd lose no time in forgetting his oath, once he was free. And there are a lot of other Confederate sympathizers here in the capital who know that the South hasn't a chance of winning. They've lost everything except their determination to keep slavery alive, if not here, then in another country."

"Antoinette Duval's gone to France," Shannon said. "Odalie told me."

"She must have gotten through on one of the last of the blockade-runners, before Mobile Bay was closed off. But it's not the Confederates who've emigrated to Paris who are of interest to the department."

"I don't understand."

"There's no need for you to understand. I can't keep you chained up in the house. Though I've been tempted. But I'm not about to give you information that could fall into enemy hands, either."

Although Shannon was silent for the rest of the drive home, she was unwilling to give up so easily. Clarisse had been right. Somehow, she would have to restore Adam's confidence in her, to make him see how unreasonable he was being.

Upstairs, in their bedroom, Shannon made another attempt to pacify Adam, saying, "I did not go to see Odalie for political reasons, any more than I had Bruce released from that prison camp to aid the Confederate cause. I only went to see Odalie again, to comfort her. She has many friends in Mobile and when I heard of the attack on the Bay, I knew she'd be frantic with worry. I thought perhaps my being there would help."

"That's enough," Adam said. "I'm tired of your excuses. I'm tired of your devotion to your sister, of your obsession with your Duval connections. You'll never forget that you're Philippe Duval's daughter."

"Adam, I don't want to quarrel with you, not anymore. I want to be a good wife to you, I swear it."

She put a hand on his arm, but he jerked away. "In that case," he said, "you can start by packing a valise for me. Not too much. Enough for a week." Seeing her startled look, he added, "I'm only going to Fredericksburg. A routine trip."

"I'm surprised you're telling me where you're going," she said, her resolve weakening under his rebuff.

"If there was any need for secrecy, I would not have told you, believe me."

Biting back a retort, she turned and went to the dresser, from which she began to remove his clean linen. How easy it was for Clarisse to advise her to make up with Adam. How could she, when he refused to trust her, when he would not even respond to the touch of her hand?

The day after Adam's departure, Shannon sat in the sun-parched garden, where the grass was dusty and yellowing, and even the flowerbeds looked forlorn, the blooms wilting on their stems. Hearing a noise at the garden gate, she rose and went to investigate. Colin, who had been playing with his clumsy, shambling puppy, looked after her, and then turned his attention back to his pet.

"Bruce," Shannon said, startled at seeing him here. Surely Odalie must have told him of Adam's anger over his release.

"May I come in?" he asked.

She hesitated. Aunt Kate would not be coming home from her duties at the hospital for a few hours. The servants might see and gossip, but that was a chance she would have to take. "Is Odalie all right?" she asked.

Bruce nodded, and, when she opened the gate, he followed her into the garden. He was no longer wearing his faded, tattered Confederate uniform. Instead, he looked handsome and elegant in a fine new suit of light gray, with a plum-colored waistcoat, and a white silk cravat. In spite of the heat, he appeared cool and unruffled, his silver-blond hair carefully brushed, his tall, dark gray hat in his hand.

He seated himself beside Shannon on a stone bench, in the shade of a broad-branched maple tree. "Does my presence here make you uneasy?" he asked. "Perhaps you'll feel better to know that Odalie and I are both leaving Washington soon."

"You're not returning to Jessamine, surely?"

"No, my dear. I don't believe that any Lathrop will ever live there again."

"But why not? Once the war's over, the fields can be planted again. The English manufacturers must be desperate for cotton by now. It will take time, but the first harvest after the war will bring a good price."

"And how are we to plant cotton or harvest it, without field hands?"

"You can hire men and pay them wages. When Adam used to lease slaves for the lumberyard in Mobile, he paid them and he said they worked better."

The mention of Adam's name brought a moment's uneasy silence between them. "That was different," Bruce said. "Jessamine, Beau Rivage, all the great plantations up and down the river are finished. Our way of life has ended. It will never be restored, not in Alabama. That's why I'm going away."

"Where will you go?"

"Mexico. Sonora. There are negotiations going on now in Paris. Louis Napoleon is in sympathy with our cause. His armies control Mexico now. We'll be given land grants there, and in time, we'll build a new Confederacy. We'll have great houses, finer than those we've lost. It will take time, but I'll build a new Jessamine one day."

"Won't it be a rugged life for Odalie in the meantime?" Shannon asked. "I don't know much about Sonora, but I should think that living conditions down there are rather primitive."

"Odalie won't be coming with me."

"You're going to send for her and Eugénie later?"

Shannon saw a look of pain and regret come into his grey eyes. "No, I'm not," he said.

"You're not walking out on Odalie and your child?"

"It's not like that, Shannon. Odalie, Eugénie and Aunt Lucienne will go to France. I've already told Odalie that she's free to seek a divorce if she wants to, and make a new life for herself. She's better suited to Paris, and the life at court there, than to Sonora."

"And has she agreed to your plans?"

"Not yet. But she'll have to accept the logic of the arrangements, once I'm gone. She'll realize that I'm doing what's best for both of us."

"I don't believe that. Odalie loves you."

He gave her a faint, regretful smile. "And I love her. She's part of me, Shannon. And there's Eugénie— it won't be easy to think of her growing up, forgetting she has a father."

"Then you've got to take them with you."

"It's too late," he said. "Even if the war had not come along, if we could have lived out our days at Jessamine, Odalie would not have been happy with me. We couldn't ever have had a real marriage be- cause Odalie's not—she can't—"

Bruce lapsed into silence, staring moodily at a dusty border of marigolds and zinnias that bordered the garden wall. He looked ill-at-ease and, Shannon thought, *He can walk out on Odalie and his child, but he's still too much of a gentleman to speak of Odalie's failure as a wife.*

Then he said slowly, "Perhaps, if I had not left you there in Colón that night, everything would be different for all of us."

Shannon smiled. "I'm glad you walked out on me," she said. "Oh, I wasn't at the time. But if I hadn't been stranded in Colón, with my money gone, I never would have turned to Adam."

Bruce looked at her in surprise. "You love Adam, even now? Yes, Odalie's told me how angry he was when he learned that you had helped to get me out of that prison camp. She said he's been making life miserable for you ever since."

"It hasn't been that bad," Shannon said. "Besides, he'll forget, in time."

"And if he doesn't? Adam's a stubborn man. And he can be ruthless."

"I know that better than anyone else. But I have to stay with him, because there can never be anyone else for me. Even if he never forgives me completely, I have to be near him." She went on, speaking more to herself than to Bruce. "I have to hear his voice, to reach out and touch him, to lie by his side at night." She stopped, and then, seeing the look on Bruce's face, she laughed softly. "Have I shocked you with my frankness?" she asked. "Maybe you don't think a lady should have such feelings."

"I might have thought so, once. But not now. Shannon, if only Odalie needed me in that way, I'd take her to Mexico with me if I had to drag her there. She's so lovely. She has grace, breeding and beauty. She's a lady, but she's never learned how to be a woman."

He rose quickly, and offered his arm to Shannon. "Walk to the gate with me," he said.

She walked with him, along the gravel path, her hand on his arm. The summer afternoon was nearing its close and a light breeze stirred the parched grass. At the gate, Bruce turned and touched Shannon's cheek lightly. "Adam's a fortunate man," he said. They stood in silence for a moment. From around the side of the house, Shannon could hear Colin's voice, as he shouted excitedly, and tossed sticks for his puppy to chase.

"May I kiss you good-bye?" Bruce asked softly.

Impulsively, Shannon put her arms around him and raised her lips to his. There was no passion between them now, only tenderness and warm affection. He stroked her tawny hair, holding her against him. Then, a moment later, he was leaving, closing the iron gate behind him.

Shannon stood looking after him, watching his easy, graceful stride as he disappeared from sight. Perhaps he had made a wise choice, after all. In Sonora, he could start over again. If only he would take Odalie with him.

Then she heard footsteps on the gravel path and turning, she saw Aunt Kate looking at her with shocked, reproving eyes.

30

THAT EVENING, at dinner, Aunt Kate was silent, her eyes fixed on her plate, her brows drawn together in a frown.

"If you would only let me explain," Shannon began, when Mrs. Beal had left the dining room.

"I don't think you have to explain anything," Aunt Kate snapped.

"But you don't understand. I was only kissing Bruce good-bye because he's—"

Shannon hesitated. To explain that Bruce was leaving Washington for Mexico would be to admit that he was breaking his parole. But unless she made some explanation to her aunt, she feared that Kate would tell Adam what she had seen.

"You're a fool, Shannon. Adam's the man for you. He always has been."

"Don't you suppose I know that?" Shannon demanded.

"Strange way you have of showing it. Quarreling

with him, carrying on with another man the minute his back is turned."

Shannon put down her coffee cup with such force that the liquid spilled into the saucer. "I am not doing any such thing. And I don't have to answer to you for what I do. I'm not a child any longer."

"You don't have to answer to me. But you'll have to answer to Adam when he comes home."

"You're not going to tell him. Aunt Kate, you mustn't."

"You want to wait until he catches the two of you together. I wouldn't care if he put a bullet into Bruce; Adam'd be within his rights. But that'd ruin Adam's future, cause a scandal."

"I'm not going to see Bruce again. He's leaving Washington. He's going to Mexico."

"He can't do that. He gave some kind of promise, swore an oath, didn't he?" Aunt Kate looked at Shannon suspiciously. "And what business would he be having in Mexico? Is he going to enlist in the French army down there?"

"He's going to settle there. He believes that there's no future for him in Alabama. That once the war's over he and the other plantation owners will be ruined. He wants to make a new home for himself in Sonora. The French emperor has said he might give support to a Confederate settlement in Mexico. Ex-Senator Gwin of California is over in Paris now. Perhaps he'll be able to persuade Louis Napoleon."

Aunt Kate shrugged but she looked slightly relieved.

"So he'll be taking his wife and child and going off to Mexico. Good riddance, I say."

"He isn't taking Odalie, or the child," Shannon said.

"Oh, isn't he now? He has a habit of walking out on his women, whether he marries them or not."

"That's not fair. He thinks Odalie will be better off in Paris, with Antoinette."

"A wife's place is with her husband," Aunt Kate said. "I stuck it out with Jethro, long as I could. I even put up with his knocking me around. He was meaner than ever after you left, Shannon. It was only when he brought a cheap little trollop to live under the same roof with me, when he dressed her up in fancy clothes and didn't even try to hide what was going on that I— No matter. Bruce ain't doing anything like that, is he?"

"Of course not."

"Then Odalie ought to go with him. Unless she has some reason not to." Aunt Kate glared at Shannon suspiciously. "Maybe you ain't telling me everything."

Shannon, exasperated with her aunt's prying, pushed her chair away from the table. "I'm going upstairs to bed," she said.

But although she went to her room, she could not sleep that night, for the August heat made the city stifling and humid. She heard the sound of distant thunder, but there was no rain to cool the heavy air, and she lay awake until dawn.

Her mind was troubled by thoughts of Bruce and Odalie. If Bruce had left tonight, what must Odalie be suffering in her house on the other side of the city? It wasn't right. Odalie loved Bruce, and he loved her, in spite of the many times she had disappointed him.

Surely, their marriage could not end this way. No matter how splendid a life Odalie might have in Paris, with Antoinette, she would never be happy there.

Anymore than I could be happy without Adam, she thought.

She sat up in bed, and wrapped her arms around her bent knees, staring at the gray light that was starting to filter through the windows. Then, acting on impulse, she got up, bathed and dressed without waking anyone in the house, slipped out into the street and found an empty cab a few blocks away. She had to see Odalie, if only to try to comfort her. Adam had said that Odalie's house was being watched, but Shannon could not let that stop her.

She found Odalie, still in the clothes she must have been wearing the evening before; her skirts were crumpled and she sat, twisting the remains of a small lace handkerchief in her hands.

"She been like that ever since Mr. Bruce left," said Reba, the little octoroon maid. "She ain't been cryin' or nothin' like that. Just sittin' there. Wouldn't go to bed. Wouldn't touch a bite of food. Even Miz Lucienne couldn't do nothin' with her."

"I'll see what I can do," Shannon said. "Meanwhile, go and prepare breakfast."

Reba nodded and scurried off to obey, and Shannon came to Odalie's side. Odalie did not look up until Shannon put a light hand on her shoulder.

"Shannon. You shouldn't be here. Adam will be angry."

"Adam's away. May I sit down?"

Odalie nodded and made room for Shannon on the sofa. The lamps still burned and the drapes were drawn; Odalie probably did not even realize that it was morning.

"He's gone," Odalie said. "Bruce has left me."

"You let him go alone?"

"What else could I do? I don't blame him, not really. I haven't been the kind of wife he needs. But—oh, Shannon, what will I do without him?"

"Has he left Washington yet, do you know? Has he told you his plans?"

Odalie nodded. "He'll be out of the city by now, surely. I don't know what route he'll be taking but he's going to go through Virginia to Wilmington, on Cape Fear in North Carolina. He's going to take a blockade-runner from there. It's a side-wheeler that's been carrying cotton and turpentine to Bermuda, and bringing back munitions and luxury goods. Bruce wasn't sure exactly when the boat would be leaving Wilmington. He may have to wait for a week or more. But he has a place to stay. An inn outside Wilmington. He should be comfortable enough there." Odalie's shoulders slumped. Her dark eyes were bleak and hopeless. "What difference does it make? I'll never see him again. He told me to go to Mama, in Paris."

"Is that what you want, Odalie?"

"You know it's not. But Bruce said I was only suited to a life of luxury, that I had to be pampered and waited upon. He really believes I'll be happier in France."

"Are you sure you wouldn't be? I'm told that life in Paris is quite splendid now, and since your mother's become a part of the Confederate expatriate circle there—"

"I want to be with Bruce. I don't care how we live,

or where. But I couldn't make him believe me. Why should he, when I've failed him so often in the past?"

Shannon took Odalie's hand. "Adam says war changes everyone. It's changed you, Odalie. I know how much courage it took for you to leave Mobile and come here. To try to see Adam and get him to help Bruce. Why, I think you would have gone to Mr. Stanton, himself, if I had refused to intercede."

"All that doesn't matter. Bruce doesn't believe that I can change in—in other ways." Odalie's cheeks went crimson, but she continued, the words rushing out. "Even on our wedding night, when I wanted so much to please him, I couldn't give myself freely. I couldn't forget."

"I don't understand," Shannon said.

"I've never told anyone. Not even Mama. I was too ashamed."

"Can you tell me now?"

Odalie twisted her torn handkerchief, pulling at the frayed bits of lace, speaking quickly. "Craig Judson. Our overseer. I was only fourteen. He said I'd led him on. But I hadn't meant to. I must have done something to arouse him that way."

Her voice was so soft now that Shannon had to lean forward to catch every word. Odalie was speaking of a night in the overseer's house, a brutal assault. "There must be something bad in me to make a man do such a thing."

"Oh, no! Odalie, no! It wasn't your fault. Why didn't you tell Bruce about it before you married him?"

"I couldn't. And now it's too late."

They heard a light tap on the parlor door, and

Reba put her head in, saying, "I've fixed breakfast, like you tol' me, Miz Kincaid, ma'am. Better come in now while it's all nice 'n' hot."

She closed the door again. "I couldn't eat," Odalie said.

"You must, or you'll be ill."

"What does it matter?"

"Are you going to give up so easily? Will you take Eugénie and go to France? And let your mother dominate your life as she has in the past?"

"What choice do I have? Bruce doesn't want me."

"But he does. He told me so, when he came to say good-bye. He loves you, Odalie."

"You're only trying to comfort me, and it's good of you, but I know——"

"He said he loved you. He meant it."

"You're sure?" Odalie's dark eyes came alive with hope.

"He said that you are a lady, but that you had never learned how to be a woman. But it's not too late to learn, if you love Bruce enough."

Odalie sat in silence for a moment, and Shannon saw that she was trembling. Then, swiftly, Odalie rose to her feet. "Come along," she said. "Breakfast's waiting. I'm going to get some food down, somehow, because I'll be needing all my strength for the trip."

"You—you're going to Wilmington?"

"There's still time. And I know the name of the inn where Bruce will be staying. If I go at once, he'll still be there. Oh, Shannon, he's got to be."

She took Shannon's hand and tugged her to her feet. "Hurry, Shannon. You can have breakfast with me, and then I'll have Reba start packing."

"But Odalie, how will you get to Wilmington? There are two armies between here and Cape Fear."

"I'll have Caleb drive me. He was devoted to Papa, and he is to me, too. He came along from Mobile with us, even though Mama tried to stop him. He's strong, and smart."

Shannon put a restraining hand on Odalie's arm. "Even so, it won't be easy. There'll be stragglers, deserters from both sides."

But a new strength seemed to be flowing through Odalie, as she left the parlor and hurried down the hall to the dining room, with Shannon trying to keep up with her. "Caleb used to drive us to North Carolina, before the war, when we went to visit our kin in Henderson."

"It's different down there now. It could be dangerous."

"He can take one of Bruce's pistols."

They entered the diningroom and seated themselves at the table, where Reba served them eggs and coffee, with biscuits and honey. "Shannon, you do think I should go, don't you?"

"You know I do. But this house has been watched in the past, and may be right now."

"I know," Odalie said calmly. "Bruce told me. But he's managed to get away."

"He must have had help. Confederate sympathizers who planned his escape with him."

"You don't think that I'll put him in danger if I try to follow him, do you?"

"It's possible. Unless—" Shannon's eyes narrowed thoughtfully. "Unless no one knows you've left before you're into Virginia." She looked at Reba, who stood at Odalie's side with a basket of hot biscuits. "There's a chance." She put down her coffee cup. "I'm going home to pack a bag for myself."

"You're coming with me?" For a moment, Odalie's voice was full of affection. Then she said, "Oh, but you can't. Adam would be furious."

"He doesn't have to know. I'll leave a message saying I've gone up North, to—to Saratoga. So many ladies we know have gone up there to escape this heat here in Washington. It's quite fashionable and—oh Lord, I nearly forgot. What about Eugénie? And Miss Lucienne?"

"Aunt Lucienne's too old to make the trip under these conditions. But I can't leave my child. Shannon, I can't."

"Your aunt will have to remain here," Shannon agreed. "I'll make sure she has everything she needs. And when you're settled in Mexico, I'll see that she gets down there to join you, if that's what she wants. Meanwhile, Reba can look after her."

Late that night, a carriage drew up at the wooden building that served as a sentry post for the Navy Yard Bridge. A blue-uniformed corporal, a skinny young man, opened the carriage door, and, holding up his lantern, peered at the two women inside.

One of them was dressed in a smart traveling costume of dark blue silk, and a matching bonnet, with velvet ribbons and saucy white ostrich plumes. The other, a light-skinned colored maid in a starched calico dress and spotless white apron, sat beside her. The corporal thought that the maid's features were remarkably delicate. She was as pretty as any of those octoroon girls he'd seen at Madam Russell's Bake Oven, one of the capital's popular sporting houses.

"You can't leave the city after dark, not without a pass, ma'am," he said to the lady in the blue silk. "The fighting in Virginia has quieted down some, but we've been ordered to take precautions."

"I do understand," the lady said with a warm dazzling smile. Lord, but she was a beauty. Hair like ripe wheat, and those eyes—golden, they were, in the light from the lantern. She went on, speaking with assurance. "I'm Mrs. Adam Kincaid. My husband is attached to Mr. Stanton's department. He has sent me a letter, asking me to join him in Fredericksburg."

"Well, now, I don't know about that. If I could see the letter, ma'am."

A burly, middle-aged man, who walked with a marked limp, came up to the carriage to join them. He wore sergeant's stripes. The young corporal turned the matter over to him with a look of relief.

"Mrs. Kincaid?" He studied her intently. "Oh, sure. My missus and I, we saw you in your box at Ford's Theater. With Mr. Kincaid, and Mr. and Mrs. Stanton. My missus kept going on about the dress you were wearing. Said it must have come straight from Paris. I don't know about such things but she couldn't stop talking about it." He gave the maid only a passing glance, but his eyes moved to the large wicker hamper at Shannon's feet.

"A few things for my husband's comfort," she said. "Fresh linen. And a supply of his favorite bourbon. He said it was difficult to get it in Fredericksburg."

Carefully, Shannon reached into the basket. "Do

take a bottle, Sergeant. Mr. Kincaid says it's excellent."

"I couldn't think of it, ma'am."

"I insist," Shannon said graciously. "Yours is a difficult and demanding post here. He'd want you to have it, I'm sure."

"Most generous, Mrs. Kincaid." The sergeant took the bottle. "I wish we could provide you with an escort, but we are short-handed."

"My coachman's most reliable," Shannon assured him.

"Big fellow, isn't he?" The massive black man sat immobile on the box. "Guess you'll be safe enough then. A pleasant trip, ma'am." He saluted smartly, and the corporal followed his example, then closed the door of the carriage. Caleb cracked his whip and the carriage went rumbling across the bridge.

Odalie gave a sigh of relief. "Thank goodness Reba thought of the soothing syrup," she said, opening the top of the wicker hamper. "Eugénie should sleep through the night." She laughed, a little shakily. "It would seem that I can pass for a woman of color," she added. "No one gave me a second glance when I left the house and came to meet you."

"Reba's clever. That berry juice and bark dye makes you look at least three shades darker."

"All the same, I'll feel better when we get as far down as Richmond," Odalie said.

Adam looked almost menacing, as he stood over Aunt Kate. The note Shannon had left him was crumpled in his hand. "How could she go to Saratoga without discussing it with me? I told her I'd be back within a week."

He had arrived home a short time before, and had been listening to Aunt Kate's explanation of Shannon's unexpected departure. Now he frowned, his dark brows drawing together, his eyes angry.

"You know how hot it's been here," Aunt Kate said uneasily. "And all them other fine ladies went off to Saratoga, friends of hers. So she made up her mind she'd go too."

"So she went off and left you behind. And Colin. Is that what you're telling me?"

"She—wanted to take us, but I told her I don't mind the heat, and I said I'd look after Colin."

Adam put a heavy hand on her shoulder. "Look at me, Kate." But she could not meet his hard stare. "Now, suppose you tell me where Shannon really went. And why."

"Don't you go bullying me, Adam Kincaid. She told me she was going to Saratoga, same as she says in that note."

"And you believed her?"

Aunt Kate did not answer, until Adam gave her a gentle shake. "We're friends, aren't we, Kate?"

"Shannon's my niece, my sister's child. I won't let you hurt her."

"Hurt her? Kate, for the love of God, she's my wife. I have a right to know where she is."

"I can't be sure, but— Adam, I came home early from the hospital one afternoon last week, and— Give me your word you won't harm her. Shannon's headstrong and willful, I know that well enough. But you've given her a bad time, these last few months. You can't blame her if— Bruce deserves what he gets, but Shannon, well, she ain't all to blame, neither. If I thought you'd hurt Shannon—"

"Kate, where is she?"

"I'm tryin' to tell you, ain't I? I went into the garden, like I said, and there Shannon was, with Bruce, standing by the gate. He was kissing her, and she wasn't trying to stop him. Later, she told me he was going away, leaving Washington. Going off to Mexico."

Adam's face was grim, and the muscles in his jaw stood out in a hard line. "There's been talk of a plot to start a new Confederate colony in Sonora. But the French emperor hasn't given his word yet, to support such a venture." His eyes were bitter. "It's like Bruce, though, taking his wife and child and rushing off to a strange country."

"He ain't took Odalie or the child. Shannon told me he was shipping them off to France, to stay with Antoinette Duval."

"And now he's gone. And Shannon, too."

"Adam, we can't be sure."

But he had turned and started toward the stairs.

"What are you going to do?" Aunt Kate asked, her eyes wide with fear.

"What do you think?" Adam demanded. "I'm going to find my wife and bring her back."

31

IN THE YEARS that followed, Shannon would never be able to remember all the details of that long, jolting trip through the war-torn countryside of Virginia and North Carolina. But certain memories would remain vivid in her mind forever.

The moment outside Richmond, when they were stopped by a troop of hard-riding Confederate cavalrymen. Shannon's connection, through Adam, with the War Department in Washington would do her no good here. And Odalie still wore the calico dress and apron of a servant. So it was Shannon who spoke to the tall, bronzed captain of the troop, using the soft, drawling tones she had come to know back in Mobile. She dabbed at her eyes with her handkerchief, as she spoke of her husband, who had been killed in the fighting at Cold Harbor, a few months before.

"My sympathies, ma'am. But you'll be able to tell your child, one day, that her father died helping

General Lee to drive Grant and his troops back out of Cold Harbor. A splendid victory."

Shannon nodded, and looked down tenderly at Eugénie, who was cradled in Odalie's arms. The child stared up, with wide golden eyes, at the man on horseback.

"I'm going back to live with my family, in Wilmington," Shannon said. "Everyone in Richmond was very kind, but—you understand—"

"Of course, ma'am. Sure you can trust these darkies of yours?" He gave Odalie a searching glance.

"The coachman's been with our family for years, and Bettylou was raised with me."

"Fine-looking wench," the captain said. Then, turning his attention to Eugénie, he said, "See you take good care of that baby, Bettylou. A pretty little thing, she is." And, to Shannon, he added, "She has your eyes, ma'am."

"Lil Missy, she look like her granddaddy, suh," Odalie said respectfully.

After the door was closed and the carriage started off again down the tree-shaded road, Shannon and Odalie looked at each other and gave way to laughter. It relieved a little of the tension that they had been under for so long.

"Clarisse couldn't have given a more convincing performance," Shannon said.

"He—he called me a fine-looking wench," Odalie said.

"And so you are," Shannon told her. Once again they burst into laughter, and even little Eugénie giggled and waved her plump arms happily.

But, as the trip went on, there was little enough cause for laughter, for they drove past neglected, and often deserted plantations. The underbrush was starting to encroach upon the cotton fields, and the gardens lay withered under the blazing sun. Bands of Confederate soldiers, their uniforms faded and torn, moved slowly down the dusty roads.

Once, Shannon and Odalie, with Eugénie, took refuge in a deserted slave cabin, while Caleb went to hide the horses and carriage in the woods beyond. "Mosby's raiders," the black man had said, as he had helped them down from the carriage. And, after he had hidden the horses and carriage, he had returned to stand guard over them, his huge hand resting on Bruce's pistol.

Still, the two women were frightened. Mosby's raiders were a guerrilla band, and while they were supposed to be fighting on the side of the South, they were known as a lawless group, who attacked isolated pickets, stole horses, derailed trains, and captured sutlers' wagons, often keeping their booty for themselves. Odalie lay stretched on a tattered corncob mattress in the cabin, soothing Eugénie, who was hot and fretful now. Shannon was huddled at the foot of the mattress, her hands balled into tight fists. She found some comfort in the sight of Caleb's broad back, his massive shoulders. But what could one man do against a whole troop?

"Mosby's men are on the Confederate side," Odalie whispered. "Surely, they wouldn't harm us. Those cavalrymen we met near Richmond were gentlemen."

"They were under strict military discipline," Shannon whispered back. Then, seeing the swift fear in Odalie's eyes, she added quickly, "There's no use taking chances. They might steal the carriage and the horses."

But it was not theft that Shannon feared. For the first time in months, she was remembering those hours of horror in Sydney-Town.

She heard the sound of Mosby's horsemen riding by, but they kept going until they reached the main house. They would wreak havoc there, she had no doubt, stealing what they could carry and smashing the rest, but that was not her concern.

It was early evening before Caleb left the cabin to reconnoiter, and when he returned he was carrying a bulky burden wrapped in a linen tablecloth.

"They took some of the food, but they didn't find it all," he said proudly. "Got us a ham, and bread and—"

Odalie rose to her feet, her eyes snapping with indignation. "Are you saying you stole those things?"

"I reckon the folks that lived there wouldn't have begrudged it to you ladies. 'Sides, if we eat along the way, 'stead of stoppin' to buy food, we'll make better time."

"He's right, Odalie," Shannon said. And, although Odalie looked disapproving, she said no more about it.

The carriage moved slowly through Virginia and down the North Carolina coast until, on an evening of mist and intermittent light rain, they came to the small inn on the banks of the Cape Fear River. "The King George. That's it," Odalie said.

Caleb got down and said firmly, "I'll go inside first

and ask for Mr. Bruce, ladies. You stay right here 'til I find him, hear?"

Caleb had taken a protective attitude not only toward Odalie and Eugénie, but toward Shannon as well. Shannon wondered if the black giant knew that she, like Odalie, was Philippe Duval's daughter.

From beyond the mist, they could hear the river lapping against the shore. Behind the inn was a swampy stretch of trees. Frogs croaked, small animals rustled through the underbrush, and a night bird made an eerie sound. The lighted windows of the inn were blurred and indistinct. An isolated spot, for those who waited to slip out of Wilmington on one of the swift blockade-runners. Although North Carolina was a member of the Confederacy, Shannon had been told that there were many citizens of Wilmington who had opposed leaving the Union: businessmen and shopkeepers who had no stake in the preservation of the plantation system. And hundreds of small farmers in the outlying districts, who had never owned a single slave.

Shannon turned as she heard footsteps and saw Caleb striding back toward the carriage. "He's here, Miz Lathrop. He's comin' right away."

The coachman helped Odalie down and a moment later, she had lifted her shabby calico skirts and was running swiftly over the wet grass. Shannon, leaning out of the carriage, saw Bruce hurrying to meet her.

Then Odalie was locked in her husband's arms, and he was lifting her off the ground, holding her against him. And Shannon thought, *I was right to urge her to come here.*

"Let me help you down, ma'am," Caleb said. "And little missy, too."

"Not yet," Shannon said, cradling Eugénie in her arms. "We'll wait here. I think Mr. Lathrop and his wife will want some time together right now."

"Reckon they will at that, Miz Kincaid," Caleb said.

"I'll put Eugénie to bed here in my room," Shannon said.

Odalie had changed her now-soiled calico dress and bedraggled apron for something more suitable, a ruffled organdy; she had also managed to remove the remains of the darkening concoction from her face and arms.

"Won't you come downstairs and dine with us?" she asked Shannon.

"I'll have a tray up here. That way, if Eugénie should wake up, I'll be with her. You and Bruce will have a lot to talk about."

"Are you sure the baby won't be any bother?"

"I'm sure." It was important, Shannon thought, that Odalie and Bruce should not be disturbed tonight.

She ate a dinner of chicken, biscuits and wine, then removed the dark blue silk dress and plumed bonnet, and put them away. After she had changed to her nightgown, she got into bed beside Eugénie. The little girl cuddled against her, and Shannon spoke to her soothingly. Then the noises from the dense growth of cypress, black gum and juniper that stretched behind the inn lulled them both to sleep long before Odalie and Bruce had climbed the stairs to their room at the other end of the hall.

"You're sure you want to come with me?" Bruce asked, as he got into bed beside Odalie. "There's still time to change your mind, my dear. Conditions are unsettled in Mexico, and Louis Napoleon has not given us a definite promise that he will support our colony in Sonora."

Odalie turned and silenced Bruce, pressing her lips to his. Then she reached up and stroked his hair, and ran her fingers along his cheek.

He took her hand and touched it to his lips. She moved closer, encircling his body with her free arm.

"Don't," he said. "If you do, I can't promise not to ask for more."

"I don't want you to promise any such thing," she said.

Slowly, deliberately, she began to stroke his back, running her hands down along the hard muscles. His mouth touched her throat, and then he was kissing her shoulder, pushing aside her nightgown.

She began to tremble but she did not draw away. Instead, she opened the ribbons that fastened the top of her nightgown. Freeing one breast, she raised it, brushing the nipple against his lips. He hesitated for an instant, then his lips parted, and her trembling deepened. She was still afraid, and perhaps she always would be, but stronger than her fear was her need for her husband.

"Will you do something for me?" she whispered.

"Anything, my love."

"Will you pretend that this is our first night together? That I'm your bride, that we've never—done this before. Be gentle with me, Bruce. Teach me, show me how to please you."

Then he took her hand and guided her questing fingers.

"Like this. And like this."

For the next two days, Shannon spent many hours strolling along the river bank, where the soft white clouds drifted lazily by. Sometimes she took Eugénie with her, and sometimes she walked alone. Always, her mind was preoccupied with thoughts of Adam. Had he returned from Fredericksburg? Had he believed the story she had told Aunt Kate, the note she had left for him?

And even if she had managed to deceive him, what then? There had been a barrier between them all these months, ever since he had come home from his trip West. If only the war would end, and they could return to San Francisco again. But perhaps, even in San Francisco. . . .

On the morning of the third day at the inn, Bruce received word from the innkeeper that the side-wheeler, *Nereide*, for which he had been waiting, was anchored now off Cape Fear.

It was half a day's journey downriver, and while Caleb was loading the baggage into the carriage, Odalie and Bruce said their good-byes to Shannon.

"The *Nereide*'s said to be a good ship. Her captain's made this run a dozen times," Bruce said confidently. "He'll wait until dark, then slip through the inlet and past the federal warships lying outside the bar. We should be about thirty miles offshore by daybreak."

"And will the *Nereide* take you to Mexico?" Shannon asked.

He shook his head. "Only as far as the Bahamas," he replied. "But the British are in control there. We'll have no trouble getting another ship to take us to Mexico."

"It sounds so far away," Shannon said slowly.

"Maybe, one day, when the war's over—" Odalie began.

Shannon nodded. "Maybe, one day." But she thought how unlikely it was that she would ever see Bruce again, or Odalie. Or their child, who looked up at her with eyes so like her own.

Bruce rose quickly and said, "I'll go out and see that the luggage is properly stowed." He took Shannon's hand and raised it to his lips. Then he was gone.

"I don't like to leave you alone," Odalie said.

"Caleb will be back here by evening," Shannon reminded her. "We'll stay the night and tomorrow, we'll start for Washington."

Shannon and Odalie sat in silence for a moment, looking at each other across the round wooden table in the corner of the inn's small taproom. The room was deserted at this hour of the morning. Even the innkeeper was nowhere to be seen.

Shannon hesitated, then spoke quickly. "There's something we must settle before you go," she said.

Odalie shifted the weight of her sleeping child in her arms.

"That money you told me about," Shannon went on. "The inheritance in that English bank. Odalie, I want you to have it."

"Papa left it to you."

"But I'll have no need of it. What with the Silver Vixen, and Adam's other investments, I'll have all I need. But you, you've got to be realistic about this. You'll be making a start in a new country. And, Bruce—forgive me, my dear, but your husband's not a—practical man."

"You think I don't know that?" Odalie's eyes met Shannon's in a look of understanding. "All the same, I can't take the money Papa left for you."

"Accept it as a loan, then," Shannon said. She knew the Duval pride well, for she had her own share of it. "Only until Bruce builds his new Jessamine down in Sonora."

Odalie bent to stroke Eugénie's dark curls, then she lifted her head. Shannon saw the strength in her sister's face. Odalie's brown eyes were soft and luminous, as they had been since the morning after her arrival here at the inn; but her mouth was firm.

Shannon thought, with a trace of sadness, that this was not the pretty, laughing girl in the rose-colored organdy who had come down to the dock at Cypress Bend five years before, to meet Bruce Lathrop and to flirt with him.

"There won't be a new Jessamine," Odalie said. "I know that as well as you do. But we'll get along. I'm not afraid."

"I'll see that you get the money," Shannon said. "I'm as stubborn as you are. We're sisters, remember. And I think our father would have wanted us to help each other."

Caleb stood in the doorway. "Time to leave, Miz Lathrop."

Shannon embraced Odalie, kissed Eugénie, and then, as she stood outside the inn, she watched the carriage roll off down the river road, to be hidden from view by a stand of cypress trees.

The inn was an isolated place, with few other guests, all men. Shannon decided to keep to her room until it was time to leave.

Toward sunset, she was surprised to hear the sound of rapid footsteps on the stairs, and the innkeeper saying, "It's that room down the hall, there. But you can't go barging in without—"

"Stand aside," she heard an angry voice saying, and her throat tightened.

She threw open the door of her room. "Now look here, mister. I don't know you or the crew of that boat you came downriver in, and I don't take to strangers here."

"It's all right," Shannon managed to say. "This man's my husband."

A moment later, Adam had pushed her into the room, closed the door, and stood towering over her, his blue eyes hard with anger.

32

"HOW DID YOU find me?" Shannon's voice was unsteady. There was something in Adam's eyes that frightened her, but she knew that she could not panic, not now.

"It wasn't too difficult. The War Department has its informers. And you did use my name to get past the sentry post, remember?"

"I had to. There was no other way. Adam, let me explain."

"Later," he said, his voice soft, but dangerous. She recognized the cold fury below the surface. "Right now, you're going to tell me where Bruce is."

"He's not here."

Adam seized her arm in a rough grip. "Tell me, damn it. Or must I search the inn and the swamp out back?"

"He was here but he's gone. With Odalie and Eugénie."

"Stop it, Shannon. Haven't there been enough lies between us?"

"I'm not lying." She began to tremble uncontrollably.

"Odalie didn't come down here with Bruce. You did. You were going to Sonora with him." He gave her a smile, cruel and mocking. "Don't tell me the gallant Mr. Lathrop has walked out on you again, as he did back in Colón?"

She shook her head, and tried to speak, but no sound would come. Adam's fingers tightened, forcing a cry of pain from her.

"It won't do any good. They've gone. Oh, Adam, I didn't want to deceive you, but I had to, for Odalie's sake. You told me her house was being watched, and I was being watched, and I was afraid that she would be stopped and held for questioning if she tried to leave alone." She gave a gasp, and said, "You're hurting me."

He relaxed his grip slightly but his hand remained on her arm. "You went through that sentry post alone. Except for a colored maid. The sergeant told me so."

She shook her head. "Odalie. It was Odalie, in Reba's clothes. And we had Eugénie with us, in a wicker hamper, along with some linens and—and a few bottles of your favorite bourbon."

His hand dropped from her arm. "I'll be damned."

"It's true, Adam."

"You were helping Odalie to get to Bruce before he sailed? So that they could go on to Mexico together?"

Shannon nodded. "You surely didn't think that I was running off with Bruce?"

"You did it once before," he said.

"That was years ago. Everything's changed since then. Surely, you must know that it's you I love."

For a moment, she thought she saw his eyes soften, but then he spoke coldly, impersonally. "One thing I do know. Bruce isn't getting away so easily. He's broken his oath of allegiance to the Union, violated his parole. He'll have to pay for that."

"You can't stop him now." Shannon's fear for herself was swallowed up in her greater fear for Bruce and Odalie.

"The hell I can't. I have a crew of picked men in that boat down on the river, men who know this part of the coast. No blockade-runner will risk leaving before dark, and by then, I'll have gotten word to the lookout ships of the Union fleet."

"Adam, wait. You've got to listen." She clutched at his arm. "I don't care how angry you are with me. You've got no reason to hate Odalie."

"I don't hate her. I feel sorry for her. She doesn't know what she's getting into. Sonora's a wilderness. It's full of lawless men, seeking silver. Hostile Indians, Apaches, Yaquis. It's no place for a woman like Odalie."

"She doesn't care. She loves Bruce. Maybe he doesn't deserve her love, but that doesn't matter, because she—" Shannon broke off in despair. "I can't make you understand, can I? Because you've never loved anyone in your life."

"You've no right to say that."

"No, I suppose not. You did love your parents. And your sister, Rachel. But after—after they died, there was no more love left in you."

She tried to stem the torrent of words, but they had been dammed up within her for too long. "You're afraid to love anyone, aren't you? Afraid of being hurt again."

His arms went around her and his mouth silenced her, his lips bruising hers. For a timeless moment she clung to him, her breasts crushed against his chest, while the world spun dizzily around her.

When he released her she whispered, "You're not angry with me any longer?"

"Angry? You bet I'm angry. How could you have risked your neck, traveling through two states where the fighting's hot and heavy? Suppose you'd blundered into a battle line? Suppose you'd been set upon by renegades or deserters?"

"We—did run into Mosby's raiders. But we hid in a deserted slave cabin until they were gone."

"My God, I always knew you were headstrong and impulsive, but this is too much. I've often been tempted to take my belt to you, like Jethro did. Maybe it's not too late to beat some sense into you now." She shrank away, then saw a corner of his mouth lift in a wry smile. "It probably wouldn't do any good. Besides, there are a number of other things I'd rather do, now I've found you." He lifted her and held her against him, then carried her to the bed. "But they'll have to wait," he said, depositing her on the lumpy mattress.

"Adam, you're not going to try to have the *Nereide* overtaken, and brought back. You can't. You mustn't."

He remained silent, and she reached for his hand, holding it against her cheek. "The war will be over soon," she said. "The South doesn't have a chance. You've told me so yourself."

Still he did not speak, and she hurried on, "Bruce believes that, too. That's why he's leaving the country, to make a new life for himself and his family. He wants to build another house, like Jessamine."

"He is a fool," Adam said. "Louis Napoleon's got more trouble than he can handle in Mexico right now, with his puppet emperor, Maximilian, on the throne there. The Mexicans will throw off French rule, and if they can't do it alone, the United States will step in, once this war's over. You don't think Louis Napoleon's rash enough to risk a clash with the United States to keep a promise to a band of Confederate exiles?"

"Then there's no hope for Bruce and Odalie, none at all?"

He sat down beside her on the bed, and put an arm around her. "I haven't said that. If Bruce can make it on his own, of course there's a chance. But there'll be no slave empire in Sonora. No new Jessamine, with an army of slaves to do the work. It'll be rough going for them."

"But you will give them a chance? You won't get word to the federal ships to stop them?"

He drew his arm away and stood up. "I'll go down and pay off the crew of that boat. They can go ahead and get roaring drunk, so long as they sober up by morning, so they can come back for us."

"We won't need them," Shannon said. "Odalie's coachman is going to return here, as soon as the *Nereide*'s safely on its way." She saw the look in his eyes. "Adam, what's wrong?"

"Sweetheart, that blockade-runner may not get through even if I don't get word to the federal warships. They've been doing a pretty good job on their own, you know."

The *Nereide*, commanded by Captain Charles Lovell, a former officer in the United States Navy, moved cautiously through the inlet, slipping past the federal warships that lay in wait outside the bar. With no lights, she headed seaward, and at daybreak, she was thirty miles offshore.

"We're safe now, aren't we?" Odalie asked Bruce as she stood beside him on the deck.

"Not quite, ma'am," said the captain, a bearded, soft-spoken Virginian. "This vessel burns coal, you see, and I was only able to buy a small amount of Welsh coal at Wilmington; that's the good stuff. I had to fill my bunkers with low-grade North Carolina coal, to make up the difference." He hesitated, then, deciding to speak frankly, he added, "We'll be changing over to the low-grade coal in a few minutes."

"But what difference does that make?" Odalie asked.

"The low-grade coal makes a hellish amount of smoke. Now, if you'll pardon me, ma'am—Mr. Lathrop."

He strode off briskly. "Bruce, I still don't understand."

"I'm afraid I do," Bruce said.

A few minutes later, black clouds of smoke were coming from the twin stacks, and within a quarter of an hour, the smoke had drawn the notice of the

Yankee warships. One of them, the USS *Iroquois*, moved out in hot pursuit.

Odalie longed to throw herself into her husband's arms, and give way to her fear, but she forced herself to speak calmly. "What will it mean if we're caught?"

"Capture and prison for Captain Lovell and his crew. And probably for me. Maybe both of us, Odalie. Oh, my dear, I shouldn't have allowed you to come along."

"My place is here with you," she said. "Besides, they haven't caught us yet."

"That's the right spirit, Mrs. Lathrop," the captain said, pausing as he went about his duties.

But the steam-powered *Iroquois* was able to add to her speed, because she was carrying sail, and the wind was favorable. White-faced, her lips set in a thin line, Odalie watched as the Yankee vessel began to overhaul the *Nereide*.

"Can't you get up more steam?" she heard the captain shout to his engineer. "We need more pressure, Mr. McCord."

"I've got the pressure up far as it'll go, sir."

"Then break out some barrels of turpentine, and soak the cotton in it. Feed that to your fireboxes."

"That's cargo, sir."

"Burn it." The captain turned to another crewman and ordered the deck cargo of cotton to be tossed overboard to lighten the ship. Odalie stared down at the bales that stretched out astern.

"Better get your child up here," Captain Lovell said briskly. "In a few minutes, this deck's going to be hotter than the hinges of hell. Begging your pardon, ma'am."

Odalie turned and hurried below, returning with Eugénie in her arms. Both officers and passengers went up to the bridge that stretched between the paddleboxes, Eugénie began to whimper, and Odalie soothed her.

But the *Iroquois* was gaining still, and Bruce stiffened as he saw that the Yankee vessel had run out her guns. Odalie saw the muzzles of the guns, too, and she gave a cry and pressed Eugénie closer.

"No cause for panic yet, ma'am," Captain Lovell said.

The engineer came pounding up onto the bridge. "My engines aren't designed to burn cotton, sir," he protested, his face fiery red, the sweat streaming down his forehead. "It's clogging the flues."

"Go back to the coal then," the captain said. "Make as much smoke as you can."

Odalie and Bruce exchanged bewildered glances. But then they heard Captain Lovell ordering a change of course. "He's trying to force the *Iroquois* up into the wind," one of the officers explained. "Look back there."

Odalie saw a cloud of black, dense smoke, saw the *Iroquois* furl sail.

"Close the dampers," Captain Lovell shouted. And, making a sharp quarter-turn, he sped away, concealed behind the oily cloud that stretched for miles.

"We've lost her," Captain Lovell reported, an hour later. "We should have clear sailing from here to the

Bahamas. You may go down below now, if you wish."

Odalie's knees were trembling beneath the concealment of her crinolines, but her voice was steady as she congratulated the captain on his daring feat.

"It's Mr. Lathrop who's to be congratulated," Captain Lovell said gallantly. "You're a cool one, ma'am. No tears, no hysterics. Not many ladies like you."

After he had turned and left them, Bruce put an arm around Odalie. "He's right, my dear. I'm a lucky man, having a wife like you beside me."

Drowsy with sleep and a night of love-making, Shannon stirred in Adam's arms, as the first light of dawn came through the window of their room at the inn. He opened his eyes, and smiled, drawing her closer. His hands caressed her body, but although she felt an answering need, she whispered, "No, we can't. Not now."

"Don't tell me you've had enough," he said, his voice teasing her gently. "No. You want more, don't you?" His fingers touched her in ways he knew would arouse her. "Don't you?"

"Yes, oh, yes. But we'll have to be leaving soon. We'll have to start for home."

"Back to Washington? Yes, I guess we've got to go there first. But as soon as the war's over, we're heading West."

Shannon smiled up at him, "I think that's your real home, out there, and it always will be."

He held her close to him. "Home, Shannon? Home is wherever you are."

Swift joy rose within her at his words. He pressed his cheek to the curve of her breast. "Those things you said to me yesterday. You were right. I never wanted to love you. And even when I sensed what was happening, I tried to deny it. But no more."

Her arms encircled him, and she moved against him, but even before their bodies joined, she knew that they were already one, and would be, forever.

Romantic Fiction

If you like novels of passion and daring adventure that take you to the very heart of human drama, these are the books for you.

☐ AFTER—Anderson	Q2279	1.50
☐ THE DANCE OF LOVE—Dodson	23110-0	1.75
☐ A GIFT OF ONYX—Kettle	23206-9	1.50
☐ TARA'S HEALING—Giles	23012-0	1.50
☐ THE DEFIANT DESIRE—Klem	13741-4	1.75
☐ LOVE'S TRIUMPHANT HEART—Ashton	13771-6	1.75
☐ MAJORCA—Dodson	13740-6	1.75

Buy them at your local bookstores or use this handy coupon for ordering:

FAWCETT BOOKS GROUP, 1 Fawcett Place, P.O. Box 1014, Greenwich, Ct. 06830

Please send me the books I have checked above. Orders for less than 5 books must include 60¢ for the first book and 25¢ for each additional book to cover mailing and handling. Postage is FREE for orders of 5 books or more. Check or money order only. Please include sales tax.

Name_____	Books \$_____
	Postage _____
Address_____	Sales Tax _____
City_____State/Zip_____	Total \$_____

Please allow 4 to 5 weeks for delivery. This offer expires 12/78.

A-20

Mary Stewart

In 1960, Mary Stewart won the British Crime Writers Association Award, and in 1964 she won the Mystery Writers of America "Edgar" Award. Her bestselling novels continue to captivate her many readers.

☐	AIRS ABOVE THE GROUND	23077-5	1.75
☐	THE CRYSTAL CAVE	23315-4	1.95
☐	THE GABRIEL HOUNDS	22971-8	1.75
☐	THE HOLLOW HILLS	23316-2	1.95
☐	THE IVY TREE	23251-4	1.75
☐	MADAM, WILL YOU TALK?	23250-6	1.75
☐	THE MOON-SPINNERS	23073-2	1.75
☐	MY BROTHER MICHAEL	22974-2	1.75
☐	NINE COACHES WAITING	23121-6	1.75
☐	THIS ROUGH MAGIC	22846-0	1.75
☐	THUNDER ON THE RIGHT	23100-3	1.75
☐	WILDFIRE AT MIDNIGHT	23317-0	1.75

Buy them at your local bookstores or use this handy coupon for ordering:

FAWCETT BOOKS GROUP, 1 Fawcett Place, P.O. Box 1014, Greenwich, Ct. 06830

Please send me the books I have checked above. Orders for less than 5 books must include 60¢ for the first book and 25¢ for each additional book to cover mailing and handling. Postage is FREE for orders of 5 books or more. Check or money order only. Please include sales tax.

Name_____

Address_____

City_____State/Zip_____

Books $_____
Postage _____
Sales Tax _____
Total $_____

Please allow 4 to 5 weeks for delivery. This offer expires 12/78.

A-11